THE GOVERNOR'S LOVER

SHE REPRESENTED HOPE FOR HER NATION

THE GOVERNOR'S LOVER

RODERIC GRIGSON

GRIGSONPUBLISHING.COM

ISBN: 978-0-6456593-3-7

Published by

Grigson Publishing

Cover design & illustration, interior formatting
Mark Thomas / Coverness.com

CEYLON

And we came to the Isle of Flowers.
Their breath met us out on the seas,
For the spring and the middle of summer,
Sat each on the lap of the breeze.
And the red passionflower to the cliffs,
And the dark-blue clematis clung.
And starred with myriad blossoms,
The long convolvulus hung.

C.F. Gordon Cummings, 1901

CHAPTER 1

THE MESTIZO GIRL

Lovinia grinned as her nimble fingers ran the thick needle through the dense weave, the crisscrossed thread closing the tear in the deep ochre and brown-coloured kilted skirt seamlessly. She had stepped on one of the panels, tearing it apart almost to her waist, causing delight among the native soldiers who had gathered around to watch her dance. The combination of her bare breasts and long shapely legs exposed to her waist had set the soldiers off, hooting and waving their hats in excitement. Lovinia had not planned for it to happen. The reaction and ensuing generosity of the lonely soldiers who tossed their coins into the basket her father carried made her think it was something she should include in her act.

She was the lead dancer in the dance troupe her father owned. They were all Mestize, people of mixed European and indigenous heritage who looked nothing like the dark-skinned natives on the island. Portuguese and Dutch soldiers and sailors stationed on the island before the British came were permitted to take local women as their wives, spawning a colony of half-breeds known disparagingly by the locals as *luncias*.

Lovinia's mother, born on the island to Portuguese parents, had given birth to a light-skinned child who held all the characteristics of her mixed race. Lightly tanned skin, glossy black hair and flashing green eyes made a striking combination. Her father was a native *Rodiya*, a caste formed by the union of a daughter of an ancient Sinhalese King and a *Veddah* hunter with whom the princess had fallen in love.

'Your father has summoned me,' a voice said, breaking her moment of amusement.

Lovinia glanced up, full lips and green eyes smiling with expectancy. Aletta was beautiful, her tanned skin the colour of copper, her dark hair hanging like a rope behind her back. Her lips turned up at the corners, making her look like she was always smiling. She had deep dimples and used her good looks to get what she wanted.

'Yes, he's been looking for you.' Lovinia nodded.

Aletta, a midwife and a skilled healer, was a few years older than Lovinia. The two traced their friendship back to when she was a child and followed Aletta around like a little puppy, emulating her in every gesture and naughty act.

'I can meet him now if he's free.' Aletta smiled at Lovinia, her amber eyes sparkling. They spoke Portuguese Creole, the language of the mixed races on the island.

'He would be in the common rooms,' Lovinia pointed, returning her friend's smile. 'He wants to talk to us both.' She folded the skirt, placing it into a cloth bag she hung on a hook inside their mud-bricked home before joining Aletta on the footpath.

Lovinia had once envied Aletta her freedom as she was permitted to leave the village, earn a few coins from her herbal remedies and contraceptive teas to keep the local women childless, and often engaged in indiscriminate behaviour with like-minded women. Lovinia eventually gained that same level of freedom when she came of age and was taken under Aletta's wing and schooled in the desires and vagaries of men.

Lovinia adored Aletta, and her affairs did not prevent her from loving her as much as her own family. In truth, her boldness made her friend more endearing.

The small native village they lived in was just south of the city of Colombo, not more than a few hundred yards from the sea, with little huts of mud and straw, sheds for milk-producing cows and working animals clustered around a village square with a sacred Bodhi tree at the centre. Tendrils of scented incense climbed from a little carved shrine supported on a thick wooden post at the base of the ancient tree. Every morning, someone in the village would place freshly picked white and yellow frangipani flowers as an offering to the statue of the Lord Buddha seated in the sanctuary.

The two girls crossed the courtyard to the shared common room next to the rice storehouse with the smooth, swinging stride made second nature to those who habitually carry burdens on the head.

The village was alive with sound. Local women were chatting around the village well, telling stories, and laughing as they washed saris, cotton blouses, petticoats, and sarongs. Here people lived and slept in the same room. They cooked outside, sheltered by the overhanging roof. A few hens scratched freely here and there, and sometimes a cow roamed freely through the village. Each family had its vegetable garden. Rice was grown in communal fields around the settlement. Through the leafy walls of cascading bougainvillaea, pink, orange, and wild purple, you could hear the clanging of metal vessels, the swishing of coconut brooms, and the pounding of the *wangediya* (mortar made from wood) as the villagers prepared their meals. Overhead, monkeys shrieked, and green parrots squawked.

The common room was quiet and sunny at that time of the day. It was a familiar design, spacious, rectangular, and windowless. But the two outside walls stopped at waist height, the *cadjan* ceiling supported by wooden columns hewn from the coconut palm, allowing light and air to pour into the room. In its centre, sitting cross-legged beside a low table, sat Lovinia's father, Banda. His brown-skinned upper body was naked, with a sarong wrapped around his slim hips and his long hair tied in a bun. He was fifty-three years old, haughty-looking, lean and supple as a sword blade. He looked up at their approach.

'Ah, I was about to come looking for you,' Banda's fine black eyes studied them intently. His voice was deep and mellow, a troubadour's voice. Lovinia flushed at the implied rebuke. She had waited for Aletta without answering his summons immediately.

'In your case, I am sure you had good reason,' he assured her, smiling to cover any hidden meaning the remark might have. He gestured for them to sit at the table. 'I have heard that an emissary from the Great King across the ocean will be here any day now, and we have to entertain him.'

Lovinia turned and looked at her father anxiously. The last time they had performed in the Fort, the British officials had not paid the total amount. After paying the dancers and musicians, there was hardly enough coinage for her father to buy a meal for the family. Her father looked at her with amused tolerance. She could see he knew what she was thinking. They had gone over this once before and agreed to ask for a retainer before any performances.

'Don't worry,' he said, glancing at Aletta, who had not performed that day. 'The Chief Steward has agreed to pay double what I usually ask. He wants something exceptional from us, which is why you two are here.'

'But he's a snake,' Lovinia shrugged, making a face at her father. 'He wanted to take me to his chambers, and it is when I refused that he did not pay the full price,' she said to Aletta, who looked amusedly.

Her father put down the cup he was holding, his eyes full of laughter. 'Listen, my pretty sceptic.' Banda leaned forward towards her, his eyes intense, his voice low and calm. 'It is for that very reason he wants us to come back and has agreed to pay double the price. He desires you, no doubt, and you must learn to use your natural gifts to hold an advantage over men like him.'

Lovinia gaped at him. 'You can't be serious.'

'We have to make something good come of this situation,' Banda's voice was cold. 'It's quite an honour,' he urged.

A voice inside her whispered that this was an opportunity, a gift that would help their family rise above their position. Lovinia dug her fingernails into her palms. She frowned. 'I think I understand,' she said slowly. Her father meant what she thought he said. 'But what exactly do you want me to do?'

Her father examined her with interest, searching her face for any sign of guile. He turned to face Aletta. 'You are older than her and know how to use your charms. I want you to teach her all you know so she'll be ready.'

Aletta rolled her eyes at Banda's words. 'Mmm…,' she glanced across at Lovinia. 'What exactly are you afraid of?'

'I'm not afraid of anything,' Lovinia snapped.

'Do you think you're not ready? It's not as difficult as you think.' Aletta said, unruffled.

Lovinia sighed. A sick feeling began building in her stomach. None of this was real. She avoided Banda's eyes, but she could see their dissatisfaction growing. It would be so much easier if she could hate them both.

'I will do whatever needs to doing.' Lovinia finally conceded, refusing to relax.

Aletta always to the point responded. 'That's good. How do you plan on seducing him?'

'You want me to seduce him?' Lovinia tingled with astonishment. She was not naïve as men often propositioned the dancers. But she had never been bothered by anyone when she danced as she was always in her father's company.

Lovinia fumbled for the words. 'If I have to, I will dance—it's what I do best.'

Banda shook his head. 'It won't be enough. It is an important official, not some soldier or sailor looking for a quick tumble.'

Aletta lifted her chin. 'Women wield a mighty power. Our power is subtle. Smooth skin, a lovely face, a whispered promise of future pleasures—few men can resist a woman's charms. Men seek to unite with, ravage, and sink themselves into our body's depths.'

Banda's eyes narrowed. 'Are you saying men have no control over their lust?'

Aletta examined him. 'They don't, and a clever woman uses this knowledge and power to her advantage.'

'She could be thrown to the *kaffirs* (blacks) once he's had his fill.' Banda was not convinced. 'He must not know that you are seducing him.'

Aletta watched Banda with amusement. 'Perhaps you do not wish my help?'

He sighed. 'The thought of using my child this way does not sit with me lightly. But I have watched you and am convinced you are the best to teach her.'

Aletta's eyes sparkled. 'You will never know for certain until it happens,' she nodded, smiling at Lovina, tapping her fingers lightly on her knee. 'I will teach you, so he will not resist your charms.'

Lovinia pondered this and wondered how her life would change. Even mortal danger could be tempting besides the oppressive poverty of their life. She had learned that excitement and risk worked on the body and soul like an aphrodisiac. Eating fish for breakfast and supper and dancing to please low-born men was not the life she wanted for herself. She would take it if she had the chance to sleep in a palace, drink the best wines, and be the lover of one of the most influential men in the Fort. So, she would do what everyone expected of her.

That afternoon, Lovinia sat quietly while Aletta, Tara, and other women from the village discussed the recent happenings. Babet and Anika had prepared *tala guli* for the gathering. The tasty roasted sesame balls mixed with coconut treacle had taken all evening to finish.

CHAPTER 2

THE GOVERNOR

They were just days from landfall, according to Captain Anderson. Thomas had concluded soon after they left England that the officer who commanded the small convoy of ships heading north to Ceylon knew what he was doing. The Captain was an imposing figure, tall and broad-shouldered with handsome well-formed features and thick dark hair tied at the back of his neck.

The spacious day room where the officers and passengers gathered for breakfast was low-pitched, usually lit by two lamps hung on chains from the thick beams above. That morning, the sun streamed into the room from large windows at the rear. Portholes ran along the two sides, a skylight in the centre. Vents in the overhead, openings for windsails to cool the cabin in the tropics, were now closed. The comfortably furnished ship's cabin had fitted racks above the mahogany sideboard holding claret jugs and several cut-glass decanters. On the sideboard was a large, well-used brass tea urn that looked out of place. Dishes containing buttered toast and bottles of jam and honey stood next to the vessel. The supply of bananas had run out some weeks prior.

A sizeable Indian carpet spread in the middle of the room had a long heavy table and high-backed dark wood chairs set around it. Beside one stood the Captain, from where he had made a statement that they would arrive off the island of Ceylon days ahead of schedule.

Lady Tarrant looked at him in surprise. 'Are you certain, Sir?' she questioned. 'I have much to do to be ready.' The lady was travelling with a companion to join her husband, Sir David Tarrant, the Head of the British East India Company in the Crown Colony of Ceylon. Lady Tarrant had sailed to England to be at her mother's side as she succumbed to a long illness and was on her way back.

'I am, indeed, madam', the Captain answered, smiling calmly at her. 'I expect to see the island off our port bow tomorrow morning.'

Lady Tarrant, who had elected herself as the spokesperson for the dozen passengers on board, regarded him suspiciously. 'How was it you did not warn us earlier?' she asked. The lady was no longer in the first blush of her youth, her features careworn but good-looking, her eyes dark and shrewd. Thomas found her to be affable without being effusive. Without assuming any airs of consequence, she had a quiet dignity of her own. She talked very much like a sensible woman.

'My confidence in reaching the island had grown in the past few days,' Captain Anderson responded positively, looking around the room and catching Thomas's eyes. 'We caught the pre-monsoon winds blowing out of the southeast just at the right time.'

Thomas nodded at the Captain without saying anything. He had noted that the strong gusts of wind which had filled out the billowing sails, had strengthened over the past few days into a steady gale driving them directly northeast.

'However, you still have the rest of today and most of tomorrow to prepare,' the Captain paused, looking at Lady Tarrant. 'It will take all day and most of the night to reach the island before anchoring off the port of Colombo if all goes well. We can anchor on the roads off the port this time of the year. Otherwise, we would have to use the port at Pointe-de-Galle, 70 miles south. It will add a few extra days to your journey, which is unnecessary.'

'How will we get ashore, Captain?'

'We will use the ship's barge to ferry you ashore, Madam.'

Mrs Juliet Hartley, her travelling companion, a slender, attractive widow who usually kept up an entertaining exchange of gossip and wit with Lady

Tarrant and the rest of the passengers, looked across the table at Thomas with a smile on her face. 'What say you, Sir Thomas?' she asked him cordially. 'You must be anxious to attend your post.'

Early in the voyage, the officers and other passengers on the ship had come to know he was the recently appointed Governor-General of the Crown Colony of Ceylon. He wished the Captain had not made the announcement on the first morning of the voyage but could not fault the man. Royal protocol demanded that the King's representative be recognized and treated with respect and dignity.

Mrs Hartley was no longer young. She was twenty-six years old and had been a widow for three years. Thomas had overheard her declare her age to one of the passengers.

'The Captain is very experienced and knows what he's doing,' Thomas answered with a smile. 'I don't have any doubt what he said was correct.'

Mrs Hartley was amusing company, and he was glad she was on board. This morning she wore an uncut bodice, cream velvet bordered with grey. Her natural grace was in stark contrast to the other passengers in the cabin.

Mr Barrymore, a plump gentleman with a morose and inquisitive mien who was travelling with his wife and daughter, a young lady of sixteen, to India to take up a senior company position, broke into the conversation. He was standing by the rear bulkhead emblazoned with the East India Company Coat of Arms, featuring waving St. George pennants and sea lions supporting a shield showing ships and roses.

'How long will we be stopping for?' he asked grumpily. 'I am supposed to be taking up my position in Bombay at the end of the month.'

An involuntary smile flickered across the Captain's lips. 'I am afraid it'll be at least another two weeks before we reach Calcutta,' he said, looking across the table. 'We need to replenish our supplies in Ceylon and give the men some time off before leaving.'

Barrymore had been putting pressure on the Captain since they left St. Helena to bypass the Crown Colony, questioning why they were not going direct to Calcutta. He based his demand because the Blenheim was an East

India Company ship, and his requirements came first. Only when the Captain had threatened to transfer him aboard their Royal Navy escort frigate sailing directly to India had he finally quietened. The Royal Navy was not known for its hospitability, and the smaller warship would be extremely uncomfortable in the rolling seas of the Indian Ocean.

Thomas stood and walked to the buffet, where he served himself two slices of buttered toast, slathering it with strawberry jam from a half-used jar. Sitting back down, he placed the saucer on the table and poured himself a cup of coffee.

Most people thought the Company owned East Indiamen vessels, but they were not. Such ships were built, manned, and hired to the Company by independent owners who held a monopoly with hereditary rights to furnish the ship bottoms for the trade. The Captain was one such owner whose years as a merchant captain had made him a considerable fortune, and he knew his rights.

Barrymore had not finished. 'Sir Thomas,' he spoke imperiously, ignoring the Captain and addressing Thomas. 'Would you order Captain Anderson here to set sail for Calcutta immediately after you leave the ship?'

Annoyance at Barrymore almost choked Thomas. He glanced at Captain Anderson beside him and saw the heightened colour in his cheeks. It was not the first time Barrymore had raised the matter. He had tired of the man's constant harping throughout the journey and marvelled at the captain's patience when dealing with this obnoxious man.

Katherine, the eldest among several young women travelling to India, spoke up in support of Barrymore. 'Yes, please, Sir Thomas. I implore you,' she asked him sweetly.

Thomas sipped his tea, giving her a guarded look. Jennifer, Kitty, Minnie, Mary, and her older sister Zoe who made up the other young ladies, were looking at Thomas expectantly. He had seen Mr Barrymore and his wife talking in low tones to them recently and realised that they were fermenting trouble now coming to a head as they drew closer to their destination.

Thomas glared at Barrymore for a moment and decided to ignore him completely. 'Dear Miss Watford,' he responded, looking at Katherine directly. 'I understand your desire to reach India in the shortest possible time, but let me assure you that you can meet many young and eligible bachelors in Ceylon too.' Glancing at the Captain, 'In fact, with the permission of Captain Anderson here, I can arrange for a suitable reception to be held in the town soon after we arrive.'

From time to time, the Company paid the passage out to India of several willing women who were neither pretty nor rich enough to make what was known as 'a good match' at home. In India, where European men greatly outnumbered European women, suitors would travel hundreds of miles to besiege these respectable young women. They would meet many prospects, some of who were more prosperous than anyone they could meet in England. Such husbands were desirable as the Company provided a generous allowance for girls who made a Company-approved match. This payment continued for life even if the woman was widowed.

Barrymore's reaction was not unexpected. 'But', he spluttered, going red in the face. 'You cannot do that! The Company has paid for their passage.' He looked at his wife, sitting pale and quiet beside her husband, for some support. 'They have a contract to live in India.'

Irritation welled up, almost tightening Thomas's throat. 'I think you are being too pedantic, Mr Barrymore.'

'There will be men waiting for the Fishing Fleet in Calcutta,' Barrymore said petulantly. 'Some of them travel vast distances.'

Thomas paused, a slice of toast halfway to his mouth. 'What?'

'A ship full of ladies, fishing for partners. They are supposed to be visiting relatives but are on the catch for a husband. You've not heard that expression?'

Thomas shook his head, frowning. 'No. It doesn't sound fitting, anyway. Or very nice.' He looked at Lady Tarrant with raised eyebrows. 'The Crown Colony of Ceylon is a part of British India, and the Company on the island is run by Lady Tarrant's husband, whom I am sure will agree to act as host for the affair.'

The idea of holding a reception had come to him suddenly. He surmised that Sir Tarrant, Head of the East India Company in Ceylon, would welcome the opportunity to procure these potential brides for eligible men under his jurisdiction. Men who worked for the Company seldom got leave, as the only possible route was via the Cape of Good Hope. This voyage took several months, sometimes much longer. With these travel difficulties, Company employees could expect to return home perhaps only once before retirement, so finding a British bride was difficult.

Lady Tarrant studied Thomas with a slight smile on her lips. 'Your Excellency,' Lady Tarrant began formally. 'I do not doubt there will be a reception in your honour soon after you take up your position. We can arrange suitable accommodation for these young ladies and look after their interests. I will be a chaperone to them if they so wish.'

Katherine evidenced little enthusiasm, evident by a downturn of her mouth. Another of the women, Jennifer, was a young lady of spirit.

'Thank you, Lady Tarrant. Of course, we must go.' she cried enthusiastically. 'What's a week or two after all this – and a chance to live in Ceylon? How wonderful would that be.' She asked, looking eagerly at her companions.

All the young women had grown as close as sisters onboard and echoed Jennifer with their affirmations.

The Governor bowed his head in gratitude at Lady Tarrant before looking sideways at Mr Barrymore. The latter looked like he had swallowed a prune. 'I think it's settled then,' he said generously, feeling quite satisfied with what had transpired.

Lady Tarrant was busy answering questions from the young women, who were excited by the news that they would stop in Ceylon. Even Katherine had put aside her objections with the prospect laid before her. They had all heard throughout the voyage from Lady Tarrant about the dust and heat of the sub-continent and how salubrious Ceylon was by comparison.

Captain Anderson, keenly observing the exchange, bowed gallantly to Lady Tarrant and nodded at Thomas before leaving the room.

Thomas wiped his mouth with a napkin and sat back comfortably. '*She would make a formidable ally*', he thought to himself, watching Lady Tarrant talking to the young ladies. By calling him by his official title, she reminded everyone in the cabin who he was. '*It would be smart to keep the good lady on my side.*'

Mrs Hartley had been watching the entire exchange. She turned her head and raised her eyes to his face in one of her clear, enquiring looks.

'You have good instincts,' she said. Her dancing hazel eyes searched Thomas's, her pretty, white teeth bared in a smile. 'That was well played.'

Thomas held her gaze and felt a momentary flare of satisfaction when he observed the rise of colour to her cheek. He had discovered almost immediately after they met that they had something in common. Juliet Hartley was a music lover and formed an instant bond. She could play the cittern, a fashionable plucked stringed instrument he enjoyed listening to. Thomas tried for the hundredth time since the voyage began to analyse his feelings and motives toward her. Granted, she was a nice, reasonably attractive woman with considerable intelligence. Yet he had met others like her in the past. Possibly, the fact that she seemed drawn to him made him reciprocate.

He was born to Scotch nobility as the second son of the seventh Earl of Lauderdale, a long line of warriors, remarkable even among the Border nobles for vigour and still more for the political craft. After his family had remained for four hundred years of knightly rank, in 1624 was advanced to the dignity of Earldom.

Although destined for the Bar, Thomas obtained a commission with the Seaforth Highlanders and was posted overseas to India. Multiple postings and his dedication to public service meant that he had never married or started a family. In truth, he was not the marrying kind. Life to him meant work, and women found him quite vigorous and peremptory once they got to know him well, which did not bode well for a dalliance of any kind.

Thomas believed it was not fair for a woman to marry a general officer serving overseas. Many senior officers who were married and whose wives seemed to thrive living in far-flung corners of the British Empire disapproved of his avowed self-justification for drawing back from having a partner. That, he concluded in private moments of thought, had no validity as an excuse. He must look deeper within himself for his inability to take a step that meant marriage.

CHAPTER 3

THE PREPARATION

Lovinia woke to the light drumming of rain on the roof. She felt more relaxed than she had for a while, but the task before her constantly intruded on her thoughts. She turned her father's words over in her mind endlessly.

She yawned and looked across to where Aletta slept, curled up on her palm-straw mat and blissfully unaware of the noise. The two of them had spent the previous evening discussing how Lovinia could entrap the English official into making her his concubine. Her father, Banda, had been out all evening attending to some business and was sleeping in the next room.

Lovinia fished around on the floor next to her mat for her *sarama* (sarong). Like every other morning, she was eager to begin her day. Lovinia slipped it over her long, shapely legs and loosely braided her hair while looking out through the open window at the garden. But she seemed to notice neither the glorious blooms nor the birds singing on their boughs, for she felt solemn and reflective. A few stray hens from the village hunted for worms in the wet puddles while a proud cockerel strutted back and forth, chasing one that took its fancy.

The morning air was hot and humid as she slipped into her flat sandals and rolled up her sleeping mat. The house was quiet. Life seemed to have come to a standstill. She went to the window and peered out while cleaning her teeth with powdered charcoal mixed into a paste. The deep, velvety blue of the night sky had grown lighter, and the shapes of other huts had come into view. A morning mist rose at the jungle's edge, drifted up to the treetops, and melted away, clearing the way for a gentle, golden sun.

As was her custom, she plucked two jasmine blossoms from the vine outside the door, tucking them behind her ear. She would put them into a container of water that night and wash her cotton blouse with the scented water in the morning. The ground was wet after the usual night rain, but the heat had hardly let up, and it increased now as the sun began to rise.

Lovinia breathed in the fresh morning air deeply. Several days passed, and she kept thinking about her father's words. She closed her eyes and called to mind her promise to him. She would do everything in her power to help their family rise above the shackles of their birthright. She was determined to play her part.

'*Maalu! Maalu!*'

The fishmonger's raucous cry alerted her from her stupor. He was almost opposite their home when she called out to him. She walked outside, avoiding clay bowls on the floor, placed to catch any drips of water that found their way through the thatched roof. She stepped lightly on the hard earth. Her calloused soles were insensible to the tiny pebbles covering the path.

The gnarled, bare-bodied older man always carried a basket laden with fish hanging off a yoke of split bamboo on his shoulder, which he placed on the ground. Sitting on his haunches with his sarong tucked in, he moved a large lotus leaf, exposing a pile of small to medium-sized fish in the woven basket. Waving the leaf at the swarm of flies that hovered around him, he prodded at the fish, lifting one by its tail and presenting it to Lovinia.

'Fresh, just caught this morning,' he grunted, squinting up at her with the rheumy eyes of a drunk. Lovinia had often watched the skilled fisherman drag nets and bait lines behind his boat.

'You say that every morning,' Lovinia teased him in Sinhalese. 'But how do I know they were not the fish left over yesterday?' The two of them had been playing the same game since her mother had died two years before when Lovinia took over the responsibility of running the household for her father.

Her mother had always taught her that fresh fish was more appealing when cooked.

The fishmonger flapped his free hand in the air. 'I would not sell you old fish, missy. What would your poor mother be thinking, accusing me like that? I would never do such a thing.'

Lovinia gestured to the man that he should move the sea bass on the top of his basket to allow her to see the ones beneath. As she suspected, the fish below had pinker gills and clearer eyes. Grinning at the abashed fisherman, she chose one and asked the man to clean and cut the fish into pieces. The man pulled a vicious-looking *wak pihiya* (curved fish knife) from his pannier and proceeded to scale, gut and chop the fish on a small wooden board. After being paid, the fisherman wrapped the bloody chunks in a lotus leaf and set out, grumbling under his breath.

Lovinia's eyes darted down the lane. Neighbours called out to each other while going about their business. Their movements, coupled with the steady creak of wagons loaded with produce from the south echoing from the road, created a rhythm that usually soothed her, but not today.

'Why didn't you wake me?' Aletta stood at the entrance to the back *verandah* (which comes from the Portuguese word *varanda* meaning long balcony or terrace), rubbing the sleep from her eyes. 'Do you want some coffee?' Aletta held out a tumbler of steaming black coffee.

The kitchen verandah was her favourite spot. It was where she spent the most time with her mother, who used to let her play with small clay pots, each containing a different spice or herb, which lined the workbench. Her mother, an *ayurvedic healer* (Ayurveda, a natural medicine method originating in India more than 3,000 years ago, meaning Knowledge of Life), taught Lovinia the medicinal properties of each of the native plants from which the ingredients came.

'Let me finish my work, and I'll join you.'

Every morning since her mother died, Lovinia took on the task of preparing their main meal for the day. Lovinia placed the bundle of fish on the wooden table next to the *dara lipa* (firewood hearth), where they prepared their meals.

She pulled a blackened cooking *chatti* (earthenware pot) from a pile under the table. Placing the chunks of fish in the vessel, she washed each piece carefully with water she poured from a *gurulettuwa* (clay pot with a long-stemmed neck) that stored and cooled the water. After pouring the dirty water out, she covered the *chatti* with a piece of hardened wood shaped as a cover.

Lovinia bent down and picked up a broken half-coconut lying next to the *hiramane* (wooden coconut scraper). The well-used kitchen implement was a low four-legged wooden stool with a sharp tooth-edged metal spur sticking out from one end. Aletta watched as Lovinia sat sideways on the *hiramane* and picked up half a coconut in her hand. The fresh coconut was plucked from the back garden the previous afternoon, husked, and cracked in half with a *manna* (heavy iron knife). The coconut water she collected in a bowl to drink later.

'I have been thinking about everything,' Lovinia said. She had not stopped going over her father's words in her head. She leant forward, cupping the half-broken shell in her hands, pressing it against the metal spur. Scrapings of tender white flesh fell in piles into the container as she rotated the nut, grating it against the tiny metal teeth. 'It's a hard life, I know, but I am happiest here. I don't want to do what I have been asked to do.'

Aletta watched her scrape the coconut furiously. 'What do you want me to do?' she asked. 'Talk to your father?'

Lovinia looked at her glumly, plucking uncertainly at her *sarama*. 'No, don't do that. Just give me time to think about it a bit more.'

Aletta watched while she soaked the grated coconut flesh in warm water and squeezed the thick creamy essence into a container. She then poured the white mixture through a fine linen sieve producing thick coconut milk she would use for cooking. A ritual she went through every morning, storing the fresh coconut milk in a *chatti* to be used that day.

Her immediate chores over, Lovinia washed her hands in a tub of water and dried them on her sarong. They sat cross-legged on the ground and viewed the sun-drenched lane at the end of the garden. A bullock cart carrying cattle fodder hurried past them.

"You seem angry," Aletta noted, looking sideways at Lovinia.

Lovinia gave her a sharp look. *She is getting better at reading my innermost thoughts.* Exasperated, she swiped her hand across her forehead and clenched her fist to keep from tapping her fingers.

I cannot do it! Was her first thought. But her second was, *Yes, you can do it—since you must. But was there any need for haste?* The thought calmed her.

At that, a new fear struck her. If she delayed, the Chief Steward would react. *Would he ban them from performing in the fort? It was the primary source of their income.*

The realisation hit her that perhaps she did not have a choice. If she said no, the whole dance troupe would suffer the consequences.

Lovinia sighed ruefully, making Aletta look at her closely.

'You've made a decision,' she declared, smiling at Lovinia's exasperated look. 'It's not an easy decision, but it's correct.'

'How do you know what I want to do?' Lovinia snapped at her, regretting her tone almost immediately.

Aletta shrugged. 'Sometimes we have to make unpopular decisions for the common good.'

Lovinia nodded, calming down. 'I am sorry I snapped at you.' She reached out and laid a hand on Aletta's arm. 'You are my best friend, and I know you care about me. It's just that he's so old.'

'So, you'll do it if he is young and handsome,' Aletta giggled, making Lovinia smile. 'Someone like Lalith.'

Lovinia glared at Aletta. 'I told you never to mention his name.'

Lalith was a dancer in her father's dance troupe, whom Lovinia had a crush on when she was a teenager. It turned out that the dancer liked young boys and was kicked out of the company when he assaulted an underage boy in the village.

Aletta's eyes softened, their colours flickering in the shade.

'Sorry, but you were asking for it,' Aletta said practically. 'You've been moping around since your father brought it up. You must understand that you're a beautiful woman and a natural dancer men lust after. You must learn to use what God has given you.'

'But all I want to be is a dancer,' Lovinia said, looking at her hands.

'Just so. You're not a complete woman until you release your feelings through dance.' Aletta paused. 'You have fine features and the grace of a dancer, and I'm sure you will pick up these special movements rather quickly. You will feel free, possibly freer than you have ever felt. Standing before an audience, silently communicating with them at a different level, you'll be happy in a way you've never been.'

CHAPTER 4

THE ARRIVAL

It was a spectacular evening, cool and invigorating. There was only the lowest whisper of water around the bows of the barge as she glided over the silvery surface. It had taken all day to arrive and berth in the small harbour.

Sir Thomas Maitland, the newly appointed Governor of Ceylon, sat uncomfortably in the barge's stern in his dress uniform with his ceremonial sword between his legs. He had debated whether to wear the full regalia, but he chose to do so, knowing that his arrival in the crown colony would be the talk of the town.

That morning, as the first promise of the dawn lightened the eastern sky and snuffed out the stars, Thomas stepped out on deck. He had been woken from a dreamless sleep by a loud knock on his door.

'Captains compliments. Eight bells.'

Thomas had given orders to be woken at the end of the mid-watch, and he dressed quickly by the flickering light of a lantern the steward had brought with him. He put on his coat, trousers, and boots, carefully parted his thinning hair and put aside the thought of shaving. There would be sufficient time to prepare for disembarkation properly.

The ship's bell struck one sharp note as he stepped on the deck hardly more than an hour before dawn. The moon flickered briefly between windblown clouds, and already leeward, there was a hint of grey in the sky. He took a deep lungful of fresh sea air, appreciating it like a fine wine. He welcomed the warmth of the wind on his face.

Thomas gave himself up to the morning's quiet, the vast expanse of blue-grey ocean stretching away in every direction. The steady surging of the sea beneath the hull, the music of the waves rhythmically pulsing over the railing, and the melody occasionally punctuated by the crack of a sail hardly broke his absorption.

Last evening, the outer picket sloop of the Royal Navy squadron off Ceylon had challenged them. Captain Anderson hoisted the recognition signal and her East India Company number as the ship plunged eastwards towards landfall.

As always, the birds gave warning of the proximity of land. A passing gull was of a species that Thomas had never seen before. The sea changed colour, taking on a yellowish hue.

The Captain explained when the passengers asked him. 'The rains of a great storm have engorged the mainland rivers and discharged their muddy floodwaters into the sea. We are close to land now.'

'Land!' The joyous cries rang through the ship.

The dawn was red and splendid; the scarlet ball of the sun rising behind a line of distant hills. The Sailing Master called a series of rapid sail changes. The crew scurried aloft, excitedly calling to one another, their spirits high with the sight of land.

Thomas lurched as the sailors adjusted the sails, the ship heeling and tacking to the north.

'We're at least two hours away from Colombo.' The Captain had crossed the poop deck and stood behind the Governor, gripping the carved rail tightly with both hands. 'I'll fly the Governor's flag, your excellency, so they know you're on board. I expect them to send a tender for you.'

Thomas nodded his thanks as the ship steadied on its new heading. He watched the land only a few miles away come to life in the early morning light. A band of almost luminous pale green sea marked the shallows and reefs stretching out from the shore. Tall palms, some hanging over nearly touching the water, merged into strips of dark green. From this distance, it was clear that the land was losing its parched brown appearance as the thirsty dry earth soaked up the first heavy rains heralding the approach of the rainy season.

They passed small indentations on the coast, which played host to a range of narrow fishing vessels. Some were anchored off the shore, bobbing on the waves. Others had been hauled up on the sands and lay tilted on their sides like beached whales. Past the yellow palm-fringed beaches revealed harder edges of rough wooden buildings opposite a group of fishermen hauling in large nets filled with a pulsating mass of silver fish. Ragtag groups of what looked like children from this distance swarmed over the upended fishing boats waving excitely out to sea.

The dark waters of the bay became limpid, then the colour of jade, the imposing ramparts of the Colombo fort overlooking the harbour dominating the entrance. The Blenheim completed a final tack that took her into the port.

'Standby to go about!' the Sailing Master yelled. As the helm went over, the ship turned into the wind, the sails disappearing from the yards.

Captain Anderson looked aloft at the sailors tightly furling the sails, then smiled briefly at his Sailing Master, a hatchet-faced man called Johnson.

'Well then, Mr Johnson, here we are. That was well done. Have you ever been to Colombo before?'

'Cannot say that I have, sire. I have, of course, been to India in the past but never had occasion to visit here, although I planned to.'

'Wonderful place, this,' the Captain muttered, studying the island through his telescope, 'reminds me of the Caribbean.' He finally turned to his First Mate. 'We'll be stopping here for a week or more,' 'We will need to take on food and water supplies, but let's send the men ashore first.'

Thomas left the rail and headed for the stairs to his cabin below. The steward had packed his belongings in a large wooden chest sitting alongside his strongbox in the middle of the room. The captain's cot, now unhooked from the timbers that crossed the cabin roof, was placed against the far wall. The barren cabin depressed him. It had been his sanctuary for the last two months or more, and it pained to see it so.

*

Thomas stepped onto the stone landing steps in the sheltered harbour from the ornate wooden barge powered by eight brown-backed oarsmen and manned by a naval Petty Officer and four ratings. It was followed closely by a launch loaded with his baggage, dispatch pouches and an assortment of mailbags.

They had moored near the ditches and masonry walls of the massive Dutch fort that dominated the Colombo harbour. The Dutch expanded the original fortress built by the Portuguese to protect the small port to include a Governor's house, buildings for officials, two churches and some private dwellings with a customs house, a hospital, warehouses and troop and naval barracks for the permanent garrison. The cannons on the forbidding battlements pointed towards the land and the sea. From beneath the ramparts stretched the city's wharves and low whitewashed houses in a curve along the shore towards the north.

The land Thomas could see seemed to consist mostly of trees. Quite a lot of trees. Even the misty hills in the distance were covered with them. A few ocean-going vessels were rolling about in the harbour, and some twenty or thirty fishing canoes hauled up on the sandy beach across from where he landed. Farther back from the sea, beyond the fort, the roofs of more significant buildings and church spires stood proud above the surrounding rooftops.

There had been the usual exchange of thundering gun salutes from the Fort, which was his due, and now there was a guard of red-coated soldiers gathering near the quayside, no doubt parading for his benefit. The heat and noise hit Thomas like a blow as he reached the uppermost stone step of the jetty.

As he stepped on the quay, awaiting him was a military honour guard of English soldiers who presented arms at the shouted command of an army sergeant major. Thomas glanced around the pier, his eyes alighting on an army officer wearing the Blue velvet facings of the Royal Engineers. The officer stepped forward, snapping a salute as he straightened to attention.

'Welcome to Ceylon, Governor Maitland. Major John Staples reporting. I trust you had a pleasant voyage.'

'Thank you, Major.' Thomas removed his cocked hat and dabbed his forehead with a linen handkerchief he pulled out of his sleeve. He was familiar with the searing slap of the white-hot sun, having experienced it on board the ship with its refreshing breezes but was not used to its intensity on land.

On board the Blenheim, Thomas had read the personal recommendation of his predecessor regarding Major John Staples. This middle-aged, professional soldier had held the position of Aide-de-Camp during his tenure on the island. Studying the man's service record and overseas postings, Thomas decided not to make any changes until he met with the man and learned whether he was competent enough to keep the role. Thomas knew from experience that many career soldiers came with political or privileged family connections, sometimes both.

'General Wemyss sent his apologies, your excellency,' Major Staples said, his bearing upright. 'The General is outstation and cannot greet you in person.'

Thomas nodded without saying anything. He needed to meet with the General who commanded all the regular troops on the island. It would have been opportune to meet him right away. He wanted an immediate briefing on the current state of the war, something he couldn't find in the months-old reports. Still, the man had taken himself away, which spoke volumes of the General's arrogance, given Thomas was the Commander-in-Chief of all Forces on the island.

Thomas let his gaze wander around the activity in the harbour. Several East India Company's smaller ships stood anchor in the calm water. All had sun-bleached sails and standing rigging that showed signs of repairs made during the long voyage from Britain. These vessels had probably just arrived and had brought the merchandise and hundreds of Britons to the island for the first time. All had high hopes, whatever their station. For every ten Englishmen who came to this part of the world, less than five would return. All hoped for wealth and position, but only a fortunate few found them even in a modest way – less than one in twenty-five. The odds for a soldier favoured an eastern grave.

As he followed Major Staples to the end of the pier, Thomas got his first look at Colombo, the city he would call home for the next few years. Jostling dark-skinned bodies crowded the long jetty filling the air with a babble of native languages, cries, shouts, and noisy chaos. Thomas spun around at loud trumpeting from a nearby timber wharf. A massive greyish-brown elephant raising its trunk and bellowing at its *mahout* (keeper) captured his total attention. Goods landed from merchant ships were being carried to the stores and warehouses in heavy drays, light carts and on the backs of stubborn donkeys.

'I have arranged for a carriage to take you to Government House.' Major Staples stood at Thomas's elbow, gesturing at an open carriage drawn by a brown horse. A squad of red-jacketed soldiers surrounding the vehicle studied Thomas with enquiring eyes as he walked towards them.

Thomas shook his head. 'No, I'll walk. I need to stretch my legs and feel solid earth beneath my feet.'

Today was the day he had been working towards all his life. Born to the purple but uneducated, he had worked himself to the bone throughout an official career of twenty-seven years, work that he doubted any ordinary man would have attempted. His life was full of his unbending devotion to duty for His Majesty's safety, honour and welfare, and dominions.

Thomas took stock once again of his qualifications for the job. The Maitland clan was one of the oldest of the Scotch nobility. They were crafty border fighters, and although they were always conspicuous figures in the fighting services, it was more in the active conduct of public affairs that the Maitlands excelled. They were busy, active public men with their share of the unscrupulousness of their age and a considerable gift of successful intrigue. In Thomas, the second son of the seventh Earl, the daring and craft of the Maitlands showed itself blended with the patience, the conciliatory temper and the habit of compromise which made him successful as an administrator. He was far from inexperienced, he reassured himself. He had served in the army in India. He had risen in the ranks by serving as a military commander and chief administrator to an anxious colony in the West Indies. He had made a name as a parliamentarian and had many friends and contacts in high places back in Britain.

The jetty ended at an unpaved road leading up a small hill. Women in the jewelled colours of their saris walked with grace and elegance, many carrying large baskets balanced on their heads with as much dignity as a dowager arriving at a court ball in a tiara. A swarm of semi-naked, brown-skinned children flitted among the crowd, offering bundles of cinnamon sticks and begging for rupees with enormous, imploring eyes.

Thomas walked several blocks to the Governor's official residence, using the nervous energy he felt. A big, cool stone building with a red roof and thick whitewashed walls stood in the centre of a walled garden. Wide, covered balconies ran all-round the ground and upper floors, reminding Thomas of a square, two-tiered wedding cake.

The impressive entrance hall, stuffed with ebony easy chairs and sofas, with a few woven-rattan recliners dotted among them, was visible when the butler threw open the doors to receive his new master. Several individuals dressed in household livery were bowing and falling back respectfully.

A formally attired man stepped forward. Major Staples introduced him as Mr Biggins, the Chief Steward. Thomas looked with interest at the man responsible for the efficient running of his household. He was a thin man who might have been good-looking in his youth. But now, he gave the impression of someone who had crushed out all the pleasures of life.

The Chief Steward bowed low to Thomas and called out the names of the servants who would deal directly with Thomas. Samuel the butler, Johnson his manservant and some others, whose names Thomas immediately forgot. He regarded them thoughtfully. He removed the cocked hat from his head and held it out, and with the other hand, relinquished his gloves and his cane into the care of a footman. His manservant Johnson took his hat from him and murmured, 'Your coat, my Lord!'

'My coat, yes, in a moment!' Thomas said, moving unhurriedly into the building. They walked past the staircase through a door into a long corridor lined with paintings leading towards the mansion's rear. An open door in the passage led to a formal dining room. To the right, through another door, Thomas could see a sizeable timber-floored ballroom with two massive chandeliers hanging from the ceiling.

They entered a spacious open foyer overlooking the shaded rear gardens at the end of the corridor. The garden was extensive, with a large green lawn flanked by several massive old trees under which giant ferns and flowering plants of various kinds grew profusely. A marble statue of the King stood proudly in the middle of the garden next to a huge boulder.

The Chief Steward scurried ahead of Thomas, waving his arm towards a door leading off the verandah to the right. 'Your office, Sire.'

Thomas followed the Chief Steward to the Governor's office. He was not impressed with the room. It was far less ornate than he'd been accustomed to in the West Indies. A portrait of the King hung above the fireplace that dominated the left wall. The governor's desk sat at the end of the room, with two overstuffed chairs in front and a sideboard in the corner.

Thomas shrugged off his coat and handed it to Johnson, his manservant. He walked to the windows. An old native man with grey hair was sweeping leaves from the withered apology for a lawn. The sun's heat had scorched the grass brown, and in places, the hard ground showed enormous bald patches, crisscrossed where the earth had cracked, as though wrinkled by age. Everything had the sad air of neglect.

Feeling fatigued by the heat and heaving humidity, Thomas went directly to his room, where he enjoyed a hot meal of mutton leg with cabbage and potatoes, washed down with excellent ale. He was suddenly weary, and while Johnson closed the blinds, he climbed into his bed and immediately went to sleep.

CHAPTER 5

THE KANDYAN

A man stood quietly with folded arms on the shady side of one of the mud-brick buildings that edged the thriving marketplace. His position gave him a good view of the dusty market and its fantastic variety of brightly coloured goods – a clashing kaleidoscope of smells and sounds—fruit and vegetable stalls, bakers, dry goods shops, cane weavers, wood carvers, and makers of sandals. Here a potter spun his wheel and shaped the clay, calling out to passing shoppers. A barber plied his trade in a shady corner, jostled by roving fishmongers.

Shoppers filled the village square—the island's white-clad, copper-skinned, black-haired inhabitants with their baskets and squabbling voices. They took no notice of the man whose ordinary white chemise and *sarama* (sarong) made him inconspicuous and whose immobility made him seem merely part of the shadow in which he stood. Outwardly casual, he was as alert as a cat at a mousehole. His eyes, the only part of him that moved, flashed restlessly over the crowd, searching, probing, overlooking nothing. He had been waiting since daybreak.

A little commotion in a far corner of the square drew his attention. A group of red-coated native soldiers, pushing officiously through the crowd, had shoved a girl against a passing rickshaw so that she collided with the man pulling the two-wheeled vehicle. He, in turn, lost his balance, staggered, and almost dropped the shafts. At that point, the English lady inside leaned forward and began to rebuke him furiously.

A glance at the sun told the man he would be noticed if he waited much longer and questioned. He was here on his King's orders to find someone willing to pass on information about what the English were planning.

The man caught sight of the girl again. This time she was near him, strolling with apparent aimlessness among the stalls. She stopped to watch a potter at work, and the man studied her curiously, unable to fit her into any of the usual categories. Unlike people from the south, the woman had a light caramel-coloured complexion, like the people from the highlands where he was born. Her face was mobile, alert, and vivid, narrow across the cheekbones, an attractive face, set with eyes as green as a field of newly grown paddy with cat-like irises, which gazed out on the world like iridescent emeralds—a rare sight in the country. Her tanned, athletic body was lithe. Her exposed breasts with their dark nipples pointing upwards like young fruit reaching for the sun.

The girl, more a young woman than he had first thought, wandered a few steps farther, and the man's eyes followed her. She was a high-spirited and lovely creature; had he not been watching closely, he would never have seen the swift glance she threw into a side alley. A shop apprentice was hurrying along, balancing his great flat basket of breadstuffs on his head, waving a palm branch over them to keep off the flies and crows.

Tongue in cheek, the man continued to watch. He was not surprised when the girl stepped innocently into the alley at the precise moment that the shop apprentice darted around the corner of the stall. There was a shout, the inevitable sharp collision, and bread, basket, and palm leaf scattered in all directions.

Instantly the girl was all remorse. She was everywhere at once, snatching up the bread and dusting them, soothing the apprentice with smiles and sympathy that caused his frown to give way to a flattering smirk. Only the watching man, shaking with silent merriment, observed a few bread rolls that found their way into her sash instead of the basket. His enjoyment increased as she began to nibble a roll absently under the apprentice's nose while chattering to him. And it passed all bounds when she took another from her sash, offered it prettily to the dazzled youth, and strolled off down the street, leaving him blushing and gaping happily after her.

The man watched the girl go down a path with that supple, swinging walk past a large tree filled with jackfruit down towards the ocean. He had spent the previous day looking for his quarry and familiarised himself with the different lanes and paths that crisscrossed the area. He followed the girl, looking around to ensure no one noticed his sudden departure.

The village was just like any other he'd visited. Landowners, cinnamon peelers, and farmers from the higher castes lived in the heart of the village. Toddy tappers, storekeepers, launderers, and members of any lower caste like the *Rodiya* lived toward the edge of the settlement. Lavatory cleaners, gravediggers and those who dealt with the dead resided outside the village, as befitted those with no caste.

In the coastal areas, fishermen risked their lives to catch fish in slender outrigger canoes daily. They lived with their family groups at the ocean's edge. They were a caste that valued their independence and would fiercely defend their territory.

Members of the noblest caste, usually the landowners, also lived in the village. However, they owned nothing more than any other village resident, cultivating their gardens and a large rice field or coconut plantation, and occupied a similar mud hut with more rooms.

A gentle sea breeze wafted through the coconut trees. The path before them was still damp from the previous night's rain, the villagers having swept them into neat, untrodden patterns. A chorus of birdsong filled the crisp morning air, just house sparrows and myna birds chirping their sweet melodies. The sun was already a ball of yellow above them, insinuating more warmth to come.

The girl ahead of him quickened her pace and disappeared around the corner. He hurried to keep her in sight. The path opened out into an open, grassy area dotted with rocks which rose gently before him to the top of a cliff overlooking the ocean.

The man looked around, trying to see where the girl was, but there was no one except a small family of goats munching on the sparse grass. Frowning in surprise at her sudden disappearance, he took a few steps forward. He was so intent on looking where the girl had gone that he jumped at the sharp, questioning voice behind him.

'Who are you? Why are you following me?'

*

Lovinia noticed the man standing by the corner of a vegetable stall. She had not seen him before and after a few minutes realised that she was the focus of his attention. Studying him from the corner of her eyes, she saw that he was tall and good-looking, with a nobleman or a warrior's posture. As a dancer, Lovinia was used to the lecherous looks she received from all types of men when she performed, but this was somehow different. When he fell in behind her on the path to the rocky outcrop overlooking the bay, Lovinia decided to confront the man.

'Who are you? Why are you following me?' Lovinia snapped out the question catching the man unaware. She had doubled back into the undergrowth, waiting until the man stepped out into the open grassland before approaching him from behind. His reaction to her unexpected presence surprised her. Despite being startled by her sudden appearance behind him, the man whirled like a trained athlete, standing perfectly balanced with his feet planted apart, prepared for anything.

Seeing the intensity in his eyes, Lovinia gathered herself, every muscle tensed for quick movement. For a moment, they remained thus, gripped by mutual surprise.

The man raised his right hand slowly, palm up. 'Do not fear me,' he said gently. 'My name is of no matter to you.' He spoke in Sinhalese but with a different intonation than she was used to.

Lovinia did not relax. 'I fear no one. Who are you? Why do you watch me?' On closer observation, she could see that the man was fairer than the people from the south.

The man hesitated as Lovinia watched him, his eyes guarded. 'Please, it was rude of me to startle you. It was not my intention. I beg your pardon. Could we begin our acquaintance all over again?' He flashed her a disarming smile as he brought his feet together, bowing slightly from the waist.

Lovinia studied him closely. He was a handsome man about ten years her senior, she guessed. Beneath a mop of curly dark hair, his light grey eyes were startling against unusually tanned skin. He was taller than her with the slenderness of an athlete, but the width of his shoulders gave promise of superior strength. His eyes roved over Lovinia's face and figure, lingering on her braided hair and unfettered breasts.

His eyes were the vigilant eyes of a hunter and caught Lovinia's attention immediately. *It's someone I must watch carefully.* The fleeting thought crossed her mind as she reacted to his smile. A tingling replaced her initial response to flee in her body that she had never felt before.

The man gestured to a rock outcropping overlooking the ocean. 'Can we sit and talk? It is something important that will greatly benefit you and your family.' His manner was perfect; it contained just the mixture of friendliness and reserve best calculated to reassure her.

Lovinia allowed herself to be guided to a flat rock by the man beside her. He smiled more engagingly than before, realising he had a powerful weapon to hold over her if need be.

What does he want from me?

The man studied her with a look she couldn't understand at all. 'What I am about to tell you will be for your ears only. My life might hang on your remembering that—yours certainly does! Do you understand?'

The man's mask had slipped for a moment. Lovinia gripped her hands tightly together, and moisture broke out on her forehead. She had no doubt what he meant.

'I am a close confidante to someone of importance, though no one knows. On the surface, I am just an ordinary merchant. I was given the task of learning what the English King's new emissary is planning. So, I must reach an arrangement with someone close to him.'

Lovinia remembered the coldness of his eyes a moment ago. The man was a loyalist rebel and, therefore, dangerous as a cobra. A little chill ran up between her shoulder blades. Undoubtedly, he was from the Kingdom of Kandy, which was at war with the English.

'All I want is that you serve me. But not as a slave. As an ally. I need someone like you, unknown, beyond suspicion—and clever. It is a dangerous task, but you have no choice, as I think I've made clear.'

So, he wants me to act as an informer. Lovinia listened in silence, hardly able to believe what he was saying. The concept was familiar and distasteful. The Kandyan court was known to hire informers who lived risky lives and were often found murdered. She was being threatened with her life, being manipulated into the position of spy and intriguer—and by those who were deadly enemies, fighting in opposing camps for opposing causes! *No, she had no intention of ever being an informer and putting her family in harm's way.*

Without answering, she leapt for the open space. But quick as she was, he was quicker. Without seeming to disturb his lazy pose, his hand shot out, and fingers like iron bands closed over her wrist.

Lovinia looked down in despair at the hand which held hers. It was lean and shapely—the hand of an aristocrat. Yet it had the strength of a labourer. 'Goat! Barbarian!' raged Lovina under her breath. She preferred to rage in Sinhalese since its heavy gutturals lent themselves perfectly to invective.

Lovinia steeled herself before returning his belligerent stare. He waited, fixing her with narrowed eyes, and Lovinia stiffened. She had never experienced this sort of ruthlessness—the sort that came sheathed in exquisite charm.

'My spies have informed me that the head of the Governor's household has shown more than a passing interest in you. He is a bachelor whose male desires include native women, which I want you to exploit.'

Mixed thoughts and emotions raced through Lovinia's body. Her pulse quickened at the idea of seducing the head of the house whose power came from a man who ruled the world. Rather than frighten her, the thought inspired her. At an early age, she realised that women were treated like chattels in their society. Unless you were born to a noble family of power and wealth, women lived a miserable existence. The English King ruled half the world, as Lovinia had heard the soldiers and sailors boast. Why couldn't she aspire for greater things than just being a lowly dancer?

It was incredible, but it was true. She could become someone who mattered. *He may be clever*, she thought. *Well, so am I! He may be important and ruthless, but he has yet to find out how heartless I can be!*

Lovinia felt his eyes upon her even before she raised her own, with an effort to meet them. Coughing to smother the quiver in her voice, 'what do you want me to do?'

The man narrowed his eyes distrustfully. 'You must use your wiles as a dancer and find a way to seduce the man. He is already attracted to you, so you must find a way to remind him of your charms. Can you do that?'

Lovinia blushed and looked away from his frank gaze. 'Yes, I can dance for him again when the opportunity presents itself.'

He acts as if I were some sheltered girl who has never ventured from her father's side, thought Lovinia. Life was no longer in any danger of becoming monotonous.

'Once you have done that,' the man went on softly, 'you will accompany the man to his quarters in the fort and remain there. Keep your ears open. Listen to whatever goes on between the Governor and those surrounding him—his nobles, soldiers, servants, and scribes. I want to know which of these people carries his orders to others outside the palace walls. Somehow, he is sending and receiving messages from within our realm. I want to know how.'

Lovinia stared at him, breathing hard; her palms felt sweaty. 'In short, I am a spy.'

'Exactly. You should have no trouble obtaining this information, given your natural ability. If you succeed, you will not be dissatisfied with your reward. But if you fail, whether by accident or design—.' He did not finish the sentence. He did not need to. He smiled, sending a little trickle of fear down Lovinia's spine.

Lovinia tried and failed. In a panic, she swallowed and tried again. 'How am I to report to you?'

'Leave that to me.'

She took a deep breath. 'Is it permitted to know your name?'

'It is not. There is no need to know who I am. The less you know, the better. That way, you will not be tempted to let your wits run away with you.' The man stood up, lifted his chemise, and pulled a large shiny coin from a belted pouch on his waist. 'Take this. It will pay for some fine clothes, some perfume. Do we understand each other?'

Lovinia looked down at a gold sovereign. She had only seen one before at the Afghan money lenders. Just that one coin would feed their extended family for weeks.

'Perfectly,' said Lovinia, looking up. She was breathing more easily now. The nervous sweat had dried on the palms of her hands. He was just a man like all the others who wanted something from her. She had learnt to accept their sweaty advances as long as they paid for the privilege she afforded them. This man just wanted her for something else.

The man straightened, satisfaction on his dark face. 'Then go. Remember, I am no stupid baker's apprentice. Enjoy your freedom, fine clothes, and contact with aristocracy—while you can. It may not last long.'

He leaned back, gesturing toward the path back to the village, and Lovinia realized he was dismissing her. She was free to make her way unchallenged to whatever her future held. Instead of poverty and constant challenges, there would be luxury, intrigue, and excitement. Once she was in, whatever this man's threats might be, there would be endless opportunities for a girl who knew how to use her wits!

The future opened before her in a vista radiant with possibilities, each more fascinating than the last. Without knowing it, she laughed aloud. The man's dry voice rasped suddenly across her daydreams.

'Be careful, Lovinia. You are still a nobody.'

She shrugged and grinned. 'I'll try to remember.'

'I will be there to remind you,' he remarked acidly. He jerked his head toward the path, and she went without looking back.

CHAPTER 6

THE CROWN COLONY

Thomas was, by habit, up before first light. When the heavy drapes were pulled open, the half-glass panelled doors filled the room with the glow of a rising eastern sun, which turned the sea from grey to blue.

The Dutch Governor's former residence, which General McDowall subsequently used, was the largest and best dwelling-house in the Fort of Colombo. Whoever had built the residence had, clearly inspired by Portuguese architecture, created a wonder of mosaic floors and latticed shutters where almost every room opened to a terrace or a balcony. It was situated on the principal street and composed of two regular stories. From the upper balcony on one side was an extensive view of the sea, the road, and shipping. On the other was a more prosperous outlook, covering the lake, bustling markets, cinnamon plantations, a wide range of inland territories bounded by a pointed peak, and many lesser mountains. Two large halls and several smaller rooms divided by an imposing wooden staircase dominated the ground floor.

'Day just breaking, Sah. A warm morning with a bit o' fog.' Johnson, his valet, was a cockney, given his accent. White hair fluttered about his ears; sharp blue eyes in a tanned, wrinkled face looked at Thomas from under white brows. Before leaving London, Thomas was offered the use of a manservant, which he had declined, preferring instead to find a local retainer after arriving at the colony.

'I knew a Johnson aboard the Blenheim. The Shipping Master. Any relative?'

'My brudder, Sah.'

Thomas studied the man with interest. 'What made you stop here?'

Johnson raised his bushy eyebrows. 'Met someone, Sah.' He watched Thomas cautiously.

'You live with a local woman?' Thomas had read about a growing number of European soldiers and sailors marrying local women on the island.

'That's right—beg pardon! Married a local woman, Sah.'

Thomas acknowledged the answer with a nod, mentally noting to learn more about the status of such arrangements. Having spent considerable time travelling in both the West and the East Indies, he understood the value a good retainer would bring, making his life much easier. But finding a bad one would do exactly the opposite, so he had resisted being rushed into deciding.

Thomas had woken up that morning feeling hot and sweaty. He had opened one of the tall windows facing the ocean but felt little relief from the still air smelling damp from a light rain that had fallen during the night.

'Get me a bath, Johnson. Make it ready while I shave.'

'Yes, Sah.'

Thomas looked about the surprisingly austere room but neat and clean, the enormous four-poster bed with decent linens and a fine net looped over a metal circle suspended over the well-stuffed mattress, the only sign of any luxury. The room also contained a wardrobe, a wash handstand with a mirror, a simple captain's desk, and an ornate straight-backed padded chair on a faded floor rug.

Thomas stripped off his sweaty night clothes and shaved at the wash handstand in the corner of the room. He kept his eyes from his naked body reflected in the mirror, from his skinny, hairy legs and slightly protuberant belly. He kept his mind from his anxiety about meeting with Major Staples that morning. Johnson and a footman entered carrying the bath and placing it on the floor near him. Thomas, shaving carefully round the corners of his lips, heard the hot water pouring into it from buckets. Compounding the mixture in the right proportion took a little while to get the temperature suitable.

Thomas stepped into it and sank with a sigh of satisfaction – an immense amount of water poured over the sides, displaced by his body, but he did not care. He thought about soaping himself but flinched from the necessary effort and physical contortions. Instead, he lay back and allowed himself to soak and relax.

Thomas found it exasperating to have a bath in this fashion. However, he tried not to allow it to annoy him. He struggled to dismiss from his mind recollections of baths taken on the deck of a ship under a deck pump powered by sailors that flung vast quantities of invigorating seawater. Thomas seized the soap and flannel and began vigorously to wash those parts of himself he could reach as water slopped over the side onto the shiny oak floor of his dressing room.

Thomas had just finished his bath when Johnson announced that Major Staples had arrived and was waiting for him in the office downstairs. Johnson hung a warm towel over Thomas's shoulders, adeptly preventing the ends from dipping into the water as Thomas stepped out of the soapy water and walked across the floor, leaving a trail of wet footprints. Thomas towelled himself and stared gloomily through the bedroom door at the garments Johnson had laid out for him there. For many years Thomas had worn nothing except a uniform. A uniform was comforting. No one could fault him if it did not flatter his figure because he had no choice. But with civilian clothes, his taste and preference were on display

Johnson helped him into his clothes, and Thomas could not help but notice that it was getting snug in several places.

'Breakfast, Sah? I could serve it 'ere or in the office downstairs.'

'Just plain toast with a cup of black coffee will do, Johnson. Downstairs if you please.' Onboard the Blenheim, Thomas's usual breakfast repast was a tankard of ale and a plate of cold roast beef.

Thomas took stock of his qualifications for the job again as he descended to the floor below. The Foreign Office was giving him a free hand – he could not complain on that score and reassured himself that he could handle it. Thomas knew he was not sent to govern an island—he was being sent to make it profitable to the Crown.

Major Staples was looking out into the garden when Thomas walked into his office. It was a large, ornate room with three tall floor-to-ceiling French doors dominating the far wall. On the wall opposite the fireplace, two overstuffed chairs faced each other next to a tall window that gave an impressive view of the garden and the sea. A coat tree occupied the corner nearest the door, where he had deposited his hat and overcoat as he entered. A small rug covered the hardwood flooring in front of the fireplace, and there was a vase with flowers on a small table near the windows where it would catch the sunlight.

Thomas dabbed his forehead with his sleeve. The intense mid-morning heat and humidity triggered by the light rain that had fallen overnight made the beads of sweat on his forehead run down his face.

'Is it always this damn hot?' Thomas grumbled. 'It's hardly noon.'

The Major turned at the sound of his voice. 'Good morning, your Excellency. The monsoon is due soon, overdue, in fact. It always feels like this before the heavy rains.'

Major Staples was a large man, squarely built, who gave the impression of someone you could count on in an emergency. Thomas strode forward to shake hands with him before turning and sitting behind the large, heavy desk.

'Thank you for coming this morning, Major. Please sit down.' Thomas motioned to the chair opposite him. 'I wish to hear from you this morning about what the last few months have been like. I read all the official despatches up to the time I left England. How goes the war with the Kandyan natives?'

Thomas steepled his hands, his head tilted to one side, listening to Major Staples give his report. Johnson busied himself around the two men, laying out a breakfast tray with four slices of brown toast, butter, strawberry jam, and a carafe of steaming hot coffee. Major Staples shook his head when offered a cup of coffee, waiting for Thomas to butter his toast and take his first sip before continuing.

Long minutes passed before Thomas raised his hand, stopping Major Staples mid-sentence. 'I can get everything you're telling me from reading the despatches from the time I was at sea,' he said, slapping a pile of documents on his table. Thomas knew that the despatches written by foreign office administrators trained to make dry statements of facts told him little of what was happening on the island. 'Tell me something I will not find in these despatches.'

The Major took a deep breath before replying. 'The most important matter that needs addressing, if I may, your Excellency, is the military forces at your disposal.'

Thomas understood what Major Staples was referring to. It was something which had concerned him. 'What is our current muster?'

'Our forces on the ground include a single European regiment of three battalions divided between Colombo, Trincomalee and Jaffnapatam.' Major Staples reported from memory. 'Local forces include a regiment of native Sinhalese and another of *Sepoys* (Indian troops employed by the British) from Madras, British officers lead both.' Major Staples paused, waiting until Thomas nodded at him to continue.

'There is a regiment of Malays recruited from Molucca and Penang, also led by British officers. We have a short regiment of a battalion of *Caffres* (blacks from Africa) and another battalion of *Sepoys* recruited from around Cochin, both of which are currently under training.'

Thomas looked up from the slice of bread he was buttering. 'So, a total deployment of how many?'

'Including artillery, garrison, supply and a small cavalry force, a total strength of around eleven thousand men, Sir.' The Major watched Thomas as he gave his report.

Thomas raised his eyebrows. 'That's quite a large force. I had no idea you have so many native troops. Has the Colonial Office approved the raising of native battalions?'

'Governor North approved, your Excellency. It was an attempt to find troops better suited to the local conditions.'

'Why?' Thomas queried. 'Has there been much illness?

'Yes, sir, and the *Caffres* are much easier to manage.'

Thomas knew there was nothing new about using former African slaves as mercenaries. The Portuguese had long employed them, as had many Indian rulers.

Thomas cast him a shrewd look. 'Are they well-led?'

The Major shifted in his chair. 'Your Excellency's presence is essential to combine the measures of the rather diverse force available to defend this colony,' he said with diplomatic restraint.

Thomas made a derisive sound. 'I have come to the same conclusion, Major.' He was pleasantly surprised with the Major's honesty. Perhaps he was worth keeping after all. 'Please arrange a meeting with General Wemyss at his convenience. The sooner, the better.'

'I shall arrange for a message to be sent immediately, Sir. If you would excuse me.' Major Staples said, rising to his feet.

Thomas nodded without responding, his thoughts far away. He was not surprised that the Kandyan kingdom entrenched in their highland sanctuary was not defeated. While the actual forces at his disposal were extensive, they were spread across the island, many around the port of Trincomalee, which the French coveted. It seemed to him that they were lucky the natives were not warlike. If they were, he concluded, the Governor he was replacing would have been the last British Governor on the island.

Thomas steepled his hands, thinking about what he had just heard. His appointment as Governor-General of the Crown Colony of Ceylon was in August of the previous year, and here he was in March, just about to begin.

Thomas remembered his brief meeting with King George III when he received his Royal commission. Rumours were circulating in London that the King was recovering from a severe illness. The Secretary of State for Foreign Affairs ushered Thomas into the Royal antechamber at St James Palace, its doorway flanked by two formidable Yeoman of the Guard. The room, lined with dark oak timbered bookshelves, held a large desk and tables covered with maps and books. A Royal Secretary was busy at a small escritoire in the far corner.

The King seated on an exquisitely carved, gilt-framed high-backed chair with arms, peering at a parchment lying on the desk, looked up when they entered.

The Secretary of State and Thomas bowed low before him.

'Your Majesty, I present Major General, The Right Honourable Sir Thomas Maitland.'

'Ah, yes. The Governor,' said the King, holding his hand for Thomas to kiss. The King was a large man with a round, pasty face and a bulbous nose, his eyes wide set and dulled with age. He wore a scarlet military-style coat over a white waistcoat and britches with the scarlet and blue mantle of the Order of the Garter around his shoulders. A heavy gold chain of the same order hung around his neck.

'His Majesty signed your commission in cabinet yesterday.' The Secretary of State announced, glancing at Thomas before slipping a roll of parchment out of his sleeve and handing it to the King. It was tied with a red ribbon and secured by a wax imprint of the Great Seal of England.

The King held the roll for a moment before leaning forward and placing the Royal Commission in Thomas's outstretched hand. 'I expect to have good reports of you before long,' He had a weak, high-pitched voice out of character in such a large form. 'The Colony is a drain on our purse, and matters need to be rectified quickly.' There was no kindliness in the expressionless tone nor life in those dull eyes.

'May I assure Your Majesty of my loyal devotion and immediate attention to the matter.'

The King studied him for a moment and made a gesture of dismissal with his hand. The Secretary of State surreptitiously pulled at his arm, indicating that the interview was over. Thomas bowed and moved to the side door leading out to the corridor.

'That was good,' the Secretary said outside. 'There weren't any awkward questions.' He held out his hand. 'Farewell, Sir Thomas. These stairs will lead you down into the courtyard. We will meet again before you sail, but I expect good reports of your governorship too.'

Later, after the strange meeting with the King and before leaving London, the Secretary of Trade had told him privately what was expected of him. It amounted to undoing his predecessor's work, who had almost ruined the colony, as rapidly and thoroughly as possible.

The island of Ceylon was now considered a Colony of the Crown, obtained for strategic reasons but retained to become profitable. Plans were in place for the island's administration to be made separate from the East India Company. They would go into effect when he arrived on the island. Due to the Kandyan wars, the negative trade balance and the disappointing revenue, the colony was in a bad financial state. The British possessions on the island consisted only of a narrow ring of territory around the coast, the island's interior under the rule of the King of Kandy. He held a strong position in his capital in the mountainous middle of the island. The Colony had become a drain on the Crown, with trade rapidly falling off, and there was an enormous debt to the East India Company under the cinnamon contract. The war with Kandy had not been anticipated, causing a massive expense increase. Moreover, the political opinion in England had turned against the extraordinary expenditures made in overseas wars.

Thomas sighed in frustration at the delay in getting to his post, but he had wisely spent the months at sea and felt fully prepared for the task ahead. Continually employed in the military and public service for twenty-five years, this experience was brought to bear on a most challenging task – running an important Colony of the Crown.

Gathering copies of his predecessors' reports from the distant colony was not straightforward. He had insisted on taking procession of every single one and eventually got what he wanted before leaving London. He had pored over the documents in his cabin for long hours and found a state of affairs hardly distinguishable from what he had left in his previous post. But there was a significant difference. In his last position, he only had delegated authority for a particular purpose and, later, no power whatsoever. Here he would be the undisputed master with a King's commission.

CHAPTER 7

SECOND THOUGHTS

Lovinia looked about her and felt another stirring of the unease she had not been able to shake off since meeting the Kandyan. A bullfrog croaked plaintively in the darkness from the channel irrigating the coconut plantation behind their hut. Lying alone on her mat on the verandah that night, Lovinia tossed and turned, trying to decide whether to tell her father of her meeting.

Lovinia had first tried to persuade herself that the Kandyan was mistaken or lying. For if his threat were real, she would have to take him seriously, which by now was a prospect she had to face. It could be true, or it might not be. She would wait and do nothing until she was sure. There was no need to do anything yet. She had dug a hole in the mud floor of their little room and buried the money that the Kandyan had given her, stamping down the earth and smoothening the mixed clay and dried cow dung floor, covering the whole surface so that no one could tell where it had been disturbed.

The hard-earthen floor was uncomfortable. The constant chirping of the crickets, which had once soothed her, had become an irritant. The familiar scent of jasmine from the vines by the doorway was underlaid heavily by the smell of dung from the cow shed.

When the cocks began to crow, she awoke from a fitful sleep, blinking at the lessening gloom. She had been up most of the night, but the rest had cleared her brain, and like a tender green shoot emerging from the black soil of the night, the solution emerged. She had to confide in someone, but it could not be her father. Aletta was the only person she felt she might be able to trust, not gossip and keep her secret.

Lovinia bathed at the well, the cold sparkling water reviving her. She donned her *sarama*, oiling and combing her hair before the small piece of polished metal in the inner room. She picked up the long-handled broom of *ekels*, swiftly sweeping the verandah of insects, dry leaves and flower petals blown in from the garden.

That morning's breakfast was a thick *kola kande*, a healthy breakfast porridge of fresh greens, garlic, coconut milk, red rice, and turmeric. Lovinia boiled the mixture on the *dara lipa* – the traditional heath on the broad back verandah where they cooked their food. She scooped a portion into a wooden bowl without the turmeric as she preferred the *kande* with a cube of *jaggery* (sugar cane) for sweetness. Then slicing fresh pawpaw from the tree in the garden, she twisted a sliver of fresh lime juice to add extra flavour.

Banda spoke from the backroom. 'Lovinia, I want to ensure that you have no second thoughts about what we must do.' He appeared on the threshold; his voice was low and unassuming. Almost kind.

Lovinia returned his gaze, hoping the colour in her eyes hid the thoughts running rampant behind them.

'Has Aletta taught you anything?'

She nodded. 'Yes, she has taught me much.'

'Are you scared?' he asked so quietly she almost missed it.

Lovinia put down her spoon. 'Do you want me to be scared, father? You know I volunteered for this. No one forced me to.'

'No. I want you to be honest.' His eyes were drawn and sunken.

'But you wouldn't know if I were lying?' Her words were patient yet wary.

'Yes, I would because you are not a gifted liar. You only think yourself to be.' Banda leaned forward, picking up the bowl of *kande* (gruel) she placed for him on the table. 'But I must alert you to the perils of this undertaking, and I can see something is bothering you.'

Lovinia's eyes narrowed. 'You're not good at reading people, father.' She held her breath as his face changed colour. She had never spoken to him so bluntly before. The knuckles in his hands turned white for a tormenting instant before he released his grip. Lovinia watched the tension leave him, a swirl of emotions colliding in her chest, wreaking havoc on her mind.

'Brave words for a girl who is putting herself in danger.' His tone was edged in ice. Lovinia imagined he knew about the Kandyan for a moment, but she immediately dismissed the thought. She sat up straight and twisted her hair to hang over one shoulder.

Looking gloomy, Banda seemed to think out loud in the distance. 'Always keep in mind that the English aren't our guests. They intended to stay, not merely as traders but as rulers. Slowly, they seek to reign over our beloved land like many foreign powers had, looting, burning, seizing properties, and subjugating us.'

Lovinia's first spy assignment sounded risky, but she did not want to miss it. 'If it will help us rise above this life, I am prepared for whatever is to come.' Lovinia knew her father went to extreme lengths to provide an income for the dance troupe, who were almost like a family. After her mother's death, her father had nearly lost his mind, and only the functioning of the dance troupe had brought him back from the edge of despair.

She reached up and coiled her wavy black hair into a knot on the nape of her neck. 'All our lives are forfeit, father. It is just a question of when.'

*

They both sat on the floor mat, knees pulled up to their chests, the oil lamp flickering between them, quiet, not looking at each other.

'Are you going to tell your father?'

Instantly wary, Lovinia tightened her knees against her chest and shuttered her expression. She had not left out anything of the encounter with the tall Kandyan.

'No!' Lovinia shook her head. 'I don't know how he'll react. You know what he is like.'

Aletta looked at Lovinia thoughtfully. 'I think you should,' she said, reaching out and holding her by the arm. 'You cannot do this by yourself. You are going to need some help.'

'That's why I am telling you,' Lovina said, looking at Aletta beseechingly. 'I need someone to talk to.'

'You realise you could die for being a spy.' Aletta tightened the grip of her fingers on Lovinia's arm almost painfully. A spark of something flashed across her face, lingering on her lips but was gone too quickly to offer anything of meaning.

Aletta was quiet for a while. When she spoke, her voice was soft and warm. 'But I would like to see you succeed. Meaning, I would like to see you live.' Her tone was filled with quiet circumspection.

'Do you think I want this? I have no choice.'

Aletta groaned when she saw the determined look on Lovinia's face. 'No, there's always a choice, Lovinia. Even if you survive this, there is nothing you can do. As a family, we must deal with this, however difficult it may seem.'

At that moment, Lovinia examined her longings in a new light. Aletta's words rang true. Much as she wanted to remain in the loving embrace of her dance troupe family, her destiny no longer lay with them. A feeling of glorious possibilities swept over her.

'Perhaps you are right, perhaps not. There's a different path for me.'

Aletta looked as though she had something on her mind. 'You'll have to carve that new path for yourself. How easy do you think that will be?' Aletta looked fondly at her. 'You know I was born not too far from here. I lived with my family next to a pond. My father, a farmer, taught me how to plough when I could barely walk. My mother was a midwife, and I assisted her whenever possible.'

Aletta stared into the distance, her eyes unfocused. 'We did not have enough to eat because of the revenue we had to pay the tax collector, but I could dance. As soon as I heard music, I wanted to stand up, smile, and move. My legs trembled; my hands moved of their own free will.' Aletta shivered at the thought. 'Dancing has always been in my veins. After my father's death, with three younger sisters to support, I had to earn a living for my family, so I sold my body to those who offered to pay. Our village used to shut their door to women such as us. It's not respectable to be out in public, to show your flesh to men and taunt them with suggestive movements.'

In the flickering yellow lamplight, Lovinia watched Aletta, a spirited woman only a few years older than her, with a spark of determination in her eyes. Lovinia envied the freedom she had, doing what she had always wanted.

'That is when I came here and wandered the streets looking for a job. I hoped to become a dancer.' Aletta's voice was thick with emotion. 'It must have been my destiny to perform. I met your father, and soon enough, I got an opportunity through him to dance in the village drinking house. It was filled with unruly men, drinking liquor, bad manners, and fights. Many customers appreciated my dancing. It came easily to me—expressing my feelings, visions, and dreams through my body.' A drop of rain struck the thatched roof. Another hit the dry surface outside, disappearing into the dry sand. Soon, the rain was falling at a steady pace.

'Your father protected me, and I became a classical dancer. For that, I must thank your father.'

Lovinia studied her for a breath before placing her bare feet on the sandy floor and rising from the mat. She walked over to the *dara lipa*, removing the lid off a clay pot of cardamom tea sitting over a bed of red coals. Lovinia prepared the tea, pouring it into two clay cups. She placed a dark, glistening cube of *jaggery* in both cups before handing one to Aletta.

Lovinia had never heard Aletta tell her life story before. She was older, more experienced, and had gone through a lot, yet she seemed to carry joy. She had always been the woman Lovinia wanted to grow up to be.

CHAPTER 8

THE WELCOME BALL

"Beg pardon, My Lord, but Chief Justice Hetherington wishes to be announced."

Thomas looked up from his work at Major Staples's knock.

Thomas stood behind his desk and took in his visitor. Incredibly, his first thought was, *I thought he would be taller than that.*

'Major Staples,' Thomas said without taking his eyes from the doorway, 'will you please excuse us?' He watched as the Chief Justice stepped aside to allow the Major to exit, which he did with a curt nod to Thomas and no acknowledgement of the visitor, which Thomas found intriguing.

Thomas walked around his desk and said, 'Won't you come in, sir? My name is Sir Thomas Maitland, and I am the new Governor of Ceylon.' He indicated the two chairs with a view of the sea. 'Won't you sit down?'

The two men bowed warily to each other, neither offering to shake hands. The Chief Justice was a stout pleasant-looking fellow, contrary to what Thomas had heard about his disposition. However, on the occasion of this first meeting, he was self-effacing.

'My lord,' he said gravely. 'I have awaited this meeting with impatience. I trust you had a pleasant journey.'

The Chief Justice ambled to the proffered chairs and sat in the one closet to the doors. 'Thank you, Governor,' he said.

Thomas studied the man as he arranged himself on the chair. He had read reports since he arrived that the Chief Justice entertained strong opinions on the dignity and inexorable righteousness of the law and had come into conflict with the military authorities on numerous occasions. He needed to assert control over him, so he had not summoned him and instead waited until the man came to him.

Thomas had learnt long ago that his best weapon was silence; the first to speak was usually the first to give ground. It was plain that Hetherington had studied at the same academy, for he said nothing, the only indication of his knowledge of the game a slowly spreading smile until finally, he realised he could not win.

Thomas noticed the expression that crossed the Chief Justice's face and the glint of steel that appeared in his eyes.

'Your excellency', the Chief Justice finally stated. 'I have not heard from you, so I took it upon myself to appear before you.'

Thomas did not respond immediately. He steepled his hands and contemplated the man before him. The Chief Justice was a man he needed to watch closely. Underneath the carefully developed exterior was a man who would not back down easily. He had already been sent back to England to clarify his duties when he crossed swords with the previous Governor and General of the Armies. Unfortunately, the man escaped reproof and returned to Ceylon as all the Home Government wanted was quietude and economy.

'Yes, I had not sent for you for the simple reason I was trying to grasp what you are hoping to attain with your harsh adherence to the laws and regulations of this country, sir,' Thomas finally declared.

The Chief Justice shifted uneasily in his chair at the harshness in Thomas's voice. He opened his mouth but snapped it shut as Thomas continued.

'You do realise that as Commander in Chief, I have the ultimate authority to decide on all judicial matters relating to the discipline of the Crown troops on the island.' Thomas knew this was not the case with the previous Governor, who did not carry the title of Commander in Chief.

Thomas glared at the Chief Justice until he nodded in agreement.

'I am assuming that is a yes!' Since there was no response, Thomas continued. 'Then why was it you ordered one of your magistrates to administer justice when he had already sent the man to his commanding officer for punishment? Furthermore, to make matters worse, you made public utterances of differences of opinion within the government.'

The Chief Justice's eyes narrowed under furrowed brows. 'I am doing my job as I see fit, your excellency. I have been vindicated by the Lord Justices in England who have endorsed my approach.'

Thomas had to struggle to keep the disagreement from his face. 'As you are well aware, the Lord Justices have no jurisdiction in this Crown colony. Furthermore, the judicial system in England is vastly different to what currently exists in the colonies.'

Thomas wondered what was going through the other's mind. The man was no fool. He held a high position in the judiciary and had the confidence to stand up to his predecessor. He might have friends back in England who protected him.

Thomas decided to lighten his tone. 'Let's agree that you will first consult with me before making any decision regarding all military forces under my command.'

The Chief Justice's eyes flashed. 'I can see now that your reputation was well earned. Very well, here's what I propose. I will correspond with you on all judicial matters involving the military. In return, I want the judicial seat on the executive council to be made permanent.'

Thomas admired the Chief Justice's courage and remembered that his job was to oversee the judicial system's administration and, as a lawyer, to hear arguments when discussing and deciding cases. His request to make the seat on the council permanent was unusual. It was exceptional for the Chief Justice to have such a position as it considerably enhanced his power. It showed a weakness for power in the man, which Thomas could exploit in the future.

'I will be honest with you,' Thomas said. 'I am still feeling my way as governor, but here is how I see my job. To be blunt about it, I am the supreme authority on this island and given the time it takes to communicate with the home government, I can, within reason, implement any change I see fit.'

Thomas studied the Chief Justice to see his reaction. Besides a tightening of his lips, he did not indicate his thinking.

'I will do my best within limits imposed on me by London to accede to your request. It need not be said that this also depends upon you making no trouble for me, and I will do my best to ensure that none is made of you. If that is not the case, I will do my utmost to make life as hard for you as possible and ensure that the Foreign Office will be notified in no uncertain terms of your role in undermining my authority.'

The Chief Justice's face wrinkled as though he had swallowed something unpleasant. Thomas was pleased to see the blow strike home, but he was under no illusions that the man would be someone he needed to watch.

So why did this knowledge not fill him with confidence?

*

Days dragged into weeks as Thomas settled into the routine of the job. He felt a surprising surge of expectation again, looking forward to the evening, eagerly anticipating the chance to sit down with Sir David and discuss the goings on in the colony from the Company's point of view. When stripped of diplomatic language and propaganda trappings, he wondered what the man's opinion of his governorship was. Thomas did not expect any significant change in the content, but the delivery should be piquant.

Thomas stared, transfixed, as the rain pattered relentlessly on the enormously tall windows of his residence. It was the beginning of March, and the monsoons had just begun. It was already swelteringly hot, but the rain made the day somewhat bearable. He breathed deeply as the scent of wet earth wafted through the air. The peacocks in the garden called frantically, and the males strutted their flamboyant plumes before the retreating hens.

Delightfully scented invitations had inundated Thomas since he arrived in the colony. It seemed that every hostess in Colombo wished to have him in her drawing room or to attend this dinner or that reception. When he did accept an invitation, he was surrounded by men and women, all eager to inspect him as if he were some strange animal, all eager to hear him speak and to obtain his opinion on any matter that interested them. He did not expect that almost all of the young females with whom he was surrounded wished to find themselves in bed with him.

However, he couldn't refuse the invitation that arrived for the official welcome ball in his honour. Thomas bathed, shaved, dined, and wore his full-dress uniform with care. He knew from his time in the West Indies that these affairs always started late after the heat subsided. Many Englishmen did not dine until ten o'clock but were often entertained until the early morning. Thomas admired the new gold epaulettes, buckled on the sword he seldom wore, and extracted from its box the cocked hat he had bought in London but never worn.

The Governor's carriage, decorated with the British Coat of Arms, its fine horses and silver accoutrements, looked very grand and was waiting under the large porch. Major Staples helped him climb into the carriage, sitting opposite him. Thomas certainly did not want to be the first arrival, but his duty was to be prompt. The function was held at a spacious villa in Hulftsdorp, the previous Governor-General's residence. His predecessor had found the official residence in the Fort too hot and confined.

Outside the Fort was a tidy world of chalk roads and white timber and stone houses of varying sizes, according to the social status of the people within, and bordered with prim English flowers and well-watered lawns. They passed a pretty white church surrounded by struggling rose bushes and low expansive windows open to the outside air, though hung with thick shutters capable of deflecting a typhoon.

The large pavilion in the villa's vast garden was ablaze with lights. Servants held flaring flambeaus outside the entrance as carriages pulled up, deposited their passengers, and drew away.

Thomas groaned as he peeked around the entrance and saw many people in the vast room. He realised he would not be the first guest, so he straightened himself, put his hat under his arm, adjusted the hang of his sword, and approached the entrance. The massive room was lit by what seemed to be hundreds of candles in chandeliers hung from the ceiling, and there was a whole company of footmen moving around the crowd with loaded silver trays.

Major Staples stepped forward with a note for the important-looking major-domo who had the tedious task of introducing everyone.

'His Excellency, Major-General Sir Thomas Maitland!' he intoned in lordly tones.

Thomas waited a moment in the doorway, then, taking a deep breath, entered the fray. Within the house, the noise was deafening. Nor was the kaleidoscope of colour any more restful than the noise. Apart from the brilliant gowns of the ladies, the men offered sufficient contrasts. The military's scarlet jackets set off the black coats of the civilians. At the same time, the footmen's pale blue livery, circulating between the guests in the most hazardous fashion with their trays of champagne held high, seemed positively sombre.

Sir David Tarrant, the Head of the East India Company and host for the evening, came up to him straight away. 'I am delighted you could come to our little welcome party, your Excellency'.

'I was glad to be able to come, David.' Thomas replied, bowing to Lady Tarrant, who stood at her husband's side. Lady Tarrant smiled and held out her hand in greeting.

Thomas bent over her hand with the same grace he would have bestowed upon the Queen of England. 'Charmed, My Lady,' he said, and with a twinkle in his eye, he added, 'I do hope my relations with you on board the Blenheim were above reproach.'

Lady Tarrant's eyebrow rose, and she smiled gently. 'That will depend, Sir Thomas, on whether you are kinder to me than you were to the gentleman in question.'

Thomas nodded his acknowledgement. 'At your command, Madame.'

Thomas caught sight of Mrs Hartley over Lady Tarrant's shoulder, standing not many paces distant. Next to her stood the six young women from the Blenheim.

Lady Tarrant followed his gaze. 'Ah, you remember Juliet Hartley and the ladies from our voyage?'

Yes, of course. Ladies!' Thomas bowed.

'Why don't you ladies come with me? Let me present you to some of our eligible bachelors.' Lady Tarrant gestured, and the young ladies shuffled to do her bidding. Mrs Hartley remained, taking a step towards him.

Thomas observed Mrs Hartley's brilliant gaze upon him. He noticed with satisfaction that she looked beautiful. Her hair was charmingly arranged, her cheeks faintly flushed, and her large eyes were glowing. There was candid speculation in it, a captivating smile slightly parting the lady's lips. Thomas returned the look and smiled. 'How do you do, Mrs Hartley?'

Thomas found a gloved hand held out to him. He took it and held it in a firm clasp, bending his head to kiss it. He had refrained from getting too close to her on board the Blenheim, but now he realised he missed her charm and intelligence.

'May I call you Juliet?'

Momentarily surprised, her beautiful eyes flew upwards to his, giving place immediately to frank amusement. An enchanting gurgle of laughter escaped her. 'Of course, Sir Thomas.'

'Are you going back to England?' Thomas recalled that Mrs Hartley had been Lady Tarrant's companion on the long voyage from England.

'I have not decided yet,' she responded. 'I hope to find a job as a governess or nanny. Lady Tarrant is helping me find something appropriate.'

Thomas nodded understandingly. He needed to conduct himself with propriety in his current position, but he could afford to flirt.

'Let me know if you need me as a reference,' he smiled at her. 'We lived in each other's pockets on the Blenheim for so long, and I am a good judge of character.'

'Thank you,' Mrs Hartley said with a most enchanting smile.

Thomas offered a half bow in acknowledgement, his eyes creasing into a smile, 'Do I have your permission to call on you? I am afraid my time today will be occupied by other matters.'

Mrs Hartley gave a small gasp and glanced up. His smile seemed to reassure her. 'I would like that, your Excellency. I am currently domiciled at Cinnamon Gardens with Lady Tarrant.'

'Please call me Thomas,' He leaned down to whisper in her ear. 'I'll see you soon.'

Mrs Hartley stole a mischievous glance at his face. 'Please make sure you do, Sir Thomas. I'll hold you to that.'

Sir Tarrant was watching the interplay between the two of them. 'Excuse me, your Excellency, Mrs Hartley.' Sir Tarrant smiled at them knowingly. 'There are a lot of people who wish to make your acquaintance. I will not bore you with many of them, but you need to meet some particularly important people.'

Thomas bowed at the two ladies. 'I am sorry to leave you like this, but duty calls.'

Sir Tarrant steered Thomas towards a small group of well-dressed men talking seriously in one corner.

'Gentlemen,' began Sir Tarrant, 'may I introduce his Excellency, Major-General Thomas Maitland, who, as you all know, is our new Governor-General, our Commander-in-Chief, and Officer Commanding all Military Forces on the island.

Your Excellency, may I introduce....' He ran through the names of the people he was introducing Thomas to.

Thomas knew that Major Staples was at his shoulder, and he would know all their names. Someone placed a glass of ice-cold Champagne in Thomas's hand, and the questions came thick and fast.

*

Thomas glanced around the vast pavilion, conscious of a glow of satisfaction. Inside the brightly lit ballroom where the buzz of conversation mixed with the clink of cut glass, it mattered nothing to him that the room was over-large for the company and that the gentlemen outnumbered the ladies by two. The music swelled out of the orchestral gallery, and the noise was deafening. Couples made their stately parade, separating and returning, arms raised high to form an arch beneath which others rushed, feet scuffing the polished wooden floor.

A group of civilians, laughing and joking, opened their ranks to admit Thomas and David. 'I have the honour to present—' began the latter. It was a lengthy introduction. Pasty-faced men and plump women seemed the norm. Merchants' wives, petty officials' wives, poorly dressed in clothes, possibly hurriedly sewn that day at the news that they were invited to the reception. Some of the fat ones panted in corsets pulled tight, and some of the slenderer ones tried to display the languorous uncorseted grace which had been fashionable ten years ago. A few were beautiful women, some bold-eyed and others languid. Thomas bowed and bowed again.

Sir Tarrant led him to the boldest-eyed and most beautiful of them all. 'Lady Catherine, I want to present His Excellency Sir Thomas Maitland – Lady Catherine Audley!'

Catherine was the most exquisite creature Thomas had ever seen. He found himself unable to stop staring, trying to imprint how the mouth, the eyes, and the cheeks all moved together to create the impression of bright interest and pure loveliness.

'You will partner Lady Catherine at dinner, Your Excellency. It's her debut, and there's no better person for her to be presented to than Your Excellency.'

Thomas felt a little skip of excitement in his chest. 'My lady.' Thomas bowed to the young woman, who curtsied. Neither lowered their eyes as custom dictated—a high-spirited and lovely creature. Under the arches of her sculptured brows, her eyes were dark and liquid, yet with a devouring fire. Her face was perfectly oval, her complexion like rose petals. She smiled—a smile of pure delight.

Thomas returned the look, smiled, and said in his most pleasant voice: 'How do you do?'

'How do you do, Your Excellency?' responded Lady Catherine slowly, still looking at him.

Thomas was distracted by her plunging décolletage, which promised a glimpse of nipple as she leaned closer to him. It did allow an inspection of a magnificent expanse of heaving blue-veined whiteness, at once compressed and projected by the tight bodice of the pale green satin gown.

Lady Catherine held out her gloved hand, which Thomas took in his, bending his head to kiss it.

'Do, please grant His Excellency one waltz, Lady Catherine,' said Sir Tarrant, amusement quivering in his voice.

Thomas's arm encircled her waist. Her gloved hand lay light as a feather on his shoulder. Thomas danced well, and she followed. Neither spoke, but Lady Catherine raised her eyes to his face. 'Why did you look at me so?'

Thomas smiled down at her. 'I don't know how I looked. Does it bother you?'

'Yes,' she replied casually. She stole a playful glance up at his face. 'That was to be expected.'

It gave her an enchanting look, but it was decidedly naughty, not a doubt of that, thought Thomas, silently adoring the pretty creature. He looked at her thoughtfully, suddenly realising that the young lady was an accomplished flirt.

'That sounds like you have played this game before,' he remarked shrewdly.

A wave of colour filled her cheeks. The corners of her mouth lifted in a smile, and her eyes glinted provocatively. 'What do you think?'

A bell announcing dinner reverberated through the noisy pavilion. 'Could I accompany you to dinner?' Thomas glanced towards the dining pavilion, where a liveried major-domo vigorously waved a handheld bell.

Lady Catherine's frank gaze lifted till she looked into his eyes. His smile seemed to reassure her. Her eyes danced. A smile quivered on her lips. 'Yes, thank you, your Excellency. You are very generous.'

'Away with your Excellency,' Thomas retorted. 'You may call me Sir Thomas or just Thomas if you wish.'

The dining pavilion was accessible through a short walkway. Catherine and Thomas joined the slow-moving stream of guests and soon found themselves in a large, brilliantly lit room with many tables. The food was served in a buffet along one wall covered with various foods; some were kept warm in chafing dishes, others cold in silver trays. Under the tutelage of Lady Catherine, Thomas went a fair way towards tackling them all. There was an excellent dish of stewed mushrooms, slices of smoked fish, various salads, different types of cheese, hot and cold eggs and what looked like a ragoût of spicy boneless chicken. Thomas helped himself and walked with Lady Catherine to a circular table occupied by his host and hostess. They had reserved two vacant places for them.

Laughter, chatter, and flickering lights; this was one of the cheeriest parties he had ever attended. He felt the warm glow of the wine inside him and realised that he was desperately hungry. There were other liquors as well. Thomas ate and drank with his spirits rising momentarily, playing his part in the conversation and feeling more and more warmly grateful toward his host and hostess for arranging the welcome.

Lady Catherine pressed his foot under the table beside him. A little electric thrill ran through him, and his steadiness vanished. He smiled and straightened away from her. She gave him a long searching look and then turned away to address a remark to her neighbour on her other side, a discreet hint perhaps for Thomas to pay attention to Lady Tarrant, whom he had hardly spoken a word to.

Despite the unusual serving arrangement, Thomas had never tasted such delicious food. His head began to spin with the liquor, which he knew was a danger signal, although this time, he did not begrudge it quite so bitterly. He checked himself in a laugh, just in time not to be too uncontrolled.

Thomas replaced his lovely porcelain plate on the buffet, among the gold dishes, and wiped his mouth with one of the silken napkins. He was full of the satisfying sensation of having overeaten and drunk enough. He hoped coffee would be served soon, and such a cup was all he needed to complete his internal gratification. Perhaps his time in the Crown Colony would not be so bad after all.

CHAPTER 9

THE FORT

The Chief Steward, dressed in a navy-blue coat with brass buttons over a tight white shirt and breeches, greeted the dozen dance troupe members at the South Gate to the Fort. Red-jacketed native soldiers carrying long rifles manning the walls looked down at them as they filed through a side postern into the fort. Torches blazed in their sconces, throwing off shadows that danced with abandon against the dressed walls of thick *kabook* (clay ironstone).

'Follow me,' the thin-faced man barked. 'We don't have much time.'

Two native servants dressed neatly in white shirts and sarongs held torches above their heads as the Chief Steward impatiently led the way. Banda and the rest of the troupe carrying packs with their dance costumes and various musical instruments, followed.

They were guided up a steep stone staircase past battlements with long iron cannons. They reached a long tunnel honeycombed on either side by niches, guardrooms and galleries that sloped upwards through the thick ramparts.

The transition from warm sunlight to cold shadow and the eerie echo under the black vault of the roof served to intensify Lovinia's unease. It seemed to her, suddenly, as though she was entering a prison from which she would never be able to escape. It was a new and troubling thought, and she shivered as though with cold.

Aletta walked firmly in her shadow, with her hand grazing Lovinia's lower back as if to remind her she was not alone. Her usually vigilant eyes appeared even more watchful than before.

The tunnel turned sharply to the right and came into a small open courtyard with more soldiers. On the far side of it, another gateway led into a square quadrangle. Beyond this lay the main bulk of the fort. A fantastic jumble of walls, stone-faced buildings, and warehouses–the more significant part screened from the city by the outer battlements.

Finally, out in the open, they walked through a heavy brass-studded wooden door leading to a side entrance of an enormous building with a bell-shaped roof. A door led directly into the eastern antechamber of the central hall. It was a small space with a low false ceiling, plastered pillars, and thick curtains. During their previous performances, the troupe had used it as a waiting space. Lovinia could see a lofty, smoke-filled hall illuminated by several tall windows through a gap in the heavy drapes.

Several English officers were smoking pipes and hookahs and drinking from ornate glasses, reclined against yellow-and-gold bolsters placed on carpets around an intricately carved wooden chair. The rest of the room was filled with red-coated English soldiers from the garrison, talking, and arguing loudly while drinking directly from large wooden tankards. Several lamps gleamed, creating a festive atmosphere.

Lovinia could feel the Chief Steward looking at her but pretended to ignore him. The man appeared to be over forty or even nearer fifty. His sunken cheeks and thin lips spoke of a *ganja* (opium) smoking habit. His large hawk-like eyes looked as though they filled his entire face. He seemed unable to take his eyes off her. The others watched them discreetly as they unpacked their belongings.

Lovinia felt Aletta's eyes on her, reminding her what she had to do. Holding the man's gaze, she spoke in the sweetest, most seductive manner possible. 'Sir, how can we make this the best evening you've ever had? Please, sir, tell me what else I can do for you?'

The Chief Steward appeared dumbstruck. He blinked like a man just woken up from a deep slumber. Lovinia blinked her beautiful deer-like eyes at the official. She smiled and caressed her right cheek with her hand, running her fingers gingerly over her hair. Her lips quivered. Her whole posture changed.

The Chief-Stewards eyes brazenly took Lovinia in. His gaze moved up her body, openly admiring the curve of her hips, the swell of her breasts,

Lovinia saw lust creep into his eyes. *Just like any other man*, she thought, *that is all they ever want; that is all they ever think about.* Hiding her disgust, she smiled invitingly at the man instead.

'*Mahathaya* (Sir),' a hoarse voice called out from the doorway. 'The *Andukāraya* (Governor) is ready.'

The Chief Steward broke contact with Lovinia's eyes and turned angrily to look at the speaker. The head of the Governor's household pursed his lips in thought, his eyes flickering to Lovinia before turning and walking out.

Lovinia breathed a sigh of relief. She picked up a vial of scented rosewater from her bag and pulled out the glass stopper. The perfume smelled heady and sweet—like a bouquet of ageing blossoms. Intoxicating and mysterious. She dabbed the stopper on her neck and arms before putting it back.

'Hold still!' Aletta commanded. Her eyes were emerald green and were lined in kohl with practised hands. Her lips were puckered into a perfect pout, stained pink with red beeswax. The white linen garment clung to Lovinia's slender frame in all the right places. A thick silver band was looped around her upper left arm.

Aletta clutched Lovinia's chin in her left hand. Then she lifted the tiny, three-haired brush to Lovinia's eyelid. 'Tonight is a night to turn heads. Make them remember you. Make sure they never forget.'

Lovinia lapsed into a sullen silence. Aletta adjusted the silver *nalalpata* (traditional headpiece placed in the middle of the forehead) and *dimiki* (hanging earrings studded with tiny gemstones), tapping her cheek gently. 'Don't pout. I can't do this properly if you make such a face.'

Lovinia tried to relax her brow, but her thoughts made it impossible. She brooded as Aletta continued to apply creams and colour to her face.

'There,' Aletta said. 'You look lovely.'

The junior dancers stretched their limbs and practised little dance moves while helping each other adjust their costumes.

Banda cleared his throat, breaking the silence. 'Musicians, be ready. Wait for my signal to begin.'

Banda nodded his head at the musicians. Upali, a bearded man with a *ravanahatha* (bowed instrument), slid the hair of his bow lightly across his instrument, checking to see if it was in tune by tightening its ivory pegs. At the same time, Anshu adjusted the reed of her *horanawa* (temple flute) one last time. Juan carried a *raban* (one-sided drum) he played with his fingers and a *thalampata* (cymbals) which he tapped with his foot.

Mahinda settled the base of his *dawula* (drum) against his left hip and struck the drum's taut surface with a curved stick called a *kaduppu,* slow, quick, quick. The drummer began pounding out a driving rhythm, and the resonating sound of the *hak gediya* (conch shell) played by Samitha joined in before all five musicians were lost in their music. They were lost to the beat.

The music was rhythmic, layered, and deep. It combined the beat of the drum with the chink of cymbals and the call of the flute rising to a crescendo of a strong pair of lungs.

It was time for them to dance. Lovinia stood at the gap by the curtains behind the four dancers and searched the faces and every corner of the room for the Chief Steward, but she could not see him. A British officer dressed in his uniform lounged on the chair in the centre of the room with a second older officer standing behind him.

Lovinia narrowed her eyes, studying the seated man. Could this be the Royal Emissary from the Great King across the sea? He was sharp-featured and oval-faced, his dark hair tied back with a velvet ribbon at the nape of his neck. A slightly old-fashioned style mainly favoured by seamen, but it suited him.

*

Beyond the door came a sudden tinkle of stringed instruments, the thud of a drum, the clang of cymbals, and a squeal of flutes. A troupe of dancers came through the door, swaying in rhythm with the music. Thomas had seen such performances a time or two before in Madras. Such dance troupes travelled about India from the court of one native rajah or nizam to another. They were sometimes employed for months to entertain the ruler, his family, and retainers.

Thomas had been reluctant when his Chief Steward invited him to a party hosted by army officers at the Fort's Garrison hall in his honour. The welcome ball in his honour had exhausted him. He only agreed when he realised he was the Commander-in-Chief and his power came from the troops under his command. Settling the current conflict with the Kandyan kingdom was as crucial as understanding the finances and administration of the colony. To do that, he needed to be seen and respected by his troops.

These dancers were creole, Thomas guessed, beautiful, petite, light-skinned women, bare above their girdles, only flowing skirts with intricate embroidery along the hem below, wearing bracelets about wrists and ankles that jangled with each movement of the dance. The mixture of French, Spanish and African natives was a common sight in the West Indian islands he had spent the last five years of his life.

A sigh went through the room, but only one drunken whoop as the dancers went through their movements, keeping time to the music from beyond the door. Thomas sat back, relaxed, and enjoyed the interlude, marking time with his foot. The women went through their repertoire, their dark eyes rimmed with kohl, flashing in the candlelight, the graceful bodies matching every nuance of the music in time. They slipped from one tempo into another and came at last to a flashing crescendo of movement and music, dominated by cymbals and drums; with a final thunderclap, they froze in statuesque attitudes.

Sir Thomas cheered with the rest as the four girls demurely genuflected, then left the room. A man slipped into view carrying a brazier filled with glowing coals, which he placed on the floor. From a pouch at his waist, he sprinkled a handful of crystals into the red-hot brazier, which burst into flames and died down almost as quickly. Thick clouds of scented smoke rose from the container obscuring the entire area.

The room grew still for a moment, and then the music exploded in a torrent of rhythm, wild and exciting yet unmistakably controlled by some rigorous underlying structure. The rhythm soared, returning after each elaborate cycle back to a forceful crescendo.

Out of the smoke burst a dancer, arms upraised. She whirled in a frenzy to the centre of the room in time to the music. Clad in a slit skirt sequined with gold and flaring around her, she spun currents of red, purple, and blue, her long slim legs flashing, her toe rings sparkling. She wore a silver headpiece with a spangle on her forehead, her hair was arranged into two long plaits secured with ribbons, and her hands were decorated with markings. She was dressed in a small open waistcoat of black silk, and her flowing skirt with intricate embroidery along the hem left little to the imagination. Her plaited hair fell past her waist in spiralling curls of ebony, with hints of silver ribbon highlighted by the torchlight. Her face was flawless—high cheekbones, flawless skin, arched brows, and a fringe of black lashes that fanned over obscenely large green eyes.

She captivated him with unguarded beauty and unassuming grace. Her hair twisted behind her like whips of ebony, and her pointed chin was turned high and proud. The silver embroidery of her black scarf cloaked the darkness of the silk beneath it. He thought this woman was unbelievably beautiful. She appeared to be around twenty years of age.

She danced with her arms gliding above her head as if composing a new melody, her hair flying in the wind as if drawing a veil over the night, her steps caressing the ground, and her gaze—from which Thomas couldn't take his eyes off for a second—sometimes embarrassed, often mischievous, and occasionally aglow with a naïve flirtatiousness.

The room erupted in a roar when the dance ended. The soldiers clapped and shouted, thumping the ground with their boots, their blood raised by the heady mix of alcohol, opium, soul-wrenching native music and rampant sexual desire. The dancer had ended in a tantric pose which Thomas knew was meant to heighten sensual awareness with those around her.

She flashed a look at him, and he saw her eyes, blazing like green jewels in her lightly tanned face. There was no submission there and not a trace of fear. As he studied her eyes, they seemed locked into his own and betrayed no notice of anyone else in the hall.

Thomas gestured at the dancer to come closer. The woman rose from the dusty floor with the trained grace of a dancer. The room quietened as she approached. Thomas felt Major Staples shift his feet behind him. The woman bowed, sinking gracefully into a submissive pose before him. He grinned down at her involuntarily. He felt an overpowering curiosity—which he had no intention of admitting.

'What is your name?' Thomas realised the moment the words came out of his mouth that she would not understand what he had asked.

She lifted her head at the sound of his voice, looking questioningly up into his face, but she replied. 'Lovinia.'

Thomas started at the sound of her voice. The clamour in the room was rising as the soldiers returned to their drinking and talking.

'You speak English.'

The dancer looked at him for a minute and got slowly to her feet shaking out her skirts. She looked magnificent, her green eyes flaming, her colour heightened, her small, dark nippled breasts framed by her tiny waistcoat heaving with her quickened breath, noticeably clear. Her skin was fair, with a warm hint of olive, and her high cheekbones stood in stunning relief. Her nose was thin and sculptured, while her lips would have been full had they not been drawn tight in response to some unspecified inner determination. Yet her eyes were clear and receptive, even warm, and Thomas asked himself if this bespoke innocence or guile.

'No—little Inglish.'

Thomas did not realise that he was staring. The dancer looked at him, blushed on meeting his eye and looked down again. The pulse in her neck quickened. Her breathing grew heavy.

So, she was a natural flirt. He found himself hoping that this woman, this half-caste dancer, did not have to pass so soon out of his life. The wish that he could see her dance only for him came into his head, irrelevant and unwelcome. He felt his cheeks burn and cursed himself for a fool. Not that he was a romantic person. He was known for being ultra-reserved, a hard taskmaster and ruthless when it suited him. He had to be because his life had not been easy. He had succeeded only by fighting every inch of the way for what he wanted and by being sure of what he did want.

'I have never seen such a dance before. What do you call it?'

Slowly, the woman raised her head. Her fearless, beautiful face mesmerised him for the second time that evening. She shook her head, her magnificent green eyes meeting his questioningly.

Thomas felt the colour rising on his face. 'Oh, I forgot. You don't speak English.'

The dancer smiled, seeing his reaction for the first time since she had appeared in the room. Something stirred in Thomas's heart. Only once had a woman been able to hold such power over him; that was a long time ago. She looked neither Asian nor European. Her cheeks were high, and her skin was light, shining, and smooth. *Definitely creole*, he thought. Her neck was slender, and she smiled through perfect, even white teeth. There was great dignity in her carriage even though she was half-dressed. She regarded him with faint amusement.

A sudden commotion at the entrance and a liveried retainer entered the room. The man walked quickly over to where Thomas was sitting.

Major Staples pulled the man aside. After listening to what the man said, the Major leant over to Thomas. 'You're wanted up at the residence. Your Excellency.'

Thomas looked over his shoulder. 'Who wants me?' He felt a rise of resentment at being interrupted at such a moment.

'There has been an attack against one of our outposts at the river crossing. General Wemyss has requested your presence.'

The Kandyans continuously probed their defences, looking for weak spots. Still, Thomas did not understand what was so important that General Wemyss could not handle it.

His body flushed with anger as he rose to his feet reluctantly. Major Staples was staring at him quizzically, and Thomas could see the doubt in his eyes. 'I don't understand what the General wants of me now. Is he like this always?' He studied the Major's face.

Thomas had read General Wemyss's reports in the regular despatches to London, which he found quite remarkable. He had met him once when the General had called on him at Government House after his arrival in the country.

Thomas found him to be an experienced general officer, older than him, who had seen much active service in America, the West Indies, Flanders and Italy. Thomas had conceded after meeting him that the General understood the difficulties of campaigning against the Kandyans but had not understood the severity of the pestilences that would beset his force. He had also suffered much under the divided system of command, which gave the previous governor so much power.

Major Staples nodded noncommittally. 'I can assure you, your Excellency, that he's very clever indeed. Even his staunchest detractors would agree on that. And he is also resourceful. Not many here are aware he has an intelligence network of his own.'

Thomas pulled himself alert. 'I had no idea. Tell me more ....'

He heard a sudden rustling behind him. He turned to see the dancer had retreated and removed the embroidered scarf from her throat. She began twirling, her legs loose, her spine flexible, her movements fluid. The decorative gemstones on her headpiece and skirt twinkled in the lamplight. A ring flashed on her third toe. She flew onto the dance floor, her hands weaving images and emotions, filling the space with her presence and compelling everyone to watch her. She whirled one arm around her head and loosened the coils of braided hair by pulling on the ribbons. Lustrous black hair streamed down her back. The sound of reawakened music and the pounding of drums rose to a crescendo.

The rhythm of her movement almost made Thomas want to join her. He was spared that embarrassment when she suddenly stopped and bowed gracefully before disappearing behind the curtains to the sound of cheers and catcalls by the intoxicated soldiers.

With a sudden urgency reviving him like a glass of brandy, he knew he wanted to see the woman again. He wanted to talk to her, to be with her and for the moment, he could think of nothing else.

CHAPTER 10

THE DUTCH

The following day Thomas breakfasted early. He had not slept much that night. He had lain awake thinking over what had happened during the evening. He had been tired when he came to bed but could not sleep. He could not forget the beautiful smiling face of the mestizo woman who had danced for him.

The feel of the cooling salves and the razor sliding over his chin restored a sense of normality. He was grateful for Johnson's silence, which enabled him to compose himself.

As the fragrance of sandalwood from the last lotion rose, Thomas stood up, running a hand over his jaw. 'Johnson, you said you were married to a local woman?'

'Yes, Sah. But not a native Sinhalese, Sah. A mestizo woman!'

'A mestizo? Are they like the Creoles in the Caribbean?' Thomas questioned.

'Yes, Sah. But of Portuguese descent.'

Thomas was familiar with the mixed race of creoles, who were persons of French, Spanish or African descent born in the West Indies. He had dealt with many as Brigadier-General on the French island of San Domingo.

'Who were the natives who danced for us in the garrison hall last night?' Thomas queried. 'They looked quite different to the locals.'

Johnson considered Thomas, his bushy white eyebrows rising, making his face look elongated. 'They are mestizos, Sah. Like my wife. They are a local dance troupe who are popular with the men.'

'Are they from around here?'

'Not far, Sah. A little village called Galkissa, just a few miles south of the fort.'

Thomas remembered that Johnson was married to a local. 'Is that where your wife is from?'

'Yes, Sah.'

'Hmm,' Thomas remarked without responding.

Thomas sat at his desk after Johnson left. He regretted the moment he was forced to leave the welcome arranged for him by General Wemyss's unreasonable request, which could have waited at least until the morning. The man wanted to send a battalion of English soldiers reinforced by native troops to attack the pass leading to the city of Kandy. The General, who was in his mid-forties, had forgotten the lesson taught to him by the complete decimation of the previous force sent against the Kandyan kingdom.

'Those were native troops, Sir,' the General had blustered when Thomas questioned him on the wisdom of repeating the same mistake. 'We'll send a battalion of our good English lads and see how they'll like it.'

Thomas sighed in annoyance. He had refused, of course, angrily sending the General away, demanding he not throw away his men's lives needlessly. However, the attack on the river outpost only a dozen miles to the north concerned him. Before the General left, Thomas had ordered the officer to recommend three possible small actions against the Kandyans for him to study.

'We will not win this war by playing into the natives' hands, General. 'I think this matter can be resolved with time by using commerce to pacify the rebels.'

Looking back at the discussions with the General, they were almost too improbable to be explained. The war was not going well from all accounts and had rendered the treasury almost empty. There were vast leakages of expenditures everywhere, and he now faced difficulty finding the money to run the colony without borrowing money from the Madras Presidency or the

Colonial office in London. Thomas glanced down at the neatly inked figures on the account sheet, turned it, and thumbed through the attached inventory when he was interrupted by Major Staples.

'I beg your pardon, Governor. You asked that you not be disturbed, but you have some unexpected visitors who crave your attention.'

Thomas leaned back and looked up at the Major, rubbing his eyes to refocus them. Rays of dying light from the setting sun crossed the room, trying to pierce the darkened corners.

'Visitors? At this time?' Thomas's mind was still processing the mass of information he had been reading, and he rose to his feet almost in a daze, stretching his arms above his head.

He waved his right hand over two unequal stacks of documents on his desk. 'I need a distraction to take my mind off all this.'

The past week had been filled with briefings and meetings with colonial civil servants who ran the island for the Crown. Thomas was determined to understand how every department on the island was run, and he was buried in an avalanche of paperwork.

Thomas shrugged on the coat he had hung on the rack by his desk, smoothening the lapels with the palms of his hands. 'Who may I ask are these visitors, Major?'

'Representatives of the Dutch East India Company, your Excellency.'

Thomas nodded at the Major. He had been expecting some form of contact from them. It bothered him that the formidable Dutch East India Company was still trading in the colony. They arrived in Ceylon earlier than the British East India Company, thus gaining a head start. They successfully built up an intra-Asian trade network in the last half-century, extending as far as Japan. They traded raw silk, saltpetre, spices, opium, and indigo dye, just like the Company. Still, their experience in Asia far surpassed it in magnitude. They had more extensive warehouses, adapted well to the nuances of conducting business here, established several trading stations, and developed an extensive network of trading relationships. The closest Dutch trading post was in Batavia, a little too close for his comfort. Their goal would be to eliminate the English as a competitor, as they had done with the Portuguese earlier.

Thomas was entirely unprepared for the four people waiting in the residence's bright and airy downstairs salon. He had expected an administrator or two, all with ruddy complexions matching the highly polished mahogany panelling and figures in keeping with the well-padded chairs and settees.

Major Staples bowed to the two men and two women with effortless grace. 'May I present the Governor, Sir Thomas Maitland.'

Thomas had time only to glance at the men and notice that one of the women was young before Staples completed the introductions. 'Monsieur and Madame Van Rijn, their daughter Mademoiselle Van Rijn, and Monsieur Maarten.'

Van Rijn looked affluent and elegant in a gold-embroidered jacket, blue breeches, and silk stockings. He walked energetically toward Thomas, extending his right hand with the gold signet ring of the VOC on the ring finger.

'We are honoured,' Van Rijn said as they shook hands. Thomas kissed the ladies' hands in turn.

'I apologize for disturbing you, your Excellency.'

Thomas waved off the apology. 'It was only a matter of time before we met. What can I do for you?'

Van Rijn seated himself comfortably and waited until the others were settled before turning to Thomas.

'Surely you are the man who distinguished himself at the capture of Palicatchery in India.'

As he spoke in almost perfect English with an accent that only hinted at his Dutch nationality, Thomas tried to think why the names had a curious – even spurious – ring about them.

'That was a long time ago,' Thomas replied. He was still trying to come to terms with his visitors, especially the two women.

The salon was surprisingly comfortable, with its large fan slowly flapping under the high ceiling, worked by a footman who had no other function than to pull the rope every few seconds whenever the room was used. Everything was on a grander scale than he had imagined - the room was more extensive than his office and kept far cleaner, and many more servants were bustling about. The furniture was comfortable and well-suited for the hot climate.

Van Rijn crossed his legs and twisted his signet ring with his left hand. 'You are wondering why we are here, your Excellency.'

'I have expected some representation from the Company, no doubt Meneer, but I must admit that this sudden meeting with the four of you is unexpected.'

'I decided to bring my family with me to help you understand the dire situation we find ourselves in,' Van Rijn said. 'Bram here', he said, waving at Maartens, 'is my secretary. He will keep a record of what is decided if you don't mind.' The young man flickered his eyes at Van Rijn but said nothing.

Thomas nodded his agreement at the arrangement.

'My husband is not completely truthful, your Excellency.' Madame Van Rijn suddenly interrupted, looking at her husband with compassion and pity. 'I have heard you have never married and wanted to present our daughter.'

'Bernadette?' said Van Rijn, his eyes wide in disbelief. 'What can you be thinking of?'

'Helena is unmarried and has quite a lively talent, Sir Thomas,' said Madame Van Rijn, touching her daughters' arm. 'She has a fine ear and will play for you when your Excellency desires.'

'I am sure you are right,' said Thomas, anxious now to turn aside this blatant advertisement of her daughter. This plain girl looked quite mortified at hearing her mother's words. 'But begging your ladies' pardon, I was hoping this meeting would lead to something more fruitful.'

'This is not right, your Excellency.' Van Rijn responded with a voice soft with desperation.

Madame Van Rijn was not in the least abashed. She shook a finger at Thomas and replied with a knowing look. 'What you need is a woman's presence, your Excellency.'

Major Staples rose from his settee, taking a step forward. 'Perhaps I could take the two ladies out into the garden?'

Thomas smiled at the Major gratefully. 'Yes, I would be most grateful Major. We don't want to bore them too much.'

Van Rijn looked at his wife with a mixture of shock and pity. 'I think it will be best to go with the Major. In fact, I insist on it.'

Madame Van Rijn got to her feet haughtily, looking like she realised that she had gone too far. 'Come with me, Helena. It is obvious we are not wanted here.'

Thomas watched as the two women were ushered out by the Major, who glanced over his shoulder at Thomas before leaving the room.

'What can I do?' Van Rijn cried, his voice rising with anger. 'She is getting impossible to live with. We must find a way to solve this problem, your Excellency,' he implored, leaning back hopelessly in his chair. 'I must apologise for her attitude.'

Thomas felt sorry for the man. Not only did he have to face the humiliation of handing the Dutch trading interests of the entire colony to the Crown but sit waiting with the rest of his company. At the same time, his masters in Batavia and Holland decided on their fate.

Thomas waved the man's regret away. 'It must be hard for them,' he admitted. He leaned forward, rubbing his hands together. 'Let's discuss what this visit is about,' he said. 'I know you have been waiting a long time for something to happen, and I would like to understand what is holding up the transfer.'

Van Rijn leaned forward, running a finger around his collar. 'I believe your predecessor did not give it much attention, your Excellency.'

Thomas had been briefed that his Governor North had promised to repatriate all Dutch prisoners, many of these both officers and men, to Batavia by boat. Nothing had been done for several years, and the pensions to which they had a right as prisoners of war and established in the capitulation had become too costly. Thomas seriously mistrusted the Dutch and considered it wise to secure their departure as a matter of security. There was also the possibility of their colluding with Kandy. But arranging their removal would amount to a heavy expense, Thomas realised.

'It is on my list of matters to be addressed, Meneer Van Rijn. But as you are aware, finding the money to hire the ships to transport these men to Batavia will take some time.'

'I am aware of that, your Excellency, and unless we do something to help these men, I am afraid that the long incarceration and rampant disease will take a great toll on their lives.'

Thomas waited for Van Rijn to continue. It was a problem that he, too, had struggled to solve.

'I have been in correspondence with the Principals of the Vereenigde Oost-Indische Compagnie back in Holland and have a proposition I would like you to consider.'

Thomas turned his head sharply to look at him. 'What proposition is that?'

'If you could send an emissary to Batavia to arrange suitable transport, the Principals will be willing to bear all expenses for the repatriation of the men and their families. I have received a letter from Holland which lays out the terms.' he remarked, holding the official letter aloft so he could see the VOC seal emblazoned on the top of the paper.

'Why wasn't this arranged before?'

Van Rijn cleared his throat, clearly uncomfortable with what he was about to say. 'Governor North was more interested in his war with the Kandyans. The men were being used to build roads and strengthen your forts. We were waiting for your Excellency to arrive.'

'You had not raised it with him before his departure?'

'Yes, I did,' Van Rijn said ruefully. 'But I did not want to get on his wrong side either, so I didn't insist.'

Thomas nodded understandingly. It pleased him to hear this. One of the significant expenses in the colony would be struck off the books.

'I will have to talk to my people, but I don't foresee any issues,' replied Thomas briskly.

Van Rijn sat back in his chair, smiling contentedly.

'How long would it take to conclude this matter?' Thomas asked.

'I understand a ship being readied for the transfer.' Van Rijn said, glancing across at Maartens, who nodded in agreement. 'It requires your official request for matters to be undertaken.' He paused. 'I think less than six months at the most.'

Thomas wondered how messages were being exchanged by the Dutch between Holland, Batavia and Colombo. He made a note to find out. He had not seen anything in his briefing notes about it.

CHAPTER 11

THE WAR WITH KANDY

Major Patterson was a tall, pleasant-faced man who looked uncomfortable sitting on the upholstered chair in front of his desk. Thomas had ordered the Major to appear at Governor's House after reading his report on the various expeditions he had experienced.

The Major had commanded a corps of pioneers who had opened a road for General Macdowal's embassy to Kandy in 1800. Again in 1803 and 1804, he was appointed to command a *free corps* comprised principally of Malays who were employed in escorting supplies to and from the different frontline depots, leading to frequent skirmishes with the enemy.

Thomas instinctively understood that knowing one's enemy was the key to dealing with them. The failure of this campaign to achieve decisive results after a heavy sacrifice of life and dividends led to the recall of the previous Governor, and he wanted to hear personally from the man about his experiences.

'Tell me all you have learnt about the Kandyans he ordered the Major. 'I have little time to get to know them personally, and I am hoping that you, and others like you, can help me understand what I am against.'

The Major took a deep breath before replying. 'The part actually in our possession encircles, like a belt, the territories subject to the King of Kandy, comprehending the whole coast of the island, in a circumference which varies from ten to twenty and thirty miles in breadth,' he started, pointing to a map of the island placed next to the desk on a stand. 'The terms of treaties concluded between the King of Kandy and successive European invaders at the end of their wars are regulating its extent inland.'

Thomas already knew that the Portuguese and the Dutch had trade dealings with the King and had tried on various occasions to use military force without much success.

'Did you conclude why they were unsuccessful in their attempts to subjugate the middle Kingdom?'

'It's a mistake to underestimate the natives,' the Major replied. 'They go about their business quite peacefully, but it was not always like that. Only by exploiting divisions between the various rulers of the five regions could they control the coastal regions. All other attempts have failed.'

'I have reached the same conclusion,' Thomas replied. 'What makes it so difficult for us?'

'Our ignorance of their passes and valleys forms one of the best safeguards of their independence. The rulers of the Kandyan nation take all possible care to prevent our acquiring information on this subject.'

'You have said that in your report,' Thomas tapped the document lying on his desk. 'What exactly do you mean?'

'They have not left us any general account of the country, nor even those parts which were the scenes of their operations. The government of Kandy, like most eastern governments, is purely autocratic. They have a small army who are generally stationed around the King. They are armed with muskets, captured at different battles or purchased from their European invaders.'

Thomas acknowledged the information with a nod.

'Although they possess little, if any, of discipline, the Kandyans have gathered, in their frequent conflicts with the Portuguese and Dutch, considerable knowledge and mastery in a class of warfare, which is best suited to the nature of their country, and to their disposition.

Thomas thought for a moment. 'Have they always fought like this?'

'They are conscious of their inability to resist the regular attack of European troops and quite aware of their advantages in being familiar with the country and the climate, they avoid close combat. They much prefer irregular warfare. They harass the enemy during his march, concentrating on his flanks, cutting off his supplies, and interrupting the communication between his regiments. They clearly understand the coolies' value by aiming at the men carrying the ammunition and provisions. Without them, a regular force can make little progress.'

Thomas tapped the despatch sitting on his desk. 'Why do we allow this to happen?'

'They occupy the heights which command the passes, from whence they fire in perfect security from behind rocks or trees. Dislodging them from these peaks is extremely difficult, as the trails are mostly on the opposite sides of the mountains and are only known to the natives.'

Thomas raised his eyebrows in surprise. 'But surely, we must have built up a bank of knowledge about the terrain and used it to overcome the enemy?'

The Major shook his head. 'That is not the case, your Excellency. They are accustomed to impeding the march of hostile troops by felling and placing large trees across the defiles as *abatis* (field fortifications). When we pause to clear these obstructions, they attack us from within the jungles, from earthen forts usually built on heights overlooking the trails. One of their tactics is seldom to press closely an enemy marching into their country; being certain that the diseases incident to us Europeans not used to the climate, and the lack of provisions, will soon fall back. The farther they advance, the better the Kandyans promote their scheme of defence, as they can throw more impediments in the way. What makes the situation of the troops even more distressing is that every man who falls into the hands of the enemy is certain of being killed,' said the Major, warming to his task.

Thomas raised his eyebrows. 'They don't take any prisoners?'

No,' the Major shook his head. 'They don't.'

'What is the morale of our troops,' Thomas questioned.

'They will follow orders,' the Major said. 'But the same cannot be said of the *coolies* (camp followers/labourers).'

'What about them?' Thomas questioned. 'I have noted a large expense for their payment and welfare.'

'I am sure there is your Excellency, but that is an area I am not qualified to discuss.'

'It may not be,' Thomas conceded. 'But you are best placed to answer the question.'

The Major studied Thomas before taking in a deep breath. 'The carriage of *doolies* (litters for the sick or wounded) and camp equipage requires an incredible number of *coolies*. These men are locals who are always gathered and ready to be used at a moment's notice. But it is not always how it works in practice. Usually, the chief seldom procures above half the required number after many delays. Therefore, the advantages we seem to enjoy over the enemy of always having a considerable disciplined force are completely lost.'

'Do they keep a watch on us?'

'There is no doubt that Kandyan spies placed amongst these men warn their masters that our detachments are being readied. In every effort I have been involved in since I arrived on station, the enemy is arrayed in force, ready to receive us.'

'Has any attempt been made to deceive them in any way?'

The Major nodded. 'Yes, we have tried various means to disguise our advances. Sometimes even attacking from multiple directions. But these tactics don't seem to work for various reasons.'

'What do you mean?' Thomas questioned. 'What reasons?'

'The *coolies* know that the Kandyans would have been warned. They also know that being caught means certain death. When they are unexpectedly attacked, from the mere impulse of fear and no doubt sedition by the Kandyan spies, they throw down their loads and rush into the jungle to conceal themselves. These disasters happen mostly in narrow valleys, and the enemy, who well know the disposition of our *coolies*, generally selects such places to attack.' The Major concluded that our expeditions lost hundreds of coolies to these attacks and many more from desertion.

Thomas stared at the Major. It was a problem he'd not faced previously.

'Does the enemy possess large numbers of regular troops?'

'Their so-called army consists of only a few hundred men, most of them European and Malay mercenaries.'

'That is all?' Thomas was amazed. 'How do they manage to keep us at bay?'

'The King can bring to the field on any emergency a considerable portion of the male population of his kingdom. Each man is provided with a musket and carries with him fifteen days' provisions and a small cooking vessel.'

'They each carry their supplies!' Thomas was familiar with the practice. 'What kind of supplies?' he asked. 'Rice?'

The Major warmed to the subject when he realised that Thomas was genuinely interested in what he had learnt. 'Rice forms the main food amongst all ranks, but in the island's interior, it is only used by the higher classes and is considered a luxury.'

'So, what do they eat?'

'Vegetables, yams, and the like. They sometimes make a gruel out of ground rice flour which they mix with greens of various types.'

'They can march and fight with such sustenance?'

'Yes. At the end of fifteen days, the citizen soldier is relieved by a fresh requisition from the village. By doing this, the army is constantly supplied with fresh troops, totally unencumbered, and the relieved men always carry home their sick and wounded companions.'

Thomas pursed his lips in thought. No baggage trains. No encumbrances of any sort. No expenditure by the Kings treasury. It was no wonder he could prosecute the war at his leisure.

The Major was watching Thomas and responded to his unasked question.

'Such a system could only work in a country like this. They know the territory intimately and what needs to be done. And most importantly, each soldier is seldom more than two, and never more than four days' march from their abode.'

'So, they have total freedom of movement within their territory!'

'Yes. They don't find it necessary to provide escorts, as they have little to fear from the slow movements of our forces, whom they can always avoid by taking a circuitous route.'

Thomas had experienced a similar situation when he was placed in charge of the forces arrayed to protect British interests on the island of San Domingo and evolve order out of chaos. After studying the situation from the time he landed in that country, he had decided that without some lull in the storm of political hate and fears that distracted the country, even an evacuation of his forces was more and more of an impossibility.

'Major Patterson, you have served in this country for several years. You have even learned to speak the language to some extent. In your assessment, how should we deal with this rebellious territory?'

The officer glanced at Major Staples sitting quietly at the back of the room. Thomas had wanted him there to ensure that the information he was being given was accurate.

'The Kandyan's are not a threat … in fact, have never been a threat to us by themselves. They could not defeat the Portuguese without the help of the Dutch and only turned against them when they refused to leave.'

Thomas nodded impatiently for the Major to continue. He had read about what had happened in the past. The island had been invaded many times and not just by the Europeans. Various empires in India, going back a thousand years or more, had attempted to conquer the island without much success.

'One may think that this makes them fearsome fighters. But the Kandyans, formidable in their jungle fortresses, are very feeble in close combat. It's not in their nature to be aggressive.'

Thomas raised in eyebrows. It was a piece of the puzzle which had been eluding him. The previous Governor nor his Generals had ever admitted to this fact in their despatches if it were true.

'And you know this from personal experience?'

'I do,' the Major nodded. 'On our last expedition, we were confronted by a large group of men situated on the banks of a great river which passes the city of Kandy. We stormed a house overlooking the ford, around 150 yards across. In a relatively short time, nearly everyone in that group, which had just before covered the opposite river bank, had disappeared into the woods. However, we still lost six Europeans, eight sepoys and thirty-five followers, killed and wounded during the crossing through enemy fire from within the woods.'

'You consider this significant?'

'They array great forces against us but delay their attack until the climate or disease take effect on us before attacking our forces, encumbered by a long train of the sick and wounded and probably destitute of ammunition.'

'That could just be the tactics they employ.'

The Major shook his head. 'I don't think so, your Excellency. They are not a warlike tribe; they only fight for allegiance to their leaders. The nobles hold their lands at the King's indulgence and are obliged, when called upon, to join the army at the head of a third of their villagers. This allows the King to dispense with a large regular force, which would be a burden to his treasury, and to bring into the field, on any emergency, a considerable portion of the male population of his kingdom.'

'Surely this will wear thin after a while."

'It is also a consequence of the reward the King of Kandy offered for the heads of his enemies and the desire to afford proofs of personal courage.'

'Hmmm.' Thomas could see that the Major had used his considerable experience and knowledge to come to his conclusions. 'Don't we have native guides to help us get through these mountain passes?'

'The Kandyans understand our ignorance of their passes and defiles forms one of the best safeguards of their independence. Their leaders are particularly careful to prevent our acquiring information on this subject. They watch the routes to their territory with continuous vigilance.'

'So, your conclusion is ….'

'Defended by their climate, mountains, and forests, the Kandyans, by strictly following the same mode of warfare, have been able to resist the incursions of several European invaders for three centuries.'

'Are you saying that this tribe of small landowners and farmers can resist the might of the British Empire?'

'Eventually, they will have to succumb. They will tire of the war, and without any trade, they will wither on the vine. We know they can be overcome in battle, as we had proven when we reached their capital. But remaining there will take considerable effort, and only after we complete the road we are building.'

Thomas steepled his hands. The Major was an important source of information which needed to be exploited. What he had heard stirred an idea in Thomas's mind.

Maybe I am approaching this the wrong way.

'Thank you, Major, for revealing your experiences. It is now beholden of me to consider what you have shared with us. I would be most grateful if you could construct a narrative to be shared with the rest of our forces which have little or no knowledge of this species of warfare.'

'Easily, your Excellency,' Major Patterson said. 'Is there something I should keep in mind when I write my report?'

'Just keep in touch with reality,' Thomas replied. 'We don't want to give anyone a good laugh at our expense. I am not going to tell you what to write. We are on the same side, with the same objective.' He stood and extended his hand to the Major. 'Let me know when your report is ready. If any problems or questions arise, my door is open.'

CHAPTER 12

THE STUDENT

Lovinia woke suddenly and completely alert. She had always been a light sleeper and heard the doorknob rattle. She was usually up around dawn, but they returned to the village after midnight, and she had taken a while to fall asleep.

Golden sunshine flooded the room through the gaps in the door as she rolled out from under the thin cotton sheet. She could hear her father's rhythmic snores from the other room. He had been pleased the Chief Steward had paid them fully for their performance.

'You made an impression,' Banda said, smiling at Lovinia. 'He even paid what he owed us.'

The members of the troupe were excited when Banda handed out their take from the evening. Many supported family groups, including their parents and, sometimes, their in-laws.

Lovinia could see that Aletta was anxious to talk to her about what happened during her performance. They hadn't had a chance to talk in private. The door rattled again, this time a bit louder.

'I'm up.' Lovinia noticed the mosquito bites on her arm as she called out, knowing who was at the door.

Aletta barged in the moment she heard the door unlock. 'You're still asleep,' she accused Lovinia, still wiping the sleep from her eyes. 'We have a lot to talk about.'

'Yes, but I am not ready yet,' Lovinia smiled at her friend, who was always so full of life in the morning. 'Why don't you get the fire going, and I'll join you in a moment.'

Aletta nodded, bouncing out of the room through the back door. Lovinia folded her bedding and put it away, taking a sip from the water jug before following her into the back verandah. Aletta had already started the fire.

'I couldn't wait any longer to talk to you,' she said, looking at Lovinia. 'You must tell me what happened.'

Lovinia could remember every single moment. She had played it over and over in her mind several times. When she danced into the room, her focus had been on the man in the place of prominence. While waiting to dance, it had become evident to her that he was the new emissary from the Great King. She had focused her attention entirely on him. She had been surprised when he addressed her.

'He spoke to me. Asked me what my name was.'

Aletta looked at Lovinia with a hint of a smile. 'He wanted you.'

Lovinia nodded. She could see that the *Andukāraya* was attracted to her. She had danced for enough men to recognise their desires.

'He tried to say more but...' Lovinia had felt a connection to the officer when it was abruptly broken.

Aletta's initial amusement of Lovinia's situation was lost. Her expression grew grave. 'What happened?'

'He received a message. Something important, I think. He was distracted afterwards.'

'Do you know what it was about?' Aletta asked gently.

Lovinia shook her head. 'They were speaking English,' she said quietly. 'I didn't understand a word of it.' She spoke Creole and Sinhalese and had a few words of English. A terrible foreboding gripped her senses as she uttered the words. She thought of the Kandyan and what he had asked her to do. How could she have missed such a splendid opportunity? The day had suddenly lost its lustre for her.

Aletta studied Lovinia, her head tilted to one side. 'I heard he's not married and has no companion. Such men are lonely and can be manipulated.' She reached out and took Lovinia's hand in hers. 'We must find a way for you to dance for him again.'

'What about the chief steward?' Lovinia asked. 'Wasn't I supposed to get closer to him? The Kandyan is expecting nothing less.'

'What Kandyan?' The question took them both by surprise. Banda stood by the door, scrutinising them both thoughtfully. 'What's going on?'

Lovinia felt the blood drain from her face. Her throat went dry. She had never hidden anything from her father, and she did not know how he would react.

Aletta acknowledged Banda's presence with a smile. 'You'll have to ask Lovinia,' she said, tossing her head. 'She's becoming extremely popular these days.'

Lovinia dug her elbow into Aletta. She hated it when her friend treated her like a child. She took in a big gulp and told her father of her encounter with the Kandyan outside the village.

'You should have come to me immediately,' Banda said understandingly. 'I know whom you are talking about.'

Lovinia's eyes opened wide. 'You know him?'

'No, but I have heard of him.' Banda walked over to the hearth and poured boiling water from the kettle into an earthenware mug. 'He's a dangerous man, I've heard.'

'He'll want to know what happened,' Lovinia said, looking down.

Banda let out a small grunt of laughter. 'It will become known around the village very soon about our performance last night. Our people will spend the money they receive and talk. It may be enough to satisfy him.' He poured a heaped spoon of coffee grounds into the mug. 'Do you want one too?' he asked them both. They both nodded at him.

'Is he able to do what he threatens?'

'If the King employs him, he can do whatever he wants. We can lose all of this,' her father said, waving his arm around their home. 'One word from someone like him, and we will have to move. These are dangerous times.'

Banda exchanged a look with Aletta.

He favoured Lovinia with a sympathetic smile. 'You should remain here for a few days,' he said, preparing two mugs. 'Stay away from the village. Do not go roaming the streets as you do. You must be careful.'

Cold, invisible fingers swept Lovinia's back. She could remember the look in the Kandyan's eyes. She needed to do something to keep him from harming them.

Aletta had been watching the interplay between them. 'I think you should forget about the Chief Steward,' she said. 'You should concentrate your attention on the man you danced for. He's the important one.'

Lovinia fixed her with a cold, hard stare. 'You can't be serious.'

'The Kandyan will not bother you if you set your sights higher,' Aletta said. 'Leave the Chief Steward to me, and you can tell your Kandyan that he now has two of us doing his bidding.'

Banda handed each of them a cup of steaming coffee. 'She is correct. It will buy you some time. But he will not be patient, so we have to devise a plan.'

His warning rang in Lavinia's head as she stirred her coffee. She felt relieved that the burden she had been carrying was shared by the two people closest to her. Her father would move heaven and earth to protect her.

'Can you come live with us for a while?' Banda asked Aletta. 'I am not always around, and I don't want her to be alone.'

Aletta nodded. 'I will move right away,' she said without hesitation. 'I have been wanting to move anyway, and this will be as good a place as any.'

Lovinia knew that her friend rented a room close to the village centre where she carried out her various activities.

'You can stay for long as you like.' Banda had always treated Aletta like a daughter and knew the two women together would make a formidable pair. 'And, I will feel better if you can protect yourself.'

Banda walked back into their hut and emerged with something wrapped in a leather cloth a few moments later. Inside the wrapping was a small, double-edged stabbing knife with an inlaid handle. 'Carry this on you at all times.'

Lovinia took the dagger from him hesitantly. It was smaller than the length of her hand. She understood the danger she found herself in sometimes when intoxicated men, their minds feverish with *ganja*, tried to grab at her. Her father or the men he employed as security would take care of the matter, usually dragging the offender away without interrupting the performance.

'Strap it to your thigh.' he said, pointing to a spot on his upper leg. 'Aletta will show you how.'

'Why do I have to wear this,' Lovinia questioned. 'There has never been a reason to use a weapon to defend myself.' She remembered that the Kandyan had grabbed her arm when she tried to leave him when she uttered those words. He could have killed her if she had not agreed to do his bidding.

'We all do.' Aletta pulled back her skirt and showed Lavinia a triangular-shaped dagger strapped to the inside of her slender thigh by a piece of linen. 'It has saved me more than once.'

Lovinia nodded, having witnessed the incident Aletta referred to. She had always thought that Aletta had got the knife from the man who had tried to fondle her.

'We still have to bring you to the attention of the English noble.' Banda's forehead creased in thought. 'I will try to arrange a meeting with the Chief Steward.'

'She'll also need to learn to talk to the *Andukāraya*,' Aletta said thoughtfully. 'I know a woman in the village who can speak the language. I'll ask her to teach you.'

Lovinia did not know what to say. She tried to gather her thoughts. It all seemed so final. She licked her lips which suddenly seemed dry. She had thought what was asked of her, first by her father and then by the Kandyan, would be impossible. Still, with everyone supporting her, it could become a reality.

'Oh, Lovinia,' Aletta said, seeing her crestfallen expression. 'Wouldn't you want to become the concubine of one of the two most powerful men on the island?'

Lovinia blinked in confusion at the amusement on her father's face. She envisioned a different kind of life opening out before her if she could ever find a way to be placed in such a position.

'I will take lessons', she agreed. 'It's the only way.'

CHAPTER 13

THE TASK AHEAD

Thomas was bored sitting in the Fort all day. He was surrounded by soldiers and retainers who jumped to obey his every request. He missed men he could converse with at his level and, above all, female company.

Last night while trying to sleep, faintly over the breeze, there was the plaintive sound of a bagpipe from the soldiers' quarters. It was beautiful and familiar, yet Thomas felt an ache of something he was beginning to recognise as loneliness.

Thomas sat at his desk, staring out the window at the gathering clouds. The enormity of the task he had been given was confronting now that he had reviewed the situation. His primary role as Governor was to restore tranquillity to the Crown Colony and curtail the extravagance of the military establishment. The regular army was small and dispirited from the recent defeat. The Kandyans, faced with a heavily armed enemy, relied on ambush, not open battle. Skilfully, they blocked pathways with fallen trees or set traps in pits disguised with thorny undergrowth and filled with sharpened wooden posts.

After almost a year of bitter fighting, the native allies and troops were in a hardly disguised mutiny. Desertions were frequent, and speculations as to the downfall of the colony were generally rife. The colony treasury was empty, and vast leakages had continually meant drawing bills on England.

Trade was rapidly falling off, and there was a considerable debt to the East India Company. It was all highly unsatisfactory.

Thomas reached across and rang the small brass bell on the desk, summoning his secretary, Mr Brewer.

'I wish to compose a report to the Colonial Office in London.'

Thomas's office allowed him to walk six paces each way. After the first halting sentences – his report naturally began with what he had uncovered upon his arrival on the island. After spending just a few months in the country, he now realised that although the island's government presented a surface appearance of uniformity and efficiency, what was a sound system had been weakly operated. Regulations were not enforced. Many just become words on a piece of paper. Inactive and lazy civil servants had been allowed the scope to give way to their failings, and many regulations were inapplicable to large parts of the territory. The previous Governor had been highly popular with the Europeans by multiplying posts in a hardly justifiable way. His government was little more than a series of wild experiments, the damage falling on the natives, not the Europeans.

Thomas paused. He felt a constriction of the throat and dryness, which he eased by taking a sip of water from a tumbler on his desk. He had decided that he would set himself three tasks. Stop the war, reduce the extravagantly inflated military establishment, and bring order to the chaotic finances of the island.

'Continue, if you please,' he ordered. 'Having regard to these conditions, I therefore proceeded— '

It was finished in the end—he was dreadfully tired—his head drooped forward at his breast where he sat.

Thomas forced himself back on his feet. 'Read it out to me,' he ordered brusquely. He felt slightly out of control, like rushing giddily down a mountain slope. But he squared his shoulders as his words were read back to him. The secretary was looking at him with eyes shining with admiration. It made him feel uncomfortable.

'If you will just sign this, sir, I will attend to the seal and the superscription.'

Brewer slipped out of his chair, and Thomas took the pen and dashed off his signature to the document. He knew that the despatch of the report would take many months before it arrived in London and perhaps a further period before it was read and digested. He would not expect to hear anything back for a considerable time—perhaps as long as a year. This thought awakened the possibilities that opened out for him.

I will make good use of this time. Thomas suddenly felt rejuvenated. He walked over to the open window, looking out into the garden. *I have been stuck in this damn room for weeks. I must get out.*

'Could you tell the Steward to have a horse ready for me forthwith,' Thomas said to Brewer, who was leaving the room. 'I must get out and breathe some fresh air.'

Thomas took his time changing into his riding gear. Major Staples stood waiting patiently for him under the porch. Two saddled horses led by a groom were being walked up from the stables at the back of the house.

'What do you have in mind, your Excellency?'

'I just want to get out for some fresh air,' Thomas grumbled at the Major. 'I feel like I am locked in all the time.'

'Would you like to visit your city lodge, sir?'

Thomas had learned that his predecessor had refused to live in the Governor's residence in the Fort, instead preferring to live in a lodge at St. Sebastian's, one of the northern outer bastions of Colombo. His Chief Steward and others had told him that the building was in wretched condition, having been transformed into a habitation from a powder magazine.

Thomas shook his head. 'I don't think so. I prefer a canter around the lake.' He had not mounted a horse for almost a year and doubted he would have got on the animal's back without the aid of a footstool.

As they clattered out of the main gate, they were approached by three armed mounted soldiers led by a sergeant who fell in behind them.

'Are they really necessary?' Thomas called out to Major Staples.

'Perhaps not,' the Major answered. 'But we are at war with the Kandyans, and we know they have spies watching us.'

Thomas nodded. *I better get used to this,* he thought as he wheeled his mount towards the entrance to the fort. The guard at the main Delft gate had the enormous wooden doors open as Thomas and his escort clattered onto the causeway leading across a wide moat filled with *caymans* (crocodiles) and through an unguarded gate into the native quarter.

Pita Kotuwa (outside the fort), known to the Europeans as 'Pettah', was a market suburb mainly occupied by the Burghers, who dressed and behaved as Europeans. They were a mixed group of people descended from Europeans, mainly Dutch, Portuguese, German, Swiss, Belgian, French and other smaller European nations who had worked and settled on the island. Many had mixed with local Sinhalese, Tamil and Moor populations and produced light-coloured children. Along the periphery were small colonies of Moor and Malabar traders, Malays, Tamils and Afghans from Persia.

Pettah was laid out in the manner of Dutch towns, in streets that ran parallel or at right angles. They were lined by native trees, which cast a pleasant shade. To the north was the area where the Dutch inhabitants resided, where Meneer Van Rijn lived with his family and friends waiting to be repatriated to Batavia. Thomas had read that prejudice existed amongst the Dutch that sea air was unwholesome. Therefore, they built all their houses in the city area that backed onto high rampart walls, protecting them from the wind.

When the British took over from the Dutch, they faced these Burghers, or citizens, in all the major towns, who were already divided by descent, occupation and social standing. Because of their position under the VOC, the Dutch Burghers had proven very useful to the British, especially in the initial changeover period. Being familiar with Roman-Dutch law and having served in various administrative capacities under the VOC, they continued to provide a similar service to the British. However, the name Burgher became an imputed racial label, a synonym for half-caste or Eurasian, which overrode any distinctions the Burghers made among themselves on either a class or descent basis.

They had now reached the more crowded streets teeming with every variety of oriental race and costume. There were the Sinhalese, the men and the women wearing their hair tied behind in knots, the women adding elaborate hairpins, and the darker-skinned Tamils from India. Hindus of every caste jostled Moormen of Arab blood who introduced coffee to Ceylon, Afghan traders, Malay policemen, long-nosed Parsees, narrow-eyed Chinese, and there were Eurasians of Dutch or Portuguese or English descent.

It was all a kaleidoscope of movement, colour, noise and confusion. Now and then, Thomas would see a Buddhist monk in saffron-coloured robes hastening along, his umbrella borne over him by a boy clothed from head to toe in white. The Sinhalese farmers travelled in wooden carts drawn by bullocks. The people seemed to be all dressed in brightly coloured attire, which led to the brightness in the air.

Thomas noted that the Sinhalese were a handsome race. Well-proportioned in both build and features, with the skin of an antique rosewood table. The men carried themselves well, almost all wearing long, neatly trimmed beards with their hair gathered behind in a knot. The beauty of the delicate featured women, their limbs wrapped in cloths of vivid colours, some gracefully carrying heavy objects on their heads, who swayed along the road, caught his attention. Quite different to the bigger, thick-lipped black and mulatto women he was used to seeing in the Caribbean.

He was roused from these musings by overhearing Major Staples ordering the small group to take the right-hand fork towards the east. They turned down a well-maintained avenue of gigantic coconut palms towards a picturesque lake.

'We are approaching Cinnamon Gardens,' Major Staples announced as a group of houses came into view. They had, by this time, covered about three miles. 'It was a former cinnamon plantation, where many of the more affluent Europeans live.'

'Where do you live, Major?'

'In the city, sire,' the Major responded, edging his mount closer. 'It's a little place I could purchase with a small inheritance.'

'So you want to live here permanently?' Thomas asked, looking at the Major.

'Yes, I do, sire,' he nodded, trying to hold his horse steady. 'I don't want to go back to England.'

'You have no family there?'

'No, sire. Three years ago, my wife and son were lost at sea when a French warship sank their transport. They were coming here to join me.'

'I am sorry to hear that, Major.'

'Thank you, sir.' The Major moved his mount away to prevent any more questions.

The houses of the European residents who made up the Colombo society were scattered along the shores of the lake and in the cinnamon gardens which adjoined it. The garden suburb was a peaceful and tranquil place dotted with pretty bungalows and handsome houses built in the European style of architecture, with the addition of a verandah or covered piazza to shade the rooms from the sun.

The single-storey houses were generally large and cool, with verandahs the whole length of the front. All the houses they passed had shutters, either open or closed; twisted frangipani trees grew in the passageways, and monkeys grunted as they swung in their gleaming branches. Social interaction was limited between the Europeans and locals, mainly to soldiers, chandlers, coachmen, grooms, artisans, shopkeepers, and vendors of sweetmeats.

Thomas allowed his horse to drop to a walk. Living inside the Fort would provide him with the security his position demanded. But he found the residence to be generally run down and in need of serious maintenance. His predecessor Governor North had abandoned the residence in favour of living in a house outside its walls. He wasn't a military man and would have found the ebbs and flows of a military garrison tedious and restrictive.

The sun was beating fiercely when they turned to the south—riding parallel to the seashore, they could see between rows of cinnamon and coconut trees. The area was primarily flat, with a canal bisecting the area. The Dutch constructed canals during their reign, linking streams, lakes, and lagoons around the city, creating a continuous line of waterways between the interior and the ports. These waterways were sheltered from the monsoon winds, making coastal transportation by sea difficult or dangerous. Thomas assumed it was used by the Dutch for transporting bundles of cinnamon, coffee, copra and timber from the southern forests to the port.

Across the canal were a village, a bazaar, and a pagoda-shaped Buddhist temple, filled with white-clothed worshippers.

With a good sense of direction, Thomas turned into a well-travelled road that ran north to south along the seashore. The road was crowded with bullock carts full of produce and people. Thomas led the small group down to the golden sands of the seashore, where a light breeze coming off the sea brought some relief from the rays of the afternoon sun.

A mixed population of more affluent Burghers, Sinhalese, Moors, and Tamils inhabited the seaside section of the town. Small houses with weathered walls were set back from narrow lanes running off the main road, their open verandahs and gardens filled with bright flowers and shrubs. The land was flat, stretching towards a small promontory a few miles south. Gentle hills led to the east, ending abruptly in blue mountains. The land was covered in a lush carpet of green as far as the eye could see.

Thomas wheeled his mount towards the north, back towards the massive walls of the Fort, which dominated the entrance to the small harbour. A Royal Navy frigate proudly flying the White Ensign lay anchored on the roads. Grey clouds on the horizon promised a shower or two of rain that night.

Thomas felt tired but happy with his little outing. Growing up in the Scottish Highlands had given him an appreciation for the outdoors. He always had a preference for exploring the unusual.

I must do this more often, he decided. *There is so much about this country I do not know.*

CHAPTER 14

LEARNING A LANGUAGE

The woman Aletta had talked about was living in their village. Juana was the mestizo wife of an English manservant working for an officer in the Fort. She learned to speak the language when she worked as a maid for one of the English families living in Cinnamon Gardens. After Banda offered to pay her, Juana agreed to teach Lovinia to speak the language.

'You're ready for today's lesson? Can you describe this verandah in English?' Lovinia tried to get her thoughts together in English with her hands on her lap. Juana was a friendly, middle-aged woman who looked after a small plot of land her English husband had bought for her. She walked from her home on the northern side of the village every morning to conduct her lessons.

Juana sighed heavily, shook her head, and said slowly, 'Repeat after me. This is a chair. That's a table.' She named at least ten more objects. 'Come! Speak! Speak. You must be quick.'

Lovinia repeated the sentences, misplacing words and biting her lips in frustration. Once corrected, she plunged in with renewed energy, her voice strong and steady.

Although Lovinia listened to English much of the day, it was much easier to weave sentences in Sinhalese. The sounds she learnt as a child were as much a part of her body as precious as her eyesight.

'Aiiyo, why is it so difficult to say?'

'It is how the language is spoken,' said Juana, smiling. 'If it's any consolation, I learnt English from a native speaker, so my pronunciation is correct.'

Lovinia sat up straighter. Words and phrases rose and fell, stormed on her tongue, exhausted her breath, and muted the birdsong. At the end of the morning, she had acquired a new vocabulary, collected the prize of several new sentences, and felt famished, but she no longer felt intimidated. The sounds were now her own and belonged to her treasury of expressions.

As they finished for the day, Lovinia was ready to step away. It had been three weeks since she had started her English lessons. *I am worn out*, Lovinia thought irritably. Her struggles with English were non-ending, but she was trying hard.

Juana wiped the perspiration from her forehead as though she had exhausted her store of energy. 'You learn quickly. It's passable, your English.'

Lovinia forgot the day's fatigue and her apprehensions. It was the first time since they started that Juana had said such a thing. 'You think so?' she asked eagerly. The last three weeks had been a burden for her. Her father had forbidden her to step outside the compound, and someone was always hanging around outside the gate.

'Yes, you've made some progress in your English conversation,' Juana said, smiling. 'I didn't expect it.'

Lovinia bowed her head and allowed the flattery to slide over her, then realized that Juana had given her a chance to express herself. 'I study whenever I have a spare moment. I practise English with anyone I can find.' She had learned to rehearse speaking English in the quietness of her home, practice, and practice until she got it right.

'I am sure you can't find many people who speak it. How many locals speak English fluently?' Juana spoke in Sinhalese. 'They ask us why we do not pick up their mother tongue. Well, we try. Most of us can speak some Sinhalese or Portuguese, but they do not seem to understand our accents. And there are so many dialects. Of course, we have no one to do the interpreting.'

'Well, I still can't say everything I want.'

'And what have you not said to me that you'd like to say?' Juana smiled, her eyes twinkling. 'Don't worry about it too much. It will come.'

'I know I have a long way to go before I speak properly.'

An impatient bunch, they are, the English,' Juana said. 'Even when you become proficient in English, don't try to give them a long explanation. Answer a question in as few words as possible. Or greet them and move on.'

Mumbling a word of gratitude, Lovinia rose and bowed respectfully. Juana had taught her English manners. 'You must learn to behave like them,' she once said. 'Only then will they show you a little respect.'

Juana nodded, seemingly pleased that Lovinia had remembered her words but the question on her mind shone in her eyes. She turned, her face catching the yellow rays of the afternoon sun. 'You have never told me why you want to speak the language. It will help me to prepare you better.'

Lovinia, Aletta and her father had discussed this before her lessons started. 'You must not tell anyone why you want to speak the language,' Banda warned.

Lovinia shrugged. 'We dance at times for the English soldiers, and my father thinks they will reward us more if we can speak to them.'

Even though Juana nodded, she didn't seem convinced. 'I learnt to speak the language working first as a housemaid and then as a nanny. The master of the house spoke Portuguese, making it easier for me to understand and learn the language. But it took me a long time. I think it will be much easier for you as you are quick-witted and don't forget. I don't need to know why you want to learn, but whatever you are planning, you must always remember that you are not one of them.'

Lavinia's heart beat wildly in apprehension. Would the woman suspect what she was planning to do? *No, there was no way she would know.* Lovinia comforted herself with the thought.

'Although your English is, shall we say, less than adequate at this point, you seem to make yourself understood.' Juana pushed herself up from her cross-legged sitting position on the mat. 'I will tell your father what I have just told you. It will be up to him if he wants me to continue.'

CHAPTER 15

CINNAMON

Thomas, seated in the window of Sir David Tarrant's drawing room, idly looking out into the street, had ceased to pay any attention to the conversation in progress. A European lady in a white *mantilla* (scarf worn by women over the head and shoulders) caught his eye among the passers-by. She was attractive enough to be observed the whole way down the street. She cast a roguish eye at the window as she passed, catching Thomas's attention.

Thomas sighed and chided himself for daydreaming. His mind was wandering more and more often of late, and it worried him. Hopefully, the tendency would pass now that he had identified some issues worthy of his complete attention.

'This war is bad for business,' Sir David said dryly. 'I am sure your Excellency understands how much it costs us.'

Thomas overhearing this last remark, turned his head and asked innocently, 'And what does it cost the Company?'

Thomas had accepted an invitation by Lady Tarrant to attend an afternoon soiree at her residence. The ladies had retired to the drawing room while Thomas sat with Sir David in his rather cramped study.

'Our commerce is down by at least half, and that's not counting the untapped potential out there.'

Thomas studied Sir Tarrant. 'Is that figure based on what the Dutch were doing on the island?'

'Certainly, yes!' Sir Tarrant declared. 'You must realise this yourself. I expect your information is as good as mine.'

Thomas nodded sanguinely. He had been contemplating how to address the three tasks he had set himself and had decided that if he could pause the Kandyan war, it would allow him to reform the military and significantly reduce costs.

'Are you considering a resumption of hostilities with the Kandyans?' Sir David asked. 'The truce is such that we are still at war. The Company is not allowed to trade with the Kandyans who control access to the harbour from the north and east.'

Thomas leaned forward. 'The Kandyan King will always quarrel with whatever power holds the coast, and being an inland nation without a need for external supplies, our great power on the sea cannot be brought to bear.'

'You have a plan, I presume?' Sir David asked.

'I do,' Thomas responded. 'But before I implement it, you and I need to come to an understanding.'

Sir Tarrant sat back in his chair attentively.

Thomas had found out during his examination of the accounts that the cinnamon trade was rapidly falling off as frequent raids and threats by the Kandyans had dried the production of the cinnamon quills to almost a trickle. This had given him an idea.

'The Crown is currently holding a large arrear of funds to the Company under the cinnamon contract. Yes?'

Sir Tarrant nodded. 'Yes, the Crown is in arrears of the contract the Company signed, which now amounts to a considerable sum of money.'

'But my understanding is that these arrears are not only due to the war.' Thomas said innocently.

'What do you mean?' Sir David sat up alertly.

'There are over 5,000 bales of perfectly good cinnamon sitting in warehouses, which your overseers have rejected for reasons I am unfamiliar with,' Thomas said, observing Sir David. 'My officials have assured me that these rejected bales are perfectly up to standard, so my question to you, Sir, what's going on?'

Sir David squirmed uncomfortably at Thomas's blunt question.

Thomas had learned that the officer appointed by the East India Company to supervise the delivery of the cinnamon, in the discharge of his duty, selected from the bales submitted to him only those that contained quality cinnamon but also good in appearance. As the contract provided for the appointment of no such official on the Crown's side to check these objections, the rejected bales occupied a large warehouse in the port.

Thomas could only conclude that this was being done deliberately to weaken the cinnamon market on the island, a view he now believed to be accurate. During his predecessor's time, 16,000 cinnamon plants had been sent to a plantation in Tinevelly in the Madras Presidency. The reason for doing so at the time was the apprehension that British occupancy in Ceylon might not prove long-lasting.

'I think you're being too harsh in your assessment,' Sir David said, sitting up straighter in his chair. 'If you have a complaint, I suggest you put it in writing to the Board of Directors.'

'I don't think you want me to go down this path, Sir David. I have been given specific instructions to review the cinnamon contract and make whatever changes I want, up to and including revocation of the terms of the agreement.'

'You cannot do that,' Sir David spluttered. 'It is the mainstay of our trade on the island.'

'You may not be aware, but your Board is displeased with the reduction in cinnamon from the island. The high-grade variety of the spice is not found in any other country and is considered the best in the world, as you know. This reduction has forced the company to transport inferior products from India, bringing lower prices in European markets.'

Sir David's face drained of colour. Thomas understood that as head of the East India Company in Ceylon, his primary responsibility was the cinnamon contract which brought considerable profits to the company.

'I believe your man is deliberately rejecting perfectly good cinnamon, so the Company has no choice but to use an inferior product from India. I suspect that he is being bribed to do this.'

'You couldn't believe I have anything to do with this, your Excellency?' An agitated Sir David got to his feet. 'If your assertion is true, I will take steps to replace the official in question.'

'And sweep all this under the carpet.' Thomas made a derisive sound, sitting back comfortably in his chair. 'I am willing to blame your peers in India if you say you had nothing to do with it, but your position carries responsibility. What did you think was happening?'

'The war, of course,' Sir David quickly responded. 'The Kandyans constantly harass the cinnamon estates around Negombo.'

'Hmm, I can see where you have come unstuck. Someone has been pulling the wool over your eyes.' Thomas was not surprised. The senior Company officials lived a life of luxury on the island, filled with elegant dinners and afternoon soirees. It was a far cry from what was happening on the plantations.

'The war has affected production in the Negombo region, but it is being made up by an increase from the newer estates in the south. This, however, has been mitigated by the rejection of good cinnamon.'

Sir David nodded his head forlornly. Thomas could see that he was struggling with the news he had just heard. He took a turn around the room, deep in thought. 'You are putting me in an anxious position, sir,' he said, finally stopping and looking at Thomas.

'I have a solution for you if you're willing to listen.' Thomas had come up with a way of ridding two of his problems, but he needed the wholehearted support of the man who stood before him.

Sir David studied Thomas intently as he walked over to his chair and sat down. 'What do you have in mind?' Thomas could see that his colour was considerably heightened, and a note in his voice warned him of a rising temper.

Thomas steepled his hands. 'My primary task as Governor is to bring the island's balance of payments in favour of the Crown. To do that, I have to raise export taxes or reduce the various expenditures draining the treasury. Perhaps even both.'

Sir David stared at Thomas without responding, his eyes fierce under jutting brows.

'However, increasing taxes alone will not entirely solve the problem,' Thomas continued. 'It will just force the Company to purchase elsewhere. So, what I am proposing is a compromise.'

Sir David beat his hand against the arm of his chair in a gesture of fretting impotence. 'I don't have much say in this matter, do I?'

Thomas ignored the small act of petulance. Sir David was a proud man who would not like the position he was in.

'The Company must reassess all rejected cinnamon stocks in storage and purchase them at the current market value. By doing this, the Company will wipe out the total amount in arrears to the Crown and make a considerable profit as the better-quality cinnamon will fetch much higher prices.' Thomas paused, studying Sir David. 'In return, I will exempt the Company from an increase in cinnamon export taxes for five years.'

Thomas sat back and watched the Head of the East India Company on the island struggle with what he had just heard. The uncomfortable silence dragged on as Sir David sat in thought, his face running through a gamut of emotions. He sighed as he reached some conclusion.

'You know, this alone will not solve your problem.' Sir David spoke in a thin voice. 'Cinnamon production is going down, and very soon, there won't be any to sell.'

Thomas nodded sanguinely. He had followed the same thinking that Sir David had just gone through. 'I agree,' he said. 'That's why I will take steps to end the war with Kandy.'

'How will you do that?' Sir David laughed uneasily. 'It's going to take a major effort to breach their defences, and you'll be faced with years of hostile occupation.'

Thomas smiled. 'I am not proposing to end the war per se. I am going to put it on pause.'

'On pause? What do you mean, on pause? How does one pause a war?'

'By removing the reason for them to oppose us,' Thomas grinned. 'We will withdraw our forces back to the Maritime Provinces and strengthen our defences. No more aggressive probes or expeditions.'

'You would do that?' Sir David looked surprised. 'I thought they sent an experienced military man like you to defeat the Kandyans.'

Thomas studied Sir David thoughtfully. 'I suppose you would think so. But my purview is quite different. There is no glory in winning here. Had I considered them a threat to the Empire, I might have gone to war with them every day since I came here.'

Sir David sat up straighter in his chair. 'The Kandyans won't stop their attacks now that they have assembled their forces to oppose us. The Kandyan King Sri Whatever-his-name-is will not allow it. Even I know that.'

'If war is what the Kandyans desire, it is a war I will not allow,' Thomas said rather arrogantly. 'There will be no provocation from us. Let them sit in their disease-ridden jungles and rot for all I care. They have no access to ports or help from anyone. Left alone, they will wither and die.'

Thomas understood that war was expensive. It was also risky as they had been beaten once and could have lost the country if the Kandyans had been more warlike. By retreating to the maritime provinces and arranging some form of a truce, he would reduce his military forces and the small army of coolies who were paid to sit idly by, waiting for the next expedition.

'I suppose you know what you are doing,' Sir David said, stroking his chin contemplatively. 'You seem to have given it a lot of thought.'

'I have!' Thomas said brightly. 'All the way from England. I am now in the process of drawing up orders for a reorganization of our forces. It will come into effect immediately.'

Thomas paused, watching Sir David. He knew his proposal was sound and would provide them both with a win.

'I would like your acceptance of my cinnamon proposal before I leave this evening. There's no need for anything we agree here to be known if you do your part.'

CHAPTER 16

THE VISITOR

At the sound of Aletta's wordless exclamation, Lovinia glanced over her shoulder. A small group of soldiers on horseback had entered the village. The two of them had come into the village that morning to look for fresh fish for cooking a curry.

All motion within the village ceased at the unusual sight of the red-coated men walking their mounts slowly across the village square. Leading them was a man who seemed vaguely familiar. He was dressed in a blue military-looking coat, white riding breeches and top boots. As the horsemen drew nearer, she was shocked. It was the same man whom she had danced for at the fort.

Aletta recognised him too. 'It's the *Andukāraya*.' She spoke softly, her voice barely noticeable over the clatter of the horse's hooves on the gravelly square. Women saw them enter the square, picked up their children, and ran away from the oncoming riders.

Horseback riders were still a rare sight in the village. The Moorish merchants, who came a few times a year, brought fabrics, cooking pots and the latest news in return for betel, cinnamon, cloves, and nutmeg. More recently, travellers from the south used their village to rest and water their animals before continuing towards Colombo.

The riders reached the village square, its ancient Bodhi tree supported by wooden posts, its canopy of leaves spreading above a small shrine with a reclining Buddha. They pulled up their horses and looked around. The leader dug his spurs into his horse, making the animal rear up, snorting.

The lead rider was an elegantly dressed man wearing a well-cut riding coat and breeches. Broad shoulders and muscular arms filled the jacket, and warm grey eyes stared down into hers when she looked up. Something was endearing about his face. Something friendly. His face was smooth, with tiny lines creasing the corners of his eyes. He looked down at the two women, his wide mouth curled in a grin and his eyes crinkled as if he was accustomed to squinting against the sun. Maybe she would have been less concerned if it had been a harmless grin. It was the smile of someone who was used to getting his way. He seemed utterly undisturbed by the disorder about them.

She felt her cheeks flush.

'Lovinia, you are staring at him.'

Lovinia heard Aletta's voice, but she did not look away. It wasn't easy to push away the feelings that had leapt to the forefront of her mind.

A woman pushed her way through the onlookers and stood before him, her chin raised in wild defiance, her hard eyes darting from left to right, appraising the scene before her. Her skin was almost black, with wild uncombed hair flaring around her sharp fox-like face. She wore her faded and torn sari blouse with a flared embroidered skirt worn low enough on the hip to show a beautiful and sensual midriff, causing a few men to stare at her with lustful looks, despite her fierce and forbidding appearance. She balanced on her bare hip a tiny girl, no more than a year old and naked except for a cheap gilt bracelet around her wrist, showing someone had thought her worthy of adornment, even though the woman held the child carelessly without love. The woman was from the gipsy clan that travelled between villages making their living by begging for alms and food.

One of the soldiers manoeuvred his horse in front of the woman, forcing her back from the *Andukāraya*. The woman was persistent. She came closer, holding the baby up for all to see, then made a sudden snatch at the soldier's leg. 'Baksheesh!'

Thomas spoke to a soldier, who threw a handful of coins at the woman's feet. The coins were snatched up in a flash with a savage snarl at anyone who might steal them. With one final disdainful look around, she dissolved into the crowd as if by magic.

After the crowd settled, the *Andukāraya* dismounted and handed over the reins to one of his escorts. He took a step towards Lovinia.

'Lovinia?' he asked, his voice low. 'That is your name, isn't it?'

Something in that voice made her warm where she should have been cold, the last thing she should be feeling. It also sparked a memory, one that hovered just out of reach. She wasn't used to the sensation of wracking her mind for something and coming up empty. *Why does he have this effect on me?* To cover her confusion, she bowed and brought her hands together in the traditional form of greeting.

'I was hoping that I would find you one day.'

Lovinia glanced at him sharply and was rewarded with an engaging smile.

'Speak to him in his language,' Aletta's loud whisper brought her back to the present. 'You won't get a chance like this again.'

'So, did you come as a friend or to find a dancing girl who aroused you?' she said, her tongue stumbling over the English words.

His eyes went wide. 'You can talk,' he said breathlessly. 'In English, I mean.' An amused grin lightened his features, and as he advanced another step. He pushed his hat back and rubbed his forehead with his fingertip, like a student struggling with a complex puzzle.

'You have been learning to speak!' he declared like he had solved some enormous problem. 'Who has been teaching you?'

'Someone in the village,' she responded proudly. 'I am still learning.'

Admiration flashed in his eyes, along with a hint of desire. 'Because of me,' he asked. He had the grace to look embarrassed.

She nodded. 'Because of you.'

Lovinia glanced away from him but knew that he still watched her. She usually hated being observed, but she didn't get the sense that he was searching for a flaw or an explanation for her existence. He seemed content to regard her, which was unnerving in an entirely different way.

'I would like to see you dance for me,' he said, keeping his voice low.

Lovinia looked at him warily. She wasn't afraid of danger. She knew how to look after herself. It had been a part of her training since she was a child. But dealing with drunken soldiers and sailors was somehow different to this.

He raised a hand to allay her suspicions, 'I want you to know you're safe in my presence. Will you come if I send for you?'

The *Andukārayas* gaze was steady as he waited for her reply. He was in earnest, and there was no doubt about that. He wanted her. She didn't need her instinct to tell her that.

Lovinia forced a polite smile to her face. 'As you wish.' She was rewarded with a brilliant smile as her words lit up his face. He gazed at her with an interest that brought heat to her face, although she was all too used to being stared at.

Lovinia wanted to be furious at his forwardness, but something of the man was purely engaging. She was unsure why it affected her the way it did. He was used to getting what he wanted, but she knew well enough what could happen to her if she succumbed quickly to his advances.

'Welcome to our little village!'

Lovinia jumped. The village *Vidane* (headman), Endira, had come up behind her and rudely interjected himself into their conversation. Appointed by the government, the man had much control over the area's people. He was responsible for keeping the peace, collecting revenue, and assisting in judicial functions.

Lovinia turned and scowled at the *Vidane*. The man was the main landowner in the area and had always treated the Mestize as second-class citizens.

'Translate for me.' The *Vidane* looked at Lovinia arrogantly. 'Tell the *Andukāraya* that he is welcome in our little village.'

Lovinia held her tongue but seethed inside. The *Vidane* was always treating her as if she were a slave, forgetting that she was a member of the popular dance troupe that brought money and fame to the village. He strutted around by day and was a drunk by night, staggering home each evening and passing out on his mat.

'Who is this man… why is he dressed like that?' Thomas addressed Lovinia, ignoring the man.

'He is the *Vidane*,' Lovinia replied in English. 'The village headman. He is dressed, how do you say…. for the ceremony.' She explained when she saw the puzzled look on his face.

The *Vidane* was wearing his ceremonial dress, which the Dutch introduced. It was a jacket made of blue fabric like a European coat closed in the front with silver buttons and frogs. His hair was drawn close with a tortoiseshell comb. He was a hefty man with a bulging belly, and the piece of coloured linen he wrapped around his waist was voluminous, making him appear even larger. He must have seen the *Andukāraya* come into the village and wore his regalia to greet him.

'What does he want?' Thomas frowned.

Lovinia sensed that the *Andukāraya* was annoyed by the man's impertinence.

'He welcomes you to the village.'

The Andukāraya studied her, ignoring the Vidane. 'You don't like him much, do you?'

Lovinia was surprised that it was so obvious she disliked the man. She closed her eyes for a moment, composing herself. 'He has money and treats his cattle better than us.'

The *Vidane* stood behind Lovinia. She could sense his impatience and heard him shifting from one foot to another. Aletta stood to the side, watching them both. Lovinia felt a tug on her skirt as the *Vidane* pushed his way past her.

'Out of my way, girl.' He stood before the *Andukāraya*, clasping his hands together and bowing his head.

Anger flared in a rush of heat up her neck.

The Vidane glanced at Lovinia. 'Ask him if he needs anything from our village.'

Lovinia looked at the *Andukāraya*, studying them with narrowed eyes. 'He wants to know if you want something from the village.'

'What I need is not his to give.' His voice hardened as he spoke, and Lovinia glimpsed the severe man who hid beneath the friendly smile. 'Tell him that I am just passing through.'

The *Vidane* turned his head and eyed her questioningly. The man's eyes held a warning, making Lovinia pause and proceed cautiously.

'The *Andukāraya* is only passing through the village and does not want to disturb us anymore.' She stared at the *Vidane*; this time, he could not hold her gaze. 'What he wants is for us to dance for him.'

'Tell him I can arrange a performance anytime he wants.' The *Vidane* said, staring hard at Lovinia.

She scowled at him and turned her back to the *Vidane*. Just because it was not true didn't mean she had to like it.

'He wants me to say he can arrange a performance anytime you want,' she said, her eyes flashing, 'but it's got nothing to do with him. My father is the one who makes the arrangements.'

The *Andukāraya's* mouth twitched, and she saw him resist a smile. He stared at *Vidane,* and his voice took a serious tone. 'Tell him I will make my arrangements.'

The *Vidane* visibly blanched when he heard the tone in the *Andukārayas* words and took a step back, bowing deeply when Lovinia translated what was said.

The *Andukārayas* gave her a grim smile as if it pleased him that he didn't have to explain further.

*

She was beautiful, her features as unfamiliar to Thomas as her language. Thomas handed the horse's reins to his escort but didn't take his eyes off her. She was an exquisite mystery to him. Her green eyes met his with a bold, assessing stare.

An amused grin lightened his features as he advanced towards the woman. He pushed his hat back and rubbed his forehead with his fingertips.

She is, curse my luck, a natural beauty. Spanish blood in her somewhere, he wouldn't doubt. Like all beautiful women, she somehow appeared underdressed.

Olive skin, hair as black and glossy as a raven's back; her demeanour was the forthright air of a woman accustomed to having her way.

The woman standing next to Lovinia, exotic and beautiful but with more experienced eyes, whispered something in creole, making Lovinia blush.

Thomas had experienced lascivious thoughts before, which wasn't what this woman inspired in him. No, it wasn't that. It was like the surprise of discovering a night-blooming orchid in the tangle of a jungle. Like discovering something so rare—knowing it was rare, knowing he'd never had a hope or a dream before of seeing such a living-and-breathing prize close enough for him to touch. And there wasn't another prize like her ever to be had. Those big green eyes, those long, long lashes, that pouting mouth, no…he wasn't inclined to take his eyes off her.

The morning sun highlighted her cheekbones and the smooth darkness of her skin. It reminded him of the newly tilled soil after a spring rain, fresh and sweet. Her eyebrows rose as she realised he was staring at her.

When he had asked her to dance for him, her lips parted in surprise, sending a rush of want through him even as he apologised. He was impressed by how she endured the weight of his scrutiny while maintaining a confusing quirk on her brows.

The time seemed to flow past like water as Thomas waited for her reply. He thought this woman was lovely. Long, light brown hair flowed down the entire length of her back, tied with a simple ribbon. And when she agreed, his heart filled with something he'd never felt.

Over her joined hands, her green eyes studied him, and they captivated him. They were deep and sparkling, shining with humour and intelligence, enchanted pools alight with character and life. Her eyes held his for a long, wonderful moment, blazing like jewels in her tanned face. There was no submission there and not a trace of fear.

Thomas knew that the colony was a harsh environment that bred tough people. He did not doubt that, if need be, she could kill a man just as quickly as – just as easily as kiss him. She was fresh and a little bold. He liked the boldness, for it was far from what he had always experienced. He was accustomed to women who fawned over him for his money or position. This woman would be unimpressed by both. She seemed to have everything she needed in her little village.

CHAPTER 17

THE OPIUM DEN

The Kandyan skirted a muddy puddle, climbed some rickety steps, and stopped outside a narrow door. It was late afternoon, and torrential rain beat down from the grey skies, creating a din against the corrugated-iron roofs that lined both sides of the street.

Despite the weather, the place was bustling. He heard a dozen languages and saw as many different styles of dress as possible. Rickshaw men charged back and forth in their bare feet, chattering and laughing.

The Kandyan looked over his shoulder to peer up and down the street, visually probing doorways and the shaded entrances to narrow alleys. Eventually, he raised his hand and knocked on the plank door. A peephole opened, and a pair of black eyes peered out. The peephole shut, and the door opened. The Kandyan stepped into the narrow entrance hall, shaking his head and wiping the rain from his shoulders.

A Chinese man wearing a high-necked mandarin jacket of shiny brocade with matching trousers and slippers stood blocking the corridor. He wore short black hair at the front and braided long down his back. The oil lamp he carried cast dancing shadows on the walls and closed doors.

A heavy curtain concealed any further view at the end of the corridor. Behind it, the Kandyan knew, in a large room were relays of professional nautch dancers. They wore nothing except gold bangles, their bodies coated in coconut oil. Thus unadorned, they perform the most sensual movements, revealing all and inviting the caresses of the far-from-sober spectators from time to time. But they were much more than mere professional dancers. Once the dancing was completed, the customers were invited to take their pick and retire to the private rooms with the dancer of their choice emerging later with monumental headaches, a lighter wallet and a memory they would carry to their dying day.

The Kandyan nodded at the Chinaman, who bowed slightly, his inquiring eyes never leaving the visitors face.

'What do you want?' He spoke in Creole, the language of the street in Colombo.

A smile, barely perceptible, played on the Kandyan's lips. 'You know what I am here for,' he said. 'Do you want us to conduct our business out here?'

The Chinaman snapped his fingers. A small, dark-skinned boy darted out of a little nook to the right, just behind the entrance. 'Take this man to my office,' he ordered, turning, and walking down the corridor, disappearing behind the curtain.

'Follow me, sir,' the boy hurried after the Chinaman, ahead of the Kandyan. Pushing aside the heavy curtain, he entered a large oblong room.

On either side of the door were small tables with weighing scales and glowing incense. Opium pipes gave off a heavy, sickly aroma filling the room.

Oil lamps on low shelves cast unsteady shadows over the guests. There were sailors, garrison soldiers, Arab merchants, members of the Sinhalese nobility dressed in western clothes, and a couple of Chinese customers. Most were men, but in the gloom, he made out one Chinese woman and two European women.

The guests lay on mattresses on the wood floor. On the walls were prints of exotic birds and flowers, yellowed by the smoke. Silence hung over the room despite the number of people. Only an occasional sigh broke the silence. Two Chinese helpers moved noiselessly around the guests, placing on the low, lacquered tables an array of long-stemmed pipes, bowls filled with lumps of the sticky, brown opium, and lamps for burning it. Some guests were still drawing on pipes, while others had already had their smoke and, their eyes glazed, stared fixedly into the dreamworld conjured by the opium.

The boy hurried to the far end of the room, pushing past a faded silk curtain that led to a corridor lined with doors on both sides. The boy pushed open the last door they came to and motioned the Kandyan to enter.

The air here was heavy, shot through with sickly incense. The walls were covered with a faded red fabric and holders for numerous candles, which cast their flickering light on a large desk that took up almost the entire room width. The desk held five long-stemmed pipes in a row like soldiers on parade. The only other furniture was a low, narrow cot, a chest of drawers, an oval mirror on a little dressing table with its chair, and a washbowl and jug on another table.

The Kandyan had been here before. He used the Chinaman to gather information from the varied clientele who visited his establishment. A combination of both a brothel and an opium den, many of his clients were soldiers and sailors who were a constant source of information about the goings on in the city and the fort. The Kandyan had learnt that the opium came from India and that the English trading company encouraged its use, allowing their ships to carry the product around the world.

The last time he had been here, the Chinaman had kept him waiting. Ignoring the chair in front of the desk, the Kandyan leaned against the wall casually. He did not have long to wait. The door opened soundlessly, admitting the Chinaman who walked past the Kandyan and sat at his desk.

The Kandyan studied the man without saying anything. He knew the Chinaman liked to play games but was not in the mood. The silence grew heavy as the inscrutable Chinaman sat perfectly still, watching him like a king cobra watches a mouse.

The Kandyan sighed. He knew it was a game he was not going to win. 'What do you have for me?'

The Chinaman smiled, knowing he had won that small battle. 'I have some news which you may find valuable,' he said.

The Kandyan nodded for him to continue.

'The English have decided not to pursue the war for the moment,' he said.

'They have been ordered back to their cantonments and will only carry out defensive operations.'

The Kandyan straightened from his lounging position against the wall, suddenly alert. Reports from the field had indicated lessening contact with the English soldiers. Their *rate mahathayas* (chiefs) had not reported a complete withdrawal of the British.

'Where did you hear that?' The Kandyan realised that if this were true, it would mean a significant change to their plans in the coming months.

'From more than one source,' the Chinaman replied. 'From both soldiers and officers,' he elaborated.

'Are you sure?'

'You know about the new road they are building towards Kandy?' the Chinaman asked.

The Kandyan nodded. 'That's not new,' he muttered darkly. 'What about it?'

'The English have stopped all work on it. They have left, taking all their tools with them.'

The Kandyan grunted in disappointment at the Chinaman. He had not heard about it. He needed to see this for himself. He had been too lax recently, thinking there would be no change in the English tactics.

'Have you heard how long this will be?' It was something that he would be asked.

The Chinaman shrugged. 'I thought you would want to know this, but no one is certain. These orders have come from the new *Andukāraya*.'

The Kandyan paced the room, lost in thought. *Why would the English do this? They have been attacking us for over a year. Does it mean they are preparing for a big attack? I need to get this information to the King.*

'You must find out more,' the Kandyan leant over the desk aggressively.

The Chinaman did not react to the Kandyan's belligerence. 'I can only make my report on what I hear. If you need more information, you must get it elsewhere.'

'You have been well paid,' the Kandyan said, pounding the desk. 'You will benefit greatly by being friends with the King.'

'Money is not the issue here. The men who issue these orders do not frequent my establishment. What we hear is second or even third-hand information. You must find someone close to one of their leaders to know what is happening.'

The Kandyan knew these words to be true. That was why he had recruited the young Mestiza dancer thinking she would make the ideal spy, but he had not seen her for a few months.

I need to find her and talk to her. I must get to the bottom of this.

The Kandyan nodded at the Chinaman. There was no point in angering the Chinaman. 'I don't want you to stop what you are doing,' he said. 'There will be more gold for you if you find out what is happening.'

The Chinaman nodded without saying anything. He picked up his flickering oil lantern and led the Kandyan into the hallway.

A young woman dressed in a silk dress stood outside, leaning against a door. She was Eurasian, skin lightly tanned, eyes dark and sensual, and hair right down to her hips. She smiled at the Kandyan. Her irresistible mouth was heart-shaped. When she leant forward slightly, her considerable cleavage drew his gaze.

The Chinaman stopped and looked at the Kandyan. 'You want to see Susy? Then have a wonderful dream?'

The Kandyan paused, almost tempted. But there were more important things on his mind. He needed to find out what was going on. His King would not be pleased if he did not have reliable information.

'No,' he shook his head reluctantly. 'I have no time.'

'Very well,' The Chinaman hurried along the hallway ahead of his guest. He stopped and drew back the faded pink silk curtain at the end of the corridor. The room was busier than when he had walked through it before. The strong, sickly odour of burning opium was pungent and intense.

The Kandyan walked through the crowded room and out into the corridor leading to the front door. He turned to the Chinaman. 'Find me right away if you hear anything,' he ordered. 'I will be in the usual places.'

The inscrutable Chinaman bowed. 'Did I ever disappoint you?' He snapped his fingers at the young boy motioning him to open the door.

The Kandyan slipped out of the establishment. The rain had eased, and it was getting dark outside. He tripped down the slippery steps and almost fell onto the muddy road. Cursing under his breath, he walked down the narrow street. Bars and bordellos had opened for the night, and the street was teeming with people. Arab merchants selling exotic spices, colourful silks and precious stones from the interior were beginning to close their shops. Money changers sat outside their booths, awaiting clients, as did the rickshaw drivers, chewing betel as they lounged against the shafts of their rickshaws. From tiny food stalls, men and women prepared rice with spicy vegetables and various types of meat, calling out to those who walked past.

The Kandyan turned north, towards the river, and then paused. He had to get across and see for himself whether the Chinaman's information was correct. He couldn't make a mistake by taking the wrong information to the King, but first, he had to talk to the mestizo woman.

CHAPTER 18

A MEETING

Lovinia peered ahead, wrapping a fold of her shawl over her head and the lower part of her face before she slipped across the deserted avenue. She had told Aletta where she was going and hoped her father would not get upset for disobeying his orders.

Gaining the shelter of a clump of trees, she saw the dim front of a building cut by one black rectangle—a deeply recessed doorway. She had come to the city's outskirts after a piece of paper with this location had been trusted into her hand by a street urchin. By the time she read what was on the paper, the boy had disappeared into the crowd.

Cautiously she moved toward it. There was no sign of anyone, no sound, only that waiting black square. And if it were a trap? Lovinia froze for a moment, fear robbing her of her purpose. Anyone, anything, might be concealed in that building. She hesitated a long, reluctant moment before deciding there was no way to avoid a trap save by walking into it. She cast one glance behind her and then darted into the doorway.

Darkness closed over her. She stood a moment with a beating heart, then began to move forward, gingerly exploring with one outstretched hand the cool rough bricks that formed the wall. There was no sound at all save her uneven breathing. Was she alone, then? Expecting to touch the smooth wood of a door at any second, her hand suddenly met air instead, and after a few more paces, she realized the passage had opened out.

Lovinia halted uneasily, trying to make out where she was. A breath of night air touched her cheek, accompanied by a whispered rustling overhead. She was perhaps in a courtyard, canopied by a thatch of dried palm leaves; she saw the outlines of the walls now and here and there around them, large, rounded objects, almost indistinguishable in the gloom. She was peering warily toward one when a pebble rolled behind her. She whirled. Someone was standing beside the wall yonder, a shape of denser black among the shadows. In a panic, she shrank toward the passage from which she had come. Then the figure moved too. Something familiar about that slender outline was the set of shoulders....

'It is you.' Almost stumbling with relief, she darted toward him.

"Hist! Not a sound.' He materialized beside her, comfortingly solid, and she felt her arm being grasped. 'Someone comes.' He dragged her into a darkened doorway, snaking one arm under her bosom, holding her close against his chest.

Lovinia had never been so glad to see anyone. She clung to his arm with a rush of affection that surprised even herself, feeling him an old friend—her only friend in a chancy, friendless world. The sculpted planes of his chest made their outlines known to her back, and the beat of his heart was like a soft, insistent knock that she could not answer. Would not. Her own was hammering harder than a blacksmith at a forge. She wanted to position herself away from his overpowering heat and scent. However, the noisy crinkling of her clothes could attract attention.

'Shh.'

Two men appeared out of the gloom, arguing quietly with each other.

'I think we can move the last of the materials over the river by night without being seen. We can station a lookout here to signal when we arrive,' the man with the skinny legs and short torso said.

'I don't know,' said the second man, taking off his hat to scratch his bald head.

Smugglers? Lovinia wondered. *Why would they be meeting here?*

They were so intent on their discussion that they passed the two of them without a glance in their direction.

The Kandyan shifted slightly, her bottom shifting over his groin, and he exhaled sharply, his breath tickling the curls at the nape of her neck.

Lovinia felt something warm and solid press into her behind. She'd felt that seductive pressure before, during dalliances with men. Her core pulsed at the remembered pleasure that had followed. Her quickened breath was audible, and she was sure he could feel the heat radiating from her, especially from the part of her that was pressed against him.

'I thought I was being followed. Let's wait a bit longer.'

His mouth was near her ear, and the deep vibration of his voice made her shiver. His lips brushed against the shell of her ear as he spoke, and Lovinia let out a soft gasp from the unexpected goodness of it. His manhood surged against her bottom once again.

'We should leave,' she said, although she didn't move. Lovinia knew if she turned around, she would see the kind of person she should be avoiding intimacy with. But he was just a man. A warm, solid man who stirred something inside her that went against everything she thought she knew of herself.

'This way. We'll talk later.'

For a moment, she longed to be back in the marketplace at Galkissa, with no more on her mind than living on her wits. But only for a moment as she hurried after the Kandyan, trying to regain her composure.

'What was that place?' she whispered as they emerged into a street. 'Those great humped things about the walls …?'

'Humped? Oh, those were the furnaces where the iron is melted. We were in the ironsmith's outer workshop. Here, into this alley now.' He led her across the street and into a narrow lane between dark warehouses.

Stumbling over invisible rubbish, Lovinia spat out her annoyance, then laughed. She had missed the excitement and enjoyment of doing something dangerous.

'I smell the river,' murmured Lovinia, drawing a long breath of the familiar, heady reek. They stepped out of the alley into a jumble of low buildings, sheds, and boathouses. A moment later, they rounded the corner of a deserted fish stall. The river lay before her, stars bobbing all along its darkly rippling length.

'Where are we going?'

'A place we can talk safely,' he murmured, 'where we cannot be observed.'

A few minutes later, they were in the street more crooked, dark, and evil-smelling than any she had been in, lined with cracked walls and dark doorways, from which an occasional cloaked figure emerged to brush past them into the gloom.

'Stay close,' muttered the Kandyan, whose hand was ready on his dagger. 'It's very much like a labyrinth. Each year it grows bigger, its alleys snaking about without rhyme or reason.'

The Kandyan walked firmly in her shadow, with his hand grazing her lower back. His usually vigilant eyes appeared even more watchful than before.

'Take care you keep your wits about you—and a good blade, too—should you pass this way alone which I don't advise. Here we are, through this door now.'

He pushed open a creaking door, like all the rest save for the weathered wooden image of a Lion swinging from a bar above it. A small courtyard was dimly lit by a flare bracketed beside another door at its far end. They made their way over rough cobblestones, past a single scrubby palm, to the tavern's side entrance. The Kandyan rapped a few times, and eventually, the door swung open.

A hulk of a man, vast of girth, dressed in a rumpled shirt, sarong, and huge brass ear hoops, stood covering the entrance. Upon seeing the Kandyan, he stepped aside and closed the door behind them, his broad face wreathed in smiles. He pattered ahead of them, the earrings bouncing and his paunch preceding him, through an entryway covered by a curtain and into a room lit by a single candle.

'You can talk here,' the innkeeper said, nodding to the Kandyan, who visibly relaxed.

Lovinia drew in a deep breath and looked around. The small windowless room reeked of smoke. A wooden table sat in the centre with stools set around it. An ashtray in the corner was filled with smoked butts of pungent *bidi*. A gust of music and laughter could be heard through the open door.

The Kandyan sank onto a stool next to the table, motioning for Lovinia to do the same.

'Can I bring you something?' The question was directed at the Kandyan, but the innkeeper studied Lovinia through narrowed eyes.

'Thank you, Lokubada,' said the Kandyan glancing at Lovinia. 'What I want is to know whether anyone is watching this place. I got the feeling of being followed, but ...' he shook his head.

'I'll take care of it right away,' the innkeeper nodded before leaving the room and closing the door behind him.

'You think you were being followed?' Lovina questioned. 'Are you sure?'

'If I were sure, then I wouldn't be so unsure,' he smiled. 'It's a dangerous game we play, and we must always be on our guard.' His reply was quick, with a hint of paternal indulgence that should have annoyed her but comforted her.

'What's your name?' Lovinia asked boldly.

His eyebrows rose, but his expression was amusement, not anger.

'Not until you answer my questions.' His gaze was speculative as he regarded her. 'What has become of the mission I gave you?' he asked. 'I have been informed that you danced for the men at the Fort. But I don't know what came of it.'

'So, you have someone watching me,' Lovina asked, the words coming out harsher than she intended. 'That has got to stop ...' Her patience was beginning to wear thin. Maybe it was the way he stared at her like she was something that could be manipulated. Or perhaps the tiny part of her didn't mind his bold examination.

The Kandyan leaned towards her. 'I will do what is necessary to keep our secrets safe.' His voice hardened as he spoke, and Lovinia glimpsed the serious man who hid beneath. 'This is not a game we play, and many lives depend on it ... including yours, mine, and your father's too,' he added. 'Now stop playing games and tell me what happened.'

'Yes, we danced at the fort,' Lovinia said finally. 'The *Andukāraya* was there, and he wants me to dance for him privately.'

The Kandyan sat back with a sudden short laugh. 'This is better than I expected. Who brought you the message?'

'He did,' Lovinia responded, explaining the *Andukāraya* visited her village and arranged for her to dance for him.

'When will this be?'

'Soon, I think.' It had been over a week, and she wondered whether he had changed his mind. 'He'll send for me when he's ready.'

The Kandyan gazed at her with an interest that brought heat to her face, although she was all too used to being stared at.

'Well, this verifies what I knew when I first saw you.' He smiled.

'What's that?' she asked.

'That you are something special.' The smile lingered on his lips.

Lovinia's heart sped up at the words, although she kept her face expressionless. She was feeling confused at the emotions running through her. She wanted to trust him, but something didn't sit right with her. The fact that he could deceive people so easily was disconcerting. She realised that despite their unfortunate first encounter, there was a sense of ease between them. It was very unsettling. *He does not need to know how I feel.* She sighed and tried to focus on the task in front of her.

'How do you want me to pass on any information I find?'

'I will make the necessary arrangement when it's time. You don't have to worry about such things,' he waved his hand.

'You don't trust me?' She didn't know why she felt the need to prod him.

'That's a reasonable question,' he said, glancing at her from the corner of his eye. 'It's not about trust,' he explained. 'I am not ready to expose the network which has taken me years to build. We have never been able to place anyone close to the centre of power. We cannot afford to make any mistakes. You may be the tip of the spear, but there are many others I must protect.'

The strange feeling in her chest coiled tighter. That wasn't what she'd expected at all. How did he know just the right thing to say?

'Why do you do it?' Many of the rebels Lovinia had encountered had been ordinary people tired of the constant state of war and wanted nothing more than to be left alone to a peaceful life.

He gave her a grim smile. 'The British came with promises, but they took away our weapons, taxed our earnings, and finally wanted our lands. The places our families had lived and died for generations. They would arrive without warning and tell you to clear out, usually passing the message with the heel of their boot or the swing of their sword. For the women, it was much worse than that.'

Lovinia had been holding her breath, drawn in by the hypnotic lilt of his voice, his words drawn to the fore by the intensity of his anger. He looked at her, those blue-grey eyes like the sea before a storm. They were mesmerizing .... and familiar, somehow.

A noise outside the door made the Kandyan rise from his stool with the quickness and grace of a leopard. He placed a finger to his lips before slinking over to the door and flinging it open.

A servant had opened the door at the end of the corridor and hurried toward them with a tray of empty plates. The Kandyan studied the man carefully as he passed but took no action.

'We need to leave,' he said after looking up and down the corridor before closing the door behind him. 'Can you find this place again?' he asked.

Lovinia nodded. 'I can find the inn—I'm used to such places and talking my way in and out of them.'

The Kandyan gave her a look that brought warmth to her face. 'It's Kumara.'

'What?'

'My name,' the Kandyan grinned. 'You wanted to know my name.'

Lovinia stared at him for a moment until his words sank in. Having a name made him more human to her. She nodded without saying anything.

'It's better we leave separately. I'll get Lokubada to send one of his men to accompany you to your village.'

CHAPTER 19

THE RESCUE FORCE

Thomas reread the despatch he had received from the Madras Presidency that morning. It was an urgent appeal to render every possible assistance in his power to the government threatened by a mutiny by native sepoys in the south Indian city of Vellore.

Thomas looked up at the sun-browned man standing before him. Commander Keats of the Royal Navy sloop HMS Egret stared back at him from under bushy eyebrows. He looked weary, his uniform dishevelled and stained with sweat and salt water.

'When did you leave Madras?'

'Ten days ago, Your Excellency,' the Commander grunted.

'You did well to get here so quickly. What was the voyage like?'

'Not an easy journey,' he growled. 'We had to sail into the teeth of the monsoon coming out of the southwest. It was not easy on the men,' he added, after clearing his throat.

Thomas nodded in understanding. Commander Keats would have had to take many risks with his ship to deliver the message quickly.

'You may sit.' Thomas waved at the chair in front of his desk, into which the Commander sank thankfully.

Thomas rang the small brass bell on his desk, which was answered quickly by his secretary, who entered from a side door. 'You called, Sir.'

'Send for the Major right away,' Thomas barked. 'He's to drop whatever he's doing and get here immediately.'

The secretary nodded and turned to leave. 'And Brewer, I want you back here along with your writing materials. I require a record of the orders I am about to issue.'

Thomas studied the Commander, who was slumped tiredly in his chair. He knew what it was to be bone-tired and took no exception to the man's posture.

'I am sure you know what's in this despatch,' Thomas said, waving the message at the Commander, who nodded tiredly. 'Do you have any additional information about what occurred?'

Commander Keats sat straight in his chair, perhaps realising whom he was addressing. 'I heard something before we sailed, but I am not sure it's true. Just barrack-room gossip, your Excellency. You know what it's like.'

As part of the military establishment, Thomas understood how news travelled through the non-commissioned officers and ranks of the British army. He had no doubt the Royal Navy faced a similar problem.

'Let me be the judge of that,' Thomas said, steepling his hands and watching the Commander struggle to decide whether he should indulge in the gossip he had heard.

'I absolve you from any repercussions you may face,' Thomas said. 'Keep in mind I could order you to tell me what you know.'

Commander Keats studied Thomas for a moment. 'I suppose you could,' he said resignedly. 'I heard that Indian sepoys in the Vellore fort had mutinied and killed over a hundred officers and men from 69th. The South Lancashire's were part of the Vellore garrison.'

'That was in the despatch I received,' Thomas nodded, tapping the manuscript with his fingers. 'Your information is accurate. But what is not obvious is why it took place. Did you hear anything which might throw some light on what happened?'

The Commander squirmed in his chair. 'I heard that the Indian regiments were not too happy with orders prohibiting the Hindoo troops from marking their foreheads with religious marks while on duty. Moslems were required to shave their beards and trim their moustaches.'

Thomas looked at the captain in disbelief. 'Is that all?'

'I also heard that the sepoys were asked not to wear turbans and were issued round caps of a European design.'

Thomas had fought as a junior officer against Tippoo Sultan in South India. He knew that the sons of the defeated Sultan were confined at Vellore. Tippoo's wives and sons, together with numerous retainers, were pensioners of the East India Company and lived in a luxurious palace within the large complex of the Vellore Fort. Thomas had learned that religion permeated all parts of life in that country and could not be set aside at the call of military expediency. Short of outraging their private lives and defiling their temples, there was nothing more damning the military could do to stir up a bloody rebellion.

'Was this mutiny limited to Vellore?' he asked Commander Keats shrewdly. 'Did you hear of any other unrest in the Sepoy regiments?'

The captain nodded. 'Just hearsay, your Excellency.'

Thomas motioned for him to continue.

'There were some incidents reported in Madras which were put down rather expeditiously if the stories were to be believed. I heard the sepoys suspected that issuing the new caps in place of their traditional headgear was an attempt by the British to convert them to Christianity.'

'It seems quite an extreme reaction,' Thomas mused. 'Is there more?'

The Commander nodded. 'Hearsay again,' he began. 'Stories were being circulated that the caps were made of cowskin and layered with pig's fat. That is all I know.'

That would do it, Thomas thought to himself. Cows were sacred to the Hindoo, and pigs were an aberration to the Moslems.

Thomas smiled gratefully at the Commander. He did not need him to elaborate further. The folly of pursuing such a course was evident to Thomas. On his arrival, he found the system's inefficiency in force in Ceylon. A small army of Europeans supported by almost triple the number of native troops and mercenaries was expected to hold the island and conduct war against the natives who were well-armed and motivated in the highland fortresses. It was not a sustainable situation. If this were a sample of the course they were about to pursue in India, there would soon be no such thing as a British India.

A further thought crossed his mind. The Crown was in trouble if news of the rebellion had already spread to Madras in the east. He could now understand the panicked nature of the message he received.

Perhaps I could use this to my advantage.

Thomas was interrupted in his thoughts by his secretary entering the room. 'I have sent for Major Staples,' he announced, setting the material he carried onto his desk in the corner. Thomas studied Commander Keats, who was looking at him apprehensively.

'You have done well, Commander,' he said, rising and offering his hand. 'My report shall reflect your diligence in getting here so quickly in adverse conditions. I suggest you get some rest and await a fresh set of orders to carry to Madras.'

The Commander shook Thomas's hand gratefully. 'Thank you, your Excellency. May I enquire as to what your plans are?'

'I am not ready to divulge that information until I talk to my Generals,' he said understandingly. 'You can be assured that I have taken this matter seriously and will respond to the request post haste.'

Thomas turned to his secretary. 'Could you see that the Commander can clean himself and get a good meal while he waits.'

The Commander looked pleased. 'Thank you, sir,' he said, turning to follow the secretary.

'One more matter before you leave, Commander Keats,' Thomas called out. 'How long will it take to sail to Negapatam?'

'Given the prevailing winds, I would say not more than three days, your Excellency.' The Commander paused by the doorway.

Thomas nodded. 'That's all, Commander, thank you.'

Thomas came around his desk and walked over to the window, looking out over the garden at the ships anchored on the roads outside the harbour. In the outer two were large Indiamen and a snow-rigged despatch vessel belonging to the Madras Marine, which Commander Keats had used for his dash to Colombo.

One ship captured his attention. The East Indiaman had arrived just a few days previously and had completed its victualling before setting sail to Madras. Its size and availability made it the ideal vessel to complement his plans.

Thomas turned away from the window. His mind was made up. He would use this opportunity to strengthen his position with the Colonial office and rid himself of some of the expenses crippling the island's treasury.

*

It had been a hectic few days since he had received the urgent request for help from India. Thomas had not delayed once he made up his mind to act. By 6:00 pm that evening, a reinforced battalion of British troops were embarked on the East Indiamen and on their way to the port of Negapatam, which acted as an important gateway on the Coromandel coast. Good roads led north and west, connecting major cities in the Madras Presidency.

Thomas's orders to Colonel Buchan were simple. Using the four hundred men under his command, the Colonel would first ensure that the mutiny had not spread into the town, which Thomas considered to be more strategic than the city of Madras, a further 220 miles to the north. The Colonel was always to safeguard his troops and not be drawn into an ambush, either in the fort which dominated the town or on the road to Vellore.

Thomas knew from his time in India how vital control of the southern town and its port was. Once the capital of Dutch Coromandel, the British conquered the Dutch-controlled town in 1781 when its fortification walls were breached after a long siege. Its sea roads had also been the scene of a significant sea battle with the French when they tried to capture the city with the aid of Hyder Ali, the ruler of Mysore, a year later.

The message Thomas had sent with Colonel Buchan to the Governor of Madras was that the men be sent back to him as soon as possible. He was keenly aware that the colony was only defended by just over a thousand British troops and various native, sepoy and mercenary regiments.

'I want all the expenses incurred by the expedition to be billed to Madras,' he ordered his secretary. 'Furthermore, as I will reduce my overall military formation by sending back all the Indian troops based here on the island, those expenditures are to be passed on to Madras.'

Thomas reread the message he had received from Lord Camden before he had sailed. It was clear that there should be no confusion about Ceylon's military position in Asia, which was no longer considered a bulwark.

It appears to me that the island of Ceylon would be considered chiefly as an outwork to the British Possessions in India, and accordingly, the military force should only be estimated about protection from internal attack and foreign European invasion; but by no means on the principle that the island would be enabled in case of necessity, to furnish material military aid to our continental possessions.

Thomas smiled grimly, feeling pleased with himself. He had been presented with an opportunity to demonstrate his capabilities and reduce the overall cost of his administration in one fell swoop. But he also understood the dangers involved in dealing with the natives through a position of ignorance and arrogance. He understood the need to understand local manners, customs, habits, religions, and prejudices. Not before you did this could you venture to move, still less to alter what is around you.

It was a system of perfect inefficiency and stupidity. Every junior ensign thinks of himself as a commander-in-chief; every writer talks as if he were the head of a government. They all write far too much, spending hours and reams of paper over matters that could quickly be settled in an interview of ten minutes.

He wowed that his government would be vastly different to that of India. Here you shall see no piles of records and stacks of

correspondence and accounts: there is nothing to be seen in Ceylon
but results. It is not as if all service members were efficient: plenty
of idle, assuming and indolent coxcombs are pushed into places
where they can harm the service.

If we do not set our house in order, there will someday come another mutiny with which we shall not be able to cope unless our system is altered.

CHAPTER 20

THE SINHALESE KING

The Kandyan guided his horse across the construction site and stopped at a point that gave him a view of all directions. Behind, the new road wound in generous curves through the foothills of the central highlands towards where he stood.

The last half-mile stretching ahead of him to the edge of the jungle had still to be filled in with gravel transported by the cartload from the south. In the distance, a vast mass of granite known as *Bathalegala* (Bible Rock) rose out of the green jungle. He had travelled from Colombo on the new road, which had cut his normal travel time to less than two days.

The Kandyan guided his horse over the uneven ground, slowly moving towards where the road ended. Small boulders the size of coconuts were piled in heaps every few yards. The ones too big to be moved were lying where they were found, waiting to be shattered by dynamite. He could see areas where the runoff from the rain had washed away the gravel and caused considerable damage.

But what unnerved him the most was the stillness. Where were the sounds of axes echoing through the jungle? Where were the shouts of the engineers as they called out orders or the rhythmic hammering of the labourers as they crushed the broken rocks into gravel? Only the harsh barks and whoops of the purple-faced langurs that inhabited the forest trees echoed through the hills.

There were no red-coated soldiers with their long muskets guarding the road. There were no mahouts shouting commands at the elephants hauling massive logs away or loud cracks of the bullwhips as overseers shouted at coolies straining their bodies to loosen boulders as tall as his horse for the engineers to crack open with their explosives. The tented accommodation along the sides of the half-built road was missing. What was left was the empty make-shift huts rigged up from a few palm leaves by the workers.

What the Chinaman said is true! The English have gone.

The Kandyan could not believe what he was seeing. He had watched the road being started many months before. He had even led attacks on the supply trains, knowing it would make it much easier for the English soldiers to attack the Royal Kingdom once the road was complete.

Isolated in their mountain stronghold, surrounded by thick impenetrable jungle and fast-flowing rivers, had kept generations of invaders away. The secret passes were known to only a few. They were fiercely guarded by earthen forts, armed with cannons captured from the Portuguese and Dutch incursions, and constantly garrisoned by men loyal to the *rate mahathayas*.

But these English invaders were different. They wanted first to conquer the jungles that had concealed and protected them. They will never win, he promised himself. He would do everything he could to defend his home. But he had first to report what he had found to the King.

The Kandyan abandoned his mount where the clearing ended, at the jungle's edge. The jungle trails, the river crossings, and steep mountain trails that only he and a few others knew could not be used by any four-legged animal.

*

As he walked through a low-ceilinged windowless corridor, the airless atmosphere, the murky shadows, and the eerie silence filled the Kandyan with a vague unease. Besides a single taper fixed on a wall bracket, the passage was so poorly lit that most of it was in deep gloom.

Fresh doubts assailed him. It was dangerous business to have anything to do with the King. *Was it wise to have returned? Perhaps he should have sent a message. Too late now.*

At the end of the corridor, two bare-footed and bare-chested sentries with round red caps and a voluminous white cloth draped around their waists guarded a wooden, metal-studded door. As the Kandyan approached, they pushed the heavy door open and gestured for him to enter.

A retainer was waiting for him. 'This way,' he murmured.

They arrived at a red-curtained doorway. The retainer swept the curtain aside and gestured for him to enter.

The Kandyan stepped into the audience chamber and the presence of the King himself. The hall was long and narrow, with two rows of elegantly carved wooden pillars crowned with lotus flowers supporting the peaked tile roof. Warm air, mingled with the sweet perfume of sacrificial offerings—lotus and frangipani flowers, ripe mango, and jackfruit—enveloped him. From the walls hung silken rugs depicting scenes of court life. These rugs also covered the floor around the gallery.

Hastily the Kandyan flung himself prostrate on the ground following the age-old ceremonial protocol of approaching Royal presence. Stretched full length, he touched the cold stone floor with his forehead reciting the ritual statement, 'May You attain Nibbana, your Divinity.'

'Arise,' the command was brusque and intimidating.

The Kandyan lifted his head and straightened up on his knees. At the end of the spacious hall was a raised platform. On an ornately carved, gold-plated throne sat King Sri Vikrama Rajasinha, the ruler of the Kingdom of Kandy, the largest and richest political entity on the island. He was attired in traditional rich apparel of presiding over state business. He had on a four-cornered hat, a vest of the finest muslin covering his chest. Over this, he had a velvet coat with puffed half-sleeves emboldened with gold thread. His lower limbs were clothed in loose trousers over which was draped a *tuppoti* (bulky waist cloth) with a dagger, its hilt studded with gems, thrust into it. A golden sword adorned his girdle, gold encrusted shoes curved upwards at the toes.

Beside him stood retainers, one holding a tasselled royal umbrella. Two others on either side fanned him with black buffalo tails. Behind him stood members of the Royal Guard in their uniform of red caps, red sash and knee-length white kilts carrying spears and *bondikula* (muzzle-loading flintlock musket). Important court figures kneeled around the gallery. Their supporters squatted behind them with standards bearing the symbols of their masters' power and honour. Ministers, officials and courtiers sat or squatted on their heels on either side of the room on rush mats.

According to court protocol, the King did not directly address his subjects, even minor officials. His instructions or questions were transmitted through the *Chief Adigar* (Chief Minister).

With a wave of the King's right hand, heavy with rings, a man dressed in ministerial regalia squatting closer to the throne rose to his feet. He addressed the King after clearing his throat.

'Divinity, I have summoned Ekanayake as you ordered so that he may report on the situation in the east.'

The King spoke a few words to the Adigar, who bowed.

'Well, Ekanayake, what news have you brought?' the man asked.

'The English have decided not to pursue the war for the moment,' the Kandyan said. 'They have been ordered back to their cantonments and will only carry out defensive operations.'

'You know this to be true?' the Adigar asked.

'Yes, your lordship,' the Kandyan answered. 'I verified this myself before returning.'

A buzz of surprise swept the room. The Chamberlain thumped the floor with his ceremonial wooden mace, immediately hushing the crowd.

The Adigar glanced around irritably, waiting until the room quietened.

The Kandyan could see the King leaning forward. His attention was fixed on the two of them.

'What more news do you bring?' the Adigar asked.

'I do bring news but only for the Great King's ears,' he said boldly, looking directly at the man sitting on the throne behind which two mighty elephant tusks framed the flag of the Nayaka dynasty: the golden lion, heraldic beast of the Sinhalese people, on a red background.

The Kandyan bowed from his waist, his arms outstretched, his head touching the cold floor. It was a risk he was willing to take. He had never met the King but had heard that he was level-headed and brave.

'How dare you speak as such,' the Adigar bristled. 'It is not your place to decide such matters.'

'I beg your forgiveness, Your Divinity, but your enemies have ears everywhere.'

His heart pounded in his chest. He was exposed and vulnerable in this place. Was he going to be executed? *I hope I've done the right thing, but I cannot make my report before all these men.* He knew that factions within the kingdom were plotting against the King and reported everything to the British.

An ominous hush fell over the room. The Kandyan heard the Adigar's footsteps shuffling away from him. He held his breath, not knowing what was to follow.

After a short silence, the Adigar spoke. 'You have done well, Ekanayake. The Lord-King has reason to be pleased with you. You will remain in the palace until summoned.'

The Kandyan relaxed, breathing a sigh of relief. Life was cheap in these times, and to the King who dispensed life and death, the cost of failure was death. He left the chamber, bent in reverence, never once turning his back to the monarch.

*

'His Divinity is here. Enter, if you will.'

After sleeping the night at the palace, the Kandyan was brought by a retainer the next morning to an ornate wooden door guarded by a Royal Guard.

Drawing a long breath to calm his nerves, he opened the door and stepped into a quiet, sunny room. It was of familiar design, spacious, rectangular, and windowless. But the two outside walls stopped some feet short of the ceiling, and through this open space, which was divided by graceful columns, light and air poured into the room. In its centre, in a chair beside a low table, sat the King. His eyes flashed dark fire under his black eyebrows.

'Well, were you observed by these spies in my court?' He laughed soundlessly at the expression on Kandyan's face and waved his visitor to squat by the table. 'I have known about them since they arrived here,' he added. 'But they are not the ones I worry about,' he said mysteriously.

The Kandyan squatted next to the table uncomfortably. He was still getting over the way he had been welcomed.

A banana leaf heaped with sticky balls sat on the table. The monarch took one and chewed on it reflectively. 'What do you know that cannot be said in public?'

'I have managed to place a spy in the *Andukāraya's* household, your Divinity,' He knew the King had been trying to get someone close to the centre of British power without success, and the news would please him.

The bristly black eyebrows lifted. 'Proceed,' the King ordered.

The Kandyan explained how he recruited a dancer to bring him information from within the British fort. Fortunately, the woman came to the attention of the *Andukāraya,* whom he expected would take her as his mistress.

'A mestizo woman, you said?' the King grumbled. 'I would have preferred it be someone from our own culture.' A frown crossed his features. 'Can she be trusted?' the King asked as he took another rice ball.

'I believe so, your Divinity. Her father, a Rodiya, runs the dance troupe she belongs to.'

The King shot a sideways glance at him. 'Indeed, you have done well. Tell me about this woman. How did you find her?'

The King's sceptical eyes met the Kandyan's across the room as he recited his tale. Gradually, the doubt cleared away from them.

'You seem fond of this woman?' observed the King, leaning backwards in his chair, looking at him long and hard with his dark eyes.

The Kandyan was startled by the King's question. He had never seen Lovinia as anything but a tool for him to use. Still, he'd come to admire her ability to do the unexpected.

'I see her only as someone we can use to get what we want,' the Kandyan finally responded, feeling intimidated by the King's penetrating gaze.

'Hai,' the King laughed soundlessly at the expression on the Kandyan's face.

'Make sure she falls under your spell and not your enemy's,' he said. 'I want you to make her your most important possession.'

'Yes, your Divinity,' the Kandyan responded. He needed to be careful how he would use Lovinia. She wasn't some pliant woman of the night who would do anything for money. She was intelligent and street-smart and required his complete attention. But first things first.

The King leaned forward. 'I require a weekly report from you. Use the Chinaman's network to send them. I will instruct treasury to make available additional funds for your use.'

'I thank you, Enlightened One,' Kumara whispered, but the King was not ready to dismiss him.

'What do they talk about me in the coastal lands?' the King asked, studying Kumara closely as he did.

'Many are still your worthy subjects, my lord,' Kumara said as convincingly as he could. He knew not to incur the wrath of the King by saying something that might send him into a rage. 'They wait for the day you will unify the whole island under your reign.'

The black eyes of the King widened, then shone with delight.

With a nod of farewell, he dismissed the Kandyan who left the chamber, bent in reverence, never once turning his back to the Monarch.

CHAPTER 21

THE ENGLISH SPYMASTER

'Two of your men are dead?' Thomas dropped the papers in his hands, letting them flutter across his immaculate desk, and leaned back in his chair, his full attention on Wilson's face.

'So, I'm told, and they cannot be found, your excellency. So, I assume I've been told the truth.'

Thomas waved his hand at the winged armchair directly opposite his own and tapped a finger to his mouth, keeping silent.

He had been briefed before leaving England that Britain's old enemies, the French, had been holding out to the Kandyan kingdom great promises of assistance. The Bay of Trincomalee, on the island's eastern coast, had become, in British eyes, the most critical part of the colony of Ceylon. Due to its unique position in the Indian Ocean, it virtually commanded the sea routes between the West and East and its extensive harbour, which could easily accommodate many seagoing ships. Its crucial importance to European trading and military ambitions in Asia was no secret among the contending naval powers of the west.

Upon reaching the island, he received further intelligence that the King of Kandy was in active communication with French settlements along the coast of India. His predecessor had maintained a growing network of well-placed contacts and informants who, both officially and unofficially, kept the British in touch with developments in the Kandyan kingdom.

There was intelligence from this network that French operatives were posing as sailors and mercenaries operating on the island. He'd been briefed that the men they were discussing were sent on an undercover mission to discover whether the French had any connection with the rebel movement in Colombo.

'Do you know who killed them?' Thomas asked finally.

Wilson had remained standing. 'I think I do, but there has been no way to verify it was the Kandyan.'

'The Kandyan?' Thomas had heard that name before. The man had been a thorn in the British side since before he came to the island. 'Why do you think it's him,' Thomas asked.

As Head of the Inland Revenue office, Wilson had ample opportunity through his revenue agents to know what was occurring across the country. 'One of my agents, one of the two who were killed, reported an increase in rebel activity around the same time this man was first spotted. It was around the time your excellency came to the island.'

'You think he was sent to gather information about my plans or was it something more sinister?'

Wilson decided to sit in the chair he had declined initially. 'If I was to take a calculated guess,' Wilsons shrugged. 'I think it would be to collect information about your orders regarding the ongoing campaign.'

Thomas regarded him sceptically. He had fought against the French-backed nationalist movement in Haiti and had narrowly escaped an assassination attempt during a routine meeting with the local chiefs.

'Why do you not think he was sent to eliminate me?' Thomas asked.

Wilson steepled his hands. 'It's not the way the Sinhalese conduct their wars. They can be a cutthroat bunch when they want to be, but I doubt they'll want the wrath of the British Empire to come down on them. I have heard that the King of Kandy has problems with the Council of Chiefs and is getting increasingly frustrated with their attitude. I doubt he'll want to fight us when he has to keep watching his back all the time.'

Thomas sensed there was an opportunity here to be exploited. 'Why are his Chiefs against him?'

'The last Dutch campaign, turned out to be quite successful, but as it has in the past, disease and the monsoon rains conspired to force their withdrawal. After years of hard fighting, both sides signed a peace treaty that left the Dutch firmly in charge of the island's entire coastline. The Dutch prospered as they negotiated full sovereign rights over the maritime provinces. However, for the Kandyans who had stagnated in their encircled mountain kingdom came only hardship and a lack of contact with the rest of the world. They have tried to break out from this situation several times, first against the Dutch and then again with us by offering to trade a cinnamon concession to the French in return for military aid but have not been successful.'

'So, there is unrest among the Chieftains?' Thomas asked.

'Yes, the *Adigars,* and we have communicated with two of them and a leading member of their *sangha* (priesthood). They support us and want to replace the King, but it's not simple.'

'Why is that?'

'The King has collected a significant force of Europeans and Asian mercenaries around him, your excellency. Most of them are from Malaya and Java. Many of them are employed as soldiers, others as officials making it extremely difficult to overthrow him. He has also grown increasingly oppressive, and any sign of opposition is put down ruthlessly.'

Thomas considered the matter and concluded that Wilson's point was well made. He poured claret from a cut-glass decanter on the table into two shot glasses and handed one to Wilson. 'What plans have you in place to capture this man?' he asked. 'You cannot allow him to collect information at will.'

Wilson nodded his thanks. 'I agree it's not ideal, but he hides among the population, and they protect him.'

'So, the people still support the Sinhalese King.' Thomas took a sip, cradling the glass between his palms.

'Yes, sir, they do,' Wilson shrugged. 'Their loyalty is undiminished.'

'There must be a way to find him.' Thomas couldn't believe, given all the resources under his command, that the man would be so hard to find. 'Do you have enough men to assign to this task?' He needed to be careful not to let the search for this man affect revenue collection. After all, fixing the drain on the Crown's coffers was his primary remit on the island.

'That's why I wanted to meet with Your Excellency,' Wilson said, shifting forward in his seat. 'I require your permission to recruit a group of Javanese mercenaries, around twenty in number, whom I want to use to track down this man and others like him. They were part of the King's palace guard and had a falling out with the Chief *Adigar*. They feared for their lives and fled to Chilaw, surrendering to the local commander. I shipped them to Colombo and interviewed them personally. Their leader, Noordeen, swears that he knows this man by sight, having seen him around the palace.'

Thomas wasn't inclined to give a direct answer. Instead, he said, 'How do you plan to use these men?'

'I will set them loose in the city to find out where this Kandyan is hiding, with a promise of a reward to those that find him. Dead or alive,' he added.

Thomas frowned. 'Are you sure we have no one else who can undertake this mission? Can't we offer a reward for information leading to his capture?'

Wilson shook his head. 'It will be like the men who were killed, Sir. Informants don't last very long.'

'So why would it be different with these men?'

'They are seasoned soldiers, Sir,' Wilson explained. 'They have lived in this country for many years and know how things work. I will instruct them to move about in groups so as not to be ambushed and killed.'

Wilson seeing that Thomas was still not convinced, continued. 'They have brought their dependants along, about forty in number. I suggest we hold them in the Echelon Barracks for a while.'

Thomas finally nodded his agreement. 'It sounds like a good plan. If we can smoke him out, we should be able to get him to talk. I will inform the Secretary of State to release some funds for you to use.' Thomas studied Wilson for a moment. 'However, I am introducing tighter fiscal controls, and you'll be expected to provide a record of how the monies were used.'

'Yes, Your Excellency,' Wilson said, finally taking a sip from the shot glass Thomas had handed him. 'Thank you, Sir.'

CHAPTER 22

THE LOVER

Lovinia peeked out the carriage window as the rhythmic galloping sound of the hooves slowed down. The sun had long set, and the city settled in for the night. Lamp lights glinted through the windows of a mansion behind a row of trees.

They were at a crossroads when the vehicle came to a complete halt. Two horsecarts were going along the road they were about to cross. The carriage rolled again, this time moving slowly, rumbling over a paved road which led to the fort's entrance.

The summons to perform privately for the Governor had come late that day. Banda had walked in on the two of them preparing dinner.

'The *Andukāraya* has sent for you.' Banda stood next to the table, studying Lovinia closely. 'You are to dance for him in his home. Are you ready?'

Nervousness gripped her insides, and her pulse quickened. Since she had met the Kandyan, Kumara, she'd wondered when this moment would come. She had never been so bored in her life. Being confined to their home and listening to the constant warnings of going out on her own took a toll. Her father had not been pleased when he'd heard she met with the Kandyan. Lovinia suspected he was a Royalist, although he had never discussed it with her. But the enforced inactivity was hard on someone like herself. She'd been allowed to run free all her life, and now, she had started to resent her situation.

But she was giving herself to a man like the *Andukāraya. Could I do it?*

Aletta, wrapping tablespoons of ground cotton bark in muslin pouches, watched Lovinia go through the range of emotions.

'He's only a man, after all,' Aletta said matter of factly, dusting her hands. 'You know what you have to do.'

Lovinia grinned at her friend's attempt to lighten her mood. Aletta never minced her words when she wanted to make a point.

'You have taught me all I need to know,' Lovinia grinned. 'It's now up to me.'

Aletta reached out and crushed her in a fierce hug.

'This is what you've been waiting for,' she whispered. 'Let's get you ready.'

Aletta looked at her closely for a moment. Lovina imagined that her friend could see right inside her and read all her guilty secrets. She felt a thrill run down her spine and was swept by an agony of shame, but there was also a hot little core of excitement within her. Aletta understood. She, too, had experienced the stirrings of sexual arousal.

Banda nodded his agreement. 'He will send a carriage for you this evening.'

Lovinia looked at their earnest faces. A tiny smile lifted the corners of her full mouth. 'I am ready for this.' She was certain of what she wanted.

*

The fort's massive walls came into view as the horse and carriage rattled over a wooden bridge spanning a large body of water. The carriage rolled to a stop at the well-lit entrance to the fort. Through the curtained window, Lovinia saw the Sinhalese soldier approach the vehicle and address the coachman. A low murmur of voices and the soldier's boots seemed increasingly louder. *He's coming to check inside.* Her heart beat fast against her ribs. Lovinia pulled the loose end of the shawl covering her head and face letting only her eyes show.

That evening before the carriage came, Aletta had laid out a variety of cosmetics. 'There is one last thing which will turn you into a local beauty. Will you permit me?'

Lovinia sat still while Aletta darkened her eyebrows and lashes and outlined her eyes with kohl, drawing the line up at the corners. She painted her lips a clear red and handed Lovinia a small mirror.

Lovinia stared at her reflection in astonishment. Gone was the natural look on her face. The dark brows distinguished her features, drawing attention to her mysterious, shaded eyes. The kohl showed the colour of her irises, making them glow a deep, rich gold, and the elongated black line gave them a fetching tilt. Her red mouth looked sensual and inviting.

'I hardly recognise myself,' she giggled. Aletta looked proud of her handiwork. She handed Lovinia the little box of kohl.

'This is my gift to you. You can practise enhancing the beauty of your eyes yourself. Lovinia had felt a surge of excitement that seemed centred in her lower belly. With Aletta at her side, might not the unknown open for her? Lovinia felt happy and hopeful about the future for the first time in many weeks.

The soldier pulled the door open. Pushing the curtain aside with his rifle, the man peeked inside. A Sinhalese sepoy – his expressionless eyes don't tell Lovinia anything. The coachman was standing behind him with folded hands, muttering something softly.

The soldier looked over his shoulder at the man and backed up, closing the door. Lovinia breathed a sigh of relief. She couldn't understand why she didn't want the man to see her face.

'Go ahead', Lovinia heard him speak. 'It's straight ahead and to the right.'

After a few minutes, the carriage started again. Lovinia rearranged the saree to uncover her face and neck. Opening the window curtain, she brought down the windowpane. Fresh air gushed inside, washing through the thin material against her skin.

Faraway drumbeats scattered her thoughts. The tempo was hurried and uneven. In the near distance, light poured from the open windows of bungalows which made up the officers' quarters. The sound of voices raised in laughter floated on the still night air.

The carriage moved ahead, passing through an open, unguarded gate and up a well-tended driveway to an imposing two-storey colonial building. Torches blazed in their sconces, lighting up the entire area. The horse cart continued past the grand entrance flanked by two red-coated soldiers, turning down a partially concealed lane to a well-lit side entrance where a livery-coated man opened the door, motioning Lovinia to step out.

Lovinia pulled the sari tight around her head and shoulders, stepping out of the cart into the circle of light. Her knees felt wobbly, but she straightened her back, took a deep breath, and looked around. The night outside was hot and humid. Dogs barked in the distance. A fluttering sea breeze carrying the fragrance of the night-blooming jasmines chilled her skin—trees bordering the building cast deep shadows on its white walls.

A long balcony over the side entrance, smothered in pink and yellow bougainvillaea, overlooked the side of the house. Someone stood by the open window puffing away at a cigar.

'I was told you speak English?'

Lovinia was startled by the sudden question. She recognised the man as the *Andukāraya's* manservant by the description she'd been given by Banda. The man studied Lovinia waiting for her response.

'I am learning.' Lovinia maintained eye contact with the man until he nodded, his eyes betraying nothing.

'Follow me.'

A chill rippled through Lovinia. She felt out of her depth in this unfamiliar environment. She breathed in, trying to calm the fluttering of her stomach, and followed the manservant. They entered a corridor leading to a small foyer with two doors and a narrow wooden staircase climbing to the upper floor. The manservant motioned her to follow him up the stairs, which took them to a long hallway with rooms leading off it. The manservant walked to a door, knocked on it, and paused, his head tilted, listening intently. Hearing a voice from within, he opened the door and stepped aside, motioning Lovinia forward.

Lovinia paused in the doorway and looked around the room. She was struck by its size and opulence: a high four-poster bed, brocade pillows, a mahogany cabinet, two chairs whose gilded legs were carved in a vine pattern, a mirror almost as tall as her, a trunk, and a teakwood desk. In this room lit by scented oil lamps, the walls were draped with multi-coloured tapestries, and the windows hung with delicate bamboo shutters. Even though the marble floor made the space cooler than the rest of the building, a swinging *punkah* (fan) was suspended from the ceiling. Two side tables, their top decorated with mother-of-pearl, flanked the bed.

Having grown up in humble surroundings, she was intimidated by the luxury of the space. Simultaneously, she also felt attracted to the prospect of wealth and its comforts.

The *Andukāraya* was seated in front of an unlit fireplace. A glass of wine glinted ruby on the table next to him in the light from a three-armed metal candle stand. A cigar with a drifting tendril of smoke sat in an ashtray on the table.

The man was stocky but not fat, and his square hands rested on the arms of his chair. In the flickering light, she could see that his face was neither ugly nor handsome, a face that was comfortable with itself and the world.

Lovinia raised her eyes a fraction, wanting, and yet not wanting to look into his eyes. The *Andukāraya* shifted in the chair. His dark eyes swept over her.

She returned his gaze, feeling like a sheep at the market, but didn't look away. Instead, she stood straight and tilted her chin upwards.

His clear grey eyes expressed solicitude, not desire. He appeared to be over thirty and held himself straight and upright. He had a broad forehead, high cheekbones and a square jaw. The jet black, neatly parted hair, brushed moustache, eyebrows and sideburns gave a youthfulness to the severe face. It could have been so much worse.

*

God, she was a beauty. The thought crossed Thomas's mind unbidden. Why was the sight of her unleashing some new temptation?

Green eyes? And skin like golden honey and hair that showed streaks of mahogany and deep brown as it fell down her back in a thick plait. She did not appear disconcerted to be alone with him, unveiled, with a strange man, but stood there and contemplated him. Her lovely body-hugging sari pulled tight around her revealed not only delightful curves and elegantly rounded arms decked in silver bangles but also unsettling bands of smooth golden midriff and shoulders.

Thomas was not a man who indulged in anything, yet at this moment, he was tempted to stroke that glossy black hair and pluck a blossom from her hair, to touch her …. all of her was temptation. He stole another look at her full breasts through the transparent cloth. He rose to his feet and took a step towards her, his feet moving by the desire welling in his heart and the twitch in his loins.

Her confident smile, streaked with submissiveness, tugged at his soul. The breeze brushed past her and carried her warm and sweet scent to his eager, flaring nostrils as she glided towards him. When they were at arm's length, Lovinia went down on her knees and touched his feet. Her hands sent a delightful shiver up to his head. She waited, folded low and hands covering his feet.

Thomas placed his trembling fingers on her shoulders, and she rose on firm muscles, her movement fluid as though choreographed to perfection. 'You were waiting, my lord,' she smiled. Her smile, innocent and trusting, robbed him of his thoughts.

Thomas smiled in delight, sat down, and gestured for her to proceed. The woman stepped back, rearranging herself into a tantric pose with her legs apart and bent at the knees. The odour of burning oil lamps and the aroma of his cigar burning in the ashtray seemed more acute to Thomas as she began to clap her hands in rhythm.

The dancer mesmerised him with movements of graceful flowing arms, the gentle swaying of sculpted hips that accentuated a slim waist, and feet that marked the captivating beats of her hands.

Lovinia swayed towards him. She looked at him through lowered lashes as her fingers loosened the silk veils swathed around her lower body. He watched as her narrow waist, flaring hips and rounded thighs were revealed.

Lovinia's skin gleamed in the flickering light, the gold and ivory of her anklets glowing against the rich colour of her olive skin. In the depression of her navel, a small red stone glinted like red fire. Thomas's blood quickened as Lovinia ran her slim hands down over her hips.

*

Lovinia could see that he was attracted to her. Despite his rigid, soldier-like bearing, she could feel an intensity in his stare that seemed to overpower his reasoning. Lovinia had seen this look hundreds of times before. He was playing at seduction, wrapped in a threat, inviting her to make the next move to incite desire.

Lovinia had no idea how to behave like an English lady, but she knew he was no drunken idiot like the soldiers she danced for. She remained standing. It gave her more self-confidence. Perhaps, gentle nature was hidden behind that solemn exterior. She had to act normal and convincing.

The *Andukāraya* rose from his chair. He approached Lovinia, and she looked down again. He was the same height as her, but his proud manner made him seem taller. Unable to counter his intense adoration, her gaze dropped. Her pulse quickened. Her breathing grew erratic.

'I am very pleased you came. Now that you're here, we must get to know each other.'

Lovinia looked up at him, blushed on meeting his eye and looked down again.

'Yes, sire,' Lovinia said, and the heat rose in her cheeks. This man would soon share a bed with her. She chased away the thought, but her face still burned.

He put his arm around her waist, pulling her closer. Then he reached for her chin and gently raised her face towards him.

It was the chance she'd been waiting for, not the time to be aggressive or assertive. Lovinia did nothing and said nothing, although her heart beat faster. She looked back at him frankly. Her deer-like eyes fixed on his dark brown ones.

The *Andukāraya* bent forward and kissed her cheek softly. Then he gently pressed his lips to Lovinia's forehead. She was taken aback but didn't flinch at his caress. Her silence encouraged him, and he kissed her lips passionately.

He held her tight in his arms, feeling the warmth of her soft skin and breathing in her delicate scent. The scent of her beautiful black hair, the softness of her arms and the curve of her light figure all seemed to ignite his soul. Before stopping, he kissed her forehead, cheeks, and neck.

The *Andukāraya* unravelled her sari and slid it off her. He did not delay loosening the cord of her flimsy undergarment, letting it drop at her feet. He smiled as his eyes ran over her tight upright breasts, flat stomach, lovely, shapely legs and exquisite thighs.

Lovinia found herself enjoying the attention. He released her and sat down on the chair to remove his shoes. Lovinia knelt beside him and took the task into her own hands.

*

She danced insanely as some unknown power possessed her. The frantic yet controlled rhythmic waving of her red costume to the clapping sound of her hands nearly gave life to the beautiful embroidery patterns of the cloth. The dance had blown her hair into her face. She brushed it back and saw the *Andukāraya* staring at her as she did.

He caught her against his chest and kissed her. The suddenness was shocking and liberating. Lovinia melted against him, her arms around his neck, her pert breasts tight against his bare skin. She could feel his nipples hardening through the thin silk she wore. Under the demands of his mouth, her lips parted without hesitation, her tongue meeting his to explore. She would have tasted of spice and something exotic.

The *Andukāraya* slid his hands down from her shoulders, past her waist, to the curve of her hips as she sat on the bed, and he lifted her so she sat across his thighs.

Lovinia gasped against his lips as she felt the hard ridge of his desire. *He wants me that much.* Thomas turned her to cup the weight of her breast.

Lovinia had always thought them too small, but she filled his palm as he teased the tight bud until she gasped into his mouth. This was arousal, she realised. She could feel her moist heat and smell the heady musk of their mutual desire.

The *Andukāraya* lifted his head and set his hands on her waist as if to lift her away. Lovinia opened her eyes and looked into his face. He had released something in her: a passion, a feminine understanding that had not been there before. This adventure gave her the courage to be free and make her world. And she knew what she wanted, a strong man who shielded her. She could not have him for long. She understood that, but ...

'Lovinia—' He stopped with a gasp as her mouth found his nipple, which contracted into a hard nub at the first stroke of her tongue. Her fingers closed over the knot that held his robe closed, and she tugged at it as he moved to hold her away from his body. The robe fell open, and she fell against him into the splendour of his nakedness.

'Lovinia,' he said again; this time, it was a groan. She lifted her face to him, lips parted, and he bent his head and kissed her. She could feel his conflict even as his mouth made love to hers. He tasted hot, male, and urgent; through the thin cotton she wore, she felt his heartbeat kick.

'No,' he muttered, lifting his head and breaking the kiss. But it seemed he did not have the strength to move right away. His breath caressed her lips, and his eyes were wide open and brilliant. 'No,' he said more strongly.

Lovinia clung to his neck, lifting one knee onto the desk and then the other, so she straddled him, her robe crumpling and leaving her wide open and exposed. Then, before he could move freely, she lowered herself slowly on the heated length of his erection, which was imprisoned along her soft hot and moist folds.

'God, Lovinia, no.' the *Andukāraya* raised his hips, but it only brought him closer, and she moved with him, moving her hips in a rhythm that made him sob with desire.

'Stop. Stop, please, while I still can—'

The *Andukāraya* was a sensual, virile man. He probably hadn't had a woman for months, and she was offering herself to him. Of course, he wanted her.

He collapsed on her as he went limp. His breath was laboured and harsh.

Lovinia tried to move. 'Wait.' He stood, lifting her with him and walked to the couch in the corner. He sat down and set her by his side. His face was sweaty as he wrapped himself in the robe and tied the sash.

'You were wonderful,' Thomas said, stroking her face.

'Yes.' her legs were shaking from the unfulfilled passion she felt.

'Come here.' He lifted her onto his lap, settled her in the crook of his arm and kissed her, all before she could react. Her legs felt even weaker as she gave herself up to his kiss. Even when his hand slipped up her leg and cupped her throbbing core, she moaned into his mouth.

How could such gentleness create such a sensation in her body? She arched, pressing against his hand as his fingers explored, stroked, and screamed into his mouth.

Lovinia stopped thinking, stopped breathing, and surrendered to sensation and heat. She was aware of being lifted and being lowered onto something soft.

'Sleep, Lovinia,' Thomas whispered as she drifted away.

*

Light streamed through the tall windows as Lovinia stood in front of the full-length mirror. Her lover had slipped out of bed before she'd woken. The tall open windows had slatted shutters to let in the breeze and give privacy and security.

She had already discarded her clothes and felt no shame looking at her naked body. The nude woman in the mirror smiled at her. Her hands ran down slowly over her neck and then over her breasts. She felt as if a beautiful young man was making love to her. Heat flowed between her thighs. She moaned and gently massaged her breasts.

Lovinia was lost in herself. Was it not the ultimate pleasure to see a strong man made weak by his lust for her? After so long, she was finally about to get something she had never imagined. She could now earn some money for her family. And no man would ever own her.

She looked at her own naked body in the mirror. A feeling of freedom and self-satisfaction tickled her skin. The *Andukāraya* had been insatiable. She had succumbed to his every whim until he couldn't anymore. It was a new Lovinia now.

A gentle knock on the door reminded her that she needed to get dressed. It didn't take her long to drape the sari around her body and adjust it for modesty. There was no need to do otherwise.

'I am ready,' she called out, waiting for the door to be opened.

The Chief Steward opened the door to a hallway where a few servants waited patiently.

'This is Nilomi, your maid,' the Chief Steward said. 'Nilomi, take Miss Lovinia to her room. The *Andukāraya* will have breakfast in an hour.'

'*Kohomada*, Nilomi,' Lovinia said as the maidservant came forwards, her *pallu* (decorated loose end of a sari) pulled forwards to shield her face.

'Good evening, Miss Lovinia,' the woman responded. Lovinia realised that she was quite young, around the same age as her.

'Sir Thomas Sahib says I must speak English all the time. My English is good, yes? The room is this way. Lessons I have learned from Lady McDonald's maid in being a proper lady's maid.'

They passed a *punkah*-wallah sitting with his back against the outside wall. He moved his foot endlessly, his big toe pulling the cord tied to the wide cloth fans in the rooms on both sides of the corridor. The maid opened a door at the end of the passage, waiting for her to go through.

Lovinia had never seen furniture like this. The high bed was draped in fine muslin netting, the padded chairs both stiff and upright. A large rug lay on the bare wooden floor beside the bed. A table with a mirror at the back was covered in little boxes, bottles, and hairbrushes. Overhead the cloth *punkah* squeaked to and fro, stirring the air. A faint buzz of chatter from outside reached her through the grillwork over the door.

'This is a nice room, I think,' Nilomi said with an anxious glance at Lovinia. 'I think the bath is filled, Miss Lovinia. I will lay out your clothes.'

'I have no clothes,' Lovinia said, peering into the bathroom. The tub was large and already full of water.

'That must have been very difficult! But Sir Thomas has readied everything that you need. See.' Nilomi threw open the clothes press, pulling out the drawers.

'Gowns and petticoats and stockings and—'

'Enough. I will bathe, and then I will put on my clothes again. I do not need these. And then I want to go home.'

Lovinia realised that she had better offer a reason why she needed to leave. 'I need to collect my clothes and inform my family.'

With one look at her, the maid opened her mouth to protest and shut it again. 'Yes, Miss Lovinia.'

CHAPTER 23

THE ARRANGEMENT

Thomas felt relaxed with Lovinia. She was exotic and enigmatic, and she was so beautiful. Thomas had never seen anyone like her. The combination of honey-coloured skin, silky black hair, and green eyes – picked up by the colours of her tunic and pantaloons – was quite devastating.

He was struck by the complexity of this woman, who spoke so frankly and whose spirit was so free, who could laugh so easily and completely enjoy herself with simple things and yet deal just as readily with her life in the next moment.

Lovinia's voice was softly accented, and her English was getting better. Besides English, she spoke Creole, Sinhalese and various other dialects. Thomas thought he had never met a woman with such charm and vivacity.

When she spoke in her native tongue, he heard authority and certainty in her voice. He listened hard, as though he might be able to understand her words even though the language was unfamiliar. Inside her infinite eyes, he was lost. That's when he knew that his control of reality had been defeated. The wild passion of this paradise he had entered had slowly started to overwhelm his soul.

One matter was always forefront of his mind these days. Given his position in the colony, it was careless of him to think that flaunting Lovinia in front of the colony's snobbish and gossipy British society was the right thing for him to do. She had told him frankly that she had no intention of dressing up like a

European woman and that he would have to accept her the way she was.

Cohabitation between local women and British men was commonplace and tolerated. He knew from his briefings in London that the growing social and sexual distance between Britons and locals was part of a growing empire's demand to become morally conscious, recognizing the demands on colonizing groups to uphold their racial, national, and religious superiority. "Going native" in his current position would be seen as a blemish on his otherwise impeccable career.

Thomas's mind roamed to the spicy gossip in the men's clubs in London and Madras when he served there. He had learnt about the *kothas* (bordellos) of Lucknow, the mansions of the famous courtesans. Kings, nawabs, royal family members, and even top-ranking British officers were their patrons. They regularly attended performances, mainly singing and dancing, often leading to more intimate dalliances.

Thomas knew European men in high positions in India maintained a *zenana* (secluded women's quarters) within their households using cohabitive relationships with Indian noblewomen from local princely courts, which paved the way for symbolic incorporation into local politics and enabled diplomatic cooperation. Largely, such alliances were discouraged and disapproved, but well-to-do men were generally able to get around the censure.

He needed someplace similar here on the island. Somewhere he could go to relax and enjoy Lovinia's company, away from the prying eyes of disapproving British society. But that very same society expected him, a bachelor, to have a wife or a mistress to run his household and warm his bed at night.

I need a stratagem to distract and obscure my relationship with Lovinia. The solution that sprang into his mind next instant was so simple, so obvious, that he all but laughed aloud. He sat up straighter, his mind going over the possibilities until he was certain.

Yes! He smiled to himself. He will maintain a presence in the city and even take a mistress as was expected, thus obscuring his relationship with the Mestizo girl. After a few moments of thought, he reached across and rang the little brass bell on the table.

'You called, Suh?' Johnson walked into the room soundlessly.

'Johnson, could you send a message to Major Staples? I require his presence immediately.'

Thomas paced the room restlessly while waiting for the Major, various scenarios playing in his mind. A knock on the study door brought him back to the present.

'Come in, come in.'

Major Staples entered, looking anxiously at Thomas. 'You called for me, Your Excellency? Is there something wrong?'

'No, no ...' Thomas laughed at the look on the Major's face. 'I have come to a decision and require your assistance.'

'Of course, Sir.'

'When I was out riding, I came across a headland about six miles south of the city, near a native village,' Thomas said. 'Galkissa, I think it was called.'

'Yes, sir, I know the place', the Major nodded.

'I want to build a country residence on the bluff overlooking the sea,' Thomas said. 'I intend to use it when my official duties don't require me to be in the city.'

Major Staples nodded, pulling out a notebook from his jacket.

'Find out from the Surveyor General's office whether that is Crown land which I believe it is. Get him to devise some plans for me to look at.'

The Major looked up from his notebook. 'Will you use it to conduct your official duties, sir?' The Major noted Thomas's raised eyebrows. 'The architect will need to understand its purpose so he can design it appropriately,' he explained.

'Ahh, I see!' Thomas ruminated for a moment. 'I suppose I will sometimes use it to conduct official business, but I don't want anything enormous. I will be using it to get away from all those boring meetings and reading all these financial reports,' he said, waving his arm over his desk.

'You mean a getaway, sir. I understand.'

'A what?'

'A place to get away,' the Major explained, looking up from his notebook.

'Several senior company officials maintain homes outside the city's walls, sir, for this very purpose. Some have even started cultivating plantations of their own using local labour.'

'Yes, that's right! A getaway, as you call it.'

'Yes, sir! I will get onto it right away,' the Major said, snapping his notebook shut. 'Will there be anything else?'

Thomas watched the Major stride out of the room. *That's one done*, he thought, quite pleased with himself for coming up with the idea. *I must go into the city to set the second part of my plan in motion.*

*

The building was a Dutch colonial-style, a wooden green-and-white mansion in Cinnamon Gardens, all louvred windows and stained glass and an open balustraded gallery with ornate columns, gingerbread fretwork, and arches all around the first storey. The bottom house, the area between the pillars on which the house rested, was shielded from public view by ground-to-ceiling latticework, open towards the garden and yard at the back.

The house was invisible from the garden, buried among the giant bougainvillaea, which climbed up trellises and trees to enclose in the verandah encircling the house. There were Venetian blinds over the windows to keep out the sun. Between the columns of the verandah were *tatties* (a screen or mat, usually made of coconut matting). Hanging from the ceilings were *punkahs*, vast fans moved by a cord and pulley normally worked by servants who tied the cord to their big toe and could keep the *punkah* flapping even when fast asleep.

Sir David, it seemed, was waiting in the private drawing room when Thomas arrived. He nodded at the footman and walked across the hall into the rather large room with a table set in the middle. Sitting deep in a well-padded armchair, Sir David rose to greet him. Lady Tarrant and Mrs Hartley stood grouped by the window, presenting a nice picture. They looked at him expectantly, like an actor emerging onto a stage. He glanced around, making a short bow.

Indian silks covered the small tables, and exotic plants graced the carved rosewood mantelpiece. Here, as elsewhere on the island, the British strove to recreate the society of London. A small fire was burning, and no fewer than four wax candles were lit on the centre table. All this luxury – the private drawing room, the fire, the wax candles – gave him uneasy delight. As the second son, he had to scrape and economise so carefully most of his life that carelessness with money gave him this dubious pleasure.

'Have you had a pleasant drive, Sir Thomas?' Lady Tarrant called out, coming forward. 'I notice you came by carriage.'

Thomas bent over her hand. 'I did, my Lady. I prefer riding, but the wet weather…' he shrugged. It had been drizzling most of the day, with gusty winds from the southwest.

'Have you noticed it's unusually cool today,' Sir David grumbled, sinking heavily into the leather-upholstered chair by the fireplace. 'My gout is playing up, and I find the fire comforting,' he said, waving his hand at the fireplace. 'I hope it doesn't bother your Excellency.'

'I find it quite pleasant,' Thomas remarked, 'It reminds me of home.'

Thomas smiled as his eyes alighted on the other occupant in the room.

'How delightful to see you again, Mrs Hartley.'

'How do you do, your Excellency.' She curtsied, head lowered demurely, but when she lifted her head again, her lips were curved into a little smile.

Thomas basked in the quick flush of pleasure which swept across Mrs Hartley's cheeks and neck as he crossed the room and took her hands.

Thomas looked at Mrs Hartley thoughtfully. They had sailed together for six months, growing in mutual respect and understanding, even as they had attempted to pretend that there could be nothing between them. He was a gentleman, and she was a widower. Thus, the explosion of passion, when it had come, had been the more exciting.

'I am glad to find you still living here.'

Mrs Hartley looked at him appraisingly, head tilted at a slight angle. 'I have been bored to death!' she said. 'I have missed our little talks onboard the Blenheim!' She blushed easily because her complexion was so fair; in repose, her features, tall forehead, long, straight nose, pointed chin, flat, wide mouth, often seemed to have been carved from marble. Only the eyes, brilliantly blue, brilliantly alive, gave that thought the lie. Her thick dark hair lay free on her shoulders and down her back; he did not suppose she had ever cut it. She wore the simplest of blue gowns, slightly tucked at the waist. Her body was not for display beneath flattering garments.

The butler appeared with a glass of wine for each on a silver platter he placed on the table, disappearing without a word.

'Shall we sit? Thomas gestured at a faded red sofa placed next to a window.

Thomas handed Juliet her wine and sat beside her on the faded red sofa. Thomas sipped slowly, allowing the liquid to refresh him a little.

Thomas darted a look at Lady Tarrant, sitting calmly while embroidering at the far end of the drawing room.

He lowered his voice. 'Have you come to any decision on your plans?'

'There is some hope of finding employment as a governess, your Excellency, or even as a companion to someone travelling back to England,' she answered quietly. 'Lady Tarrant has generously invited me to remain here until my plans come to fruition.'

'You do know you don't have to address me so formally,' Thomas smiled. 'We are old friends, after all.'

Her lively blue eyes locked with his. 'Perfectly!' She laughed. 'But how do I address you?'

'In general, my friends call me Thomas.'

'I cannot be expected to do so, however!' she said warmly. 'I shall call you Sir Thomas.

'Well, if you call me Sir Maitland or Your Excellency, you will undo me,' he pointed out.

'Then you must call me Juliet.' She smiled at him, a wide smile that lit her eyes so they shone with brilliance.

Thomas chuckled. His mood seemed much improved from that morning. Already the conversation was easier. Perhaps he had been anxious for no reason.

Thomas swung his gaze to the wet, manicured gardens outside the windows. Beyond its confines, a city teemed with local people carrying their bundles. Barefoot. Backs bent. Perhaps hungry. Were they hungry?

'Have you travelled outside of Colombo, Juliet?'

'I would love to see what it's like, Sir Thomas.' She leaned forward. 'I have been warned that most English outside cities contract malaria within the first months, often in the first weeks.'

'Nothing a good gin and tonic won't fix, my dear Juliet.' Sir David's deep voice rumbled from his seat by the fire.

Juliet turned a puzzled gaze on him.

'It's a cocktail introduced by the Company in India to help British officers manage the effects of malaria.'

Juliet stared at Sir Tarrant before turning to Thomas. 'Goodness, was that a joke?'

'It's the tonic water, you see.' Thomas grinned at Juliet's confusion. 'It contains quinine which is a natural remedy against the disease.' When he was serving in India, the soldiers were given a regular gin ration with tonic water mixed with sugar and lime to make the bitter drink more palatable.

Lady Tarrant spoke from the distant armchair. 'You should escort Juliet on one of your investigations, Sir Thomas.'

'It's an excellent idea, my Lady, but it's not easy unless you're an accomplished horsewoman.' Thomas looked at Juliet. 'These are not roads as we know them. They are more like tracks, and there are wild animals and plenty of diseases we don't know how to cure.'

'I am not… a good horsewoman, I mean,' Juliet said, a laugh flashing in her eyes. 'I wish I did, but I am hopeless on a horse!'

'Perhaps a palanquin then.' Lady Tarrant peered over her glasses. She seemed distracted, and her tone was mild, but Thomas suspected she was more keenly interested than her demeanour suggested.

'I can arrange one quite easily,' Sir David contributed from his position by the fireplace. 'When would you be available, your excellency?'

Juliet turned to him enthusiastically. 'I would love that. Not many of the women here have been outside the immediate area.'

'I had planned on exploring further south,' Thomas replied. 'Will tomorrow morning be suitable?'

Juliet clapped her hands and laughed in delight. Her open and natural laughter was full of humour and unrestrained.

Lady Tarrant looked up from her embroidery with a smile.

'Yes, I am free ...I've nothing planned.' Juliet lowered her voice. 'Frankly, I am bored. I hear these bored women complaining about their servants and how things are done so much better back home.'

Thomas almost choked on his breath. 'Well, that's settled then. 'I'll be here around ten if that is suitable?'

'Do you miss home, Sir Thomas?'

The question took Thomas by surprise. 'There are moments I miss England a great deal.' He set down his glass. 'But this is my home now.'

Juliet's dancing eyes searched his, her pretty white teeth bared in a smile. She nodded thoughtfully. 'Can we visit the Fort? I've heard so much about the Governor's mansion.'

'I'm afraid where I live is nowhere near as grand as here.'

'Are you planning on living in the Fort?' Lady Tarrant asked. 'Governor North found it quite dull and limiting.'

'He wasn't a soldier, Lady Tarrant.' Thomas responded. 'I am used to living amongst soldiers, and my quarters are more than adequate.'

'What are you planning to do with the Governor's Lodge at St. Sebastian's?' Sir David questioned. 'The Company are looking for additional warehouse space and will be prepared to take it over if it is unused.'

'I haven't spent time thinking about it.' Thomas knew he needed to address it but dismissed it as not needing immediate attention. An unbidden thought crossed his mind. He wanted to find a way to keep Juliet from returning to England.

'I've visited the Lodge, which requires much work to make it habitable as a lodging,' Thomas said, looking at Sir David. He had visited the country lodge at St Sebastian's situated prettily on a fresh-water lake, which was a part of the

Fort's northern fortifications. He found the house in a wretched condition, having been transformed from a powder magazine.

'Yes,' Sir David nodded. 'I couldn't understand how North was able to reside there. But then the man only used it as an office and entertained elsewhere.'

'Perhaps I could look to restoring it for the purpose it was meant for,' Thomas mused, pausing for a few seconds, thinking.

'I just had a thought!' he said finally, looking directly at Juliet. 'You are looking for something to do. Would the task of making the Lodge liveable be interesting to you?'

Juliet looked confused for a moment. Then a small smile formed on her lips. 'You mean you're looking for a housekeeper?'

'No,' Thomas shook his head. 'I want more than a housekeeper. It has to be someone who will oversee the restoration of the property and be a hostess at official government functions. Of course, the Crown will provide a budget for the restoration works, and I will arrange for a generous annuity. You could live there once the work is complete. I intend to use it for visiting dignitaries and senior officials from England.' Thomas tilted his head, considering Juliet. 'However, it may not be quite up to standard until the entire renovation is complete.'

'I don't require grand living,' Juliet blurted. Her cheeks flushed when she realised what she had said. Their gazes met, and they both became keenly aware of the obvious. Her gaze was focused on him as her mouth curved in an uncertain smile.

'So, you would consider it?'

'I cannot answer without knowing what Sir David and Lady Tarrant think.' Juliet said, eagerly turning towards Lady Tarrant. 'They have been so kind and patient with me.'

'I think it's a splendid idea,' Lady Tarrant responded without hesitation, putting her embroidery aside and rising to her feet. 'I am sure David can assist you in finding the right tradesmen, won't you, dear? Juliet could live here until the work is complete, of course. It's only a short palanquin ride away.'

Sir David nodded, seemingly satisfied with the arrangement. 'I know just the person who could handle the task for you. We use him quite a bit to maintain and restore our properties.'

Thomas turned to Juliet and reached for her hands. 'Well, what do you think?'

An involuntary smile flickered on Juliet's lips. 'You are all so kind,' she said with an uncertain laugh. 'I suppose I can only try, given everyone's support.'

Thomas breathed a sigh of relief. 'Well, that's settled then,' Thomas squeezed Juliet's hands. 'I'll get my secretary to make all the necessary arrangements.'

CHAPTER 24

THE MISSION

Lovinia rose early on the day of the harvest festival. Around the country, fields were in bloom, and hope was alive for a productive harvest. The harvest celebration brought out all castes and genders as people celebrated with colours and merrymaking. Buddha's followers honoured him by imitating his playfulness.

She had spoken to Banda and Aletta the previous evening about going into Colombo for a meeting with the Kandyan. Banda decided to accompany her. She wrapped a saree around her body and covered her head and face in a shawl. Travelling in a rickshaw, the two soon found themselves in a labyrinth of dense streets to the north of the Fort.

The colourful city bazaars were always raucous with vendors' cries and the fierce bargaining of shoppers. The streets were narrow and confined, the buildings huddled together, supporting one another. The shops and domestic dwellings were open to the streets, the bustle of living and selling happening out in the open. The air was suffocating with the odour of spices, over-ripe fruit, dried fish, meat, and fresh gore from slaughterhouses running into the open drains. The roads were crowded with people and farm animals amidst the constant flutter of scavenging crows.

The place was a confusing web of shoulder-width alleys and houses packed tight with terraces that leaned on one another. Leathers and fabrics stretched and sagged overhead and connected the opposing terraces, giving cover to the walkway. Lovinia, who always kept to the larger and ordered roads, never knew these places existed in Colombo.

Groups of *farangi* (foreigners) and locals stood outside gaudy-coloured doors. Some watched them but turned away when they saw Banda staring at them.

They arrived at the laneway. Banda stepped up to the brightly coloured door emblazoned with a symbol of a lion carrying a sword and rapped on it with his fingers. The door opened creakily. A burst of noise and golden light flowed out around the bulky figure of a man who blocked the entrance.

'What do you want?' he growled, staring at Lovinia, who stepped forward when she saw it was Lokubada.

'We are here to see the Kandyan,' she replied.

The man's beady eyes studied her carefully. 'Hai, he's here. He told me to expect you,' grunted the innkeeper. The man looked past Lovinia at Banda. 'He's only expecting you, not a crowd.'

'He's my father. I couldn't come alone,' Lovinia shrugged. 'He can remain outside if you wish.' She had already discussed the possibility of the Kandyan only wanting to meet her.

'It is better if he does,' Lokubada agreed. 'You won't come to any harm in here.'

Lovinia glanced back at Banda, who nodded at her.

'I will remain on the street,' Banda said.

The innkeeper stepped back and motioned Lovinia past him. 'Come in, come in!'

He closed the door behind them, his broad face wreathed in a smile. He pattered ahead of Lovinia, the earrings bouncing and his paunch preceding him, through a tiny entryway and into a large square room which was smoky with torchlight and smelled of beer and roasting meat.

All around the walls were cubicles, divided by shoulder-high partitions but open to the room, and the charcoal fire blazing in its centre in a great pottery pan. In the cubicles, kneeling on reed mats before low tables, were customers—

men, mostly, with a scattering of women and an occasional bearded foreigner. They were eating, drinking, gambling noisily at 'odd and even,' or talking in low tones over cups of local beer or arrack. One group roared drunken approval of the antics of a juggler performing his feats beside their table. On the opposite side of the room, a dancing girl swayed and postured to the jingle of her tambourine and the wail of a blind musician's flute.

In the centre of all, stirring the contents of a kettle bubbling over the fire pan, stood a tiny, dried-up woman. A metal loop with ring coins and copper and silver rupees hung from her sash. A curious necklace of shells weighed her narrow chest. She had the brightest, most suspicious eyes Lovinia had ever seen. Her long spoon was motionless as she watched them cross the room.

'My wife, Sakuntala,' puffed the innkeeper, noting the direction of Lovinia's glance. 'Wonderful woman. She runs the place here. Hai, they'd rob me blind were it not for her. God's truth! A babe of innocence, she calls me, trusting anyone, even these sailors—' With a breathy laugh, he dug Lovinia in the ribs, then detoured around the beribboned dancing girl to head for a table in the farthest corner.

As they passed, Lovinia glanced at the girl, whose languid movements now concealed, now revealed, the cubbyhole behind her, in which a scribe sat cross-legged before his inkstand in earnest conversation with a shaven-headed, yellow-robed priest. At that moment, the scribe looked around, and the firelight fell on his face. It was the Kandyan.

Lovinia caught her breath, hesitating. But his eyes met hers only an instant, then moved calmly back to his writing block. The dancing girl whirled between them again, and Lovinia walked on. Her cheeks burned as she slipped past the innkeeper into the farthest cubicle and sank to her knees upon the woven mat.

"He'll be with you when he's ready," Lokubada said. "I'll fetch a *toddy* (palm wine) to cool your throat." Giving a hitch to his ample sarong, he waddled away.

Lovinia looked around. In the next cubicle, two solemn older men, one fat, one thin, played an absorbed and silent game of *dum* (checkers), a group of rivermen gaming in another corner.

Lokubada was back almost immediately with a ceramic jug filled to the brim and a wooden cup. Lovinia took the jug from the perspiring innkeeper, who beamed and paddled off again, his earrings bobbing. She poured the fermented king coconut juice into the cup, and its gentle fragrance filled her nostrils. She watched the cloudy liquid gurgle into the cup when a shadow fell across the table.

'You wished my services?' Kumara said smoothly. 'A contract written? Perhaps, a letter to a lover?' he smiled.

He was leaning in the entrance to their cubicle, his inkstand under one arm. Two reed pens stuck jauntily behind his ear. Even in the long robe and coarse linen headcloth of a scribe, his pose was as easy, his grace as careless, as in the court of the King. He grinned down at Lovinia, and her retort died on her lips. She struggled to regain her composure as he turned to murmur something to the innkeeper who had come up behind him. What was it about his smile? Its warmth? Its sudden intimacy? It rushed to the head like strong wine.

Lovinia was aware of nothing but him as he stood there outlined against the noisy, torchlit room. All day she had nerved herself for this meeting, fearing to find him again, the curt stranger he had been in the village. Now, all in a moment, her fears had vanished. *There was no dangerous spy, but her companion in espionage—warm, teasing, dangerous.* Her spirits rose like a sail.

Kumara slid in beside Lovinia. 'So, you accomplished it,' he murmured, seating himself cross-legged, in the scribe's manner and setting his inkstand on the table.

'Better than you hoped, I think,' she said wickedly.

'Was it such a task?'

'Task? At first, I knew not even know how to start! A hard master you are.' Lovinia grimaced. '"Get into the man's bed," you said, then away you stroll, with never another thought of it—"

Kumara laughed, handing her the cup she had filled and pouring another for himself in a cup he carried. 'But why should I think of it? I have every confidence, my green-eyed one, in your capacity for guile, not to say cheating—' Kumara regarded her with amusement. 'I have seen you at work, and I'll wager

I could learn guile from you. Now, pull in your claws. Were you not as you are, you'd be no use to me.'

Lovinia sipped from her cup, feeling a glow that had nothing to do with her drink. The flautist's sweet wail threaded through the jovial uproar of the tavern; laughter was warm about her; the juggler's balls spun brighter than shooting stars—even the message she must deliver slipped like a ghost into the farthest outskirts of her mind.

'You've not told me,' Kumara said, watching her, 'what you think of the Inn of the Lion.'

"Ahh, I like it well! Save for that old woman with the beady eye out there.'

'Sakuntala? No, no! She's worth all the rest put together. A marvel of a woman.' Kumara laughed.

'So, her husband said,' remarked Lovinia sceptically.

Kumara nodded, turning the cup in his hand. 'Perhaps it is all in the point of view. I'll admit her virtues would be less apparent to one attempting to snatch a loaf or two from under that beady eye.'

'I'm done with loaf snatching! But she could watch me no closer were I after her money ring.' Lovinia said, shivering dramatically.

'Well, she has reasons. First, you are new here. Second, she is jealous as a she-leopard of every pretty maid who comes near her husband.'

Lovinia stared at him in amazement, making Kumara laugh outright.

'A lesson you must have already learnt is that all is not what it seems to be, and if you haven't learnt it yet, make sure you remember it.'

'You mean there is more to her than meets the eye?' Her curiosity was thoroughly aroused. This had all the earmarks of a tale not intended for her ears—therefore, she had every intention of hearing it.

Kumara leaned towards her. His eyes were intense, his voice low and conspiratorial. 'Look around you.' Kumara waved a hand towards the crowded room. 'These are all rebels in British eyes, all loyal to the Sinhalese King.' A slow smile curved his mouth. 'That little woman is the one that holds it all together.'

Lovinia was surprised, not by what he had just said, but by the fact that he trusted her enough to say it. She twirled her wine cup thoughtfully. *Would this make it more dangerous for me?* Passing information is one thing but knowing about the rebel movement and one of its main meeting places was another. She shivered and took a sip of the wine, trying to dismiss the idea as impossible. But her thoughts were restless now, leaping back to that message she had yet to deliver. It was warm and pleasant here, with the good smell of meat and the torchlight flooding the room with smoky gold. She set down her cup and spoke in a low voice.

'It grows late, and my companions will be worried. What is it you want from me.'

Kumara hesitated, playing with the amulet on his wrist. 'First, let's talk about you,' he said. 'Has the *Andukāraya* taken you into his bed yet?'

Lovinia sucked in her breath. 'How did you get this information?' She shook her head, dismayed that he already knew what she had come to tell him. 'Do you have spies watching me?'

'I will be foolish not to,' he said gravely. 'I don't trust easily; otherwise, I wouldn't be doing my job.'

'I'm not surprised to hear that,' Lovinia responded. 'But, if you truly want answers, you have to learn to trust me.'

Kumara's face darkened in response to her statement. Something flashed across his face but was gone too quickly to offer anything significant.

'Give me your knife,' he said. 'I am sure you carry one.' His voice was quieter than it had been.

Lovinia scoffed. 'You must have your own.' She was not going to be taking any orders from him.

Kumara moved and sat beside her, his hand reaching for her leg. It wasn't done quickly. It was slow and deliberate, not to scare or intimidate her.

Although she pushed him away, that didn't stop him from reaching the sheath strapped to her thigh and pulling out the knife. He avoided touching her skin with his own, but his finger grazed her thigh as he pulled his hand away, and Lovinia felt it. Everywhere.

As she watched in confusion, Kumara positioned the sharp tip of the knife at his breast, right where his heart beat beneath the tunic he wore. His other hand gripped one of her own and closed it around the hilt of her knife. This was all done with the same controlled anger that had carried him beside her.

'If you doubt my commitment to the King or the words I spoke to you on that bluff, you may as well get this over with now.'

He exerted the slightest pressure on her hand, pushing the knife's tip through his jacket. She knew it pressed into his skin and glared up at him.

'What trick is this?' she asked, her face tightening.

'This is no trick,' he said gravely. 'You may scorn me, but if you doubt me— if you cannot trust that I mean what I say to you—I'm already a dead man.'

Lovinia looked into his eyes. She sensed no malice or ill will, but the intensity of his gaze was an undeniable force that held her in her place.

'If your life expectancy rests on me, I hate to tell you this, but you haven't much longer to live,' Lovinia said, annoyed at his attitude.

Kumara's mouth twitched, and she saw him resist a smile before continuing. His voice was still serious. 'If your opinion of me is still so low, we will accomplish nothing together.'

Lovinia made a sound of irritation. 'It's we, is it? I didn't get that feeling before.'

It was strange. His warm hand was still wrapped around her fingers and the knife hilt, and she was still spitting mad, but something else was there beside her confused annoyance. The air throbbed with something dark, fierce, and unknown to her despite all her knowledge. Lovinia pulled her hand and the knife from his grip and slipped it back into its sheath with shaking hands. She'd thought to shock him with its revelation earlier, but he'd turned the tables on her, as he seemed to each time they met.

'You have quite the flair for the dramatic.' Those were the only words she could manage. She looked around the room. It seemed busier. Laughter rang out from the cubby next to them. She could feel Kumara watching her.

'I want to put all this behind us and start again,' he said. 'It's just I have a job; without you, the task is much harder.'

Lovinia wanted to be furious at him, but something about Kumara was just pure engaging. She could see why he'd be a good spy.

Lovinia scowled at him. Just because he was getting on her good side didn't mean she had to like it.

'If you want me to spy for you, then I want to know your mission,' Lovinia said archly. She didn't know why she wanted to provoke him, but she had never cared for people like Kumara, who treated her people like dirt.

Kumara shook his head. 'There's nothing sinister about my mission. I received it directly from the King. He knows about you, and it will be unwise to incur his wrath.'

'He knows about me?' Lovinia's heart skipped a beat. This news put her and her whole family at risk. *Why did he do that?*

'Yes, I told him about you,' Kumara said grimly, watching Lovinia struggle with the news. 'You have nothing to worry about as long as we do his bidding.

His people will know the King only punishes those who displease him.'

Lovinia leaned back, her pulse pounding. Kumara was telling the truth, that much she could discern, and it made her realise how dangerous a situation she was in. The two most powerful men on the island were interested in her.

Despite herself, she felt an overpowering curiosity—which she had no intention of admitting—about what these powerful men wanted her to do.

Kumara waited. His smile had hardened into something so implacable that she felt a tremor of fear. 'I have a very special duty for you. But,'—he leaned forward to emphasise his words— 'It's so dangerous a duty that you must have your wits about you at all times.'

Lovinia gripped the table. She had reached a conclusion. Her mind had no hesitation, but it took a moment to control her wild excitement. 'Yes, I will do it,' she whispered, 'but you must protect me from harm.'

He gave a faint smile. 'I will do my best. You are my total focus. The King will reward both of us handsomely if you succeed. But if you don't—'

Lovinia nodded, understanding what he left unsaid. 'What service am I to do?'

'Now that you've enticed the *Andukāraya* with your wiles, you must get close to him,' he said, lowering his voice so Lovinia could lean in closer. 'Men like to talk. Listen to everything he says. The King has ordered me to find out what the British are planning. Are they preparing their forces for an invasion? What is on their minds?'

He sounds different, Lovinia thought. She focused on the details she needed to remember. Details were useful. Details were safe.

'It will be an easy assignment, a simple passing of information, one that a person of your talents should be able to handle.'

CHAPTER 25

THE COUNTRY MANOR

The bungalow was a modest one-story wooden building with a vast thatched roof that covered a wide verandah running along all four sides of the dwelling. It was situated on a bluff overlooking the ocean. Latticed terrace doors stood in the wide-open invitation for any breeze inclined to stir the muggy afternoon. It was built for him to use when he visited the site where his country mansion was under construction.

The deep foundations of a two-storey mansion were complete in the same guarded compound, just a few yards away. A small army of workers swarmed over the worksite laying thick walls of dressed kabook stone transported from a nearby quarry. Piles of various building materials covered by yellowed canvas lay scattered around like mounds of sand blown up from the beach.

I'll be able to move in soon. The thought pleased him. Far away from the incestuous and intricately layered social hierarchy that was Colombo society, his mind was certainly not with the food or about the ongoing construction of his manor, or for that matter, any of the various issues he had to deal with in his office.

Lovinia, yes. She was the cause of all this trouble. The emerald green eyes with a hint of lively sparkle, the glowing skin and untamed jet-black hair, the voluptuous curve of her sultry body with its perky breasts, the playful calmness, and the stubborn obedience. He couldn't understand how these starkly differing qualities peacefully existed in person. He had never seen or known someone like that before.

Thomas dipped a papadum into a dish of coconut chutney and transferred it to his mouth. The first time he'd been served local food, he had looked at it doubtfully.

'What is this you are serving me?' he asked, raising his eyebrows at Johnson.

'It's what the locals eat, Sah,' Johnson grinned. 'I think you'll like it.'

And surprisingly, Thomas did, enjoying the unusual flavour and the bite on his tongue.

Lead-coloured clouds filled the horizon, and thunder rumbled in the distance, portending rain. Long rolling waves thundered ashore after breaking on the exposed rocks of the reef. Thomas's attention was drawn to two curiously constructed fishing boats just beyond the waves, only a few hundred yards from where he was sitting. It seemed to him that they were hurrying back with their catch before the afternoon storms.

The fishing boats were weighted down by the nets they were dragging. The boats, carved out of a hollow tree, were extremely narrow with high sides. They were shaped like a long canoes with a plank of wood across the middle to give them strength. A bamboo mast with an old mat or piece of coarse brown cotton served as a sail. Across the boat were two narrow beams, twice the vessel's breadth, with a thick wooden beam to hold the sail poles, balance the boat, and prevent it from oversetting. A wooden oar tied to one end but often held by the boat master steered the vessel through gaps between the rocky reefs. The ocean's murmurs were hushed enough for him to hear the fishermen's songs as they pulled in nets filled with silvery fish below him at the foot of the peninsula.

Chewing slowly, he savoured the spicy relish. Small bowls held a variety of food, some savoury like the dhal cooked with cumin seeds and lime juice and string beans flavoured with a black spice mixture. Other dishes were sweet, made of semolina and boiled milk. His favourite was the jalebis – luscious syrup-filled fritters, a taste he had acquired in India.

Thomas had received the good news that morning that the Dutch prisoners of war who were still on the island would finally be repatriated. The pensions to which they had a right as prisoners of war and established in their capitulation had become too costly. He also seriously mistrusted them, fearing they would conspire with the King of Kandy. He had taken the unusual step he had discussed with Monsieur Van Rijn of sending a personal emissary under a flag of truce to Batavia, which was then in French hands. He suggested that the prisoners should be sent for. Much to his surprise, a Dutch commissioner arrived to pick up these Dutchmen, ridding himself of the expense and anxiety.

Full of good humour, he rang the bell, instructing Brewer to send for Major Staples. After hearing that the Major was in the city at an important meeting and was only expected back that evening, Thomas decided to explore the area around his new estate. He ordered for his horse to be saddled. While pulling on his riding boots, he briefly pondered what important meeting Major Staples could be attending. As far as he knew, there was nothing of any importance.

I'll find out soon enough. Thomas had come to trust the Major and expected to be briefed if the matter was serious.

Thomas waited by the entrance until his mount was walked over. He mounted the animal with the help of a lift from the stable hand and cantered down the narrow dirt road towards the east. Two mounted troopers fell in behind him as he left the compound, and even though he resented their presence, he knew it was a burden he'd have to bear.

Finally slowing his horse to a trot, he crested a small hill overlooking the native village. The searing slap of the white-hot sun made him wish he'd brought a hat. There was always something he hadn't seen before. Thomas passed a grove of coconut palms and watched while a bare-bodied man with his sarong tucked around his waist shinned up the narrow trunk with only a leather strap around his feet. He cut the ripe *thambili* (king coconuts), letting them fall to the ground with a thump.

Thomas walked his horse slowly down the hill into the village where Lovinia lived. The villagers were accustomed to seeing him coming and going from the capital. Some welcomed him with warm smiles, while others paid little attention.

As he approached the perimeter, the jewel colours of the women's saris, the jostling dark-skinned bodies, the babble of native languages, cries, shouts, and noisy chaos assaulted his eyes and ears. But above all, the smell. The smell of people, dust, and dryness mingled with spices, rotting fish, strange food cooking, and the smoke of the intoxicating weed called *ganja* curling from communal water pipes known as *hubble-bubbles* because of the gurgling sound they make.

As he guided his horse through the village, the smell from the cows that wandered the main road and side streets, the tame elephants that laboured about the village, the wild monkeys that scampered and darted along roofs and walls and the pungent odours of warehouses, bazaars, drains, and sewers made his nose wrinkle in disgust. In contrast, he enjoyed the sweet smell of incense wafting from the shrines and temples and the aromatic scents of jasmine, frangipani and cinnamon. The smell of the island he was beginning to enjoy was the smell of Ceylon.

After spending a pleasant couple of hours riding, he returned to his bungalow, letting his horse lead the way.

He poured himself a large glass of Madeira, sat down to work on a draft of his report to London, and waited for the Major.

*

The sound of a galloping horse pulling up outside and the stamp of boots at the entrance heralded the arrival of Major Staples from his meeting in the city. The Major walked into the room unannounced. He nodded at Thomas while pulling off his riding gloves, then shut the door firmly behind him.

'I apologise for not being present when you called for me, your excellency. I was summoned for an urgent meeting at the fort.'

Thomas had not seen the Major this flustered before. He was a man who never hurried and was always in control of his emotions.

'And what of this news that has you so concerned?' Thomas asked calmly.

Major Staples took a deep breath. 'My first mission here under the previous governor was to inquire into the existence of a Kandyan informant within our ranks. This was during the war when we were preparing to launch a surprise attack to catch them unawares, but the campaign was unsuccessful, and we lost a lot of good men in the process.'

Thomas nodded. He had read about the unsuccessful campaign and how many soldiers the army had lost.

The Major began to pace the room. 'We never caught the bugger, and I thought it was all a made-up story to excuse the sorry state the army was in at the time.'

'Are you certain?' Thomas was shocked. 'I read the despatches and reports from that campaign, and nothing was written about any spy.'

'The War Office hushed it up although they are certain it came from our side. There has been no formal accusation. I remember they wanted further evidence, which we couldn't give them.

'Surely not someone in the regiments?'

The Major shook his head. 'No! Not from the two British regiments, sir. Nor from the Indian Sepoy regiment. But it could have been from the Malay regiment or the Lascarin Regiment. That's where we focused our attention. We now think it was someone from within the Company itself. We need to tread very carefully and begin an immediate investigation.'

'The Company!' Thomas sat back in his chair, his mind exploring all the possibilities. The East India Company had numerous trading concessions within the country and had used previous military governors to try and conquer the rich heartland of the island before it became a crown colony. The Company would certainly have ties to the Kandyan King as they would enormously benefit from a cessation of hostilities. He suddenly remembered his discussion with Sir Tarrant when he broached his decision to stop road construction. *It requires further investigation..*

'What has prompted this sudden interest?' he questioned. 'The only security briefing I have had is by Inland Revenue about a man called the Kandyan who is making a bloody nuisance of himself.'

'This is more a military matter, sir. We have received information that the Kandyans have appropriated our latest muster role. This is not good news as they now know we are short a frontline regiment, having sent a reinforced battalion to India.'

'I see,' Thomas said as he digested this news. 'You don't think this Kandyan fellow has anything to do with it?'

'No, sir, we don't,' The Major responded. 'There's no way he could get those muster rolls unless they were given to him by someone with access. We believe a spy among us is feeding this information to Kandy.'

'What does high command recommend?'

'We need to tread very carefully and begin an investigation to find the leak.' The Major stopped by the window and took a deep breath.

'Is that all?'

'No, sire! They also recommended we immediately recall the battalion we sent to India and request the War Office to send us two more British regiments. The French are sniffing around Trincomalee again, and I am certain they are in communication with the Kandyan King.'

Thomas kept quiet, his mind going over what the Major had just said. After a few moments of silence, his mind was made up. He looked up at the Major.

'Get Mr Brewer to prepare a draft request to the Home Office requesting two additional line regiments be sent to the island.' Thomas steepled his hands, going over his decision. 'Make the justification clear. Include the French sniffing around whipping up the Kandyans, etc., so they understand the urgency.'

Major Staples nodded and turned to leave the room.

'Tell Brewer I have almost halved the Crown's expenditure on the island since I arrived, so there won't be any additional strain on the Home Office coffers.'

*

It was the end of the rainy season; the sky was clearer, and the beaming breaks between showers lasted for longer during the day. Latticed terrace doors stood in the wide-open invitation for any breeze inclined to stir the muggy air.

True to her intention to learn as much as possible, she had begun reading newspapers and listening to the *Andukāraya* discussing plans for the colony. Lovinia knew that there had been a war with the Kingdom of Kandy and that, following the British victory, a peace treaty had been signed.

It was amazing how much information people talked about freely in front of their household staff. Lovinia didn't know why it still surprised her—after all, it was why she had been assigned that mission—but each fresh realization incited a confusing mixture of both glee and contempt. She felt a flicker of excitement, too, at times.

Lovinia turned restlessly between the hot sheets. She had crept in through the back door, which had been kept open for her, waiting for the *Andukāraya* to come to bed. The clattering of swift feet above her head reassured her that the tiny gecko was busy hunting insects and cockroaches that inhabited the building.

Frustrated, she untangled herself from the thin sheet and the mosquito net and flung open the shutters to the sultry air. Thick with dew and the sweet perfume from the night-blooming jasmine tree, slightly tainted by cigar smoke, it stuck to her skin.

With the constant chirping of crickets, an owl called somewhere in the garden. Closer by, lowered male voices, conspicuous in the stillness, leaked from the open library doors in the next room. Lights streamed onto the lawn, and a tall shadow seemed to pace before the windows.

Her father had once told her that silence was the key to making a good deal which she had not understood at the time. But silence, she had learned, was key to being a good spy. The rustle of the leaves in gusts of sea breeze and the sound of the sea advancing and retreating up the beach made the words indistinct. She held her breath and pressed her ear as close to the curtains as she could.

The Major was talking now. Lovinia barely recognized his voice; the man she knew to be always good-humoured now sounded grim and authoritative.

'...my mission here...inquiry...Kandyan informant...during the war...

'Are you certain?' the *Andukāraya* sounded shocked, Lovinia thought. She strained to listen by leaning against the windowsill, but her heartbeat pounding in her ears made it hard to hear what was being said. Her hands curled into fists, nails sinking into the flesh of her palms. She strained her ears, trying to hear what was being said.

'The war office is as certain as possible... no formal accusation... further evidence...'

'...surely not... the regiment...'

'No, ...within the Company. ...tread very carefully ...investigation to find the leak.'

The Major must have moved closer to the window. 'That we immediately recall the battalion we sent to India and request the War Office to send us two more British regiments, your excellency. The French are sniffing around Trincomalee again, and I am certain they communicate with the Kandyan King.'

Lovinia suppressed a bitter laugh as she recalled Kumara's request from a few days before. *It will be an easy assignment, a simple passing of information, one that a person of your talents should be able to handle.* Her skin prickled with unease as she pressed against the window drapes hoping it would help her blend into the shadows. The rumble of deep voices continued, but Lovinia could no longer make out the words. Not long after, steps over the tile floor told of somebody leaving the house.

Exhaling, she sunk onto a chair. Guilt twinged inside her, but she pushed it back. She had been given no choice. She closed her eyes and focused her thoughts inward, taking a deep breath to quell her racing thoughts. She focused on the details she needed to remember. *They want more soldiers to come to the island. That would be something the Kandyan would want to know. What could it mean?* A prick of guilty conscience stung her for a second as it occurred to Lovinia that she was not supposed to hear this conversation. Were they involved in something risky? Was Kumara in danger? If that were the case, wouldn't she be in danger too?

She needed to get this information to Kumara. *But how?* Her nimble mind danced through a list of possibilities.

Had somebody on their side betrayed secrets to the enemy? Worry fluttered in her stomach, and her frustration grew. It was late in the night when she finally conceded herself, defeated by her inability to protect him. The gecko's clapping staccato lulled her into a troubled sleep.

CHAPTER 26

THE CHASE

Lovinia had just finished telling Kumara what she had overheard at the governor's residence when a sandaled foot came crashing to a stop on the empty seat nearby.

'If it isn't the beautiful girl with the barbed tongue,' a voice slurred from above.

When she gazed upward, her eyes thinned in disgust. It was the drunken lout who had accosted her a few days before.

'For drunken bastards for sure,' Lovinia retorted under her breath.

'Apparently, you are well known here,' Kumara said, the tension banding across his features.

'What?' the young man drawled, the wine impairing his comprehension.

"Never mind. What do you want?' Lovinia asked with a spark of annoyance. The young man was handsome in a vague, unmemorable way.

He leered down at her. 'I may have been a bit cheeky earlier, but I'd like to share an observation my friends and I have.' He gestured toward Kumara with his thumb. 'This one here? He seems entirely unsuitable for a woman like you… too old and ill-tempered by the looks of him. I think you're much better matched with a man with charm. Such as myself.'

At this, Kumara made a motion to stand. Lovinia placed her palm against his chest, her flashing eyes never wavering from the young man's glazed stare.

'You seem to have forgotten—in a rather short time. I might add—that you called my mother a whore. In what world do you think I would prefer you to any man, grumpy or not?'

He grinned at her, his friends behind him laughing at her audacity. 'Don't take it to heart, beautiful girl. What if I told you my mother was a whore? Would that make it better? In any case, I greatly appreciate women of that ilk.' He winked at her.

The laughter behind him grew louder. Again, Lovinia felt the fury beneath her palm as she pressed against Kumara, keeping him in his seat with nothing more than the force of her will.

She nodded. 'I can't say I'm surprised. As for me? I believe I'll leave this set of goods on the rack, as well. I have no interest in … tiny cucumbers.'

At this, Kumara's head twisted to hers, his eyes registering shock. And the edge of his lips twitched.

The silence around them was deafening for a painful beat. Then a wild chorus of amusement filled the air. The young man's friends slapped their knees and pounded one another's backs as they guffawed at his expense.

His face turned several shades of red once he comprehended the full breadth of Lovinia's insult. 'You—' He lunged for her.

Lovinia bolted out of the way. Kumara grabbed the man by the front of his vest and hurled him into his cluster of friends.

'Kumara!' Lovinia shouted. Once the young man managed to scramble to his feet, Kumara reared back and struck him in the jaw so hard he staggered into a table of rough-looking men, heavily engrossed in their dice match, with the betting at an all-time high. The coins and the dice crashed to the ground as the table shuddered under the young man's weight. The gamblers roared with rage as they shot to their feet, everything around them falling to shambles. Their precious game was destroyed beyond repair.

All eyes turned on Kumara. 'Oh, no,' Lovinia moaned.

With grim resignation, he reached for his sword.

'No, you idiot!' Lovinia gasped. 'Run!' Lovinia had often seen how such clashes usually ended. These hard-bitten men would use every dirty trick to overcome their opponents, and Lovinia didn't want to see Kumara die.

She grabbed his hand and spun away, the blood pounding through her body. 'Out of the way!' she shouted as they dodged past a vegetable cart, her feet flying above the dirt. The sound of the men after them only spurred her to go faster, especially with Kumara's longer strides driving them along the narrow thoroughfare of the market.

She pulled him back when he yanked her down a small alleyway. 'Do you know where you're going?' she demanded.

'For once in your life, could you stop talking and listen.'

'How dare you—' He wrapped his right arm around her and pressed their bodies together in a shadowed alcove. Then he thrust his index finger onto her lips.

Lovinia listened as their pursuers ran past the alleyway, still shouting and carrying on in a drunken haze. When the sounds faded away, he removed his finger from her lips. But it was too late. Because Lovinia could feel his heart beating faster. Just like hers.

'You were saying?' He was so close, his words more a whisper than sound.

'How dare you say that to me?' she scolded.

His eyes glittered with laughter. 'Are you implying you caused this mess?'

'Me? This is not my fault!' Lovinia snapped. 'This is your fault!'

Kumar opened his eyes wide. 'Mine?'

'Yes,' she said. 'You know, you have quite the temper.'

'No. You and your mouth.' He traced his finger across her lips.

Lovinia's heart thudded against his. When she peered up at him through her eyelashes, his hand at the small of her back pulled her closer. *Don't kiss me, Kumara. Please … don't.*

'They're here! I've found them!'

Kumara grasped her hand in his, and they again took off down the alleyway. 'We can't keep running,' he said over his shoulder. 'They will eventually catch us. We might have to stand and fight.'

Lovinia tugged on Kumara's arm, yanking him into a back alleyway leading away from the river. 'They won't find us here.'

They twisted and turned down the narrow passages until the pursuit noise died behind them. They finally stopped, huddled together in a darkened alcove.

'We are not far from the Inn of the Lion.' Kumara puffed out.

Lovinia trembled, still gasping for air. *They were safe.* Just as she was about to open her mouth to speak, Kumara closed them by kissing her hard. He shifted into her, trapping her against the brick wall of the alcove. His cloak was dark, his trousers, and his hair. With his head bent and her trapped before him, entirely shielded by his body, they should be invisible in the shadows. Even her lightly coloured face could catch a gleam from the smoky street flares.

Through the sensual haze of her brain, she heard the men's pounding footsteps nearby, heard them halt and swear at their disappearance.

'We'll never find them in this haze ... let's go back and start a new game.'

'Cunts! All of them,' one of the men swore. 'I was winning.'

'No way,' said another, panting. 'You never win.'

Kumara didn't lift his head until the men's voices were fading.

*

Kumara had to fight the distraction of her lips beneath his, ignore the temptation to taste her, try to blot out the sensation of her exceedingly feminine body pressed along the length of his, and concentrate, focus all his senses on what was happening in the street behind his back. He waited until the men's voices faded before lifting his head

Registering Lovinia's silence, Kumara looked down at her. Despite the shadows, he fell into the dark pools of her wide, stunned eyes. He felt her breasts quickly rise and fall, mashed against his chest. Saw her lips, lush and ripe, full and parted in the poor light. Beckoning.

He saw the tip of her tongue glide over her lower lip, making the lusciousness glisten. He didn't need to kiss her again, yet he did. It wasn't a simple kiss but one fuelled by anger and relief. And by something he didn't understand—that something she and only she evoked and set pounding in his blood.

Her lips had been parted; he filled her mouth, stole her breath, and then gave it back. He deliberately lingered, tasted, and explored. He tightened his fingers on hers, kept their hands safely locked, arms down, even though every instinct pushed him to free his hands and seize her, hold her, bring her close—much closer.

He wanted her, and that want was open, undisguised, in every bold stroke of his tongue, in the demanding pressure of his lips on hers. In the hard ridge that pressed against her belly. Yet she couldn't back away, pull back—end this unwise kiss because she didn't want to. Because there was, it seemed no force within her was powerful enough to counter the pull of it and him.

Kumara found himself in the unaccustomed position of forcing himself to end a kiss that promised so much more, leaving him aching and hungry for much more. A 'more' he now was sure he could have, but while this seemed the right time, it wasn't the right place.

Drawing back from the exchange, limited though it had been, was hard enough. Lifting his head, Kumara looked down into her face at the fluttered lashes that lifted, revealing eyes clouded with rising passion. Her lips were lightly swollen, sheening from his kiss.

Stepping back was much harder, losing the elementally feminine cushion of her curves. This evocative softness cradled Kumara's hard frame. Easing back, subduing his rising clawing need, took more effort than he'd imagined, but he finally moved back. Then, releasing one of her hands, he turned and stepped out of the alcove.

After checking that they were safe, he drew her out without a word and led her by her hand. They reached the end of the alley and stepped into a wider street.

Looking left, he saw the spires of a Christian church rising through the low-hanging fog and thanked heaven for a forester's sense of direction. He glanced back down the lane, then pulled Lovinia toward the church, assessing the possibilities. He was so intent on the news Lovinia had brought and what he was doing that he didn't notice the men who followed them.

CHAPTER 27

THE TUNNEL

The country mansion was a charming residence overhanging the sea, with all the beauty of a small hill and valley, woods, rocks, a beautiful beach, and a fine open sea.

The recently whitewashed walls gleamed in the sunlight. The heavy front doors and the shutters on the windows were teak. Above them were elaborate, floral-patterned fanlights of stained glass. Inside, a wide wooden staircase with a red carpet in the middle rose from the foyer to a large landing. Doors led into the ballroom and the banquet hall on either side. Sunlight streamed down onto the landing through a stained-glass skylight.

From the landing, two sets of stairs curved in each direction, only to meet again on the next floor. There was a large foyer with doors to the bedrooms on either side. French doors opened onto the balcony above the front porch at the far end, commanding views of pretty hills and valleys filled with tall palm trees. Another set of doors led to a long balcony overlooking the ocean.

Thomas had arrived from Colombo the previous evening. It had become dark before reaching Galkissa, but the woods suddenly blazed to life upon passing a village. Eighteen or twenty villagers ran out of their houses with bundles of lighted palm leaves and preceded them to the next hamlet. They were relieved by others and so on until they arrived at Galkissa.

Thomas learned that the provision of illumination at night for persons of consequence in government was a tribute from the fishermen, which started during the Dutch government, which required the fishing colonies on the road to Point de Galle to provide such a service. The illumination surpassed anything Thomas had ever experienced.

To distract himself, he let his eyes wander about the room. Its walls were decorated with tapestries; fine rugs lay on the marble floor. A large window filled the room with light, catching the golden hues sweeping the sky before sunset. The window looked down to the sea beyond, stretching out in a gilded blue across the horizon. On one side of the room were two long chairs with several plump silk cushions arranged around a low table.

On the other side of the room stood a pair of bookcases, sagging under the weight of their tomes. Between the bookcases, a purple curtain concealed a doorway leading to another room. A well-ordered writing desk and accompanying chair occupied the corner beneath the window so he could sit and gaze across the water when he lifted his eyes from his papers.

He had returned to his office determined to put his worries behind him, but he had no sooner sat down when someone knocked at his door, and his secretary stuck his head in. 'Sir, have you got a moment?' he asked.

'Certainly, Mr Brewer,' Thomas replied as he sat back in his chair. 'Come in. Please sit down. What can I do for you?"

Brewer took his seat in front of the governor's oak desk and looked down at his hands, uncertain how to begin. Thomas decided to wait him out. He had never seen the young man this unsure of himself, and he wondered what the cause could be.

'Your Excellency,' Brewer hesitated. "Umm, I have come into possession of some information I feel you should know, although I fear I may lose your confidence when you learn how I got it.'

Thomas was mildly puzzled by Brewer's statement but decided that speculation would be a waste of time. 'Please go on, Mr Brewer. What is the information?'

Brewer straightened in his chair and looked at Thomas. 'My Lord, I have reason to believe that a plan is afoot to compromise your position with the foreign office in London.'

Thomas's eyebrows shot up in surprise. Whatever he had expected Brewer to say, it was not this!

'Compromise me?' he questioned. Thomas studied Brewer, who was looking down at his hands. 'I think perhaps you had better tell me the whole story.'

'Aye-aye, sir,' Brewer said, taking a deep breath before launching into his story.

'I have been seeing Mister Hetherington's daughter for a few months without her father knowing,' Brewer said, watching Thomas. 'She happened to mention the last time we met that she had overheard her father talking to one of his men about your excellency, sir.'

Thomas could see that the young man was fidgeting in his chair. He was struggling to say what he wanted to say.

'Spit it out, man,' Thomas snapped. 'What is it that bothers you so much?'

Brewer took a deep breath. 'He wants to investigate rumours of a relationship between your excellency and a local woman.'

Thomas looked at his desk, his mind trying to understand what young Brewer had said. His affair with Lovinia was not something he wanted to be made public. However, he was under no illusion that such a relationship would be used against him. It seemed plausible that the girl had overheard something her father had said. Still, it was just as possible she'd overheard nothing. Unfortunately, whatever it was she had overheard, it was not something he could afford to ignore.

'You were right to bring this to my attention,' Thomas said, looking up. 'Was there anything more?'

'I asked her who it was her father was speaking to, but she did not know. That was when she changed the subject, and I did not want to press her.'

Given his proposal to reform the civil service, Thomas realised that the Chief Justice could and would try to discredit him in the eyes of the foreign office. He had underestimated the man, and it was only by sheer luck that his scheme to undermine him had come to light.

Thomas leaned forward on his chair, silent for a moment. 'Thank you, Mr Brewer,' Thomas said. 'You did well not to push the lass. I count on your absolute discretion on this matter.'

'Aye-aye, Sir,' Brewer said as he rose to leave the room.

Thomas's voice stopped him. 'And Mr Brewer, be very careful when next you see this girl. She must not go back to her father with tales of your curiosity about what she told you. One remark from her within those walls and our only source of information will dry up.'

'Yes, your excellency,' Brewer nodded.

After his secretary left the room, Thomas got up to pace his office. He used pacing as a time of intense concentration, during which he tore a problem apart and looked at it from every angle. He wondered who was passing information to the Chief Justice for a moment but immediately discarded the line of thought. He was sure there were people in his household who were paid to report on his movements, and looking for them would not solve the problem as others would be recruited to replace them.

Thomas opened the door to the balcony overlooking the sea and stepped outside. It was a hot and humid morning with tall rain clouds looming on the horizon. Not a breath of air assisted the heaviness in the air. From where he was standing, he could see labourers, sweat pouring down their backs, working on the garden surrounding the building, which was nearing completion.

I need to take some action! He wished he could bring in the Hetherington girl and press her for more information, but he knew that would yield him nothing and would only serve to alert her father. *No, I need to be careful.*

He swatted at some insects that suddenly swarmed around his head. They seemed attracted to his white skin, and he'd recently been bitten by a few mosquitoes. He returned to the coolness of his study, shutting the door firmly behind him.

*

The feel of the cooling salves and the sharp razor sliding over his chin restored a sense of normality to the day. He was grateful for the barber's silence, which enabled him to compose himself.

As the fragrance of sandalwood from the last lotion filled the air, Thomas stood up, running a hand over his jaw. He stared into the empty fireplace, trying to organize his thoughts. Reluctantly he concluded that he needed to stop seeing Lovinia until he could find a way to meet her without anyone knowing.

After a late breakfast of fruit, buffalo milk curd, and hoppers–lacy, biscuity baskets with eggs inside, which Thomas dug into with muted enthusiasm, his mind was busy formulating a plan.

Thomas rang the bell on his desk and waited, tapping the arm of his chair until Brewer entered the room. 'Could you bring me the plans for my country residence and a topographical map of the area?'

Thomas carefully studied the map by spreading the two documents Brewer brought to his table. His fingers traced the contours around the hilly outcrop where he lived, finally stopping on the road to Point de Galle.

'Hmmm.' The distance, he estimated, was less than a third of a mile.

It would work, he decided, straightening up. He had participated in campaigns in Saint-Domingue and India on various sieges where experienced military sappers bored long tunnels under enemy fortifications to undermine and collapse them.

Thomas rang the bell on his desk, summoning Brewer.

'Could you ask Major Staples to join me?'

Major Staples must have been out riding as he eventually appeared dressed in riding breeches and boots. 'I am sorry for the delay, your excellency. I was breaking in one of my new mounts.'

Thomas waved away his apology. He did not expect his staff to wait for him to call them. He recalled when he was a junior officer in India in the service of the Governor in Bombay. The man used to berate his officers mercilessly if they did not appear immediately after they were summoned.

'Please sit down, Major,' Thomas indicated the empty chair at his desk.

'You are from the Royal Engineers and have been serving on the island for a few years,' Thomas stated. 'I presume you know all the units which serve on the island.'

'Yes, sir,' the major nodded. 'It's been almost four years since I was assigned here.'

'Are there any sappers in our muster roll?'

Major Staples looked surprised at his question. His brows creased as he searched for an answer. 'I don't think so, sir. We have a pioneer battalion, but we've not needed sappers on our campaigns.'

Thomas was not surprised by the Major's answer. He couldn't remember any such unit on the military register. He steepled his hands while holding the Major's gaze. 'Are there any Welshman on any of the regiment rosters?'

Thomas had served with the Royal Welch Fusiliers in Santa Domingo. He had come to appreciate their ability to tunnel under fortifications that had withstood constant bombardment.

'I know a Captain Davies who is from Cardiff, your excellency. There may be others I am not aware of.'

Thomas studied the Major contemplating whether he should take him into his confidence. Making up his mind, Thomas stood and walked around his desk.

'You know I am friends with a local woman who visits me in my quarters.' He let the question hang in the air for a moment.

The Major looked up at Thomas standing next to him. 'Err, yes, I do, your excellency. It's my job to know everyone who meets you.'

Thomas nodded. It was what he had expected.

'I have been advised that news of this, ummm, friendship has reached the ears of the Chief Justice, who wants to use it against me.'

The Major jumped to his feet. 'I hope you don't think it's me, sir.' He looked like he had just swallowed something unpleasant.

'That's not what this is about,' Thomas said but was interrupted by the Major before he could complete the sentence.

'I wouldn't do any such thing. I can assure you, sir. What anyone wants to do privately is his business and no one else's.'

'I know it's not you,' Thomas said placatingly. 'You have proven to be a valuable aide, and I have recommended a promotion which I am sure will be approved in due course.'

Thomas noticed a shadow pass over the Major's face before he took a deep breath. 'Thank you, your excellency.' However, his gaze remained fixed on Thomas. 'How can I help, sir.'

'I asked about the Welsh because I know they are excellent miners. In my last posting, I served with the Royal Welch and greatly regarded their tunnelling abilities.'

'Tunnelling, sir?' The Major's brow furrowed as he thought about what he had just heard.

'Yes, Major,' Thomas said, pursing his lips. 'It seems I cannot be open when meeting my local friend, but I don't want to stop seeing her, so I've decided to see her without anyone knowing.'

Major Staples looked confused but nodded without saying anything.

'I want a tunnel built from the cellar of this house to a point near the village where she lives. A tunnel that could be used by my lady friend to visit me without being seen.'

The Major raised his eyebrows but kept quiet. Thomas could see that he was thinking about what he'd just revealed.

'I need you to arrange for the tunnel to be built secretly,' said Thomas observing the major as he spoke. 'You can tell anyone who needs to know that it is an escape route I requested as part of the safety arrangements being put in place. That's why it's better to use some Welsh lads and order them to keep their mouths shut.'

The Major nodded in agreement.

'I will lighten your duties until the work is done. I will talk to the quartermaster about seconding the men you choose under your direct command.'

A few moments of silence ensued.

'John, you must keep this matter entirely between yourself and me. Tell no one else, do you understand.'

CHAPTER 28

THE ESCAPE

Lovinia closed her eyes and focused her thoughts inward, taking a deep breath to quell her racing thoughts. She barely had time to recover her composure before they hurried down the alley to a broader street. Her pulse was still pounding with suppressed anger and unslaked passion.

She recognized both and knew which was the safer to address. While she could understand, even without his explanation, why he'd kissed her the first time, she couldn't explain and didn't want to think about why he'd kissed her again. The second time. That second, much more thorough time.

Lovinia had no difficulty reading his desire, recognizing it—along with the response that raced through her. Hot, spontaneous, and strong. She wanted him, and that was dangerous. But this was not the time to dwell on it. They were still not out of danger.

They hurried down the street, leading to a broader, more used thoroughfare towards the south, towards her village in Galkissa. The road became less crowded as they moved out of the city precincts into the cinnamon gardens dotted with the homes of wealthy Europeans.

Lovinia's cat-like senses did not miss the stealthy footsteps behind them. 'Don't look back,' she whispered. 'Someone's following.'

There weren't any places to hide on the road lit by smoky flares. She reached between her legs and pulled the dagger strapped to her thigh.

'Urgh,' Kumara grunted without looking back. Lovinia saw him place a hand on the hilt of his sword.

They hurried forward, closing the distance between them. Kumara put his arm protectively across her shoulders and pulled her close. 'Can you tell how many they are?'

'A few,' she whispered. 'Not more than two or three, I think.'

They hurried up a small hill until a church loomed out of the fog, a faint light shining through the tall narrow windows. Kumara quickened his pace, pushing her ahead of him. She felt herself leaning into him, accepting his protection. He smelled of sandalwood. Strange that she'd never noticed before—

They had arrived at the building, its thick crenellated stone walls inviting, offering a place of refuge. It was surrounded by a garden on one side and a cemetery on the other. They slipped inside the half-open door and pushed it shut behind them, the hinges squealing softly.

'There's no bolt,' Lovina said, looking around. The inside of the church was bare and functional, empty of any furniture. Its only redeeming feature was the stained-glass window above the pulpit. Light from the tall candles on the simple altar left deep shadows along yellow-washed walls and round wooden pillars holding the roof up. Two lavender and black doors on either side of a red-flagged floor diagonally picked out with lime gleamed in the flickering light.

'I know this place. Come.'

Kumara dragged her by the arm to a small wooden door in the darkened corner of the large room where the candlelight didn't quite reach. It opened quietly at their touch. Kumara closed the door behind them, and they felt their way up a narrow dark staircase leading up to a flat landing from which ropes disappeared into the darkness above.

'They may not have seen us enter the church,' Kumara said, his mouth close to her ear. 'We should be safe here.'

Lovinia felt safe in Kumara's arms, but their position signified so much to her. *Much to lose.* Her lips pressed tight, her eyes scanning her new surroundings. She pulled the *pallu* of her saree closer, tucking the dagger into the waistband of her underskirt. *Much to fight for.*

A faint light filtered from a small window that overlooked the church's nave.

'Do you know these men who follow you?'

Her eyes adjusted to the alcove's darkness, and Lovinia could see Kumara shaking his head. 'No. I don't know who they are. I was warned that men were hunting me,' he said. 'They must be working for the British.'

Lovinia tensed, hearing a noise from below her feet. The door. *Someone was opening the church door.* Her stomach gave a nasty tumble, and she inhaled sharply. She felt the panic rise and wanted to scream but forced the feeling down, knowing it would do no good.

Kumara pulled her close, sensing her disquiet.

Soft footsteps and the sound of a man's voice.

'*Adakah mereka dating ke sini?*' Did they come here?

'Malays ... soldiers, I think.' Lovinia had heard Malay being spoken but didn't understand the language. She knew that professional soldiers from the islands in the east who sold their swords to the highest bidders usually spoke it.

'Yes,' Kumara whispered in her ear. 'They're not sure where we are.'

Lovinia was not surprised that Kumara could understand the language. He seemed to be a man with many talents.

'*Jom Cari tempat.*'

'They want to search the church,' Kumara said in a low voice. 'We can watch from here.'

They shifted to the narrow window overlooking the church nave as two men came into view. They were dressed in ragged military coats and pants. Both carried swords in their hands, and one had a musket slung across his back.

The two men spread out, looking behind the pillars and searching behind the altar. '*Tiada sesiapa di sini.*' There's no one here. '*Jom cari tanah perkuburan.*' Let's search the cemetery.

The men opened a side door and slipped out without noticing the low turret door hidden in the dark corner.

Lovinia had not realised she'd been holding her breath. She gasped, filling her lungs with air. 'Why are these men looking for you?' she questioned. 'They are *ja-minussu* (mercenary soldiers from Java), not men who serve in the British army.'

'Yes,' Kumara agreed. 'Which makes it stranger. But seeing them has given me a thought.'

Lovinia waited for Kumara to say more, but he didn't say a single word. Fuelled by a senseless fury, she snapped, 'Is it something I need to worry about?'

'This habit of yours putting yourself in danger has got to stop,' Kumara said, changing the subject.

'This has nothing to do with what occurred in the market,' Lovinia said, pushing him away. 'And you know it.'

'There was no need to provoke that young man which led to all this,' he shrugged. 'It's my job to keep you safe.'

'Is that what the kiss was all about, then? The second kiss. Protecting me?' Lovinia heard her voice rise.

Kumara tightened his grip on her arm. 'Keep your voice down,' he cautioned. 'Those men may not have gone far.'

'Why are they following you?' Lovinia asked again. She wouldn't let him treat her like some piece of meat that could be discarded at any time. She was risking her life spying for him, and she wanted to know why.

Kumara sighed, realising she would not allow him to hide the truth. 'They look like soldiers who served the King in Kandy,' he said. 'There was a group of them who fell out of favour recently, and it seems the British are using them to hunt me.'

Lovinia arched an eyebrow. 'Can they recognise you?' she asked, knowing the answer.

'Yes, they would have seen me at the palace.'

'What are you going to do about it?' Lovinia asked anxiously. 'You cannot lead them to me or my village.'

'I cannot,' Kumara agreed. 'But let's try and solve one problem at a time. We must get out of here before they bring more men to search the area.'

They left the sanctuary of the church without being spotted. Kumara led them in silent haste through a warren of alleys and streets, twisting back down the hill to Galkissa, all thoughts of spending any more time together forgotten.

Only one thought constantly preyed on Lovinia's mind. The desire.

CHAPTER 29

THE ILLNESS

It was dark when Thomas returned to his residence. He found a packet of letters from England awaiting him. He left them where they lay, too tired to read them now. He had a thumping headache, and there was plenty of time the next day to find out what was happening outside the East.

He had spent the entire day drawing up plans with his general staff to send a contingent of troops to southern India to quell a mutiny. The request came from the recently appointed Governor of Madras. It was not a rebellion by the Indian sepoys as it had been in the past but a revolt by their discontented European officers against a series of ill-judged and repulsive actions in the name of the economy. These measures caused great dissatisfaction among every European officer of all ranks in the Madras army, leading them to revolt against the civilian government.

During the night, a reinforced regiment of mixed *Kaffir* and British troops were scheduled to embark on their way to Travancore to support loyal troops from the government in their effort to overcome the rebels. He signed the orders against his better judgement as it would leave the island dangerously vulnerable with only a single British regiment and a collection of Malay, *Sepoy* (Indian) and *Lascarin* (Sinhalese) battalions to defend the island. Thomas decided he would write to the foreign office the next morning asking about his request to station two more English regiments in Ceylon, especially if he was expected to keep supplying troops to India wherever there was a problem.

Thomas suddenly began to feel sick, very sick. He began sweating profusely and was soaked to the skin. His head thumping with pain, he rolled up in his cloak and flopped down on his bed.

He awoke before daybreak feeling cold. His bedclothes were saturated in sweat, and he shivered uncontrollably. The sunblind was raised from the night before, and the air was still cool. Feeling damp and dirty, he attempted to get out of bed, but the pain banged inside his head. He felt weak as he reached for the cord summoning his manservant before collapsing on the bed.

Thomas awoke with Johnson bending over him, a hand on his brow. He blinked in puzzlement, unable to understand why his manservant's face was shrouded in fog.

'Fever,' Johnson said, turning to the steward beside him. 'Make speed an' tell Surgeon Anderson that the Governor is lying in filthy clothes shiverin' and shakin' with fever.'

Thomas must have drifted off again and awoke when Surgeon Major Anderson arrived at the double, his face white with apprehension as he examined his patient.

'Malaria,' he said finally.

*

Johnson stared hard at the Governor, at the dark patches under his closed eyes. His tanned skin had a grey hue, his face drenched in sweat, and every breath he drew sounded like a strangled rasp. Johnson guessed he was dehydrated by the way he kept licking his lips. He had seen men suffering the disease before, and he knew some did not recover.

Johnson whispered. 'Will he make it?'

'Hopefully,' Dr Anderson replied. 'He is fit and strong, which always helps. I've given him a large dose of quinine, mercury, and a few opium pills to relieve the headaches. But he is dangerously ill and could take a fatal turn for the worse. He will need someone to look after him day and night. I'll try and get one of the nurses from the hospital to come over.'

'He's already got one,' Johnson said stoutly. 'He's got me, hasn't he?'

After a pause, Dr Anderson nodded tiredly. 'Very well, I shall arrange it with Major Staples to relieve you of all your other duties.'

'Aye, do that,' Johnson said. 'And while you're at it, mebbe ye could tell him to arrange for a couple of coolies to come and help me clean up this bed.'

'I'll send some coolies,' Dr Anderson said, leaving.

'An' a few blankets,' Johnson called after him. 'He'll need a few more clean blankets to keep him comfortable when the shivering gets bad. And water! I'll need water to keep his face freshly sponged and cool. You'll see to that an all, will you?'

At the door, the military surgeon stopped in his tracks, staring at the audacious manservant, eyeing him up and down as if unable to believe his insolence.

'Oh – and some tea!' Johnson added. 'If I'm stayin' here awhile, I'll need a drop of the auld life saver.'

Johnson grinned as Dr Anderson turned and thrust himself out the door before his patience and temper escaped him.

*

'The *Andukāraya* has *Kale Una* (Forest fever),' Juana said, clasping Lovinia's hand in her own.

The mestizo wife of the governor's manservant came around from time to time to converse with Lovinia in English. Lovinia had never seen her so distraught when she answered the knock on her door that morning.

'What do you mean?' Lovinia responded, her mind not quite making the connection. She had been awaiting the *Andukāraya's* summons but had not heard from him. It was not unusual for him to neglect her for days at times when he was busy.

'English army doctors are treating him,' Juana said, her mouth tight. She tightened the grip on Lovina's hand. 'But the treatment does not seem to be working,' she added.

Juana's words suddenly registered with Lovinia. No one was immune to the mosquito-borne disease, which always appeared during the rainy season. It was not common for people to suffer from the disease along the coastal belt. Lovinia remembered the lake and canals surrounding the city, which would be a breeding ground for mosquitos.

'How long has he had it?'

Juana explained that the *Andukāraya* had fallen ill a couple of days ago and that her husband was looking after him. The English doctors had been treating him with western medicines, but he was not responding to them and was getting worse. 'He has lost a lot of weight, and they cannot get his fever down.'

'We need Aletta,' Lovinia cried. 'She'll know what ayurvedic medicines we could use to help him.'

Aletta had gone to the market that morning, and Lovinia and Juana paced the room as they waited for her to return.

'*Rasakinda* (giloy), *inguru* (ginger) and *kottamalli* (coriander).' Aletta didn't wait for a response. 'We must prepare an infusion of all three, but it will take time.'

Aletta hurried into her room to get two small baskets of dried palm leaves. She handed one to Lovinia. 'Go to the market and get five or more of the freshest *inguru* (ginger) you can find,' indicating the size she wanted with her hands. 'I got some *kottamalli* (coriander) for us this morning, but it won't be enough. Get three more bundles. We need to make more cups of tea over the next few days.'

Lovinia nodded. She had seen Aletta when she was like this. Nothing would distract her from what she was doing.

'Juana! You must go back to your husband and ask him to make sure the *Andukāraya* drinks lots of water. He needs to replenish the liquids in his body.' When she saw Juana nod in acknowledgement, she continued. 'Tell him we will need about twelve hours to prepare the infusion.'

Her orders given, Aletta picked up the second basket and headed out the door. 'I will get the *Rasakinda* myself. I know where it's growing.'

By midday, both Aletta and Lovinia were back with their respective purchases. Banda was commandeered to collect wood for a fire while the two women washed and finely chopped the herbs. Aletta immediately began crushing the chopped pieces into a thick paste using a granite hand mortar and pestle.

'This has to be a fine paste,' she grunted, alternately pounding and grinding the pieces into the heavy stone implement. Once it was ready, she used her hands to form the thick paste into an aromatic *gulli* (ball)

Banda had built a low fire outside the back door by the time the mixture was ready. The ball of fine paste was stirred into a clay pot with eight cups of cold water and placed on the fire.

'It must boil slowly until it comes down to one cup,' Aletta said, stirring the concoction. 'It will be bitter and much easier to drink if we add some honey.'

Lovinia nodded as she hastened back to the market. She had seen a woman selling small jars of bee's honey that morning.

Various thoughts were running through her mind as she walked down the street. *I need to get this news to Kumara.* But she didn't want to go into the city looking for him. They were supposed to meet the next day, and the information could wait until then.

*

Thomas woke with a bad taste in his mouth. The fog in his mind had disappeared, and his eyes focused on the rectangular punkah swinging slowly above him. He must have been sick. He could ascertain that much by the weakness in his body, but he couldn't remember much. The days were all blurred into one. He only remembered being forced to drink a foul-tasting liquid, hoping he would not endure that again.

Thomas tried to remember what day it was, but his head hurt with a dull throbbing ache which erased any thoughts. He turned his head slowly to see Johnson staring at him with a concerned look.

'How are you feeling, Sah?'

'Was I sick?' he croaked. The effort of speaking made him breathless.

'Malaria, suh,' Johnson responded, his eyes crinkling. 'It was uncertain there for a while, but you seem to have gotten past the worst.'

Thomas closed his eyes. The effort of keeping them open tired him immeasurably.

'Let me get you a sip of water.'

Thomas felt his head being lifted. A cup nudged his lips, dribbling the water onto his parched lips, allowing him to sip the cool liquid.

'Don't drink too much, Sah,' Johnson admonished from above. 'Doctor's order, Suh.'

Thomas opened his eyes a crack. The cool water made him feel a bit better. "How long have I been like this?' he whispered.

'Over a week, Sah.'

'That long!' Thomas couldn't comprehend that he had been sick for so many days. He couldn't remember anything.

'Yes, Sah,' Johnson grumbled. 'You only turned the corner after we gave you some herbal medicine prepared by one of the local women.'

Before Thomas could ask Johnson what he meant, he was interrupted by an authoritative voice.

'Rubbish, man. Don't fill the governor's head with all that mumbo jumbo.'

Dr Anderson's face replaced Johnson's above him.

'Quinine is what saved you, your excellency. The new wonder drug makes all the difference in treating malaria patients. How are you feeling?'

Dr Anderson fussed around him, taking his temperature and using his stethoscope to listen to his lungs. 'Better, he muttered, 'much better.'

The doctor's face withdrew from Thomas's view.

'Has he been complaining of any pain?' he heard the doctor ask.

'No, Sah. He just woke up.'

'Good, good,' the doctor said. 'Give him an opium tablet if he complains of a headache. I will administer another draft of quinine....'

Thomas closed his eyes. He felt so tired ....

CHAPTER 30

THE MANHUNT

If Ceylon was an island whose shores the peoples of half the known world washed up, then the Hellfire Tavern was where the scum settled. It was a drinking establishment located off an alley that ran to one side of the dead end of a side street in the heart of the oldest, filthiest quarter of the city. It not only sold what passed for alcohol but also satisfied the most depraved fantasies anyone could think of. The payment of large bribes to several individuals contributed to the tavern's continuing existence since the individuals in question were regular patrons.

Captain Noordeen was getting impatient. He had been given a job, and it offended his sensibilities that he could not finish the task. He sat near the back wall with his lieutenant on one of the tables.

The tavern's main saloon played host to a motley assortment of mercenaries, smugglers, slave traders, merchants and seamen of every type, rank, and race. They were attended to by tired-looking, disease-ridden whores circulating the room. The air was thick with the pungent aromas of tobacco smoke, *ganja* weed, unwashed bodies, stale liquor, and the sinus-clearing perfumes with which the ladies doused themselves after every customer.

The Captain was an intimidating figure with a thick neck and calloused hands. He had only one eye, the right socket simply a pit covered with scar tissue. His skin was pockmarked. He was dressed in a faded green military coat, tight pantaloons displaying well-muscled thighs and wearing a round cap on his head. Sharp-featured and oval-faced, his dark black hair cascaded in loose curls over his shoulders. A stained white scabbard with a military sword hung on a leather sword belt strapped over his shoulder.

Earlier that day, he had met with the man who held the future of his men and their families in his hands. It won't be long before we find him, he had tried to reassure the Englishman, but Noordeen could sense the other man's scepticism.

His men had been looking for the Kandyan, but he was like a wisp of smoke that came and went before you could grasp it. Even the fortune in bribes they had doled out around the city had not made any difference.

The Kandyan had always been an enigma to the Captain. He remembered when working in Kandy for the King. He seemed to have almost a magical ability to sense danger, making him extremely valuable as a spy. He had been allowed access to the Royal quarters at will and blamed the man for the misfortune that had led the King to turn against him and his men.

'We'll get him, don't worry,' Puteri, his lieutenant, said. The two were waiting for a local man who had passed on a message saying he knew where the Kandyan was hiding.

'We should have eliminated him when we had the chance.' Puteri said, taking a long drink from his tankard of beer. He wiped his frothy mouth with the back of his hand, giving a loud burp.

His lieutenant was referring to the time they had crossed the man when they had refused him access to the King. After that, the Chief *Adigar* went out of his way to make life hell, finally leading to them leaving Kandy and escaping to the coast.

'Don't be stupid,' Captain Noordeen said. 'If he was already dead, why would the Britishers give us money to find him?'

The Captain shook his head in disgust. With men like this, it was no wonder the Kandyan could easily elude them.

A man dressed in a stained banion suddenly appeared in front of them. He had a thin long skinning knife tucked into the waistband of his sarong. He was dark and weather-beaten, his wrinkle-lined face framing deep-set eyes.

'Are you the men looking for the Kandyan?' He spoke in Sinhalese and stood waiting, looking from one to the other.

'And you are?' Captain Noordeen nodded, gesturing for the man to sit down.

'I am Ashok, from Preethipura,' the man said, accepting the captain's invitation. 'I was told you will pay for the information you seek?'

'Yes,' Captain Noordeen reached for the purse tucked into his waist, pulling out a silver coin which he held up to the man. 'Tell me what you know.'

The man reached for the coin, but the captain pulled his hand away. 'You get your reward, but I want first to know what you know.'

The man looked around the room before lowering his head, indicating for Noordeen to do the same. 'I have seen him with my own eyes,' he whispered. 'He comes and goes, sometimes for days, but he always returns to the same place to rest.'

'And where is this place,' Noordeen asked, glancing at Puteri. This was the best information they had received so far.

'I will only tell you once I get paid,' the man said. 'And one coin won't be enough.'

'That wasn't the deal,' Captain Noordeen said.

'I'll take you to where he stays,' the man offered. 'You pay me one coin now and another when you catch him.'

The Captain thought for a moment and flipped the silver coin onto the table. 'If you're lying, you won't see the night out,' he said.

He stood up, stretching his arms. He felt suddenly at ease, knowing he was close to catching the Kandyan. The Englishman had ordered him not to kill the man but injuring him severely was not mentioned. He smiled, already looking forward to when he got his hands on the man.

CHAPTER 31

THE AMBUSH

Jampettah Street was a jumble of shops, kiosks, and stalls where bakers, ironsmiths, and bootmakers traded next to potters, spice and garment merchants. There were wine merchants, goldsmiths, jewellery, ornaments made by the town's silversmiths, and intricately carved ebony elephants. In the bazaars, haggling was heard in Sinhalese, Tamil, Hindi, Malay, Arabic, Farsi, Dutch, and Creole over sugar, salt, flour, rice, spices, vegetables, porcelain, rugs, and silk.

Kumara dodged through the traffic, the noise and the smells overwhelming. Fleeting impressions of street performers, wretched beggars, and swift pickpockets fused into a racket. Fresh fruits, spices, and animal droppings took turns to tease and sting his nose. He passed chophouses, cabinetmakers, and undertakers. Outside a weaver's shop, a rainbow of sheer sarees floated in the wind, translucent and glimmering like jewels.

He walked through a dusty market and its fantastic variety of brightly coloured goods – a clashing kaleidoscope of smells and sounds. Kumara stopped outside a shop with a glass window with beautifully embroidered goods on sale to see whether he was being followed. He could not spot anyone on the crowded street behind him and continued. He stopped at a food stall to buy a packet of rice and curry wrapped in a banana leaf, held together by a thin strip of plantain bark, which he tucked into the cloth bag over his shoulder.

The news Lovinia had given him that the *Andukāraya* was badly ill with malaria was unexpected, and he needed time to think of all its possible ramifications. One thing was sure. Lovinia would not have access to him until he recovered – if he did recover. He had heard of *parangi* (white men) catching the disease and being sent back to their country to recover. He knew nothing of what Lovinia had overheard about the English spy. Kumara had always suspected that someone high up was feeding the Chinaman high-level information but had never questioned the man. It was not his place to do so.

Lost in his thoughts, he found himself approaching a small square shaded by a makeshift palm roof next to a neglected Catholic church built by the Portuguese. Fishermen always sold the night's catch here. Baskets of prawns, shrimp, lobsters, and squid were already displayed. Huge, silvery tuna lay on the ground, their scales still shining, and white-bellied skates were ready for gutting under the critical eye of local women. Crows and egrets hovered, ready to pounce, scavenging for fish scraps. The overpowering stench of rotting fish masked the salty-sweet tang of the sea.

Kumara had to cross this square to get to his hideaway. It was empty this evening except for sleeping mongrel dogs, but the smell was even more pungent than usual. His head still lowered, holding his nose with one hand, and waving away flies with the other. He quickened his pace between the dead fish and through slicks of blood and sludge.

The sun was slowly setting as he opened the gate and approached the small hut he rented from the fishing clan. Two fat pigs grunted contentedly from their pen in the corner of the yard. A clutch of plump hens scratched in the dirt under the coconut trees, and a small white goat bleated for attention as it strained against its tether.

Kumara strode up to the door, then hovered uncertainly. There was an itch between his shoulders which made him feel unsafe. He looked over his shoulder back at the way he came. *Nothing.* He had chosen this place to hide because of the clannish nature of the fishermen. They would not let anyone within the perimeter of their village for no reason.

Unless it was for money! The thought came unbidden to his mind, and the more he thought about it, the more it made sense. The Javanese mercenaries who had escaped from the Sinhalese king's wrath. The number of people being paid to look for him. The British must have been spending money for his capture.

Instead of opening the door to his hut, he stepped around the corner into the backyard, which he crossed in three long strides, pushing aside the flimsy *cadjan* (plaited palm leaf) fence, which he rearranged carefully behind him.

Kumara lowered himself to his haunches and studied his surroundings. The fishing village backed onto a large grove of coconut trees which led to a canal about a hundred yards away built by the Dutch. Close to the village, the floor was sandy and dry, stamped down by the passage of many feet. He couldn't see anybody, which was strange. At this time of the day, the men would prepare to go out to sea for the night, storing their nets in the boats pulled up on the beach. He strained to listen to anything unusual, but the only sounds he could hear were the domestic yard animals and those of insects and birds high above in the tops of the coconut trees.

I'll have to leave this place. I've stayed here too long.

Of course, he will have to leave the village and find somewhere else. But he needed to be sure that he would not be followed.

Dusk came quickly as the day's heat and humidity created beautiful clouds on the horizon that picked up the sun's fading colours. Kumara retreated to the edge of the coconut grove without raising himself and positioned himself behind a mature coconut tree trunk.

Above him, the night sky was almost clear, the black shadows of the clouds partially obscuring the half-moon that tried to shine through. It provided enough light to glimmer off the dark sea, lifting and dancing on the small crests of wavelets that advanced and retreated on the white beach. The smell of the seaweed and seawater was strong with the taste of salt while the light breeze rustled the leaves of the coconut palms above him.

He had not eaten all day, so he opened the packet of food he carried in his bag and ate with his fingers, discarding the wrappings after wiping his hands. Feeling a bit better, he decided to retreat into the coconut grove to continue to watch the village, especially his hut, which was just a dark blob in the moonlight.

Kumara's eyes started to close, his chin dropping to his chest as the night dragged on. The fishing village was strangely silent. No fishing boats had set sail that evening despite the partially clear night and light sea breeze, which would have been ideal for fishing. *Was I being too fearful?* The thought had crossed his mind a few times, but he had learned to trust his senses.

It would have been well after midnight when he awoke to a dog barking somewhere in the village. He raised himself from his sitting position, squatting by the thick tree trunk a few yards into the grove. He sensed before he saw some movement by the cadjan fence behind his hut. Dark shadows flittered across his vision in the moon's light, which appeared from behind a cloud.

They are here. He gripped the handle of his *kaduwa* (sword) and gently pulled it out of the sheath. It was a short stabbing weapon with a sharp edge, excellent for close-quarter work. He watched as a group of men, some carrying torches above their heads, approached his hut at the edge of the village. He swore to himself when he saw that one of the leaders was the village headman carrying a large, curved fishing knife customarily used to chop fish.

The men moved silently, the swords and long guns they carried gleaming in the light of the torches they carried. He could see them when they surrounded his hut, the torches lighting up the space. They all wore short black coats and baggy pants, some with a four-cornered hat on their heads. Exactly like the two men he saw from the church spire. These were not men who could be trifled with easily.

Kumara retreated further back into the coconut grove. He needed to be careful as they might search the area once they found that he was not in the hut. He was not too concerned as he was in his natural element. He had killed many times in conflicts against his King's enemies in the forests and mountains around his home. But the canal at his back concerned him. *I will need to cross it somehow.*

A shout from inside the hut confirmed his fears - *they know I am gone.* The bright torches scattered as the men searched the village. A few of them came into the coconut grove, the flames from their torches brightening the grove around him. He retreated silently, keeping outside the circle of light as they searched around the bases of the coconut trees.

Kumara was doing well until he tripped over a fallen branch and fell. The sound alerted the men closest to him.

'*Ada seseorang di sini,*' There's someone here. The shout echoed through the night.

Kumara scrambled to his feet and moved back as the circle of light caught him briefly.

'*Itu dia, Itu dia,*' There he is, there he is.

A musket flamed in the darkness, and Kumara felt a sharp pain under his left arm, driving him to his knees. *I've been hit.* When he was back on his feet, one of the mercenaries was almost on him with his sword raised, ready to strike.

Kumara was at a disadvantage as he had not regained his balance. He barely managed to block the downward strike of the soldier's sword, warding off the sharp steel blade in a shower of sparks. The man stumbled forward, his momentum making him trip over the same tree branch that had impeded Kumara.

It was almost a reflex action. Kumara used his sword sideways, chopping at the man's exposed neck while on his knees. A spurt of dark blood indicated he had sliced the soldier's jugular vein, effectively taking him out of action. As Kumara turned to run, another musket flamed, his sudden movement taking the mercenary by surprise, making the lead ball miss its target.

Safely back in the darkness, Kumara ran towards the canal, dodging trees and fallen branches he could see in the filtered moonlight shining through the branches above him. The lights and sounds of pursuit were getting close as he reached the canal bank. He could go upstream or downstream but didn't fancy his chances, given he would be losing blood from the wound he received, so he slipped into the stinking water without diving in so as not to alert his pursuers.

'*Mana dia pergi?*' Where did he go?

Kumara had just managed to duck his head under the overgrown weeds and grass lining the canal's edge by the time the men arrived. He could barely touch the muddy bottom with his outstretched toes and would not be seen from above unless someone got into the canal. He would be safe if he remained completely still.

Kumara could hear the men on the bank above him arguing. Some wanted to go upstream, while others argued the opposite way was more likely. A couple of them began swiping at the overgrown vegetation lining the bank with their swords, searching for him beneath their feet. He just managed to duck his head under the water as a swinging sword nicked the top of his head, almost drawing a gasp from him. Luckily the man wielding the sword had not felt the contact. He kept his head underwater for as long as he could before slowly coming up for air.

The men searching for him had moved along, some still swinging their swords at the undergrowth lining the banks. He couldn't stay here as the men would return when they couldn't find him, so he decided to cross the canal and find a place to hide on the opposite bank. Waiting until a passing cloud covered the moon, he dog paddled across the canal, keeping his head just above the murky water's surface.

Now on the other side, he could see the light from the torches in both directions as they searched the canal bank for him. He tried to get out of the water, but he couldn't get any purchase with his feet, and there was nothing for him to hold onto that he could use to pull himself out.

Kumara continued downstream, looking for a place he could get out of the canal. He was beginning to feel weak, and the use of his left arm was restricted. The men searching the opposite bank were returning. Still, he felt relatively safe as the light of their torches wouldn't reach across the canal for him to be spotted. But he couldn't remain in the water as dawn wasn't far away.

After what seemed to be an hour of paddling, he saw a fallen branch of a tree at the canal edge. Resting under its foliage for a while, Kumara pulled himself out of the water and lay on his back, trying to get his breath back. The sky was lightening above him as the stars winked out one by one at the approaching dawn. He looked around until he spotted a hole in the tangled mess of thornbush and scrub grass only yards from where he lay. He crawled into the dense mass of undergrowth, feeling the barbs of thorns catching his clothing and making the bushes shake above him.

CHAPTER 32

THE REFUGE

Lovinia hopped from one foot to another as she waited for Kumara. The cool sea breeze made her wish she'd brought a warmer shawl. She leant against the side wall of a run-down hostel on the street corner whose sign in bold green lettering above the door proclaimed in four languages that the establishment specialised in Halal food.

They had agreed to meet in the Muslim quarter, not for the first time. Kumara liked to vary the places they met in case he was followed. And she liked it because she could hide her face and blend in with the other women who frequented its markets.

Lovinia studied the ebb and flow of the crowd as it swirled around one stall and then another. Colour and sound seem to explode everywhere. The smell of people, frying fish, tea, perfume, hair oil, fruit and flowers. Traders were touting their wares along the kerb. Women, some wearing hijabs, were haggling over clay pots ranged according to size, with the largest at the back and the smallest at the front. Rush baskets full of sardines freshly caught and packed in the sand used by unscrupulous traders to make extra weight on the scales, scrawny chicken in wooden crates piled one on top of another added to the cacophony of noise in the shanty quarter.

Lovinia's attention was drawn to the glass window of the hotel displaying an array of pastries, some triangular, others oblong, some resembling nests of fine yarn, others consisting of wafer-thin layers, crisp, golden brown and saturated in honey. She loved sweet things and felt her mouth water at the sight.

Kumara is late. Annoyed with herself for being distracted, she looked up and down the street, hoping to see the familiar figure of the man she thought she was falling in love with. It had taken her a while to come to that conclusion, but after that encounter in the church, it had just felt right when he kissed her.

Lovina looked down the street, and her heart skipped a beat when she thought she recognised the figure walking slowly towards her. *He looks tired.* The prowling walk she was used to was missing. There was also something about how he hung his head which alerted her. *Is he ill?*

The closer he came, the more certain Lovinia felt something was wrong. Usually a neat dresser, his clothing looked wet and rumpled, like he had slept in them. A piece of cloth was wrapped around his head untidily. He had his right hand on his sword, which was tucked into the waistband of his sarong. His left hand hung down limply.

Lovinia resisted the urge to rush out to meet him. It would attract too much attention. She waited until he was a few steps away and went to him, supporting him by wrapping her arm around his body with a rush of affection that surprised even herself. He was sweating profusely.

His eyes looked gauntly at her. 'I have been shot,' he grunted.

'Where?'

'Under my arm,' he said weakly. 'I've lost a lot of blood.'

Lovinia looked over her shoulder as they staggered into the alley next to the hotel. No one was paying them any attention. The men who had shot him had not been following. Feeling more confident, she peered at him. She could see that he was close to losing unconsciousness. He needed to go somewhere his wounds could be tended.

'Take me to the Lion Inn,' he croaked. 'They will know what to do.'

Lovinia nodded and helped Kumara lean against a wooden siding behind a pile of lumber. The Inn of the Lion was many streets away. She didn't think he would get that far in his condition, even with her help.

'Stay here,' she ordered. 'You cannot be seen from the street. I'll find someone to help.'

Kumara flopped to the ground, his head on his chest. Lovinia saw that the cloth on his head was bloody, and she had blood on her arms. Wiping her arms with her shawl, she hurried out of the alley, still unsure whether she should leave him alone in his condition.

For a moment, Lovinia longed to be back in the marketplace at Galkissa, with no more on her mind than snatching a honey cake. But only for a moment. The solution to her problem presented itself when a hand cart half filled with coconuts pushed by a market worker came into view. Lovinia adjusted her head scarf around her face, composing herself before approaching the muscular young man.

Lovinia saw that he had seen her and was observing her as she approached him. He was young, still in his teens. She smiled flirtatiously at him, making him blush. He stopped pushing the cart when she was alongside him.

'Would you like to make some extra money,' she asked, smiling at him. It wasn't the first time she had used her femininity to attract a man.

'What do you mean?'

'My friend has fallen and hurt himself,' she said, indicating the alley. 'I need someone to help me take him to his lodging. Can you help?'

The young man scratched his head. Now?' he asked.

'Yes, now.'

Lovinia could see that he was not sure. 'What's your name?' she asked, laying her hand on his muscular forearm.

'Sunil,' he gulped, glancing nervously at her.

A virgin, Lovinia thought, not used to a woman's touch. 'Well, Sunil,' she said, smiling into his eyes. 'Would you like to make a silver coin?'

'Silver coin?' His eyes lit up when he heard her words.

'Yes,' she said, leaning close to him. 'You can use it to visit a *nautch* house.' Lovinia knew that a boy like him would only earn a few copper coins for pushing a cart around. A silver coin would get him into a dance house where the hostesses could be persuaded to help him lose his virginity.

The boy blushed, understanding the hidden meaning in her words. 'What do you want me to do,' he agreed, nodding his head eagerly.

'Follow me,' she said, pointing at the entrance to the alley. Now that she had got what she wanted, her one thought was to get Kumara to the Inn of the Lion as quickly as possible.

CHAPTER 33

THE SURPRISE VISIT

Catherine leaned out of the little horse-drawn carriage as they approached the entrance to the Governor's country mansion. It was after ten o'clock, and the air was still cool and redolent with the smell of jasmine and lilies. She felt nervous and excited. The fact that she was flouting convention by going unescorted to a bachelor's house added the thrill of danger to the escapade.

She had been disappointed that the Governor had not been seen for a few weeks. Rumours swirled that he had fallen ill, others that he had fallen from his horse and hurt himself. Others gossiped about an affair with a local woman he had met while riding.

Catherine wanted to see for herself. From the day they had met at the Welcome Ball, she had entertained hopes that the Governor would see her as his lifelong partner. She had felt at the time that he showed considerable interest in her and was disappointed that nothing came of it. She had tried to engineer several instances where her friends would arrange parties on her behalf and invite the Governor, only to be disappointed when the invitation was not accepted. The Governor seemed to spend most of his free time at the residence he had built a few miles to the south, which made it almost impossible to meet him casually.

Finally, she decided to take matters into her own hands and confront the Governor in his own home. She only hoped they wouldn't run into any of the officer's wives as they returned from their morning rides. It was also when some people made their morning social calls – before it got too hot and humid to be outside.

Reaching out her gloved hand, she squeezed Madeline's fingers. Madeline returned the pressure, giving Catherine one of her devastating smiles.

'Almost there now,' she said. 'You haven't changed your mind?'

'Oh, no. I'm looking forward to seeing Sir Thomas on his home ground.'

Madeline, the wife of Colonel Landers, who had served in India and was second in command in the cantonment, was a little older than her. Catherine had overheard other wives talk unkindly about Madeline having a 'touch of the tarbrush'. She was only tolerated because of her husband's position in the garrison. The two of them had become firm friends after they both realised they were kindred spirits living in a ruling class ill-prepared for the ancient eastern culture they found themselves in.

Catherine smoothed the wide collar of the black velvet jacket that fitted her well over the waist and hips but was too tight across her bust. She was conscious of the way her breasts swelled against the shaped jacket. Below her waist, Catherine was wearing a riding habit and boots. She had dressed carefully, choosing the daring riding dress she had worn only once.

Madeline looked beautiful in a Western-style riding gown of dark-blue combed cotton. Her gleaming black hair was looped over her ears and then swept into a chignon on the nape of her neck. Only her honey-coloured skin and small straight nose betrayed her Indian blood.

Madeline ordered the driver to pull up before the residence and to wait in the shadows of a grove of tamarind trees for their return. Alighting with care, they shook out the folds of their habits. A cooling breeze blew in from the sea, dispersing the smells of dust and heat. Before they set off, Madeline gave the driver some money. 'I'll pay you the rest when we return,' she said, ensuring his reliability.

The driver nodded and settled down happily to sleep until he was needed again.

*

Thomas got out of bed and pulled on a robe. His headache had left him entirely, and he was smiling now at the thought of finally being productive. The illness had drained him of all his energy, and he had lost all desire to eat. Constant vomiting and nausea had weakened his body so that his clothes just hung on him.

Johnson stopped sleeping in the cot next to his bed after he began to show signs of recovery. Thomas felt grateful to the man for looking after him and made a mental note to show his gratitude somehow.

The rest of the house was still sleeping when he went to his study. He collected the reports left on his desk by Brewer. Then found himself a glass of mango juice in a jug in the pantry next to his room, then returned and propped himself against the pillows to read them. His secretary had summarised reports from various departments and had left a few confidential reports unopened, bearing an unbroken seal for him to read.

One of them was from Wilson, the head of Inland Revenue. Thomas broke the seal eagerly, wanting to know what had happened in the search for the Kandyan spy. The report from the day before was short and not pleasing. The man had been tracked to his hideout but evaded capture after killing one of the men sent to catch him. He was on the run, and Wilson surmised that he was possibly injured by traces of blood they had found where he had been hiding. The chase continued without any success.

Thomas was still reading when Johnson came into the room.

'You're feeling better, Sah,' Johnson said, looking questioningly at Thomas lying on the bed with papers strewn around.

'Yes, very much so,' Thomas remarked warmly. 'And I awoke feeling hungry, so I helped myself to a glass of juice I found in the pantry.'

'You should have rung the bell, Sah. You are weak, and moving around too much will tire you.'

'I cannot remain in bed forever, Johnson. I am feeling much better.'

Johnson was smiling as he fussed around Thomas. 'Is there anything I can get for you, Sah?'

'What about a sponge bath and some breakfast, Johnson, some real food for a change? I am heartily fed up with all the potions you have been feeding me.'

'Aye, aye, Sah,' smiled Johnson, turning to leave the room.

'Oh, Johnson, before you go. Have you heard from Miss Lovinia?

Johnson had mentioned to Thomas that the women from Lovinia's village had prepared a local brew which seemed to have helped him recover from the parasitic disease he had been suffering.

'Joanna, my wife, Sah, always brings Miss Lovinia's felicitations when she delivers the native medicine. It is prepared fresh every day. She is looking forward to seeing you when you feel up to it.'

Thomas nodded his thanks. 'Please thank Mrs Johnson on my behalf. And pass on a message to Miss Lovinia that I am recovering fast and will be back at my normal duties shortly.'

After his sponge bath, Thomas sat on the front garden balcony. He ate breakfast with an appetite for the first time in weeks. It consisted of a poached egg and lightly buttered toast. A cup of freshly brewed tea sat on the tray next to a bowl of sliced fruit. He had come to love the local fruit, which was both sweet and succulent at the same time.

From his raised position, he could see a long group of feathery-fronded coconut trees which grew in abundance in the coastal areas. The thatched grey roofs of village houses were distinguishable below the palms, nearly concealed among the plantain trees and other bushes growing about them. Above these stood several tall, deep green, pointed-leaved mango trees and, higher still, a few wide-spreading tamarinds and tall, slender trees of a variety he was unfamiliar with.

Flights of pigeons wheeled and swooped in unison in the air currents above the peaceful scene, a group landing near the property entrance.

A movement near the front gate made the pigeons take wing in a noisy cloud of grey. Two ladies dressed in fashionable riding clothes appeared, walking towards the building.

He wondered why they had not ridden or driven up to the entrance like he would expect any normal visitor to do. Thomas was not prepared to entertain any guests in his condition, so he retreated into his room without being noticed and rang the bell, summoning Johnson.

'Are we expecting anyone?' he asked Johnson, who looked surprised by his question.

'Guests, sir?' a puzzled Johnson replied.

The two women had reached the gate to the property and were talking to the guard at the sentry post.

'Look, there,' Thomas pointed. 'There are two women, dressed for a garden party by the look of it, trying to get the guard to open the gate.'

A flustered Johnson peered out of the window. 'Oh, my goodness,' he said upon spotting the two intruders. 'I'll go and see what they want.'

'Make sure you send them on their way,' Thomas growled. 'I am not ready to be entertaining anyone, especially those rude enough to appear without an invitation.'

*

Linking arms, the two women walked through the thick vegetation until they came to the swept sandy track which led to the Governor's country mansion.

The residence, with its white façade and stone pillars on either side of the door, gave it an imposing appearance. The gardens around the building were still incomplete, the flower beds just a pile of turned earth and manure. A substantial wooden gate guarded the entrance to the property. Next to it stood an open sentry hut with a thatched cadjan roof. A British soldier, startled by their sudden appearance, stood up from the wooden bench he was sitting on, adjusting his uniform before stepping out onto the path behind the gate.

'Hello, the gate!' Caroline called out as they stopped by the entrance. The two girls giggled at the look on the young sentry's face when he saw them up close.

'Umm, are you lost?' he asked, his eyes fixed on the rounded tops of Catherine's breasts pushed up by her riding top.

'No, I think we know where we are,' Madeline responded, grinning at Catherine, who pushed her chest out further. 'Is this the Governor's mansion?'

'Yes, ma'am.' The soldier's eyes snapped up at Madeline's question, his face blushing red at being discovered. 'Are you expected?' he stammered.

'I think the Governor will want to see us,' Catherine said, smiling flirtatiously. The young man had broad shoulders and a look of innocence that appealed to her.

'My orders are to not let anyone in without permission,' he said, seemingly getting over the shock of seeing two beautiful young women standing before him.

'We're not just anyone, as you can see. We are here to speak to the Governor. Will you let us in, please,' Catherine added, smiling up at the tall sentry.

The soldier shuffled his feet, looking over his shoulder at the building behind him, unsure what he should be doing.

'Ahh, someone is coming,' the sentry said, relief obvious in his voice.

The front door to the mansion had opened, and a man dressed in a butler's uniform walked down the gravel path towards them. He was not young. White hair hung over his ears, and sharp blue eyes in a tanned, wrinkled face looked at them from under white brows.

'How can I help you, ladies?'

'We have come to see the Governor,' Catherine said aloofly. She wouldn't let any of the governor's staff get in the way of her mission.

'He's not expecting any visitors, ma'am.'

'Well, he's not. I am sure,' Catherine snapped. 'This is meant to be a surprise.'

'You'll have to come back some other time, I am afraid, ma'am,' said the English butler, seemingly unaffected by her outburst. 'Preferably with an invitation.'

Catherine was taken aback by the man's attitude and lack of respect. She was used to getting her way, so she tried a different approach.

'What's your name?' she smiled at him.

'Johnson, ma'am.'

'Could you please inform the Governor, Johnson, that Lady Catherine Audley and Madame Madeline Landers are here to see him?

'He is aware of your presence, ma'am,' said Johnson waving his arm behind him. 'But as I have said, he is too busy to entertain any visitors.'

Catherine examined the building closely but couldn't see anyone watching them. 'But we have come all this way for nothing,' she fumed. 'Why has he hidden away for so long? Is he injured or sick?'

Johnson observed her without saying anything.

Catherine opened her mouth to speak but felt Madeline pull her by the arm. 'Let's go, Catherine. I don't want to get into trouble. Now is not the time,' she said softly.

Catherine glared at the two men before turning reluctantly and following Madeline back the way they had come.

Tears of frustration pricked her eyes. She missed England and despised the person she'd become in Ceylon. She recognised that she would not have it her way this time, but she would not give up and find another way of getting what she wanted.

CHAPTER 34

THE ASSASSINS

The three men moved like wraiths across the rooftops of the town. Barefoot and silent as shadows, they leapt a small gap onto the house's flat roof behind the Inn of the Lion.

They had been searching for the Kandyan spy for days, finally tracking him to this place. By chance, one of their men had spotted an injured man being carried in a handcart through nearby streets two days after the unsuccessful ambush at the fishing village. He had followed the cart, accompanied by a woman, to the inn they were observing. They were unsure whether he'd still be here, but their Captain, under pressure from his masters, decided to send in a team to either capture or kill him.

Getting this far had not been easy. Some of the roofs they had crossed had been covered in tiles that either clinked underfoot or were treacherously loose so that now and then, one would slide off with a heart-stopping grating noise. It had been only the men's long experience of similar missions that had prevented them from falling to their death. Yet they had got this far, at least without being observed to a vantage point perhaps five feet higher than the roof of their target.

In contrast to the front of the property with its narrow wooden door and thick walls, the rear of the two-storey inn was not as stoutly constructed. But there were windows cut into the wall and ledges below them. And lower down, some windows had narrow balconies with simple wooden balustrades. One of these would provide its way in.

'Can you see anyone?' Jamail whispered.

Nur's eyes, which had always been keen as a hawk's, sifted the dark for any movement. There were no lamps away from the main streets, and the night sky had filled with clouds through which the moon rarely penetrated to cast the rooftops in fleeting moments of silvery light.

'Yes,' Nur said. He could see the sentries, two men standing by the gateway in the middle of the side wall that would provide entry to the property for tradespeople and servants. The sentries carried blunderbusses, a shrewdly chosen weapon, Nur thought, because it roared like the devil when fired, alerting everyone that there was trouble.

Jamail and Aziz crawled up beside him. Two more men were slowly pacing the roof opposite them from one side to another. None of these guards had been there when they had passed here during the day. But then, they had heard that Lokubada was always a man who looked after his own.

'There!' Nur hissed. The fourth man on their team had taken a different route because Hassan was on the roof opposite, bent low, knife in hand, moving as fast and smooth as a bird's shadow and coming up on one of the guards from behind.

Nur held his breath. He was certain the guard would turn around and that he would fire that blunderbuss. But Hassan was already on him like a leopard on an antelope. He clamped his left hand over the man's mouth and nose and thrust the knife into his neck below the ear, and Nur saw the blade protrude from the other side. Then Hassan slashed outwards through the throat, and as the sentry's legs buckled, he lowered him to the floor without a sound.

Hassan was already moving again. But the other sentry was turning now, having come to the eastern edge of the roof, and Aziz cursed under his breath.

'He won't make it,' Jamail muttered.

Up came the blunderbuss, but the guard was not fast enough, and Hassan punched the knife up under his ribs into the heart, then hauled the blade out and slashed it across the man's neck before he could scream. Then Hassan was somehow holding the blunderbuss as the guard stood choking on his blood, already dead before his legs knew it.

Hassan stepped behind him and laid the man down, then strode over to the roof's edge and shrugged off the length of rope he'd coiled like a sash across his body.

Nur sighed. 'Allah knows I love him like a brother, but he's deadlier than a cobra.' They stood now as Hassan came to the roof's edge and, holding one end, hurled the rope coils up to Nur, who caught them before they could fly over his head. Hassan tied his end of the rope around his waist before edging out over the side and hanging full length by his hands for a moment before dropping down to a narrow ledge outside a top-floor window, where the servants' quarters would be.

If anyone within heard him now or saw a shadow at the window, Hassan would surely be done for, they'd never get into the house, and they might never learn where the Kandyan had been taken.

'Allah be with him now,' Aziz said. 'Something to tie that rope to would be more useful,' Jamail said, and Nur feared his friend was right, for there was just the ledge and the window through which a warm yellow glow seeped into the night. But no sooner had the words been spoken than Hassan dropped off the ledge, landed silently on one of the small balconies ten feet below, then took the rope from his waist and tied it to the wooden balustrade. No light came from the tall, shuttered windows behind him.

'Now it's our turn,' Aziz said, tying the rope around his waist and striding backwards until the line was taut. There was nothing on that flat roof to tie off on, so Aziz would be the anchor, using all his enormous size and strength to take Nur and Jamail's weight as they climbed across.

'Are you sure you are strong enough?' Jamail asked, half grinning.

'You'll soon know if I'm not,' Aziz replied.

'And so will you, Jamail, if that knot's not up to scratch,' Nur said, steeling himself for what they must now do. 'I'll go first,' he said as Hassan waved his arm, gesturing at them to come across.

Nur wrapped his arms and legs around the rope, for a moment hanging there like a deer strung up after the kill, Aziz heaving back, those great arms and oak-strong legs straining to keep the rope taut.

'Off you go then,' he growled, and Nur began hauling himself out into the night, his sword hanging beneath him, the two pistols snug in the sash around his waist. There was no talking now, only concentration, muscle, and ligament. Keeping his legs crossed over the rope and using them as a grapnel, he pulled himself out along the line, high above the street below. He was unafraid of falling, but if one of the remaining guards came around the back of the house or if someone happened to look out of a rear window, then all Nur's skill at climbing would not be enough to save him.

Suspended in the darkness as he was, Nur could see very little around him. But he could hear his heartbeat in his ears, the barking of dogs in the streets, the chirruping of crickets and the soft sighing of the sea away in the distance. He waited for a shout of alarm or crash of gunfire. But none came, and then he had reached the far end of the rope, alive and undetected.

Nur swung a leg onto the balcony and hauled himself up, scrambling over the railing to stand face-to-face with Hassan. The two men nodded at one another in recognition of their night's work so far, then looked back across the divide to watch Jamail come across.

The cloud broke, and the city's rooftops were bathed in the moon's cold light. So too, was Jamail, who froze for a heartbeat. Then he was moving fast, pulling himself along the rope hand over hand, the corded muscle of his arms glistening in the moon glow. But the sudden speed jerked the rope, and Nur heard Aziz curse as he lost his footing and was hauled, skidding, to the roof's edge. Jamail dropped sharply but clung on, and Aziz, a great hulking shape in the half-light, leant back and pulled the rope straight again.

By the time Jamail climbed onto the balcony, Hassan was standing by the windows, holding the dagger he had used so skilfully on the guards. Now he punched its hilt through one of the small diamonds in the leaded glass and thrust his hand to draw the iron catch from the casement. The window swung open, and Hassan sprang into the room, his knife in a fighting grip, ready to deal with anyone inside.

A gun blasted from inside the room, folding Hassan in two and throwing him back the way he had come. While preparing to follow, Nur and Jamail lost their balance on the narrow balcony when Hassan flew back, toppling into the street two floors below.

Muffled shouts came from inside the building as orders were given. Dazed by their sudden fall, Nur and Jamail tried to rise to their feet as the side door to the inn slammed open, and the two sentries ran out, their weapons pointed in their direction. Nur's leg gave way under him as he tried to get up, and he grabbed hold of Jamail, who had already risen to his feet.

From the front of the building, a single voice raised in alarm and pounding footsteps made the two men realise they were surrounded. They had failed in their mission, and their Captain would not be pleased.

Nur hoped that Aziz, who was on the roof, would be able to get away and report what had happened. He pulled a pistol from his waist, cocked it and pointed it toward the two men by the side gate.

The roar of the blunderbuss firing was the last thing he heard.

CHAPTER 35

THE SUMMONS

I t was a hot, cloudless day. The prolonged drought had parched the landscape, sapping the land of its energy. Tall rainclouds on the horizon promised the monsoon rains were not far away.

Lovinia had received a message from Juana that morning saying the *Andukāraya* was ready to meet with her. Her husband, Johnson, would make the necessary arrangements as a certain level of discretion would be required for her visit. She had not seen the him for a few weeks and was anxious to see how he was doing. Juana brought reports from her husband daily, and it seemed Sir Thomas was feeling stronger every day.

Lovinia spent the morning preparing, bathing at the well behind her home and drying her long hair before combing it. Aletta was not at home that day, attending to a woman giving birth and her father was at the village practising a new routine with his dance troupe.

With no distraction in the house, the thoughts that constantly intruded were of the Kandyan, Kumara, whom she had left to recover at the Inn of the Lion. She had not heard from Lokubada, which concerned her, but she took it as a good sign as he would have sent a message if anything had gone wrong.

The sun had started to set when the summons arrived in the form of Juana. 'You are to come with me to the *Andukāraya's* home.'

The two women headed towards the seashore using trails that bypassed the village. They finally arrived at the seashore just as the sun set. They followed the wide beach until the promontory loomed out in the fading red light. They climbed up the side of the cliff along a path used by the village children who played on the sandy shore.

They approached the property from the south, opposite the main entrance and away from the sentry post, which was manned at night. The side door to the building opened at their touch, and they quietly entered the kitchen lit by the glow of the dying embers of the cooking fire.

Johnson, seated at the large, rectangular cooking table, rose as they entered the room. 'Perfect,' he said in a low voice, walking over and kissing his wife. 'Thank you, Luv. You can remain here until I am back.'

The house felt cool after the heat and dust outside. Johnson motioned for Lovinia to follow him. The house was quiet as he led her up the back stairs to an open landing. Lamps illuminated a long corridor with doors on either side. The place smelled of fresh paint and wood polish.

'There's no one here except the Governor and me,' Johnson said as he stepped into the hallway. 'I gave the staff the evening off.'

Lovinia wondered at the secrecy that seemed to have been put in place since she was last here. *What were they trying to hide?*

'It's because the *Andukāraya* doesn't want anyone to know about you,' Johnson said, reading her mind. 'He has enemies who will use the information to discredit him, so you must be careful not to talk to anyone.'

Lovinia nodded. She understood about keeping things to herself.

'One more thing before you go in,' Johnson had stopped by a door and waited till she came close. 'He's feeling much better, but he is not strong enough to exert himself too much. You must be careful not to overtire him.'

Lovinia was glad the flickering lamplight hid the blush that warmed her cheeks. She had left him exhausted and prone on his bed the last time. He was quite virile for his age but could not match the exuberance that Lovinia brought to their lovemaking.

Johnson knocked on the door and waited a moment before entering.

'Miss Lovinia, Sah,' he announced, ushering Lovinia into the room. He waited a moment before backing out, shutting the door behind him.

The *Andukāraya* was sitting at a small desk that had been moved into his bedroom. The door to the balcony was wide open, letting in the cool night breeze. The room was lit only by a three-pronged lamp on the desk which also contained a tray with a half-finished bowl of rice pudding pushed to the side. He stood up when Lovinia entered, motioning her to come forward into the light.

Lovinia was shocked at his appearance. He had lost a lot of weight, and his clothes hung off him loosely.

'Yes, I know, I know! I am quite a sight to see,' he said in a weakened voice, watching her reaction. 'Hence the low lighting.'

Lovinia crossed over to him and hugged him. It felt like she was hugging just flesh and bones. She felt him return her hug, but it wasn't with the normal vigour she was used to.

'I have been thinking of you every moment I was lying half-dead in my bed,' he said. 'It was the thought of not seeing you again that kept me going.'

Could it be that he's so affected by me? How awkward it would be if he became too attached to her now that she was in love with someone else.

She looked directly at him, squinting slightly in the flickering light. His face was gaunt, but his eyes were sharp and clear. He bent towards her slowly, his parted lips just brushing her forehead. He gently ran his fingers through her luscious hair, something she knew he liked doing.

Lovinia held her breath, absorbed by his slow sensual movements. There was a moment of calm, of complete silence when he just looked at her.

'Let me sit down,' he finally said. 'I get tired quite easily.'

Lovinia helped him sit down and kneeled at his feet. She took his hands in his. 'Is there something I can do for you?' she asked.

He shook his head. 'Just stay with me,' he said, closing his eyes.

*

It was after midnight when Lovinia opened the door to her home. She had helped Johnson carry the *Andukāraya* to his bed before leaving with Juana.

The night was dark with scudding clouds, the only illumination a flaming torch Lovinia carried, lighting the familiar tracks back to the village.

Banda must have woken to the sound of her entering as he stumbled out of his room, grumbling. He muttered as he lit a lamp while Lovinia was getting ready for bed.

'How is the *Andukāraya*?' he asked, taking a drink from the water jug.

'He's still recovering,' Lovinia shrugged. 'He gets tired easily.'

Lovinia looked around but couldn't see Aletta. 'Aletta's not back?'

Her father didn't answer, looking at her over the jug rim. 'I received a message from Lokubada this evening,' he said, taking a sip.

Lovinia's felt a stab of panic. 'What did he want?' she asked as calmly as she could. *It must be about Kumara.*

'He wants to meet with you tomorrow at the market near the Inn,' he said. 'It's something to do with the Kandyan.'

Various thoughts raced through her mind, some making her worry even more. She shook herself mentally. *It doesn't do any good to imagine what may be wrong.* She'll find out soon enough the next day.

'What are you thinking about?' her father asked.

'That I must be careful,' she said. 'It won't be good to be seen and recognised.'

CHAPTER 36

THE FUGITIVE

'He cannot stay here,' Lokubada hissed, his eyes constantly checking his surroundings. 'It's too dangerous.'

Lovinia came to the market near the Inn of the Lion when she received a message from the innkeeper. They had agreed when she brought Kumara to the inn that she would stay away, and any news would be passed through an intermediary.

'What happened?' Lovinia asked. The innkeeper had assured her that Kumara would be safe at the Inn.

Lokubada quickly updated her on the previous night's attempt by a group of Malay assassins to penetrate the Inn and kill the Kandyan. 'We know how to deal with these people,' he growled, spitting into the gutter, 'but I am afraid we have to move him in case the British come looking for him.'

Lovinia felt a shot of raw fear grip her body. 'You think they will?' She couldn't bear to think about Kumara being either killed or captured. He would be tortured, and the entire network of spies would be threatened. *Including me,* she thought.

'Yes,' Lokubada nodded. 'It's possible, but we have a bit of time before they do. Noordeen will want the reward for himself and try again with more men, possibly tonight. He won't succeed, but we must get him out of there before it happens.'

'Where will you take him?'

'We can smuggle him out of the area without being observed. But he must stay outside the city while recovering from his wounds. It will be too dangerous for him to remain here.'

Again, the ripples of fear played against the furthest reaches of her mind. *I must think, think.* Where could he recover without being discovered? The answer was so obvious she wondered why she had not thought of it before.

'What if he is sent to Galkissa, to my village?' She gasped as the words came out unbidden, but she knew it was the correct thing to do as she said it. 'We will look after him and keep him safe.'

Lokubada stared at her for a moment. 'I can see why he is so enamoured by you,' he said. 'They will never think of looking for him there.' He thought for a moment. 'Go back and prepare a safe place for him. He will need care for a few days. I will make sure he gets there tonight.'

*

Her father was not sure it was a good idea when she told him what she had proposed.

'We cannot keep him here,' Banda said, pushing his hair back on his forehead. 'People come and go all the time. And if the *Vidane* finds out, you know well what he'll do.'

'Oh,' Lovinia was deflated, wondering how to respond. She gave a rueful sigh and looked down at her hands. She hadn't considered the implications on her family if they were found nursing a man wanted by the British. 'So, what can we do?' she begged, looking alternately at her father and Aletta, who was looking out of the window. 'If the British catch him, they will force him to reveal what he knows.'

'Don't blame yourself,' her father comforted her. 'I know you meant no harm.'

Lovinia nodded, feeling a little better after hearing her father's words. But that still did not solve the problem they were facing.

'We can take him into the forest and leave him at the *vidiya*,' Aletta said suddenly. 'No one ever goes there.'

The *vidiya* was a place no one went to. It was a place the villagers shunned as it was thought to be the abode of demons.

Banda gave a sceptical grunt and paused for a moment's thought. 'Yes,' he finally agreed, frowning. 'It's a good place to hide, although it always gives me a bad feeling. We must make sure that it's not in use now.'

'Leave that to me,' Aletta said. 'I am one of those who prepare the *vidiya* for the *rata yakun natima* (devil dance ceremonies) and have no fear of the place.'

Lovinia reached out and clasped Aletta's hand while giving her a brilliant smile. She trusted her friend implicitly. Once again, Aletta had demonstrated her ability to think differently.

Lovinia had known since she was a child of the *thovil* ceremonies that took place in the dead of night in the deep forest. A typical *thovilaya* was performed only by women to bring blessings to an expectant mother or to cure a serious female illness. The demonic exorcism rituals practised as a healing ceremony for men, communicating with demons or departed beings, were not spoken about much. The ceremony was a form of exorcism carried out in the *vidiya*, which was only used for this purpose.

Her father nodded, standing and stretching himself. 'There is much to be done before he gets here tonight, and we don't have much time,' he said. 'I will spend some time in the village before I guide them to the *vidiya*. The two of you take whatever you require from here to make him comfortable and prepare a place in one of the smaller huts.'

'I'll prepare food to take with us,' Lovinia said, feeling better already. 'I can pluck some *thambili* (king coconut) from the garden.'

'Make sure no one follows you, and don't forget to take your medicine chest,' Banda said, looking at Aletta. 'I don't want anyone in the troupe to know.'

The two women spent the next few hours preparing. They talked about using little-known paths through the forest, shunning the more direct way the villagers used to get to the *vidiya*.

It was late afternoon when they left their home. Lovinia carried a cloth bag and a rolled-up mattress on her shoulder. Aletta slung her heavy medicine chest, which was held by straps, across her back. She lifted a net bag with a few cooking utensils on a long pole balanced on her shoulder.

'It's not heavy,' she said when Lovinia raised her eyebrows questioningly.

'We can take that track there.' Aletta pointed. 'It cuts through the forests, and it will be deserted now. We'll make better time. I am sure no one will see us.'

A flock of green parrots rose from the branches screeching and chattering with excitement as they entered the cool shade of the forest. The loud, hoarse cries of large grey forest monkeys resounded through the trees as they walked the leaf-strewn path. Ceasing to feed on the succulent leaves, they shook the rustling branches in their bold leaps to reach higher branches in the forest canopy. A sudden stillness soon followed as they mysteriously concealed themselves, vanishing as though by magic among the dense foliage.

'You have never talked much about what happens in the *vidiya*,' Lovina said to Aletta, who was walking in front of her.

'It's a healing ceremony like any other,' Aletta explained. 'Since the times of our ancestors, it's believed that every minute of a person's life is governed by supernatural powers, either good or bad. If good forces are protecting you, everything goes well. But the moment illness occurs, a family member dies unexpectedly, or some disaster occurs, it is the work of evil forces caused by particular demons.'

'So, what happens?'

'Well, man alone cannot subdue these forces, the Gods must be won over to do that, and the *thovil* ceremony plays an important part in summoning those powers.'

To Lovinia, Aletta seemed to embody all the sensuality and mystery of the island. She was an enigma, able to live in two worlds, and she spoke of things Lovinia did not understand but was willing to learn.

'I want to watch one of these ceremonies.' Lovinia declared. Her mother, raised a Christian, had never allowed Lovinia to attend. Banda had followed her mother's wishes, although she knew that various members of his troupe did.

After following a trail that Aletta seemed to know, they reached the end of an embankment of a village *tank* (reservoir). It was a shallow sheet of water covering twenty to thirty acres of land, which the villagers used to water their fields during the dry season. At both sides of the tank and along the outer toe of the dam grew lofty trees, with grey trunks often strengthened by wide buttresses where they entered the earth. Water buffalo wallowed in the shallow water, content to chew at the nutritious weeds that grew profusely underwater. Birds of various types wheeled in the evening sky above them as they proceeded along the embankment, disturbing large brown frogs sunning themselves or catching flies near the water's edge.

They plunged back into the forest, long shadows from the rough-stemmed tamarind trees making the forest gloomy in the evening light. After a few minutes, they reached a clearing with a cluster of low, dilapidated wooden huts with thatched roofs, each with a cultivated area at the back overgrown with banana plants and coconut trees. At a slight distance from the others was a larger hut in better condition with an open side overlooking a central yard with a firepit full of burnt logs and ashes. A small bathing well with a mudbrick wall sat to one side.

Dark clouds filled the sky, and light rain began to fall, the kind that dampened the dust but did not wash it away. 'Mango showers', Lovinia declared. It was what the villagers called these showers that helped ripen the fruit to a richer yellow.

Aletta guided Lovinia to a hut farthest from the main structure, slightly better than the others. 'Let's use this place,' she said, removing the medicine chest from her back after placing the cooking utensils on the floor. 'It's away from the entrance, and no one will come here.'

The hut was cluttered with various items, some covered by dusty woven mats. The two women began preparing the hut's interior, knowing they had just a few hours before Banda arrived with the injured Kandyan.

*

Lovinia was asleep when Aletta shook her awake. Her stomach tightened as she sat up, shooting Aletta a look.

'Someone is coming up the path,' Aletta whispered. 'It must be them.'

Aletta had agreed to keep watch and promised to wake Lovinia when she felt tired. They had swept and cleaned the hut, moving some of the stored items, including an assortment of drums, masks and costumes representing demons, into other huts. Lovinia had been reluctant to handle the ritual masks representing both good and bad demons.

'They are only masks,' Aletta explained dismissively. 'Their power comes from the ritual, the chanting of ancient verses, the dancing and drumming which is as old as the hills. They have no power of their own. The Gods must be won over first.'

Lovinia handled the masks with care, not wanting to evoke any of the spiritual deities that may reside in the object.

Aletta had prepared two torches by wrapping rags around long, straight branches from a tree she had freshly cut in the forest. The flickering light dimly lit the *vidiya*, giving it a smoky eerie appearance.

Lovinia wound her hair into a knot at the nape of her neck before stepping outside the hut and following her friend towards the entrance. The normal night sounds of the forest seemed magnified by the tension she felt and by wondering how Kumara fared with his wounds. She hadn't had time to think about it much, but now that she was about to see him again, her anxiety increased tenfold.

Lovinia examined her feelings as dispassionately as possible, realising that she couldn't separate the feelings she had developed for him as a man from those she had felt for him before.

The glow on the path slowly got closer until she saw two men, one supporting the other, stumbling their way down the track. One was the familiar figure of her father, who had his arm under the shoulder of the other figure.

'Come, let's help him.'

Aletta hurried forward, followed closely by Lovinia.

Banda was gasping for breath when they reached him. Perspiration poured off his body, making him slick to the touch. Kumara's head was slumped to his chest, but his eyes were open, watching Lovinia as she took the torch from her father's hand.

'I almost didn't make it,' Banda puffed. 'It was longer than I remember.'

'It's only a few steps further,' Aletta cried as she guided them towards the hut at the back of the vidiya. 'You'll be safe here.'

*

Kumara opened his eyes to the sound of rain pounding on the thatched roof above his head. He felt tired and hungry. He remembered not having eaten for some time.

Where am I? His eyes took in the surroundings, which did not reveal much. It was a rectangular room with its roof resting on plain round wooden poles. Its walls were woven palm leaves resting on a raised earthen floor. A village hut of some kind, like many he'd been in before.

His mind was still groggy, and the last thing he could remember was being half-carried somewhere, *perhaps to this place,* he thought. The pain in his head had subsided to a dull ache, but the wound under his arm still throbbed relentlessly. Something tight across his chest made breathing laboured.

A rustle of movement made him turn his head. His eyes focused on a figure sitting silently on a three-legged stool beside him. It was Lovinia. She sat erect, waiting for him to speak. Gone was the playful look he was used to, replaced with a steely-eyed stare. He'd never met a girl so resilient, so spirited. He looked again at her lovely, young face. She was elegant and had a way of maintaining her poise even in the situation she found herself in.

'Where am I?' His voice sounded raspy and dry.

'Somewhere safe,' she said, reaching down beside her. She edged closer, stretching out and propping up his head while holding a container to his lips. 'Drink this,' she said. 'It will help purge the poisons from your body.'

The drink was bitter, making him cough as the liquid went down his throat. He wet his lips with his tongue. 'How long have I been here?'

'Two days,' she said. 'You needed to rest, so we left you alone.'

'Who knows I am here?'

'Only my father, who brought you here, my friend Aletta and I,' Lovinia assured him. 'No one ever comes here, so you'll be safe.'

'What is this place?' Kumara asked, looking around the room. There was nothing much to see. A brown earthen *chatti* (a water jug), a cloth bag with some belongings, an open chest holding stoppered vials and packages wrapped in paper sitting on a small table.

'It's a *vidiya*, where a *thovilaya* is performed.'

Kumara had heard about the dance ceremonies the people of the south performed, invoking various demons to heal those sick in the mind and soul. Where he came from, these types of ceremonies were more refined and followed Buddhist practices.

A gust of wind shook the hut, whipping a spray of rainwater through the open door, wetting the mat he lay on. Lovinia wiped the drops of moisture using the corner of her sarong.

Kumara tried to sit up and failed. Finally, he had to be assisted by Lovina, who supported him with an arm around his shoulder. His upper body was wrapped in long strips of white cloth, compressing his chest tightly.

He could feel her softness and smell the freshness of her hair and body, breathing it in deeply while appreciating her closeness.

'How do you feel?' she asked.

Kumara reached up and touched the top of his head. 'My head does not hurt as much,' he grumbled, 'but my body is very painful, especially when I move.'

'You were shot, Lovina said. 'Aletta had to remove the musket ball, lying just under the skin on your back. We think two of your ribs are broken where the ball was deflected. You're fortunate that it happened like that.'

Kumara closed his eyes, feeling faint.

'You need to eat something,' Lovinia said, helping him lean against the side wall.

He could hear her moving around the room before she came and sat next to him again. 'I have prepared some rice *gullies* (balls) mixed with dhal, which will give you nourishment', she said matter of factly. 'Aletta will be here later to give you medicine to ease the pain.'

Lovinia fed him balls of rice and dhal from a banana leaf packet alternating with sips of cool fresh water that refreshed him.

After he ate his fill, Lovinia picked up the *chatti* on the table and shook it. 'I'll draw more water,' she said as she left the room.

A stingy ray of sunlight slunk into the room through the open door as the rain ceased. Kumara sat silently on the mat, watching the specks of dust drifting in the shaft of light illuminating the room. A feeling of melancholy drifted over him. At times like this, loneliness tightened around him like a vice. He had no family, as his life was at his monarch's bidding.

Kumara regained composure when Lovina returned to the room carrying the heavy pitcher on her hip. Kumara smiled affectionately at the woman he had chosen as a spy. He initially had doubts, given her independence and stubborn nature, but she had proven resilient and trustworthy.

Lovinia came and sat down on her stool after she had cleaned up the remains of the food and swept away the puddles of water by the entrance. She looked him straight into his eyes, examining his face for any sign of illness. She blushed when she saw him watching her with interest in his eyes.

Her eyes flashed. 'What are you looking at?' she asked with perfect composure.

Kumara reached out and took her hands in his. They were firm, warm hands with long fingers.

'You have grown on me since we first met, Lovinia, and I cannot think of anything more pleasing than to be with you all the time.'

A smile spread across her lips, revealing a set of neat white teeth. 'I see,' she replied in her alluring voice. Her gaze now caressed his face with a gentle inner warmth as she spoke. 'You may take me as your woman wherever you choose to have me, Kumara.'

Kumara felt a warming glow engulf his body. She grew more and more desirable with each moment. He took her with infinite care into his arms and kissed her lingeringly, in silence, then tilted her chin and looked down into her face.

'I will talk to your father when the moment is right,' he said. 'We have a mission to complete, both of us, and once that's over ….'

Lovinia laughed softly, delightedly. 'Yes, Kumara,' she replied with a sureness and self-confidence of a woman who understood her worth.

CHAPTER 37

THE INSPECTION

Thomas slowly resumed his duties as he grew stronger. His appetite had returned completely, and he was beginning to put on weight. Dr Anderson brought him a bottle of medicinal tonic water from India, which he swore was a preventative for contracting malaria. Thomas found it palatable, especially when mixed with a touch of gin which was becoming popular on the island.

Major Staples resumed his normal role after reporting that the requested tunnel had been completed. It ran from the storage room in the lower cellar to a point about a hundred yards away from the village where Lovinia lived.

'It wasn't as difficult as we thought,' he said, seemingly pleased with himself. 'It's limestone through its entire length that made it much easier.'

Thomas nodded his thanks. 'I'll make an effort to inspect it when I feel a bit stronger.' He knew Lovinia had been using the tunnel, visiting him almost daily, with local delicacies she had made for him and fresh fruit from her village.

Thomas adjusted the cushion on which he was sitting. His once well-padded bottom had shrunk in size and no longer protected him as it had in the past.

'Have we heard back from the Home Office about our request for more troops?'

'It's too soon, your excellency,' Major Staples replied. 'It's the monsoon season, and we cannot predict how long it will take. However, the men we sent to India have disembarked and are being allotted to their posts.'

'Have you heard anything from Wilson,' Thomas asked. 'I saw a report from him about a week ago but nothing since.'

'Neither have I,' the Major said. 'I will request a report right away.'

Thomas sat back on his chair, contemplating his future. Getting sick had given him many opportunities to ponder what he was doing with his life. There was no doubt that meeting Lovinia had changed everything. He no longer felt an overwhelming sense of duty which had always driven him in the past. He knew he could be happy doing what he was doing now, here in this country, with Lovinia. But he also realised that she would never be accepted by the snobbish society he so willingly served.

Thomas must have dozed off, waking to the footsteps in the hallway. The sky outside his balcony was clearer, and the sunny breaks between showers seemed longer. The latticed doors stood wide open for any breeze inclined to stir the muggy afternoon.

Johnson came into the room after knocking on the door. 'Sorry to disturb you, your excellency. A messenger has brought a package for your eyes only.'

Johnson handed the package to Thomas.

'Would you like some afternoon tea, Sah? There are still a few sweets Miss Lovinia brought last evening.'

'Yes, thank you, Johnson.'

Thomas opened the package with the letter opener on his desk as Johnson left the room. Inside was a sheaf of papers with a report from the Head of Inland Revenue.

After apologising for not delivering the report personally, Wilson's report covered the hunt for the Kandyan. Captain Noordeen's men had still not caught the man who was confirmed badly wounded. He had not been spotted for over a week, and the assumption was that he had been spirited out of the city, perhaps to Kandy, to recover from his wounds.

Thomas sighed in disappointment. The man must be very experienced, having eluded many mercenaries, soldiers and agents looking for him.

One good bit of news in the report was that during their investigation, the revenue agents had uncovered what seemed to be the headquarters of the

Royalist network in the city. A tavern called the Inn of the Lion in Pettah had been raided, and its proprietor, a man, called Lokubada, had been taken into custody.

We've made some progress, Thomas thought, *but it's not enough.*

The remaining sheaf of papers was a record of a few years of cinnamon contracts signed by the East India Company. Thomas leafed through the paperwork, which detailed the quantity of spice transiting through various ports on the island for which taxes were liable. A circled note on one of the margins caught his attention. The note questioned an increase in the shipment of cinnamon from Jaffnapatam, located in the north of the island. This increase occurred when the Crown Colony was at war with the Kandyan Kingdom, which seemed odd to Thomas.

Thomas sat back thoughtfully. It was obvious to him since he arrived that the commercial aims of the British East India Company were dictating the development of its policies on the island. But would they stoop so low as to share confidential military information with the Kandyans to gather additional cinnamon concessions? He doubted that it was the Company's policy to do that, but what about its operation in Jaffnapatam? *Would they?*

Making a note to speak to Major Staples, he also dashed off a note to Wilson requesting him to open a confidential investigation into the trading affairs of the Company in Jaffnapatam. He knew that the Government Agent who held the post was relatively young, and questions were raised in the past about his capabilities since he didn't speak any of the local languages.

A gust of wind twirled through the open door setting the old punkah in motion. Thomas glared up at it. He was hoping to spend some time outside taking in the rays of the afternoon sun. It seemed like the weather was changing, bringing inevitable afternoon showers.

Feeling bored, he left his room and walked down the stairs, meeting Johnson, carrying a tray holding a glass and a jug of water halfway.

'Can I help you with anything, Sah?' Johnson asked, stepping aside to let Thomas pass.

'I decided to see what the Major and his Welsh lads have built in the cellar,

Johnson. Would you be good enough to guide me since the Major is not here?'

Johnson hurried down the stairs behind the governor, leaving his tray on a side table, before directing Thomas to the rear of the house. Like the others in the hallway, a wooden door revealed a set of stairs leading down into the cellar.

'Could you remain here, Sah, till I get a lamp?'

Thomas nodded, peering into the darkness with interest until Johnson returned with an oil lamp.

'You must be careful, Sah,' he cautioned. 'It's quite steep.'

The two of them descended, led by Johnson, who carried the lamp aloft, illuminating the narrow staircase.

The cellar room they entered was lined with rock. The earthen floor underfoot smoothed down to almost a polished surface. Square stone columns supported the thick wooden beams of the mansion above. The light didn't quite pierce the far corners of the room, which was mostly empty. Besides a few large trunks, various bits of household furniture, portraits and wall hangings, the only other contents were two wooden racks containing wine bottles and a large iron-bound wooden cask often found on ships

Johnson led Thomas to a closed door on the eastern side of the room. Opening the door with a key he produced from his pocket, he stopped at the narrow entrance.

'The entrance to the tunnel is in this room,' he explained. 'Major Staples decided not to go down another level which made it more difficult and would have taken longer to complete.'

Thomas walked into a chamber about the size of his bedroom. It had been dug out by hand, as indicated by the pick and shovel marks on the chalky rock. The floor was rough and unswept. The opening to the narrow tunnel was at the far end of the room, its arched entrance dark and uninviting.

Johnson brought the oil lantern closer to the tunnel entrance.

'I usually leave a torch at the other end of the tunnel for Miss Lovina to use,' Johnson said. 'Only my wife and I know where the entrance is,' he added.

'Where does it lead?' Thomas asked.

'There's a disused well behind her property which has run dry,' Johnson explained. 'There's an entrance at the bottom of the well which leads to the tunnel. It's not easy to find,' he added.

'How does one get down there?' Thomas questioned.

'You must climb a ladder hidden in the tall grass near the well. It's the only way to get down.'

Thomas nodded at Johnson's explanation. 'I am glad I don't have to be climbing up and down ladders at my age,' he chuckled. 'We can leave that up to athletic young ladies like Miss Lovinia.'

As Thomas turned to leave, 'One more thing, Sah,' Johnson said. 'Major Staples has arranged for an iron gate to be constructed across the entrance. It is being built, and the Welsh lads will be back to install it when it's ready. Only I will have the key to let anyone in.'

In his room, Thomas lay on the divan and closed his eyes. He felt pleased that everything was falling into place. Expenditure was under control after the reforms he had instituted, and his situation had improved considerably since he had first arrived on the island. Building the country retreat had been a masterstroke giving him access to Lovinia whenever he wanted. Juliet was an excellent housekeeper at his official residence in Colombo, and everyone thought she was his mistress.

And to make matters better. No one suspected anything about Lovinia.

CHAPTER 38

THE SEARCH

The streets and taverns of the city were rife with ugly rumours as the search for the Kandyan entered its seventh day. Not just about the manhunt but the clash outside the Inn of the Lion, which had left three men dead. People gossiped about it while they supped, lounged on the verandah, drank in the taverns or smoked their hookah pipes in a cloud of ganja-infused fumes.

'You've been paid enough gold to find him,' said Wilson, scowling, 'but here we are, still none the wiser of which hole he is hiding in.'

'We have paid the price, too,' Captain Noordeen snapped. 'I've lost four of my men and have to pay blood money to their widows.'

'Spare me the platitudes,' Wilson snarled. 'I am under pressure from the Governor to deliver something.' He shook his head in disgust.

A deep uneasy silence descended between the two men. The mercenary captain was the first to speak.

'I have a plan to capture him,' Captain Noordeen said, only his eyes betraying his disquiet. 'I am going to withdraw my men from the inner city, and I suggest you do the same with your British dogs.'

'How is that going to work?' Wilson asked incredulously. 'If we take our foot off, it'll only beholden him further.'

'Exactly.' Captain Noordeen leaned forward impatiently. 'That's exactly what I expect to happen.'

Wilson thought about what the Captain had said for a moment.

'I see now,' he said, leaning back and smiling. 'You are a cagey bugger. You want to draw him out. Lay a trap for him,' he smiled, 'Clever!' He picked up his glass of ale and raised it. 'To a successful undertaking!'

'It won't be that simple,' Captain Noordeen said, glaring at the man.

'No, it won't,' Wilson agreed. 'If it were that simple, we would have caught him by now. Have you heard from your contacts in Kandy?'

'I know he has not returned to Kandy. That's what I hear, anyway. What news have you heard?' Noordeen growled.

'The same as you,' Wilson agreed. 'That means he's either dead, too wounded to travel, or hiding somewhere close.'

'I'll put my money that he's hiding somewhere close, licking his wounds.' The Captain said. 'Have you been able to get the inn's owner to talk?'

Wilson shook his head. 'He's being difficult, or he doesn't know anything. He swears that the Kandyan left the inn the same night three of your men were killed.'

'One of my men saw what happened,' the Captain said furiously. 'It was the guards who shot them.'

'Yes, they did,' agreed Wilson. 'He says his guards thought they were under attack by a rival gang and defended the place. He lost two of his men during the attack, it seems.'

'He's lying, and you know it,' the Captain muttered angrily. He knew it would be foolish to challenge him further, not wanting to face the Englishman's displeasure.

'I believe he doesn't know where the Kandyan is,' Wilson said. 'That's all that matters. Our methods are persuasive, and he would have told us. Now tell me. How do you plan to lure him into a trap?'

*

Kumara was bored. The wound under his arm was healing well, and the ache in his head had almost disappeared, making his thoughts much clearer. He couldn't leave the hut as the dark skies showed no signs of letting up the downpour that relentlessly battered the forest.

Someone from Lovinia's household visited him daily, bringing food, medicine and company. Apart from the daily contact, Kumara was beginning to feel lonely.

Kumara touched the long scar which parted his hair at the top of his head with his fingers. The wound had healed, but it was sensitive to the touch. His fingers felt sticky, so he wiped Aletta's ointment on his sarong. He was lucky the sword had not cracked his skull open. He had spent the morning doing light stretching exercises in the hut. He ran through a series of movements which strengthened his sword arm, recognising he couldn't let his stamina decline.

The news that Banda had brought that morning did not please him. British troops had raided the Inn of the Lion, and Lokubada had been arrested. He had been taken away in chains, and no one knew where he was.

'It's too dangerous for you to return,' Banda stated. 'All the roads into the city are being watched by soldiers. If you wish to travel anywhere, keep yourself well covered.'

The warning rang in his head. 'What about Noordeen?' Kumara asked. He was not concerned about the British soldiers, but Captain Noordeen and his men were a different matter. They had almost got him twice and had left him in this state. Kumara realised it would be foolish to show himself in the city if Noordeen was still looking for him.

Banda shrugged and shook his head. 'I heard nothing about him, but his men are still searching for you.'

Kumara thought for a while. Lokubada had promised the night he left the inn that he would send his men to search for the mercenary hideout.

Kumara shared that information with Banda. 'Could we send a message to discover what they have learnt?' Kumara asked. 'Taking Lokubada away will only delay things. Sakuntala will know what's going on.'

Banda had left him, promising to find out what he could.

Kumara also realised he had to get word to the Chinaman that he was wounded but alive. He was sure rumours of his close escape from the Malays would be around the town, and he needed to let his King know that he was still alive.

I'll worry about that later, he thought. I don't want anyone to know where I am hiding. The Chinaman, though in the King's employ, was not a man to be trusted completely.

With nothing else troubling his mind, his thoughts inevitably went to Lovinia. The dancer turned spy who had become his lover. The days he looked forward to most were when Lovinia would come alone and spend time together. He had his fair share of women in the past, but the feeling the Mestizo woman gave him was nothing he had ever experienced.

Looking back, he tried to understand when his feelings for her had changed. *It was that kiss.* But it was more than sexual attraction, he decided. Holding her lithe body in his arms that night had affected him physically.

His thoughts stirred him into movement. He walked out into the open yard through little puddles of rainwater, feeling the wet earth between his toes. The rain had stopped, and rays of sunshine struggled through the clouds sending little wisps of steam into the air.

Kumara knew what he felt for Lovinia were a distraction to his mission for the King, but he couldn't think of any way to separate the feelings that clashed within him. He needed her to provide insight into the *Andukāraya's* thinking and any other information she could collect. But his affection for her conflicted with that mission. *What if she gets caught?*

The King valued his services but had his detractors in the Royal court. What would happen if the King died or was overthrown by one of the *Adigars?* Where would that leave me? He was not a rich man with landholdings. Where would we go if we had to leave this place suddenly? All these thoughts came rushing into his head. He had been so focused on his work for the King that he had never thought about his future.

Kumara had been following a path and found himself at the village tank. He was so lost in his thoughts that he did not remember how he got there. Mentally resolving to think about his problem further, he walked to the top of the *bund* (embankment) and looked around. The reservoir was full, and water leaked over the dam, cutting deep grooves in the earth. The hoarse scream of a White-tailed Fishing Eagle perched on one of the higher branches of a tall tree overhanging the water echoed across the water.

Kumara didn't want to be seen by any of the villagers who maintained the reservoir, so he hurried back down the path into the forest, which protected him from observation.

*

She slept a little. Not much. When she woke, the house was quiet. Right now, Lovinia wanted to be by herself. Nothing more. She went to the living room, bare feet silent against the cool earthen floor. She stretched her limbs, which were stiff with tiredness. She took slow breaths, moving her body through gentle exercises to warm the blood. Then she raised her hands above her head and began her dance exercises. Even though her body had grown unused to the activity and her muscles were sore, falling into the familiar pattern felt like coming home.

Lovinia had responded to the *Andukāraya's* summons the previous evening and had found him fully recovered and happy to see her. They made love for the first time since he got sick. The *Andukāraya's* libido and strength had almost returned to normal. A lightening of the eastern sky was the only indication that dawn was close when she crept into her bed, hoping to get some sleep.

When Aletta woke, Lovinia was covered in sweat, her hair tangled. Aletta gave Lovinia a significant look but did not say anything. Instead, she went to the back verandah, where Lovinia heard her filling a bucket with water from the well.

'You were out all night,' Aletta commented as she entered the room. 'Have you slept at all?'

'Not much,' Lovinia responded. She could feel a headache building. 'Have you?'

Aletta made a dismissive sound. 'I always worry when you go out at night,' she said. 'I don't like you using that tunnel in the dark.'

'I don't like it either, but what choice do I have,' Lovinia replied. 'It's the only way to see him.'

'It's for your protection, but you must be careful,' Aletta agreed. 'He has many enemies who wish to use your relationship against him. Always have your dagger with you, and don't hesitate to use it if you must.'

Lovinia nodded. She was used to Aletta trying to mother her.

'I've prepared a bath for you,' Aletta said. 'I'll help you comb your hair when you've finished.'

Later, after Lovinia completed her morning ablutions, they sat around the kitchen table having sliced pawpaw for breakfast.

'How is Kumara?' Lovinia asked, wiping the juice trickling down the side of her mouth.

'He's almost fully recovered,' Aletta replied, 'he's started exercising. He wanted your father to get some information from the city.'

Lovinia nodded, scooping a slice of the yellow fruit and placing it in her mouth. 'He's like that. Never stops. I am supposed to go to him today but don't feel quite up to it.'

Lovinia could feel Aletta studying her as she ate.

'Hmmm, I can go in your place, I suppose,' Aletta grinned.

'Thanks,' Lovinia said, looking up. 'Tell him I'll be there tomorrow,'

Aletta nodded, but she looked worried. 'I hope you are taking the potion I gave you regularly. You don't want to get pregnant.'

Lovinia stared at Aletta. Heat flared in her cheeks. 'What made you bring that up?' she asked. 'Of course, I am taking it.' She didn't need Aletta to keep reminding her of it. She needed to rely on herself first and foremost.

Aletta reached out and held her hand. 'You are like a sister to me, Lovinia, and this is not a game you are playing. These are serious men who will discard you when you are useless to them.'

Lovinia suppressed a flinch. The warmth of Aletta's voice had disappeared, replaced with a seriousness she had not heard for some time. Lovinia took a deep breath. Treachery, spies, danger, lies. And she had thought her life had been so tranquil, so ... boring.

Aletta was watching her, saying nothing. The silence was no longer inviting.

Lovinia mulled over her words. Her friend was very astute and only wanted to protect her. Then she met Aletta's eyes. 'Yes, I know you are worried about me, and I will do what needs to be done.'

Aletta's gaze met hers and held it. Her eyes softened. 'There have been so many demands and expectations placed on you,' she said softly. 'I am amazed at how you've handled them all, and you've grown as a woman too.'

Lovinia's throat constricted at Aletta's words. She hadn't realised how much she valued her friend's support until that moment. She reached out and wrapped her arms around Aletta, her eyes moist with tears.

CHAPTER 39

SETTING A TRAP

Thomas had received news of a significant sea battle off the Spanish mainland. The British Royal Navy had triumphed over a combined French and Spanish fleet at the Battle of Trafalgar near Cadiz. It took over three months for the news to reach Madras before travelling to Ceylon.

Understanding the victory's implication, Thomas decided to hold a victory ball at the official Governor-General's residence in the Royal Navy's honour. He toyed with the idea of sending an invitation to the King of Kandy to remind him of the power of the British Empire. Still, he resisted the impulse, doubting the King would see any humour in the situation.

He was staying at his official residence in the city and sent for Major Staples. Thomas was sitting at his desk when the Major entered.

'You sent for me, your excellency.'

Thomas considered the Major standing before him. He had been everything Thomas had wanted in an aide-de-camp and had come to depend on his competence and devotion to duty.

'I have an issue I must discuss with you, Major, one that concerns you,' Thomas began. 'Why don't you sit down.'

Yes, sire.' The Major settled comfortably into the chair opposite Thomas's desk. The stiffness he had displayed when Thomas first met him had disappeared, replaced by an air of easy competence.

'I remember a conversation we both had shortly after I came here about your plans for the future.' Thomas began. 'Do you recall it?'

'That I want to make this place my home, your excellency. Yes, I do.'

'Well, you also recall my telling you I recommended you for a promotion. A well-deserved one, I may add,' Thomas said, steepling his hands.

The Major's eyes narrowed. 'Yes, sire, I do.'

'Well, your promotion has come through, Major,' Thomas smiled thinly. 'What I did not foresee is that the War Office has reassigned you back to England to your old regiment as Lieutenant Colonel.'

The Major frowned, his face etched in stone. He didn't look like a man who had received good news. 'I see, sire.'

'And here lies the conundrum, Major,' Thomas said. 'In my recommendation, I specifically requested that you remain in the country as my aide, given your knowledge and experience of the local conditions. But someone in the War Office in London has decided to overrule my request, for which I am not pleased.'

The Major sat silently, looking down at his hands. Thomas could see that he was struggling to reconcile the situation he'd found himself in.

Thomas decided to put him out of his misery. 'I have decided to ignore the order to reassign you to Home command,' he said. 'As Commander in Chief, I have the right to choose my officers. I will inform England that you are an irreplaceable asset, given our current manpower shortage. You will remain with the rank of Major until I hear back from England. However, I will instruct the provost marshall that you will be paid as a Lieutenant Colonel until your rank is officially gazetted.'

The Major's eyes lit up, and his face brightened. 'Thank you, sire,' he said. 'It would have placed me in an extremely difficult situation. I have met someone here whose hand I want to ask in marriage. I believe she will say yes, so returning to England would have complicated things immensely.'

Thomas smiled at the Major's reaction. 'Congratulations, Major. Do I know the lucky lady?'

'Well, it was something I wanted to discuss with you, your excellency,' the

Major looked at Thomas earnestly. 'It's Mrs Hartley, your housekeeper.'

'Juliet!' Thomas was surprised but not shocked. He had seen the two conversing around the house and felt a sense of relief that she had found someone like the Major to look after her.

'That's wonderful news,' he said, smiling broadly. 'I spent many months with her on our journey over, and I couldn't think of a more level-headed and capable woman.'

'Thank you, sire.' Major Staples looked like a weight had been lifted off his shoulders. 'With your permission, sire, I will propose to Juliet, I mean, Mrs Hartley, as soon as I get a chance.'

'Congratulations, Major, and pass on my best wishes to Juliet.'

The Major nodded and stood up.

'Before you go, Major, I have a job for you,' Thomas said. 'I intend to hold an official ball to celebrate our win at Trafalgar. I have chosen you, Major, as the event manager,' Thomas told his aide.

Being the competent aide, the Major reached for the notebook he always carried.

'You will, of course, have the assistance of a platoon of duty aides,' Thomas added. 'And I want a good show. Plenty of dancing and feasting and no expense spared. Something to delight the women and give them something to write home about.'

Thomas watched the Major scribble in his notebook.

'I also want to come up with some entertainment that will delight and entertain our civilian guests. Yet I'm damned if I can think of anything. Any ideas, Major? A man like you should be able to come up with something exciting.'

The Major thought for a moment, and then his eyes became fixed and distant as an idea seemed to cross his mind.

'How about a fireworks display, sir?'

'Fireworks display?'

'It would be very easy to arrange. And it would give our civilian guests some idea of the battlefield's rocket flares and cannon explosions.'

'A fireworks display! Why that's an excellent idea!' Thomas beamed. 'We are the military, after all.'

Thomas rubbed his hands together in anticipated pleasure. 'Well, I shall leave all the arrangements in your hands, Major. I suggest you get together with Mrs Hartley to do the planning. A woman's touch, you know!' He chuckled in approval.

*

The arrangements and organisation for the ball at Government House were carried out with all the precision and efficiency of a battle campaign. On the night, a guard of *Lascarin* soldiers uniformed in red stood to attention around the house's lawns. At the same time, a battalion of uniformed native servants waited in readiness to serve.

At precisely seven o'clock, the guests began to arrive in streams. Officers resplendent in scarlet coats with gold loops and chains, others in the pale blue and gold of the Light Cavalry or the green and red of the Rifle regiments; all every bit as colourful as the ladies in their shimmering gowns of every hue and shade.

The ball was in full swing by half past seven, with guests still arriving. Thomas moved around the ballroom, conferring with the guests, occasionally pausing to speak and joke with some of his fellow officers.

As the night progressed, the room became unbearably noisy with hysterically happy laughter, ladies shrieking greetings across the room and men bowing graciously in response. On every female neck and hand, jewels blazed garishly. Some of the civilian gentlemen of the East India Company were almost as bejewelled as the ladies, with ruby and diamond rings dazzling on both hands.

At the far end of the room, a group of men stood together, arms around each other's shoulders and singing a faintly disreputable jingle from one of London's faraway music halls. Martial music bubbled over the din.

Everyone filed to the lawn after supper to watch the fireworks display. Cries of delight greeted a series of loud bangs. Fireworks erupted over the moonlit sky, whistling a tune and shooting out silver stars, which fluttered down with a rainbow flash of lights. The air was quickly filled with thick swirling smoke and the acrid smell of gunpowder.

'Magnificient,' Sir David remarked, his eyes shining in the light of the exploding pyrotechnics. 'It evokes the senses of what a real battle must be like.'

Thomas didn't have the heart to tell him that it sounded nothing like a real battle. The sound uppermost at the time is the unrelenting screaming of injured men and horses cruelly cut down by the explosions.

He finally managed to escape the clutches of several matrons who towed their daughters along to be introduced. His legs, in breeches and well-polished boots, stretched before him, and a half-full wineglass tilted his hand. On the table by his elbow stood a carafe with an inch or two of pale amber wine. He raised the crystal glass and sipped, intent on the garden outside the window. But Thomas's gaze was directed at nothing. He had spent the last two weeks in Colombo in a whirlwind of activity, approving various lists and attending tea parties and soirees organised by various groups of ladies. He looked at the recent and past and, with increasing curiosity, at the future.

The sound of laughter, conversation, and clinking goblets drifted in from the packed ballroom down the corridor. He knew that his time on the island was limited. These were not lifelong positions, and he wondered whether the war in Europe would require his services in the future.

Thomas drew in a breath of the warm moist air which had found its way through the open terrace door. He could smell the delicate scent of night jasmine that grew in abundance up the wrought ironwork pillars supporting the upper balcony. When he was in England, it was easy to laugh at the descriptions he had read of the island paradise according to the followers of Islam, where Adam and Eve had sought refuge after being driven away from the Garden of Eden, or the Greeks, who called it the Land of Lotus Flowers. However, the mystique of the climate and the country made him realise they did not exaggerate.

Someone tapped tentatively on the half-open door.

Deep in his thoughts, Thomas suppressed a sense of irritation, realising he was no longer alone with his thoughts. It was a feeling that seemed to have grown over the past week he had spent in Colombo. He missed the solitude surrounding him like a protective blanket in his country mansion. Life in the grandeur of the official residence made him immune from the commonplaces of everyday life outside of the city. The lovely palm-fringed coastline, chants of the fishermen as they pulled up their daily catch, the comforting rhythms of drums beating at a nearby temple, and the sounds and smells of the forests. He could live an elegant and leisurely life without the pressures constantly around him in the city.

'Yes?'

The door creaked open, and Major Staples poked his head through the opening.

'Oh, there you are, sir,' he said, looking over his shoulder while sidling into the room and closing the door firmly behind him. 'I was wondering where you had escaped to.'

'How perceptive of you,' Thomas said, forcing a smile. 'Your choice of words.'

Major Staples nodded glumly. 'I made sure not to be followed, your excellency.'

'Congratulations are in order, Major. You've done a magnificent job tonight. Please pass on my thanks to everyone who was involved.'

The Major nodded, walking over to where Thomas was sitting. 'Thank you, sire,' he said tiredly. 'There is a reason why I came looking for you.'

Something in the way he spoke made Thomas look at him sharply.

'I am afraid, your excellency, that I have some grave news. There are whispers on the street that the Kandyan is back.'

Thomas sat up straight as he absorbed the news. 'Has Wilson been able to verify this?'

The Major shook his head. 'I'm not sure, sir. Wilson sought me to arrange a meeting in the morning. He only told me what it was about when I said you won't be available as you were leaving for your country estate.'

Thomas sat back in his chair, his mind settling on the day. He was not surprised. In his experience, men like the Kandyan rebel never died. History was littered with stories about such men. They usually reappeared in physical or spiritual manifestation to lead their people to greater things. He had met one such man when he was Commander in Chief in Sainte Domingue in the West Indies. Toussaint Louverture was a prominent leader of the Haitian Revolution. He was born enslaved in the French colony. He became an outstanding leader, displaying military and political acumen that transformed the slave rebellion into a revolutionary movement against the French.

Thomas nodded. 'Schedule it for tomorrow at a reasonable time in the afternoon before I leave.'

Later, as he drifted off to sleep under his mosquito net, his mind was restless. It flitted from the anxiety he felt not seeing Lovinia for so long to wanting to know about the important news that Wilson was bringing.

I am not going to let this man delay my departure. I have wanted to go back ever since I got here.

*

Wilson looked rested and refreshed when he arrived at Government House for the meeting the next day. The same could not be said of Thomas, who had hardly slept a wink. There were so many thoughts whirling around in his mind.

It had just turned noon, and the heat from the day had already begun to penetrate the room. Not a breath of air stirred the flimsy cotton drapes keeping the glare of the noonday sun at bay.

Wilson cleared his throat and opened his folder. He was seated on the sofa next to the Major while Thomas sat on the chair opposite them. His first report was not about the Kandyan.

'Your excellency, I want to begin with some good news. My men have discovered the person leaking vital information to our enemies. Unfortunately, it is one of our own.'

Thomas and Major Staples exchanged glances. This was not what they had expected.

'You mean an Englishman?' Major Staples sounded outraged.

'Yes, indeed,' Wilson nodded, handing a sheet of paper to Thomas. 'Young

James Hardwick from Lancashire, who works in the Company Head Office, has found himself deep in debt – too much opium and expensive women, I am afraid. They used that to force him to hand over information, mostly of a trading nature, but some of our military dispositions too.'

Thomas's lips tightened as he scanned the report.

'How did you find out?' Thomas asked, handing the report to Major Staples.

'He came to us, sir,' Wilson looked pleased. 'He got cold feet when we started asking questions and came clean.'

This was excellent news that would please the Home Office, Thomas decided. The report said he had been passing vital secrets for several years.

'What do you recommend we do with him?' Thomas tugged at his ear. 'I don't want this to become a scandal and a barrier between the Crown and the Company.'

'I can arrange to send him back to England, your excellency. They can deal with him over there. No one outside this group needs to know.'

'I agree, Wilson,' Thomas sat back, trying to absorb the news. He looked across at Major Staples and then back to Wilson. 'I want to know every bit of information he has passed over. We could even use this news to our advantage if we acted swiftly.'

'Yes, your excellency,' Wilson replied. 'I've started that process already.'

Thomas nodded. He was pleased with Wilson. The man had proven to be quite capable. 'You've done well, Wilson. I'll make sure it is noted in your record.'

'Thank you, your excellency,' Wilson smiled. 'The other reason I am here, of course, is to give you an update on our hunt for the Kandyan.'

'Yes, please do,' Thomas said instantly. 'The man's been a thorn in our side even before I arrived.'

Noting that both men were waiting for him to speak, Wilson continued.

'I've received one report that a man calling himself the Kandyan met with a group of rebels a few days ago,' Wilson said. 'Coincidentally, this sighting happened simultaneously with lots of questions being asked about Captain Noordeen and his men.'

'That's the Malay officer who deserted with his men from Kandy, your excellency,' Major Staples reminded Thomas.

Thomas nodded. 'What does all this mean?' he questioned Wilson. 'You've had time to think it over.'

'Undoubtedly, the Kandyan is alive. He must have been wounded hence his absence, but he is back and is being extremely careful. I believe he is planning some mischief against the Malay and his men, who were the ones who injured him. That's my assessment, your excellency.'

After completing his report, Wilson sat back, looking at Thomas expectantly.

'Oh, I believe you, Wilson.' Thomas leaned forward. 'But allowing him to roam around freely is not acceptable. What is your plan to bring him into custody? I presume you have a plan of some sort?'

'Yes, your Excellency. I do,' Wilson replied.

'Well, spit it out, man! We don't have all day.' Thomas had felt irritated from the moment he woke that morning. He wanted to get out of the city and resented delaying his departure, but he was glad he did, given the news.

'I have asked the City Commander to pull all our troops back to barracks and only keep the city entrances under observation,' said Wilson sensing the Governor's mood.

Thomas nodded impatiently. He had signed the order, so this was not news to him.

'This was done deliberately to loosen our grip on the citizens and make the Kandyan think we're not looking for him anymore.' Wilson glanced at the Major and continued. 'Captain Noordeen's men are being held back until he is sighted, and we'll use them to deal with the Kandyan. The Malays know what he looks like and are likelier to catch him.'

'What about your idea that he's going after the Malay?' Thomas queried.

'That's a part of the plan, sire. It doesn't matter how we draw him out. We'll be ready for him.'

CHAPTER 40

PREPARING

'Do you realise you will be walking into a trap?' Banda asked. 'The soldiers have been sent back to their barracks, but they have quietly doubled the guard at all the gates. They want you back in the city.'

It was evening, and the smoky fire kept the mosquitos at bay. They were meeting at the vidiya three nights before a scheduled dance ceremony. He needed to be gone by the next night, so Kumara had asked Banda and Aletta to join the two of them to discuss the plan he had come up with. He needed their help for it to succeed.

'What do you plan to do?' Aletta asked. Always the direct one, she wanted to get to the point of a matter.

'I cannot complete my assignment for the King unless I have easy access in and out of the city,' Kumara said, standing up while looking at Aletta. He understood the feeling of uncertainty amongst the small group, the enormity of the task, and the feeling of something hanging in the balance.

'It's vital to our network, the way we operate.' Kumara paused, looking around the group, before continuing. 'It's got much harder since the Malays arrived from Kandy. They are part of the group that guarded the King and have seen me come and go from the palace. The Britishers have heard of me but have no idea what I look like, so it makes it easier to move around amongst them.'

'So, it's obvious,' Banda said. 'You have to get rid of them.'

Kumara paced around with restless energy. 'Yes,' he replied. 'Or discredit them somehow. But they are under the protection of the English in the fort.' He had received news from Sakuntala that her men had tracked the Malay mercenaries to the fort.

Banda nodded. 'She also said she's gathering a few capable men you can use when the time's right. According to her, their numbers are low, given the two failed attempts at the Inn of the Lion. She's a dangerous one, for sure.'

'She's worth her weight in gold and more,' Kumara agreed.

'Ok, so you know where he is hiding,' said Lovinia, looking at her friend, who was shaking her leg impatiently. 'So, what do you plan to do?'

'Wars are not always decided on the battlefield,' Kumara said, 'but by deception and cunning. That's the Kandyan way of fighting, and we'll follow that same principle when we deal with Noordeen and his men.'

Banda poked at the fire with a long stick.

'The British will use the mercenaries to do their work for them while they watch and wait to see the outcome,' Kumara said. 'It's the British way of doing things. We need a big distraction to draw the British's attention while dealing with the mercenaries.'

Kumara was convinced that the men Sakuntala had assembled could deal with the mercenaries if they were less than a dozen fit men. Captain Noordeen was the key. He needed to be killed for the plan to succeed.

'What if we start a fire near where they store their ammunition by the outer gate in the north,' Banda asked. 'Maybe more than one fire. Wouldn't that keep the soldiers distracted?'

Kumara thought the idea was certainly worth exploring. Fires were taken very seriously by the inhabitants of cities. Most of them lived in houses or dwellings built of wood.

'Yes,' Kumara agreed. 'That will certainly focus their attention.'

"How will you deal with Captain Noordeen,' asked Lovinia anxiously. 'He's supposed to be a real beast, and you're not strong enough to fight him.'

'This is where Aletta comes in.'

Kumara studied the woman who was Lovinia's best friend. He was unsure whether she approved of his new relationship with Lovinia, but she was key to his plans.

'What do you want from me?' She was studying him without giving away any of her thoughts.

'As a healer, you must know a lot about poisons,' Kumara said. 'Am I correct?'

Aletta blinked in surprise. 'Yes, I suppose I do,' she said after a moment's hesitation. 'There are many poisonous plants in the forest which people come into contact with by mistake. I need to know how they work to heal the victims.'

Kumara nodded. It was what he expected.

'I have a task for you,' he said, watching her eyes, watching her reaction. 'Prepare me a small potion, when taken, will deaden the senses but not kill.'

Aletta wrinkled her brow and did not speak right away. 'How will you use it?' she finally asked. 'Some are ingested by eating, others are mixed with liquid.'

'Something that can be mixed in a drink which cannot be detected.' Kumara said. 'I know a way to immobilise the Malay Captain without him finding out.'

'How will you do that?' Banda questioned. 'He always has his men around him.'

'Leave that to me,' Kumara waved him off. 'It's going to take some planning and a lot of gold.'

Kumara looked at each of them in turn. 'Whatever happens to me, what's important is that we protect Lovinia's relationship with the *Andukāraya* at all costs. Not even a whisper must get out.'

Seeing that they all understood his words, he finally relaxed. He needed their support to do what he had planned.

'When do we have to leave this place?' he asked, turning to Lovinia.

She gave him a look filled with meaning. 'The villagers will be here during the day to prepare,' she said. 'Aletta and I will make sure there are no traces of you being here.'

*

Captain Noordeen looked around the room at his men, who wore dusty grey cotton pantaloons, wide leather belts, and curved cavalry swords. Some carried rifles heavy with silver and intricate carving. Less than half the number that had come with him from Kandy. They occupied a large room set aside for them in the fort. Alcohol was prohibited, so the men lounged or kept busy cleaning, sharpening their weapons, and playing *dum* (Malaysian checkers) while sipping toddy, a fermented drink made from coconut water by adding sugar and a pinch of yeast.

He quietly swore under his breath but was careful not to show them how he was feeling. He had been hoping to use the gold from the Englishman to buy some land outside the city, but he would have to use it instead to hire more men. He shifted in his chair, moving his sword between his legs.

'We need more men,' Puteri said, startling Noordeen as if he had read his mind.

The Captain had not seen Puteri approach and almost snapped at his lieutenant, but he bit back his words before they came out. Puteri was loyal but did not possess a sharp intellect which is why he was still around. He studied the man in front of him. Puteri had a large head and a heavily pockmarked face, with eyes which looked too small. He was a big man with broad shoulders set on a substantial frame and was deadly in a fight which is why the men respected him.

'I agree,' the Captain said. He didn't need to assert his authority until the time was right. 'Do you know of any who are available?'

Puteri tugged his left ear, which was missing a large chunk. 'No one wants to join us,' he said in his gravelly voice. 'They don't like us working with the invaders.'

The men must have been talking about it, which is why Puteri raised it with me, the Captain thought.

'How about our men,' he said, waving his arm around the room. 'Are they dissatisfied with all the gold we are making?'

'It's not about the gold, captain,' Puteri shifted uneasily, looking around the room. 'The men are not happy living here. Their families are complaining that they want to live in Kampong Kertel.'

Captain Noordeen understood the men's frustrations. He, too, felt the need to get away from the rigid discipline the British army enforced in their fortress. But he knew the reason they were being held here.

Captain Noordeen pushed back his chair and stood to face a man of a height equal to his own. He was aware of his lieutenant's bunched fists with their swollen well-used knuckles. If there were going to be a challenge to his authority, it would never do to be caught sitting down.

'We have talked about this before,' the Captain raised his voice. 'The Englishers won't let us leave until we find the Kandyan. It's the price we must pay for leaving Kandy.'

Outside the alcove, the rest of the room had gone quiet, the babble of indecipherable conversation dying away; all eyes were now on the two men facing each other. In anticipation, it became a crowd who seemed taken by the fact that there might be a contest, while those closest were wondering if it was safe to stay within the orbit of its coming violence.

A moment followed when violence was on the cusp—the two men standing locked eyes. Puteri was the first to break contact. His eyes flicked a glance at Captain Noordeen's sword at his side.

Sensing a reduction in tension between the two men, the room slowly returned to life. 'How long do we have to stay here?' a voice called out. 'It's easy for us as we come and go as we please. But our women and children don't like it.'

'That is all we want to know,' Puteri said in a strained voice. 'The soldiers treat us like we are uncultured savages. It won't take much for one of them to lose their head.'

A growl of assent from the men made Captain Noordeen realise the problem was more serious than he had thought. They talked with each other in low voices, occasionally glancing at him angrily.

I need to settle this now before it gets out of hand.

He raised his arm, waiting until the room quietened.

'It won't be much longer,' he began, trying to project his voice across the room. 'We have set in place a trap to catch the man.'

'What makes you think we will catch him?' Puteri asked. 'He has eluded the British for years, and we have had no better fortune.'

'I will not be turned from this,' he said with a grim finality that silenced Puteri. 'We are mercenaries, men for hire, and we are being paid to do a job.' He looked around the room. 'You have already forgotten how the Kandyan King treated us when he wanted to kill us all,' he paused, looking into the eyes of the men around him, 'including our families,' he shouted.

The Captain saw that some of the men were nodding. He was getting through to them. It was time to shut down the dissenters.

He lowered his voice. 'And in any case, the British will now double what they pay if we catch the Kandyan.' He had been trying not to tell his men about doubling the payment, but he realised he had no choice.

A buzz of sound erupted as the men conferred with each other, some nodding as they absorbed the news.

The Captain sat down, gulping a glass of *thambili* (King coconut water). He had bought some time, but he had nothing more to offer. *They must catch the Kandyan soon.*

CHAPTER 41

THE HEALING CEREMONY

Lovinia and Aletta spent the entire day preparing for the *tovil* ceremony. They arrived early and found Kumara had left during the night. They cleaned out the hut he had been using to recuperate, removing all signs of his presence.

Lovinia had spent the previous evening with Kumara, and when it was time to leave, she had no desire to go but knew that she must.

'I have to leave,' she whispered, stroking his bearded face. 'Although I would rather stay.'

His expression softened as he encircled her wrist with lean fingers. She was surprised at his strength. He had been so gentle in his lovemaking.

'You must do what you must,' he said. 'Sometimes we have no choice in what happens next.' His arm encircled her narrow waist and gathered her against him. Her high, firm breasts pressed against his naked chest as she lifted her chin and kissed him.

Lovinia shook her head, trying to dispel her thoughts. Her emotions were confused, and she didn't want to examine them too closely.

'I've never participated in any of these ceremonies,' Lovinia said, reaching for the broom. 'You know my mother forbade me to join, and my father followed her wishes.'

'Your mother was a Christian!' Aletta replied as if it explained everything.

'They don't believe in supernatural deities. False gods, they call them.'

'I thought Buddhism does not recognise supernatural beings either?' Lovinia questioned.

'It doesn't, but Buddhism has been immersed in Hindu beliefs, which existed before the religion was brought into this country,' Aletta explained. 'In the villages of the south, these ancient beliefs are still practised in secret.'

They were ready when a group of villagers arrived later that morning with an assortment of supplies required for the night's ceremony. The object of the *daha-ata-paliya* (eighteen-form dance) ceremony was to cure a woman ill with fever by exorcising the demon whose presence in her body was believed to be the cause.

The main structure of the vidiya was covered on three sides with the bark of the banana tree, decorated with various shapes and figures made of the banana bark and tender young coconut leaves. Torches made by wrapping clean rags around a long stick were prepared and left in a pile for later use.

Women swept the compound of leaves and debris while men collected wood for the main fire. Some women rolled out reed mats in a large circle facing the main structure, while others prepared food and palm toddy for the occasion.

A group of men mended and cleaned all the masks and ceremonial clothing. At the same time, others attended the *yak bereya* (devil drums) used for the exorcising ceremony. They tightened the sinew thongs, which stretched the drum skins made from the stomach lining of cattle, giving the instrument its unique tone.

The enclosure had gradually filled with villagers and their children who treated the ceremony as a social gathering. The patient's family served food and sweets on banana leaves. The crowd gradually quietened and settled on their reed mats as the ceremony approached.

The constant, raucous cacophony of evening birdsong quietened as the evening light faded with its strange dimensions. In the darkness, there was a sense of things stirring, aligning, and a stage dressing for the action to begin.

Torches were lit, giving the area an eerie atmosphere representing an unknown world.

Lovinia sat with Aletta at the circle's edge, where she could watch without having to peer over the villager's heads. She knew that a few of her father's troupe performed in these ceremonies and hoped she'd recognise them in their costumes.

Two drummers dressed in white sarongs with a wide red band tightly wrapped around their waists positioned themselves on either side of the *vidiya*, where the patient, dressed completely in white, sat slumped on a low seat wrapped in white cloth and raised upon a table in the patient's hut. The torches were fed with oil and wood resin, burning brighter, and creating clouds of fragrant smoke as the drumming began.

The ceremony began with felicitations to the Buddha and propitiations to the Gods. These took the form of stylised prose accompanied by drumming until a dancer appeared garbed in an embroidered flounced skirt reaching just below the knees, a coarse loose shirt, bells around his legs and on his head a crown of palm leaves with long streamers. He brandished a lighted torch in each hand, above, below, and before, sometimes kneeling. Then his body was fumigated with the fragrant smoke. The dancer held the torch against his face, neck and body without apparent harm. Becoming much exhausted by his movements, he had to be fortified occasionally with drinks, including a considerable amount of palm toddy.

Another dancer followed, dressed similarly but wearing a hideously painted wooden *vesamuna* (mask), with hooded cobras and tusk-like teeth and pupils bulging out, holding a long torch by the middle lit in his mouth at each end. The dance steps were similar, but Lovinia noticed the pace of the drumming had begun to intensify as the performers ingested more toddy as the night wore on.

After a while, the masked dancer seized a young rooster of tawny red colour and, brandishing a knife, ran around furiously with savage howls making signs of beheading the fowl with his teeth. One of the drummers sang an invocation to the tormenting spirit. Then, the third and last dancer, with a different *vesamuna* and garments, imitated a furious bear with hideous noises and outlandish movements.

Excitement was high, and the place had filled even more. Around midnight, the dancing became more frenzied. The leading dancer's maskless face was even more frightening. Children screamed and clung to their mother's bodies at his very sight. His face, surrounded by long black hair, was painted black, with immaculately white teeth about double the normal size. He gyrated wildly around the patient, who was beginning to shiver in fright.

A white non-transparent cloth held by two people was pulled in front of the patient covering her view completely. The dancer and the drummers withdrew, and a deep rhythmic chanting started behind the vidiya, accompanied by the low beats of drums. Bells jingled off and on, symbolising to the audience that the *Mahason Yaka* (Devil Mahasona), played by the *Yakadura* (chief exorciser), was getting ready to enter. Suddenly a fearful cry was heard, signalling that he was almost ready. Again, a scream - this time even louder and the sound of beating drums increased in a frenzy.

The moment the drums started their frenzied beating, every hair on Lovinia's body stood up as if she had been struck by lightning. At such volume, the beat of the drums and the pace of the repetitive phrases were entirely different from any sound, any music she had ever heard. She looked at the calm faces and detached manner of the villagers who sat in family groups, maybe a dozen people in each group ranging from the middle-aged to some only ten or eleven years old - they were all so relaxed, even smiling and communicating with their eyes as if they were doing nothing more remarkable than preparing a meal. This contrast only heightened the abstraction. Their familiar, casual manner created a sense of security. If not framed by such a reassuring sense of the ordinary, Lovinia might have been scared by the music's effect upon her.

Since the sides of the vidiya were covered with bark, no one in the audience knew where the *Mahason Yaka* would emerge. The drumming ceased, and with a piercing scream, the *Mahason Yaka* dressed all in white, wearing a ritual *kolam natima vesamuna* (wolf-headed mask), pulled apart the banana bark and pushed his head through while screaming again and again. Eventually, he brought his entire body into the vidiya, advancing step by step while screaming at each step.

From where Lovinia and Aletta were sitting, they could see the gyrations of the *Yakadura* performing for the villagers. The patient behind the white cloth whose head kept turning, eyes roving nervously, waiting for the moment the demon appeared in front of her. The patient cowered back, hearing his voice getting closer and closer. Suddenly, the *Mahason Yaka* stopped screaming while continuing to entertain and frighten the onlookers with his frenzied dancing.

The jingling of the bells on his feet made the patient aware that the *Mahason Yaka* was close at hand. She looked around nervously, pushing herself upright on her chair.

After advancing towards the patient, *Mahason Yaka* pushed aside the concealing cloth and jumped on her with a loud yell making the patient scream. The patient, shocked by his sudden appearance, her face contorted with fear and emotion, fainted, her head lolling forward on her chest.

The drumming resumed at full vigour and intensified the whole atmosphere. The *Mahason Yaka* continued spinning vigorously around the unconscious patient, with hideous shrieks building into an intense moment as he chased the demon from the woman's body. Four strong men from his ritual team held him as he fell in a tremor, his teeth chattering against each other, fists clenched, his body stiff as a board.

After this intense moment in the ceremony, the spirit was soothed by the offering of *thambili* and food by the patient's family, loud chanting and hymns sung by the ritual team requesting the demon to leave the woman alone.

Finally, the head of the rooster was cut, and its body was taken away to be thrown into the sea, symbolising that the demon had been thrown out and suggesting that a greater force had devoured the spirit.

The end came soon after, at dawn, when the *Yakadura* finally brought blessings on everyone while chanting verses before a moulded demon figure.

The hushed audience, transfixed by the spiritually and emotionally charged experience, broke into small groups whispering to each other as they left the compound.

CHAPTER 42

LOVINIA

Lovinia awoke with a start from a vivid dream, her heart pounding wildly in her chest. The room was dark but for a weak glow of light streaming through the shutters thrown open to let in the night air, the sweet fragrance of frangipani, and the salty tang of the nearby sea. A rumble of thunder sounded in the distance. The wind was picking up and fluttered the curtains covering the window.

I have overslept.

It was the day that Kumara had chosen to set his plan in motion. She wondered whether the dream was a portend of things to come.

The floor was cold under her bare feet as she scrambled out of bed, the night air cool on her skin. She crept out from under the billowing mosquito netting tent, picking up her clothing from the dark wooden floor, trying not to make a noise. It had been almost dawn before they had finally slept, so it would be not kind to wake him now. She should leave before the household woke up.

'Do you have to leave?'

The voice from the bed startled her. At his summons, she had come to the *Andukāraya's* bedroom, and he had tired her out with his demands. Afterwards, they sat talking. Lovinia was hungry to know everything he could tell her about the celebratory ball in the city, and he did not hesitate to answer her questions. But as they talked, she sensed a change in him and wanted to explore it more.

'No, but it will be daylight soon.'

Lovinia walked back, pushing aside the netting, and climbing onto the bed. The *Andukāraya* was watching her, his eyes lingering on her body, taking time to appreciate her shapely form. His eyes flickered over her, and she was suddenly aware of how her nipples had peaked in the cool air.

She shifted above him, leaning on her elbow, gathering her hair to trickle it across his face as she smiled. He touched her lips with his and found her mouth open, tongue licking his teeth and exploring as her hands searched his body. He closed his own hands over hers, trying to withdraw his mouth without success. Her tongue shyly caressed his. Each light, teasing pass was a gift.

Lovinia laughed a gentle gurgle of amusement deep in her throat and slid away from him. She could feel his desire begin to grow.

'You cannot go yet.'

Dawn had begun its slow creep through the house. The faint clatter of pots indicated that the cook was awake and preparing the morning meal.

'You should go away more often,' she said, kneeling on the bed, looking down at him. 'I've not known you to be so aroused after our night.'

'That's what I want to tell you,' the *Andukāraya* said, propping himself on his elbows. 'I will be spending most of my time here now.'

Lovinia drew in a deep breath and studied the tousled head of the most powerful man in the colony. He was not one to make frivolous comments, and she wondered what had changed to make him utter those words. She reached out and took his hands in hers. She kept silent, looking at him with keen interest. She had learned that most people craved attention. Showing someone the smallest bit of interest could get them to reveal much about themselves. He glanced at her, found her a willing listener, and did just that.

'I have realised I am unhappy when staying at the Government House in Columbo. The air is unhealthy from the canals and lake. I suspect it's where I caught that dreaded disease. I have arranged for this to become my official residence immediately.'

She continued to gaze at him and then slowly released his hands. This was news Kumara would want to hear. Her face was outwardly serene, but inside her head, her thoughts were in turmoil as she constantly ran through the endless things that could go wrong with Kumara's plan. She cringed inwardly at the thought.

'By God, you're lovely.'

Lovinia felt a stab of guilt at his words.

She was struck afresh by his power. She would always be awed by him, which was dangerous.

Then the light caught his face, and she could see him. After all, he was only a man who had suffered and come through his illness with signs of that struggle in clearly etched lines around his mouth and a new painful understanding in his eyes. It seemed his old cynical arrogance had been replaced with something else. He was still proud, and the regal manner was there, but there was now compassion to moderate that pride. She put out a hand to steady herself and clear her head,

'You're a special friend,' he said, smiling at her. 'And I'm acting boorish. How many men would be jealous of what I have? My life has changed so much after coming here. There is always the promise of more excitement. I shouldn't complain. What about you, Lovinia? What is your ambition?'

She lifted an eyebrow. This was not something he had ever asked her before.

'No one has ever asked me that question before,' she said honestly. 'All I have ever wanted is to dance.'

'Have you ever thought of getting married?'

Lovinia shook her head without answering. She was beginning to feel uncomfortable with the change in the *Andukāraya's* behaviour. She was used to men using her body for a physical release, and until she met Kumara, she had not met anyone with whom she had felt a special bond.

'Are these questions making you uncomfortable?'

Lovinia searched his face. The fleeting tenderness of just a moment past was gone, his thoughts already moving on to other matters.

She nodded, deciding not to speak. Could that be a hit of anxious uncertainty in his eyes?

He leaned back on his pillow, his eyes leaving her face. 'We will have time to talk about it later,' he said. 'I want you to come to me every night.'

His face darkened as his brows shot together with an unpleasant thought. He turned to look at her again. 'That is if you want to.'

Lovinia nodded, although her heart wasn't in it. She would do whatever it took to keep her family safe. 'I want to,' she said, hoping he would not hear the hesitation in her voice. 'But I have to help my father sometimes. It is our only means of support,' she explained.

'I understand,' he said. 'I will ensure your father is adequately compensated.'

The first crash of thunder sounded overhead and echoed around the hills. Heavy drops spattered against the shutters and drummed on the roof in a continuous roar.

'I must go now,' Lovinia said quietly.

He nodded as she slipped out of bed and put on her clothes. She didn't see him watching her as she slipped out of the room.

CHAPTER 43

KUMARA

An alarm went off in the back of his mind as it always did when he was in dangerous territory. Any false move he made would be his last.

Kumara had purchased passage on a small coastal trading vessel in the town of Kaltura just south of Columbo. As the boat left the town, his thoughts were further to the north, at the little village of Galkissa where he'd left his heart.

His breath left him in a long sigh as he remembered their time together. Lovinia was special in so many ways. He had felt that the moment he laid eyes on her, but now the future was uncertain. He knew she wanted to be with him, but there would be difficulties, but he wouldn't allow doubt to shadow his mind. Kumara cleared his mind of Lovinia and any negative thoughts. There would be time for brooding later. First, he must focus on his mission. *He couldn't afford to fail.*

Within an hour of the boat docking in the capital, Kumara walked out of the busy harbour filled with tall ships and boats of all kinds. As he had anticipated, no soldiers were watching the harbour entrance. Several rickshaw men, bare-bodied with turbans and knee-length sarongs, crouched between the shafts of their rickshaws, chewing *betel* (nut from the areca palm used as a stimulant), waiting for customers.

Kumara pulled the tail of his turban round and tucked it in snugly to veil the lower part of his bearded face. As he walked out, he realised he had made a mistake leaving the harbour alone when he saw a group of rough-looking men idling outside the gates. The gangs roaming the harbour and its surroundings were notorious for preying on travellers arriving by sea. Kumara could feel them eyeing him as he walked past and knew he was in trouble. He was hoping to enter the city secretly after dark by not using the land gates, which were closely watched. He had not bargained, running into a gang of cutthroats.

The sound of loud laughter made him instinctively look over his shoulder. A group of sailors were leaving the harbour through the same gate he had come through, drawing the attention of the gang he'd just walked past. Kumara quickly ducked down a side street, hoping that his sudden disappearance would not be noticed and would confuse the gang members about his whereabouts. But he was under no illusion that he was completely out of trouble. The gangs knew their territory well and would know how to find him.

The first thing he needed to do was determine if he was being followed. He hurried to a nearby tavern frequented by sailors, which was loud and rowdy. He ducked inside, immediately going to the kitchen and walking past a bewildered cook before exiting out the back. In the alley's shadows, he made his way past a chicken coop, through a short gate with squeaky hinges, and then walked a little distance to the next alleyway and turned the corner. There, he waited, listening, opening the hood of his cloak to hear better.

After several minutes, where all he heard was the scrape of leaves being dragged by the breeze and the nearby bluster of the tavern, he heard the gate squeak.

He carefully looked around the corner, spying two men standing in the dim light by the gate. They looked confused, unsure of which way he had gone. They decided to split up because one went the other way while one came in his direction.

Divide your opponents' forces. Remove the lesser pieces one by one.

It was a lesson his father had drilled into him when he talked about the many campaigns he'd fought for the Kandyan King, first as a young man against the Portuguese and later against the Dutch. He was a minor chieftain from the eastern highlands whose allegiance to the King required him to provide fifty armed and provisioned men from his holdings every time the King demanded it.

Kumara pressed his back against the wall pulling a narrow dagger from under his cloak, which he fitted to the palm of his hand, closing his fingers around it. The needle-sharp point of the stabbing dagger stuck out between his fingers, making it an ideal close-quarter weapon. He listened for the sound of advancing footsteps. The man was cautious, but he made out the subtle scuffing sounds that increased in volume as he approached the corner. He was walking quickly, which meant he was trying to catch up, believing Kumara was much farther ahead than he was.

His shadow suddenly appeared around the corner. He had a wicked-looking knife in his hand with the blade pointed forward. He saw Kumara, but it was too late. Kumara gripped the man's wrist to control the bladed weapon and jabbed his dagger against his neck, piercing his skin and causing a spray of blood when he jerked back in surprise. The man's elbow jutted at his face, but he dodged it, keeping his wrist gripped firmly. The man grunted at the pain and tried to call out in warning. Kumara twisted and covered his mouth with his hand, the ring he wore on his middle finger slashing part of the man's lip.

The cutthroat was strong, vigorous, and terrified, which added to his strength. He tried to twist the dagger around to stab Kumara in the stomach, and it took all his effort to keep the blade pointed away. Then the blood loss from his neck finally worked, and the man slumped in a heap on the cobblestones, but Kumara still held his wrist and neck and gently laid him down.

Although his heart was racing at the sudden violence, he listened keenly for the sound of the man's partner pursuing him. But he heard nothing. He quickly disarmed the man, taking the knife for himself. He dragged the body deeper into the shadows to make it more difficult to find in the dark. They might not discover him until daylight when he'd be well away. Then he left the alley.

*

After carefully negotiating the side streets and alleyways without incident, Kumara reached a spot he could observe the side door of the Inn of the

Lion without being seen. Two men sat on chairs in the alleyway scrutinising everyone who passed them. They were chuckling and laughing as they played a game of dice while passing a bottle between them. He watched them, listening to their banter and studying the bottle they continued to pass to each other. It looked full, which meant they intended it to last through the night.

Kumara retreated, going back around the block and approaching the inn from the main street. As he expected, the front entrance was also being watched by a group of men. Patrons continued to stream in and out of the establishment, some rejected by the doorkeeper while others were let in.

Realising he needed a diversion of some sort to get into the inn, he crossed the thoroughfare into a side street and approached a small tavern a few doors down. He had worn clothes he normally wouldn't wear, disguising himself as a Mohammedan sailor from the islands to the west. He wore a dark *thobe* (a long shirt worn as a robe) belted at the waist with loose pants and a keffiyeh to cover his head. A short sword hung at his hip.

Kumara slipped into the tavern, which was crowded at that time of the night. The proprietor didn't recognise his bearded face. However, he'd been there several times before, gesturing to a table at the far side of the room. A serving maid brought him a tankard of frothing beer which was the entry price, waiting until he gave her a copper coin.

Looking around the room, he spotted the man he was after. He sat amongst a group of men huddling over a table, talking amongst themselves. Kumara beckoned the serving maid with a flick of his fingers.

'Give that man a drink,' he pointed, holding a silver coin out to her. 'You can keep the change if you keep your mouth shut.'

Kumara watched as the maid carried a fresh tankard to the table, handing it to the man who looked in Kumara's direction. He nodded, whispering to the person seated to his right, then stood up and headed to the side entrance where patrons relieved their bladders.

Kumara followed, looking around to see whether anyone was watching. The enclosed courtyard to which the door led stank of vomit and bodily fluids, making him gasp in disgust.

The man who had preceded him stood in a dark shadow, waiting. 'I thought you might come here,' he said, clasping Kumara's hand. 'Sakuntala warned us that the inn is being watched, and you would find another way to make contact.'

Indika was one of Sakuntala's men Kumara had used in the past. He was from a village not far from where he'd grown up, and Kumara trusted him completely.

'Have you seen any of Noordeen's men around?' he asked.

Indika stepped back into the shadows pulling Kumara with him, when someone opened the door and stepped into the yard. The man was drunk, muttering as he relieved himself in a steady stream against the wall before going back into the tavern without noticing them.

'We are watching out for them, but we haven't seen them for a few days,' Indika whispered. 'I think they are waiting for something to happen.'

'Yes,' Kumara whispered back. 'They are waiting for me to show myself. How many men are with you?'

'There are six with me here, and I can gather twelve or more experienced men if you give me a few hours.'

Kumara remained silent and pulled at his beard. 'That should do. I will send instructions through Sakuntala, where I will need them. Make sure they are all well-armed and ready to face the mercenaries.'

Kumara could sense Indika nodding. 'I will do as you ask.'

'Any news of Lokubada?' Kumara asked. He had felt bad when he heard that his old friend had been taken by the British and was hoping to hear some good news.

'Nothing new,' Indika responded. 'The last we heard was that he is being held at the fort.'

'Ok, let's get out of here,' Kumara said. 'I'll be in touch.'

CHAPTER 44

FESTIVAL OF LIGHT

Lovinia had convinced Thomas to attend the village celebration of *Vesak* (festival of light), which he had learned, was one of the most important Buddhist festivals celebrated throughout the island.

'You have brought prosperity to the village by your presence, and the villagers want to thank you,' Lovinia explained. 'There will be a *dansala* (place of almsgiving) built in the village square. You have been invited to attend a small ceremony and partake of the offerings.'

Thomas had been intrigued by the offer and had accepted. He had known about various Buddhist celebrations since he came to the island but had never paid much attention.

From early that morning, the sound of *pirith* (chanting) from a nearby Buddhist temple had drifted in the wind carrying with it the unmistakable mystique of the island and its inhabitants.

As dusk approached, the sense of anticipation seemed to grow in the household. Most of the staff were given the day off—the remaining lit *pahanas* (clay oil lamps) in every residence window. An elaborate Vesak *kudu* (paper lantern with a lit candle illuminating it from inside) with smaller *kudus* hanging off it, built by one of the stable grooms, hung on a long pole near the gatehouse, attracting a small crowd of locals who gathered outside the compound to admire the decoration.

The streets were thronged with people as he rode to the village. He had decided to wear a semi-official uniform; a light blue high-necked, waist-length cavalry coat, white shirt and breeches with thigh-high leather boots. A white leather strap carrying his sword crossed his chest. A row of campaign medals gleamed on his chest.

Everyone he passed was dressed in white, even the children, who walked with their parents towards the village. Flickering paper lanterns, some in the shape of stars and lotus flowers, hung outside every dwelling, some decorated with garlands of colourful flowers. Lights sparkled everywhere as Thomas and his ever-present escort of soldiers entered the village.

In the centre of the village, an elaborate structure with painted panels depicting scenes from the life of Buddha was illuminated by hundreds of *pahanas* placed in rows on narrow wooden shelves.

The men from the village, all dressed in white, had gathered under the village Bo tree, the older men squatting, their sarongs pulled tight around their haunches, their toes digging into the dust; the young ones standing or leaning against the thick trunk of the tree, the smoke from their cigarettes winding up into its branches.

The women and children were gathered separately, sitting in family groups watching as the *Vidane* (village headman), dressed in his finery, greeted Thomas, bowing and scraping as he guided him to an open cadjan hut built with waist-high walls. It was decorated in streamers of linen and palm fronds, giving it a festive look. On one side were low tables groaning with the weight of clay pots filled with various local foods.

The heady aroma of curries mingled with wood smoke filled his senses. The sounds of people quietly talking, laughing and singing *bhakti geetha* (religious songs) rose and fell in the breeze. Behind the structure, women using long wooden ladles stirred bubbling pots on open cooking fires tended by sweaty bare-bodied men.

Lovinia and two women he thought he recognised were in the shelter when he entered. All three were dressed in white sarees. Thomas held Lovinia's eyes for a moment. He glanced away when the Vidane beckoned the older woman, who came forward with her palms pressed together in respect. She studied Thomas before glancing at the Vidane, who spoke to her in Sinhalese.

'The Vidane wants me to welcome your excellency to the village and thank you for gracing us with your presence,' she said.

Thomas nodded his thanks to the Vidane, who looked like he had more to say.

'I think I have seen you before,' Thomas said, addressing the woman. 'But I cannot remember your name.'

'It's Joanna, your excellency. Joanna Johnson.'

'Ah, of course,' Thomas said with a twinge of embarrassment. 'I must thank you for assisting Johnson during my sickness. I understand you made the potions which helped me recover.'

'Not me, your excellency,' Juana said. She looked over her shoulder and beckoned Aletta forward. 'This is Aletta, who prepared the potions with her own hands. She is a midwife and a healer in the village.'

Thomas recognised the woman who had been with Lovinia when he had visited the village for the first time. 'Thank you,' he said, looking at her directly. 'I believe you saved my life.'

Juana translated, making Aletta smile and respond in her language.

'She says she is a healer and will do the same for anyone who is sick.'

The *Vidane* interrupted, making Juana look at him sharply.

'The *Vidane* is anxious to get started,' Juana said. 'He wants me to direct you over there, where you will be served a simple meal.'

Thomas allowed himself to be guided to an area with floormats made from dry palm leaves spread on the floor. A chair decorated elaborately with palm fronds twisted into various shapes was placed on the mats for him to sit.

The crowd fell silent as three priests dressed in saffron robes entered the *dansala*. They recited incantations over the food, blessing the offerings and accepting the first serving into bowls they carried under their robes. With just a curious glance in his direction, they shuffled out of the pavilion.

'You may sit now,' Lovinia whispered as the priests left.

Lovinia placed banana leaves on a low table in front of him. When Aletta started serving steaming rice on the banana leaves, Thomas glanced curiously at Lovinia, thinking this was a religious ritual of the *dansala*.

She smiled. 'Aren't you hungry?'

Thomas watched as Aletta served a thick yellow liquid on the rice, which Juana explained was called *dhal* (yellow lentils). There was a third item, too— some cooked vegetables.

When Lovinia and Aletta started eating with their fingers, Thomas tried to imitate them, making the women smile. Lovinia demonstrated how to pick up the food using just the tips of his fingers.

'You're doing well,' she spoke in a low voice, not looking at him.

Villagers crowded outside the *dansala*, peering over the cadjan walls while they ate. The Vidane strutted around the room, making comments to the crowd, undoubtedly explaining the importance of having the *Andukāraya* attend the village function.

'What is the significance of all this,' Thomas asked Juana, waving his free hand around.

'It's a festival commemorating the birth, the enlightenment and death of the Lord Buddha,' she explained. 'People prepare food as an act of merit for the needy.'

'Is it an old custom?' he asked. He had never found it necessary to learn about the local culture and customs, something he thought put him at a disadvantage.

'The concept of *dana* or almsgiving is a fundamental discipline of Buddhists and began when the ancient Kings donated food and provided shelter for people who undertook pilgrimages during this full moon period,' Juana said. 'I am a Christian myself, and even we follow the practice of giving alms to the poor.'

Thomas nodded, finding the whole experience quite remarkable. He had never been a religious person, but the devotion displayed by the villagers during this holy day touched his heart.

The food tasted delicious, and he promised himself to ask his cook back at the residence to prepare a few local dishes for him to try. He watched as people began to line up outside the dansala waiting patiently until they were seated. They were served food on banana leaves which they ate sitting cross-legged on mats. Women moved around the seated diners offering drinks and sweets or collecting the used banana leaves. Others waited until it was their turn to enter the *dansala*.

He washed his hands in a clay bowl with a slice of lime and cleaned his fingers on a piece of white linen handed to him.

'Please thank the Chief for inviting me to share in your celebration,' he said to Juana. 'It has been most enlightening.'

For the first time since he arrived, Thomas noticed a genuine smile cross Lovinia's face.

CHAPTER 45

THE SHOWDOWN

Captain Noordeen walked down the unfamiliar street with Puteri. It was in an area near the harbour he had not visited before. The streets were noisy and colourful, with merchants calling in high-pitched voices to the brightly-clad citizens who jostled and haggled over prices. All paused to look at the two men who walked amongst them.

Buildings on both sides of the street advertised themselves as ship chandlers. One was very obviously a place to recruit hands, given the clutch of sailors of all colours milling around outside. There would be competition for the more experienced, those who could hand, reef and steer. Numerous tables were laden with several varieties of fish with the seawater smell of freshness. Others held piles of live crabs and lobsters, manned by females of such brutish appearance and formidable build that they looked sure to get the best of any bargaining.

He was not in a good mood. They came to meet a man who said he had information to sell. He had sent word about a passenger they had picked up at Kaltura two days prior. He kicked aside a crate of live mud crabs that had fallen on the footpath, glaring at the stall holder when he opened his mouth to complain.

The east-side houses turned into an untidy set of more trading emporiums, each with its beam and double block to raise and lower goods from the upper floors. Like the front, all the trades serviced seagoing ships were here;

sailmakers and purveyors of canvas by the bolt, business's selling rope from whip lines to multi-stranded anchor cables, businesses supplying vinegar and turpentine spirits. There were woodyards, bakeries for ship's biscuits, and a slaughterhouse for meat. Interspersed with these shops was a ready supply of places to buy a drink.

The tavern was crowded with sailors, prostitutes, mercenaries and locals who looked like they would cut your throat for a gold coin. Scantily dressed women circled the tables, sitting on the laps of men who showed any interest. It was raucous and rowdy, fairly typical of such harbourside establishments.

The Captain identified himself to the innkeeper, who pointed to an empty table at the back of the room. A young woman with a low-cut dress displaying her bulging charms walked over as they sat down.

'Two beers,' Captain Noordeen ordered before she could say anything. The girl, who had a no-nonsense look about her, stood waiting with a hand on her hip until he placed a silver coin in her hand. Then she flounced away, swinging her hips as the two men watched.

Captain Noordeen's eyes darted around the room, lit by smoky torches adding to the haze of hand-made *bidi* and cheroots, some flavoured with spices, and the occasional unmistakable smell of *ganja*. Not seeing anyone interested in them, he leaned back on his chair, his back against the wall.

'Do you know what he looks like?' Puteri asked, looking around. 'He could be any one of these men.'

The Captain shook his head. 'We are early, so let's just wait.'

He had a good feeling about the message ever since he received it. It made sense that the Kandyan would enter the city by sea as the land gates were closely watched.

I wish I'd thought about it. It would have been easy to position some of his men to watch the harbour gates.

The serving maid brought two tankards of frothing beer to their table. She held out a few copper coins of change which the captain waved away.

'Thank you, sir!' The girl pocketed the coins with a smile.

Puteri tried to run his hand up her leg, but she slapped his hand away.

'I can get someone more inclined to visit you,' she said, laughing at him. 'There are rooms upstairs you can use.'

'Leave her be,' the Captain growled, reaching for the tankard. 'We are here on business.' He took a sip, wiping the foam from his mouth.

A mixed group of sailors and mercenaries were becoming rowdy at the next table. The innkeeper walked over, trying to calm them down. 'More beer, more beer,' the group chanted. Two serving maids hustled over carrying trays full of tankards which they distributed among the group.

A bearded Muslim sailor stood up. 'To the death of the Kandyan King,' he called out, slurring his words. 'Then, my friends, we shall live in peace. Let's drink to it.'

'To peace,' everyone shouted, raising their cups.

Captain Noordeen drank his down, smacking the tankard on the table. Puteri followed, then waved his arm at the serving maid across the room.

*

Kumara watched the two men drink their beers and smiled. The trap was sprung, and the game was over, but they did not know it yet.

It had taken a few days to organise everything, and he knew it would work when he saw the captain and his lieutenant walk into the tavern. He was expecting the Captain to have more men with him, so he had come prepared, scattering his men around the room and guarding the two exits. It would have been a blood bath, but he felt he had no choice. He was glad the choice was made for him and that no lives would be lost. With these two men out of the picture, it would be easy to move around the city without being recognised.

Kumara watched and waited, stroking his beard and studying the two men who had called for more drinks to be brought to their table. They had not recognised him when he proposed the toast. It was the only moment it could all have gone wrong. But his disguise held up.

The Malay Captain must have felt something was wrong as his nostrils flared. He leaned forward, his eyes darting around the room. His brow wrinkled in concern. Beads of sweat formed on his forehead.

Kumara kept watching his face, realising the symptoms he was now feeling had alerted him to the poison running through his system. The poison he had drunk with his beer.

Tremors began to seize Captain Noordeen's muscles. He reached across the table but couldn't coordinate himself, overturning the tankard and spilling the beer on the table.

His lieutenant must have had a stronger constitution as he reached out to help his captain but then seemed to realise what was happening. He stood up, his hand reaching for his sword, but tripped over his feet and crashed onto the floor.

The innkeeper bustled over. He'd been warned about the possibility of a fight breaking out in the tavern and under no circumstances was he to call the watch. He would be fully compensated for any damage caused. But he wouldn't have expected this.

'Are you well, Captain?' asked the innkeeper. His face looked worried.

The tremors began to convulse through the two men.

'Someone fetch the apothecary!' the innkeeper shouted in concern. 'These men are sick!'

Kumara rose from his table and approached the innkeeper. 'They are from our ship,' he said. 'We have a doctor on board who can treat them.'

'Help them! Help them!' the innkeeper said, looking relieved.

'Carry them to the ship,' Kumara said to his men at the table. Several lifted the two semi-conscious men and carried them out of the side entrance. The rest of the tavern's patrons, watching the drama unfold, returned to what they were doing. It was not uncommon to see men being carried out of a tavern when they got too intoxicated and lost control.

Kumara handed the innkeeper a purse of gold coins. 'This is for the trouble we caused you,' he said. 'Buy a round of drinks and keep the rest for yourself. I don't want a whisper of what happened here to be repeated. Otherwise, I'll be back.'

The innkeeper nodded, quickly pocketing the purse as he ushered Kumara to the side entrance. 'You won't hear a word from me.'

Kumara handed a smaller purse to the serving maid, who followed them. 'You did well. I'll keep you in mind if I need your services again.' The woman nodded, tucking the purse under her dress and hurrying back inside.

Kumara walked down the alley behind his men. He had one more task to do. He had to pay the Captain of the vessel that would carry the two mercenaries away from the island. A ship was leaving for Cape Town that night carrying cargo and spices to the west. The two men would be chained below deck and released penniless when the ship reached Cape Town, hopefully never to return to the island.

He had contemplated for a moment whether to have the men killed while under the poison's effects but pushed aside the thought. Aletta had warned him that the poison would leave the men with nerve damage, unable to use their limbs to their fullest capacity, making it impossible for them to remain mercenaries.

Kumara sighed, knowing he had condemned the men to a harsh life. In a small way, he had contributed to them being banished from Kandy when he complained to the Chief *Adigar* about how he'd been treated. It had changed their lives, and he felt they had suffered enough in his hands.

CHAPTER 46

THE CONSEQUENCE

'What do you mean they have disappeared?' Thomas was meeting with the Head of Revenue Collection at his country residence. Wilson had requested a meeting and had arrived on his horse.

'Captain Noordeen and Puteri, his lieutenant, have absconded with the gold, your excellency,' said Wilson matter of factly. 'We have tried to track their whereabouts, but they seem to have vanished into thin air.'

'People don't just vanish, Wilson,' Thomas growled. 'Even here in the mystic east. There has to be another explanation.'

'I agree, sire,' Wilson said, sitting back uncomfortably. 'They could have decided to leave the city and hide from their men who were getting agitated by their forced confinement,' he began ticking off his fingers. 'Two, they could be dead, killed by the rebels they were hunting, although I find that difficult to believe as we would have heard about it by now.'

'You mean the Kandyan killed them,' Thomas snorted. 'I notice you've still not caught him.'

'The Kandyan, if he's alive, is keeping a very low profile,' Wilson said. 'Some say that he's dead, and he's just been kept alive in people's minds to keep us off balance.'

Thomas steepled his fingers thoughtfully and leaned back in his chair, looking perturbed. 'Have you had no sighting of him?'

Wilson shook his head. 'No, sire, we haven't. The rebel network is still in place, as we can tell, but the Kandyan is not running it.'

'How can you be so sure?'

'We cannot, but whoever it is, it's not him. The modus operandi is completely different. For all you know, the network is being run directly from Kandy through intermediaries.'

'What about that chap you caught when you raided the inn?'

'Mr Lokubada,' Wilson sniffed. 'He has given us nothing. It couldn't be him, as we had him in custody while all this was happening. We released him a few days ago.'

Thomas shook his head disbelievingly. 'Any good news?'

Wilson sat up straighter. 'Yes, plenty, your excellency. Our problems with the Company have been resolved to everyone's satisfaction. They are extremely grateful to us for not charging James Hardwick and shipping him back to England.'

Thomas nodded. He could use it as leverage to get a better deal with Sir David when the cinnamon contract came up next.

'We have had a positive response from Kandy about sending an emissary to discuss a truce of some sort,' Wilson said. 'I suggest it be someone from the civil service. A Revenue Collector, perhaps.'

'Make sure it's someone who speaks the local language,' Thomas said. 'We must use people who understand and appreciate not only the local dialects but also the people's customs, manners, and civilisation. Eventually, the civil service should not only deal with trade and commerce but also work to make British rule acceptable and palatable.'

Wilson noted on a pad he carried. 'They will need to be trained properly.'

"We must ensure that these Collectors have a good knowledge of local affairs and intimate knowledge and understanding of the provinces and districts under them,' Thomas agreed. 'There's a college in Fort William, where young recruits of the Indian Civil Service have to spend three years learning about the country and how to govern it correctly,'

Thomas watched as Wilson jotted more notes into his pocketbook. 'Is there anything else?' he asked. The meeting had gone longer than he expected, and he wanted to sit outside and watch the fisherman setting out to sea on the evening tide.

'I have had a preliminary look at the operating expenses,' Wilson said. 'You will be pleased to hear that expenditures have been reduced by a third. This reduction came about after the military stopped their operations against the Kandyans, the inland service administrative reforms were enacted, and the Dutch prisoners were sent to Batavia.'

Thomas smiled, motioning Wilson to continue.

'Revenue will increase by a third, now the cinnamon tax has increased, and paddy cultivation has doubled.'

'That's good news indeed! Thank you, Wilson.' Thomas swiped his hand through his greying hair. 'I have been thinking recently about ways of increasing our revenue. Being sick clears the mind wonderfully,' he grinned. 'I want you to put some bright minds together and devise a plan to open the country up to European entrepreneurs investing their capital here,' Thomas said. 'There is a great deal of land that could be used for cultivation, and an injection of European capital would stimulate the country's economy.'

Wilson's eyes widened.

Thomas knew what was going through his mind. It would make his job more important. 'Yes, I know what you're thinking,' Thomas said. 'But first things first. Let me see a report on the effect it will have on the island before I make up my mind.'

'Yes, your excellency. Let me get onto it right away.'

CHAPTER 47

DOUBLING DOWN

The village vegetable gardens basked in the brittle heat. The sun bore down on the neat rows of vegetables, bathing them in its light and feeding them with invisible goodness. Nothing stirred, neither the stems of maize with their silken-whiskered fruit, the broad-bladed leeks, the dark green bushes full of long red chillies, nor even the feather-topped carrots.

Few animals braved the sun. Birds sought the shade of trees, while insects crawled into the cool shelter of leaves or burrowed deep into the fruit's flesh. Even the lizards, basking on stones and tree trunks, were still exercising their tongues in pursuit of food. Only scorpions, clad in protective armour, rattled about in the open, unconcerned.

'It's over,' Banda said, walking through the front gate smiling. 'His plan worked. Both Noordeen and Puteri are on a ship bound for Africa.'

Lovinia and Aletta were seated on the front verandah sifting through a bag of rice for tiny pebbles some traders mixed in to increase the bag's weight. They had been to the market that morning which was busier than usual. The village benefited from its proximity to the *Andukāraya's* residence as all the meat, fish, poultry, and vegetables for the household were purchased locally. The local staff working at the residence, recruited from the village, also brought unprecedented prosperity.

Lovinia's eyes moved across his face. 'Is he okay?' she asked. Her mind had been restless all morning, thinking about what could have gone wrong.

'Yes, he's fine,' Banda responded, placing the bag he carried on the floor next to them. A slow grin spread across his sun-drenched face. 'He's keeping low until everything settles down.' His grin grew wider. 'The English are going crazy looking for them.'

Banda sat on the verandah, his back against the pillar. 'Your potion worked perfectly,' he said, to Aletta, 'there was no need for violence.'

Aletta nodded without saying anything.

Lovinia knew she had been worried whether the potion she made was potent enough to do its job. She inhaled and shook the *kulla* (wicker tray) to separate the tiny stones.

'I have some news to give you,' she said, looking at her father. 'The *Andukāraya* has decided to make Galkissa his official residence.'

Banda's amusement vanished as he considered what Lovinia had said. 'Well, it cannot be bad for the village,' he said. 'We'll have more traffic from the city and elsewhere, which will only bring prosperity. The *Vidane* will be pleased.'

Lovinia nodded. 'Yes, but he wants me to visit him every night.'

'And that bothers you?' her father asked, looking at her inquiringly.

'She's worried that she'll be unable to perform with the troupe,' Aletta said, glancing at Lovinia. 'It's something she has always done.'

'I said that to him,' Lovinia said. 'I told him that I cannot leave the dance troupe as it's our only means of livelihood.'

'Well, what did he say?'

'He said that he'll compensate you for my loss.'

'That's exactly what I would have expected him to say,' her father nodded. 'I can always get another dancer unless Aletta wants to do it?' Banda looked at Aletta with raised eyebrows.

'It's possible, but you know I get called often when people are sick or when there is a childbirth,' Aletta said, reaching out and holding Lovinia's arm. 'I'd rather spend time at home with Lovinia, who will need someone around during the day.'

Banda nodded. 'That's settled then. I will talk to Johnson and tell him what the *Andukāraya* said. He can make the necessary arrangements.'

'There's still the question of Kumara,' Aletta said, looking at Lovinia. 'What do you want?'

'I am not sure,' Lovinia said. 'I need time to think about it.'

'You will have to lead two lives,' her father said matter of factly. 'Kumara wants you to continue this relationship with the *Andukāraya*, so he will have to accept what that means. But you must ensure that it never gets to the ears of anyone other than Juana and the three of us. He must never visit you in the village,' he warned, 'never.'

Lovinia chewed on her lower lip. It was going to be difficult, she realised. She found them both attractive in their ways, but they'd also filled her with apprehension.

'We will have to make it work.' She heard the pretence in her voice.

Aletta's expression softened in understanding. 'Don't worry. We are here to help you.'

'Well,' Lovinia huffed. 'That's a relief, isn't it?'

Aletta's shoulders pulled back, and she cocked her head to one side. 'Don't underestimate my usefulness, Lovinia, and I won't underestimate yours.'

Lovinia already wished she could have snatched her remark back. She sighed. 'I am sorry, Aletta. I don't mean to snap at you. It's just that I've tried so hard to be careful. I don't want Kumara hurt by my friendship with the *Andukāraya*.'

Aletta shot her a withering look. 'If he cares for you, he will find a way to live with it.' Her tone dared Lovinia to push her further, but her eyes faltered for a fleeting moment.

Lovinia reached out and held her arm. 'Don't be mad at me. I am just trying to come to terms with what this all means.'

Aletta's expression softened. 'Remember, it won't last forever.'

Lovinia blinked. Could Aletta see it in her eyes? That sad, lonely longing of hers? She nodded and looked at her hands. *But how long would it be?* There was a cold emptiness in the pit of her stomach. Her face must have revealed her thoughts.

Aletta reached out and stroked her face. 'The *Andukāraya* won't be here forever. Once he leaves, you will have your life back the way you want it. You are doing this for your family, Lovinia. Keep that foremost in your mind; whether they know it or not, our village has benefitted in many ways. People are happier than they have ever been. You have changed so many lives for the better.'

Lovinia looked up and saw her father smiling. 'With this new arrangement, we will not need to travel great distances to perform. That will please everyone.'

'We have to prepare for the time that the *Andukāraya* will be no longer here,' Aletta, always practical, said.

'Yes,' Banda responded. 'I have been thinking of starting a dance school to teach our young people the finer arts. I can do it now.'

Lovinia knew that her father had always wanted to teach dancing but could never afford it. She took a deep breath and let it out slowly. *Maybe it was all for the better.* She was still young and had a whole life ahead of her.

'Please let me help," she begged. 'I'll go mad if I have to sit around all day.'

Banda studied Lovinia before answering. 'Yes, I'd love you to help. Both of you. But your focus must be on the *Andukāraya* as your relationship with him has made our lives easier.'

Her shoulders slumped. 'So what? Play the concubine and keep my ears open?' As soon as she said the words aloud, she was startled to realize their truth.

'Yes. We'd be both blind and helpless without you.' He chucked her chin gently. 'But you need to be careful. He must never find out.'

'Well, then,' she said as she struggled to keep her voice under control, 'I will do what you ask, but I don't have to like it.'

'I hope you understand what that means. If the *Andukāraya* finds out you're worthless to him, all this will be gone in an instant.'

CHAPTER 48

THE END

Lovinia wanted to talk to Kumara despite her father's insistence that she didn't. She decided to ask for Aletta's help.

'You want me to go against your father's wishes,' Aletta seemed almost alarmed. 'I cannot do that!'

'All I want you to do is to get a message to him,' she pleaded. 'I won't risk travelling into the city, but I can meet him in the forest.'

Aletta shook her head. 'What makes you think he will come?'

'He will come,' Lovinia said confidently. 'I am his greatest asset, and he won't risk upsetting me.'

Aletta laughed. 'I see you are learning to use your power as a woman, which is all well and good, but if your father finds out I helped in this madness, he will banish me from the village.'

Why does he need to know?' Lovinia shrugged. 'If he finds out, I will say I sent the message.'

Aletta studied Lovinia for a moment before answering. 'Okay. I will do so, but only if I am there when you meet him. It would be easier to explain your absence if we were together.'

Lovinia nodded her assent, reaching out and hugging her friend to her tightly.

They decided the best place to meet without being seen was at the *vidiya* where Kumara had recovered from his wound. They would ask him to meet them in the late evening when they were sure no one would be around. They picked a time two days hence when the dance troupe were scheduled to perform at a wedding ceremony away from the village, knowing that Banda would not be around to keep an eye on them.

Lovinia couldn't wait for the time to pass. She visited the *Andukāraya* that night and spent most of the day sleeping or sitting on the verandah doing her dance exercises. She sensed her body was filling out into the full bloom of womanhood, stirring a deep sense of power. She was no longer a helpless woman depending on her father or any man. She felt independent, living on her terms.

Finally, the time arrived for the two women to enter the forest. As the shadows lengthened on the ground, the sun had begun its long descent to the sea. The forest was quiet as the birds and animals sensed the approach of darkness.

The *vidiya* was empty as the two approached the hut they had used to look after Kumara.

'I thought he'd be here,' Aletta said, looking around the empty compound clean of detritus after the healing ceremony, only fallen leaves fluttered around in the evening breeze.

There was no sign of Kumara, so the two sat outside the hut with their backs to the wall. At that time of the evening, the forest seemed to come alive. Flocks of birds roosted in their favourite trees, calling each other as they settled for the night.

'Let's find a *pahana*,' Lovinia said as the light faded. 'It will be enough.'

Aletta lit an oil lamp she found in the room, which still had some oil, using a flint she carried in a pouch on her waist. 'Remember, we cannot stay too long,' Aletta said. 'You cannot keep the *Andukāraya* waiting.'

The darkness descended suddenly, and the forest came alive with the sound of night animals leaving their burrows in search of food. Tiny bats flittered in and out of the light as they hunted insects attracted by the brightness.

The two friends sat together, each wrapped in their thoughts for a while when Aletta finally broke the silence. 'Maybe he's not coming.'

A similar thought had been creeping through Lovinia's mind. She had been sure he would come but was now having doubts. Anxiety bit into her, gnawing at her until she could sit still no longer. Grunting, she kicked her legs out and stood. The ground was cool beneath her feet, and she welcomed the tremor that came with the chill.

'Thinking of this will do me no good now,' she muttered, ignoring her slippers to walk barefooted. She just needed to get the anxious energy out of her system.

Aletta watched her pace outside the hut without any comment.

Lovinia was eager to plant her fist into something and let the pain spread from her knuckles into her mind. It was her unbearable attraction to him that she realised caused her to act this way. She wasn't fooled enough to disregard the heat she felt in her belly whenever she thought of him or the tingling in her blood that erupted whenever he was near. It was desire, as simple and as unwelcome as it could be.

Her father was right. She didn't have the time to be attracted to him; she needed to focus on what she had been asked to do. And Kumara knew that more than anyone. He wouldn't jeopardise his mission for the sake of love.

She knew that now.

'What do you want to do?' Aletta's voice broke into her thoughts.

'You're right! He's not coming,' she said, stopping in front of Aletta.

'I am sorry, Lovinia,' Aletta said, rising to her feet. 'If we leave now, you won't be too late.'

*

'I am glad you came tonight.' the low voice jolted her out of her deep sleep. The *Andukāraya* was watching her, his back against the door. He had entered the room and closed the door without her hearing him.

He was wearing a robe of heavy silk, belted at the waist. Lovinia could see his skin and a curl of hair peeping over his neckline. His feet were bare, and his hair was loose on his shoulders.

He was beside her when she turned, so close that she could smell the familiar tang of his skin. She was dizzy in reaction to the shock of his appearance and closeness.

'Lovinia.' He gathered her to him, into the softness of silk, against the hard strength of his body. She buried her face into the fabric and felt skin against her cheek, his heart beating against her ear. Every fibre of her being told her he was safe, protected, and desired. Every instinct told her he was danger and betrayal. A sense of guilt whispered at the edges of her mind.

He made no move to caress or touch her as she relaxed. She became aware of his arousal, firm against the softness of her belly as she rested against him.

'Are you happy?'

The question surprised her, but she was too far aroused to reason too much. 'What do you think?' Lovinia pulled his head down for a kiss.

Her kiss became a series of tender, teasing brushes of his mouth against hers. As he deepened his kiss, she leaned into him, sliding her hands up his shoulders until she teased her fingers through his hair. He moaned softly, then, with a growl, he caught her in his arms and lifted her body against his. Her feet barely scraped the floor. His bold tongue stroked hers, and she couldn't catch her breath as the heat built between their bodies, welding them together. His hand gathered and pulled off her slip. He wasn't guiding them any longer but overwhelming her instead. Perhaps that was his intent. To hide behind intimacy and draw her close to hold her at a distance. Strange. She would have to think about it further once it was an option. At that moment, his kisses were erasing her mind.

Suddenly, he set her back on her feet. As they parted, her impulse was to back away. However, she forced herself to stand her ground and meet his gaze.

'Honestly? I do not know,' he said finally, drawing away and tracing his index finger down her nose, along the line of her lips, as though he had never seen them before.

Lovinia searched his face for any hints of approval or disdain. His expression revealed nothing but confusion. Then, his hand gripped her shoulder and pulled her closer until they were lovers in an embrace.

AUTHORS NOTE

Let me share the story of how this book came about. Ever since my childhood days in Colombo, I was fascinated by the story of Major-General Sir Thomas Maitland, the British Army General who had fallen in love with a local woman named Lovinia Aponsuwa. She was the half-Sinhalese, half-Portuguese lead dancer of her father's dance troupe that performed at a welcome party when he arrived in the Crown Colony of Ceylon to take up his post as Governor-General in 1805.

The Governor General, smitten by her obvious charms but wary of the disapprovals of a narrow-minded British society, built a stately country mansion on a promontory overlooking the sea close to the village of Galkissa, just a few miles south of Colombo, where she lived. An underground tunnel from the mansion's cellar allowed Lovinia to visit him regularly to conduct their affair in secret.

For many years I went to a school not far from the Mount Lavinia Hotel, a heritage establishment over 200 years old and one of the oldest in Asia. I often walked past the hotel's elegant colonial façade, which includes the original mansion the Governor General built to be close to his lover. Later, when I was older and confident enough to enter the imposing building, I was shown the entrance to the tunnel Lovinia used, which exists to this day.

None of their love affair, which lasted over six years, was recorded in detail. All that is known is that the Governor General was eventually recalled to England in 1811 after suffering two severe bouts of malaria. He went on to play an important role as a Governor General in the Mediterranean until he died of a stroke in his 60s, still very much a bachelor.

What became of Lovinia has been lost in the mists of time. Some stories say she died of a broken heart after her aristocratic lover left. Others say she became a wealthy landowner in Attidiya, close to her village of Galkissa, the land bequeathed to her by the departing Governor General.

Although I have tried to stay true to the historical facts of the time—Governor Maitland was sent to the island to arrest the crippling expenditure that previous Governors had incurred administering the Crown colony; the British East India Company held a monopoly on all the island's cinnamon concessions; the repatriation of the Dutch VOC prisoners and their families to Batavia; Governor Maitland clashing with the Chief Justice and forcing judicial reform in the Maritime Provinces; the alarming Sepoy mutiny in India for which troops were despatched from Ceylon to quell; and the never-ending and costly war against the middle Kingdom of Kandy—the story is a product of my imagination.

However, there are a few exceptions. I have remained true to Governor Maitland's character traits and actions on the island, as noted by many historians. He has been described as a despot and an Empire Builder who implemented civilian and military reforms on the island, which eventually led Ceylon to be known as the Jewel in the British Crown. I've also shown his interest in the local culture, which was quite unusual for a high-ranking European at the time.

And finally, I haven't concerned myself only with kings, generals, the well-to-do and the ne'er-do-wells. I have tried to show the island's unique culture and how ordinary people lived, laughed, suffered, and even managed to thrive under the yoke of colonial rule.

Thank you for taking part in this historical journey with me.

ACKNOWLEDGEMENTS

A book of this nature is never the work of one person. Thanks to all my readers who have supported me over the past three years as I researched and wrote this story which has been haunting me since childhood.

Special thanks to my wife, Menaka, for her counsel and endless support during this period.

I also wish to thank several members of my writing group, the Scribe Tribe, for their assistance during the final stages of completing the book. Diane, Lauren and Hannah, I couldn't have done it without you.

And finally, my book cover designer, Mark, your awesome cover design has brought the narrative to life.

ABOUT THE AUTHOR

Roderic Grigson was born in Colombo, Sri Lanka, where he was educated and lived till he was twenty-one. Rod's family were Burghers, descendants of the Portuguese, Dutch and British colonials who ruled the island nation for 450 years.

With no prospects in the former British colony of Ceylon, which had become a socialist state run by Sinhalese nationals, he left the country of his birth with a few dollars in his pocket. He entered the United States on a tourist visa. He found work at the United Nations Headquarters in New York, where he worked for the next twelve years.

After studying information technology at New York University, he volunteered and joined the United Nations Peacekeeping Forces in Egypt and Lebanon, serving on the Suez Canal during the signing of the Israel-Egypt Peace Accord and South Lebanon and Beirut during the Lebanese Civil War.

After spending two years in the field, Rod returned to New York in 1980 and joined the UN Technological Innovations team. He spent the next six years helping develop and implement office information systems in six languages in UN regional offices worldwide.

Rod migrated with his wife to Australia in 1986, where he became a senior executive for a global IT company with responsibilities across the Asia Pacific region. In 2012, after choosing to retire early from corporate life, Rod completed a 6-month Creative Writing course and began writing his first novel.

This book, 'The Governor's Lover', is Rod's fourth book. His first book 'Sacred Tears' was released in 2014, his second, 'After the Flames', in 2017, and his third, 'The Sullen Hills', in 2018. All of his books are available for purchase on Amazon.

Rod keeps himself busy facilitating a long-standing writing group called the 'Scribe Tribe', which includes several published authors. He launched Grigson Publishing in 2020 to help new writers take the next step in their writing journey by mentoring and guiding them through the editing and publishing process. He also teaches creative & memoir writing courses and, more recently, computer and employability courses to new migrants and refugees.

To keep up to date with Rod, his writing, please visit:
rodericgrigson.com

For information on Rod's mentoring and publishing services, please visit:
grigsonpublishing.com

www.ingramcontent.com/pod-product-compliance
Lightning Source LLC
Chambersburg PA
CBHW030526120726
47904CB00005B/1638